Red-Hot Raves for Louisa Edwards' Recipe for Love series

JUST ONE TASTE

"The third addition to Edwards' contemporary, culinary-based love stories is a rare treat that is certain to satisfy readers with its delectable combination of lusciously sensuous romance and irresistibly clever writing."

—*Booklist*

"Laugh-out-loud funny, *Just One Taste* is a surprisingly tasty story of two unlikely people meeting and falling in love . . . A fun, light read with plenty of humor and passion, *Just One Taste* makes it to my keeper shelf and has me searching for the book preceding this one."

—*Affaire de Coeur*

"Awesome characters, delicious food and even more fabulous sex makes for a super-sexy and fun read! Edwards does it again. Her stories are fun but so meaningful, and I will definitely be reading her next book!"

—*The Book Lush*

"This is a wonderfully tasty series. Once you take the first bite of this story you'll be hooked to the very last bite."

—*Once Upon A Romance* (5 Stars)

"There are a lot of elements in *Just One Taste*, and Edwards juggles them like a pro. The addition of mouthwatering recipes at the end of the book enhances the excellent reading experience, and draws you into the world of cooks and cooking. A very enjoyable contemporary romance with plenty of bite and heart."

—*Sacramento Book Review*

"I absolutely love *Top Chef* and *Iron Chef America* but have never really picked up a food/chef-related novel before. I'm happy to report that *Just One Taste* was fun, sweet, and deliciously romantic."   —*PS I Love Books*

"This is my first 'taste' of a Louisa Edwards book, and I'll be going out for the others in this series. If you want a story with sweet romance, definite sensuality and enough laughs to make your day, then you need to read *Just One Taste*."   —*Long and Short Reviews*

"Rosemary is probably one of the most intricately sketched heroines I've ever seen in a book, and the romance is, in a word . . . intense, and the blending of the story was richly presented. Make it a point to read this Perfect 10 today!"

—*Romance Reviews Today*

"Rosemary and Wes are each so very charming on their own, and together they just capture your heart. *Just One Taste* by Louisa Edwards has plenty of clever teasing between characters, and the tension and emotion keep those pages flipping like flapjacks!"

—*The Romance Readers Connection*

"Funny, entertaining, and simmering with sexual chemistry."   —*Bookloons*

ON THE STEAMY SIDE

"*On the Steamy Side* is an instant re-read, a fresh, emotions-first take on the food-infused romance and, quite simply, a stellar example of the health and vibrancy of the American contemporary romance. I'm betting it ends up on any number of Best of 2010 lists."

—Michelle Buonfiglio,
Barnes & Noble's *Heart to Heart*

"A delight from cover to cover . . . My favorite aspect is how skillfully Ms. Edwards weaves emotional subjects throughout the novel . . . *On the Steamy Side* is much more than a sexy romance. It [has] depth and humanity. This series is headed for my keeper shelves."

—*A Romance Review*

"Edwards cooks up the perfect combination of compelling characters and an intriguing plot that delivers a marvelous confection of irresistible details about the fascinating world inside the kitchen of a gourmet restaurant."

—*Booklist* (Starred Review)

"The snappy, fun-loving dialogue and overall camaraderie with this cast of characters makes for great reading."

—*Babbling About Books*

"The plot, the humor, the angst and the romance are superb, and Edwards' writing style is as crisp and clean as a freshly starched toque-blanche. Reader, party of one, your novel is ready."

—*Reader to Reader*

"Louisa Edwards continues her Recipe for Love series with her latest book, *On The Steamy Side*. And boy, is it ever steamy! You could fry an egg between these pages of bubbling hot romance! With the popularity of the

Food Network, Louisa Edwards' delicious series will be a huge hit with foodies and romantics alike."

"Steam up your reading with *On the Steamy Side* by mega-talented Louisa Edwards."   —SingleTitles.com

"Fast-paced and scintillating . . . Boiling and searing love scenes aside, the complex relationships and self-discovery shared with the unique backdrop of the cutthroat and competitive culinary arts forces the reader to consume page after page as voraciously as the chefs can dish it up."

—*Romance Readers Choice*

"Louisa Edwards' fast-paced, sparkling *On The Steamy Side* has sizzling sex scenes, complicated relationships, and unique settings, with an undercurrent of humor."

—*Long and Short Reviews*

"If you need a real feel-good, make-your-heart-sing, and your-body-tingle kind of afternoon this is the perfect recipe for success."   —*Coffee Time Romance*

CAN'T STAND THE HEAT

"Exceptional culinary detail and page-singeing sexual chemistry combine with a fascinating group of characters to produce a sophisticated modern romance."

—*Library Journal*

"In her wickedly entertaining debut, Edwards dishes up a captivating contemporary romance expertly seasoned with plenty of sizzling sexual chemistry and deliciously tart humor."   —*Booklist*

Too Hot to Touch

LOUISA EDWARDS

St. Martin's Paperbacks

This is a work of fiction. All of the characters, organizations, and events portrayed in this novel are either products of the author's imagination or are used fictitiously.

TOO HOT TO TOUCH

Copyright © 2011 by Louisa Edwards.

Excerpt from *Some Like It Hot* copyright © 2011 by Louisa Edwards.

All rights reserved.

For information address St. Martin's Press, 175 Fifth Avenue, New York, NY 10010.

EAN: 978-0-312-35648-4

Printed in the United States of America

St. Martin's Paperbacks edition / August 2011

St. Martin's Paperbacks are published by St. Martin's Press, 175 Fifth Avenue, New York, NY 10010.

10 9 8 7 6 5 4 3 2 1

To my Gram, who first introduced me to romance novels. I wish you were around to tell me what you think of this one! I'm pretty sure it wouldn't be too racy for a broad like you.

Acknowledgments

This book wouldn't have been possible without the faith and vision of my wonderful editor, Rose Hilliard. Thank you for believing in the Rising Star Chef series and for all your help along the way in making this book what it is. Jules is your girl! I hope you're as proud of her as I am.

Big love for my agent, Deidre Knight, who really went above and beyond on this book. Thank you for always taking my call, always holding my hand, and always making me a better writer! You're the best, savviest, funniest, most inspiring guide a girl could have on this wacky journey through the world of publishing.

They say writing is a solitary pursuit, but I've never found that to be the case. Thank God! My writer friends save my sanity every day, and provide invaluable support (in the form of slumber parties disguised as writing retreats), encouragement (in the form of nagging), and information (in the form of gossipy emails). I would be lost without you all!

Candy Havens, Jaye Wells, and Ann Aguirre—you got me through this book in one piece, and mostly on time.

Kate Pearce, Nic Montreuil, and Bria Quinlan—your

comments on drafts of *THtT* were invaluable to me. I hope you can spot your fingerprints all over this story as clearly as I can!

Megan Blocker, and Matt & Jaime Bartlett—anyone who cooks and enjoys the recipes in the back of this book should direct their compliments to you.

As for my soul sisters, Roxanne St. Claire and Kristen Painter—without your company in the trenches, day by day and hour by hour, I'd be a total wreck. And I'd probably never write a word. Whenever anyone asks me about my muse, I think of you two.

Thank you to my parents, Jan and George, who started reading romance because it's what I write—but who, I think, are enjoying it more than they ever expected! And thanks to my sister, Georgia, who's been my partner in reading for nearly fifteen years. Love you guys!

Biggest love and thanks of all goes to my husband, Nick—you push me to do more than I think I can manage, and you believe in me when I forget how to believe in myself. Thank you for being the love of my life.

As always, any errors in the book are mine, and mine alone.

Too Hot
to Touch

Prologue

Juliet Cavanaugh wrapped her arms around her ribs for warmth and stomped her feet as she walked. The stomping had two benefits; it kept the blood flowing, and it relieved some of the pent-up freak-out simmering in her chest.

The boots she'd grabbed on her way out the door were her mother's—stealing them was a last act of defiance, and she refused to feel guilty about it.

Besides, they fit Juliet perfectly. At seventeen, she'd been as tall as her mother—and taller than most of the boys in her class—for the past three years already. Most of the time, it was a pain. But at the moment, with leather and shearling wool protecting her toes from the slushy sidewalk, Juliet was glad.

She stomped on in a furious haze, not even sure at first where she was headed, until she was thrown from her trancelike march when her boot hit a patch of ice and nearly slid out from under her. Wobbling precariously, she managed to find her balance, and looked up to discover that she was on a very familiar corner.

Barrow and Grove, tucked away in the heart of Greenwich Village.

Old brick town houses lined the narrow street; only a few windows were lit. The biggest source of illumination was the large plate-glass pane at the front of the building on the corner across from her. Warm, yellow light spilled out and sparked along the edges of the words "Lunden's Tavern," scrolled across the glass in a splash of antique gold.

The light seemed to beckon her forward, hinting at things like warmth and friendship and safety and home. Juliet clutched her elbows close to her body and tried not to think about that last thing.

Home. The place she wasn't allowed to go, anymore.

Her mother's flushed, angry face flashed against Juliet's eyelids every time she blinked wet snowflakes out of her lashes, but she pushed it down and buried it deep, right beside that other thing she wasn't thinking about, never wanted to think about again.

Her left shoulder throbbed where it met her neck, as if she could still feel the imprint of rough, too-tight fingers grabbing and holding and pulling her closer . . .

Shuddering, Juliet forced her eyes open and her mind as blank as the snow before it hit the dirty Manhattan streets.

Lunden's Tavern. Of course this was where she'd end up. Her best friend, Danny Lunden, lived above the restaurant. Danny had the kind of family Juliet had always dreamed about. Happy mom, dad who was always around . . . and, oh yeah, ridiculously hot older brother.

The idea of running into Max Lunden brought her up short. Her heart stuttered at the thought of his wide, easy smile and laughing blue-gray eyes, but even her diehard crush couldn't stand up to the humiliation of having him see her like this. She must look like . . . well, like a scared kid who'd been tossed out to wander in the snow.

If only she'd looked this much like a drowned rat earlier

tonight, when Oliver got home. Maybe then he would've ignored her, instead of coming into her room . . .

Paralyzed indecision kept her hopping from one foot to the other for an agonizing minute until a cab drove past, going fast enough that its tires fanned out a spray of cold, dirty water. Jumping back to avoid the impromptu ice bath, Juliet decided she was being dumb.

From her oh-so-subtle probing, she knew Max was home from culinary school, but that didn't mean he was *home* home. On a Friday night? No way. He was probably out with his friends. Or maybe a girlfriend.

In spite of everything that had happened tonight, the thought of Max with some pretty girly girl slid between Juliet's ribs and pricked at her heart.

But either way, it was beyond lame to stand around freezing to death just because a hot guy might see her looking less than her best.

As if Max ever noticed her, anyway.

Stumbling forward, Juliet headed for the comfort of the restaurant and her best friend.

Danny will help me figure out what to do.

But when she went around to the side entrance and pushed the buzzer for the Lundens' apartment above the restaurant, no one answered.

"Come on, come on," she breathed, the words puffing from her in clouds of condensation. Blowing on her fingers to warm them up, she debated for all of ten seconds before marching back to the front of the building.

She and Danny were supposed to keep out of the restaurant dining room during business hours. But this was totally an emergency, she decided.

I'll just peek in and see if Danny's there.

When she nudged open the heavy wooden door, a wave of lovely, welcoming heat rushed out. Unable to resist, Juliet sidled into the restaurant and looked around.

The dining room was empty.

Are they closed? she wondered, blood pounding in her ears. But the door wasn't locked.

Standing in the entryway, Juliet shifted her weight and scowled at the uncertainty flooding her chest. She hated feeling like this, her emotions so close to the surface all the freaking time. Being a teenager sucked.

Being at the mercy of the grown-ups in her life? Sucked worse.

Drawing in a breath and feeling her lungs start to thaw, Juliet stared around the small, deserted room. Black-and-white tiled floors gleamed under the golden lights. Red leather booths curved invitingly against the walls, making her long to sink into one and just veg. There weren't many tables; she thought the place might seat fifty guests at a time, but not too many more.

A Manhattan institution for decades, Lunden's was known for grilling the best steak in the city. Danny had given her a tour of the kitchen once, announcing his intention to take over as pastry chef one day, and make the best ever chocolate cake for the Broadway stars, politicians, and other famous people who came to Lunden's.

Juliet had been impressed by the speed and efficiency all around her as the chefs worked, but more than that, she'd been caught by the sense of camaraderie and friendship between them. They seemed almost like a big, loud family, and she'd longed to be part of it.

While Juliet was trying to decide if she had the guts to curl up on one of those banquettes and rest there in the warmth for a while, a man poked his head out of the door at the back of the restaurant, the one that led to the kitchen.

Juliet's pulse leaped for an instant—*Maybe it's Max!*—before she recognized Gus Lunden. Chef/owner of Lunden's Tavern, and her best friend's dad.

"I thought I heard the door," he said, a wide smile creasing his friendly face as he emerged from the kitchen, wiping his hands on a white side towel. "How's it going, kiddo? Danny's not here—he and Nina are checking on my wife's mother. She lives up on eighty-first, doesn't get around too well, even when it's not snowing and sleeting out. I told 'em to go ahead. After the fifth canceled reservation and the third no-show, I'm going to be closing up early anyway. Sorry you missed him."

"Oh," Juliet said, feeling awkward. "I'm sorry to bother you. I should go."

"No, no," Mr. Lunden protested. "Come in and get warm. It's a mess out there. Where are your scarf and gloves? You kids, I swear. Gallivanting around Manhattan in nothing but a jacket over—what is that, a dress? Without any sleeves, even. And all the weather forecasters warning us about Snowmageddon!"

"I didn't have much of a choice," Juliet muttered, tugging down the hem of the hated yellow dress. She wished she'd had time to change. Her skin prickled as warmth began to return to her body. Weirdly, she was shivering harder now than she had been outside, and of course, Mr. Lunden noticed.

"You're nearly blue!" Alarm widened the man's eyes. "Come on, why don't you take a seat. Let me get you something hot to drink. Right? That's what you do when someone's got a chill, isn't it? I wish Nina were here. My wife always knows exactly what to do."

Mr. Lunden came forward with his hand outstretched, and even though she was sure it made her look like a spaz, Juliet hustled sideways to avoid being touched. She didn't even mean to, exactly, but her skin felt jumpy and too tight for her body, as if she were trying to squeeze into last year's jeans.

He didn't seem to notice, waving her over to a corner

table and watching her drop down on the banquette, scarlet leather creaking under her.

"Thanks, Mr. Lunden," she managed. "Maybe just for a second, then I'll get out of your way."

"Aw, kid," he said, staring down at her, sympathy bright in his blue-gray eyes. His weathered face showed the lines of premature age, years spent in a professional kitchen, bent over hot cooking surfaces, but he still looked a lot like Danny and Max. The Lunden men all had strong jaws, storm-cloud eyes, and wide mouths, quick to grin.

"I've told you before, call me Gus! Nobody calls me Mr. Lunden. Around here, it's 'Chef' this and 'Chef' that, but 'Mr. Lunden' makes me look behind me for my old man."

There it was, that big, friendly smile, the same one that had first convinced her to set aside her shyness, just once, and say hi to the boy sitting next to her in math class. She'd gotten a distracted, absentminded version of that smile from Max once, and kept the memory in a treasure box in her mind, bringing it out every so often when things were bad to make herself feel better.

She trusted that smile.

Whatever tension or fear Juliet had been holding on to suddenly released in a torrent. A shiver raced through her, chattering her teeth together, and Gus frowned. "Right! That hot drink. You just sit here and concentrate on getting warm, and I'll be back in a jiff."

He marched into the kitchen, a man on a mission, and Juliet leaned her head against the stiff leather cushion of the banquette to catch her breath. She blinked up at the intricate pattern on the stamped-tin ceiling. There were stylized roses, she saw, worked into row after row of diamond shapes. She'd never noticed before. Pretty.

A clatter from the kitchen startled her into a jump but when the door swung open, it was only Mr. Lunden—Gus—with a round tray holding two steaming white mugs.

"Here you go." He slid one of the mugs across the table with a practiced move, the dark brown liquid inside sloshing but never spilling. Then, to Juliet's surprise, he pulled up a chair and took the other mug for himself.

"Um, thanks," Juliet said again. "But you don't have to . . . I mean, I'm sure I'll be good to go in a minute."

"I'm sure you will," he said, blowing on his drink. "But a little company never hurt anything." Leveling a sharp look over the rim of his mug, he went on, "Seems like maybe you could use the company, too."

Nodding, Juliet took too big a swallow of molten hot cocoa and burned her tongue.

"Careful, kiddo." Gus's gentle concern tightened something in Juliet's chest to an aching knot.

"It's good hot chocolate," she said, hating the hoarseness of her own voice. "I like it."

It was better than good, actually, thick and not too sweet, the rich, complex flavor coating Juliet's tongue with liquid comfort.

"Excellent," Gus said, putting his mug down and pinning her with a serious gaze. "Now, supposing you tell me what a kid your age is doing wandering around in a snowstorm like this?"

"I . . . wanted to hang out with Danny?" she tried, not sure what to say. Could she really tell him the truth? Shame burned lines along her cheekbones at the thought.

His eyes sharpened like a set of the chef's knives Danny had gleefully demonstrated on that kitchen tour. "I don't doubt you were hoping to find Danny at home, Jules, but what sent you out in the storm in the first place?"

Only the Lunden family ever called her that. The nickname made Juliet's throat close tight, as if she'd suddenly become allergic to chocolate. What was next, hives?

"I had a fight with my mom," she told him, hiding her

expression by dipping her head for another sip of hot chocolate. She glanced up through her eyelashes to check his reaction.

"Hmm," was all Gus said. "I thought it must be something like that."

His calm acceptance gave her a burst of confidence. "Actually, it was worse than a fight. It was . . . I'm never going back there."

That made him press his lips together in a tight, flat line. "Family is important," he said slowly. "Are you sure there's no way—"

"Not ever," she said fiercely, wanting to make him understand. "I left, because I couldn't stay, but now I don't have anywhere to—to go . . ."

To her absolute horror, a loud, ugly sob choked out of her before she knew what was happening. Covering her mouth with one hand, Juliet slid down in the seat and wished she could disappear under the table. Tears wet the top edge of her hand, but she managed to force the rest of her sobs into whimpering breaths.

"Hey now," Gus said, looking alarmed. "No need for that. Here." He leaned to one side, grabbed a linen napkin off the table next to them and handed it to Juliet.

"Thanks," she said when she could speak again. "Crap. I didn't mean to get all girly on you."

Gus shrugged, concern still filling his expression. "Nothing wrong with a good cry. I've been known to indulge, myself."

For the first time since she came in, Gus looked tired, and Juliet blinked her tears away. Maybe she wasn't the only one having problems.

"How about you, Mr. Lunden? Gus, I mean. Are *you* doing all right?"

Gus's head reared back, his eyes wide and shadowed

with something Juliet couldn't understand. "What, me? Right as rain, kid. I'm . . . oh, fine. Just fine."

For the first time since she came into the restaurant, Juliet didn't believe a word out of Gus's mouth. Before the welling suspicion could set her jittery nerves jangling again, he sighed and said, "Okay, so I'm not fine. Had a little fight with Max tonight, and it's got me on edge." He gave her a determined smile. "But maybe my problem is your good luck."

Juliet blinked, thrown by the reference to Max. "What? I mean . . . what?"

All the weariness melted out of Gus's expression. His smile was only a little forced, and the kindness behind his gray eyes was real enough. "You need somewhere to crash, right? And as of an hour ago, I've got an empty room upstairs that's yours for the asking. Maybe just for tonight; could be, tomorrow you'll see things differently and want to give your mom a call."

Juliet shook her head instinctively, but Gus held up a hand. "That's something to think about later. For right now, we need to find you a hot shower and some dry clothes, then bed. I think that's the procedure. You'll have to bear with me; my wife is the one who usually arranges things when we have guests come to stay."

"I don't understand . . . what room? Are you . . . are you serious?" Juliet had been over at Danny's lots of times. It was a nice place, bigger than her mom's apartment, but Juliet had never noticed a spare guestroom.

"Nothing to understand." Gus clapped his hands together once before gathering up the empty mugs from the table. "You need some space from your mom. And hey, whattaya know! We happen to have some empty space to fill. Come on, up with you. We can work out the details later. You need to get some dry clothes on."

Juliet stood, and didn't flinch at Gus's gentle grasp on her arm. She swayed on her feet, weariness dropping over her like a heavy blanket, muffling the world around her. Everything was happening so fast.

"Why would you take me in? Just like that. How do you know I'm not lying about my mom and everything?"

Gus smiled, and in that moment, he looked so much like his sons that it took Juliet's breath away. "My wife, Nina—she's the one who does the hiring around here. She's got a sense about people, Nina does. She can tell if a waiter's going to be the type to liberate ribeyes from the freezer or take bottles of wine home to his girlfriend. She sees under the surface. Me, I take people as they come. I look at you, and I see my son's friend, a nice kid with blond hair and brown eyes. I see someone who's taken a solid hit, but isn't down for the count. I see a good girl in a bad situation, who's smart enough to let me make her situation a little bit better."

"I don't even know what to say . . ."

Gus nodded decisively. "It's settled, then. You'll stay with us tonight, and tomorrow, we'll see what's what."

He strode off toward the back of the restaurant, giving Juliet an impatient glance over his shoulder, clearly expecting her to follow along like a duckling after its mother.

"Come on, Jules," Gus said. "The last thing we need is for you to catch a chill. My wife would kill me, and when she was done, Danny would take his turn."

Something bloomed in Juliet's chest, a warm, expanding balloon of emotion too huge to fully understand. All she knew for sure was that she'd never felt safer in her life.

She smiled, and took her first step into a new future.

Chapter 1

6 years later

The dining room was deserted, the cracked red leather of the banquettes sagging sadly over the snowy white tablecloths.

From here, she couldn't tell that those linens were all fraying at the edges, but she could see every chip, every indelible scuff mark, in the gorgeous black-and-white tiles covering the floor.

Jules Cavanaugh peered out the round glass window cut into the kitchen door and remembered another night when Lunden's had been empty, just like this. Only tonight, there was no blizzard. No storm. No snow.

And no customers, either.

Mind full of the worries that had become all too common over the last year and a half—*is it time to talk Gus into shutting down lunch service? Do we really need four servers on Thursday nights if we don't get more than ten covers all night long? What am I going to tell Gino when he calls about next week's beef order? They're not going to extend our credit forever, even if Gino's great-grandfather supplied the first steaks ever cooked at Lunden's*—Jules had managed to tune out most of the commotion behind her.

A kitchen full of chefs with nothing to do was a recipe for trouble, and the Lunden's crew was no exception.

The long, dull hours of boredom and inactivity, interspersed with pockets of chaos and action when a customer did happen to wander in wore on the men and women who kept Lunden's back-of-the-house operations going.

Well, mostly men, Jules acknowledged, turning around to survey her ragtag makeshift family.

It was quite the sausage fest in the Lunden's kitchen, she mused. And sure, it was weird for her sometimes, being the lone hen in a crowd of cocks, but mostly she felt like one of them.

Winslow Jones, always the first to get antsy, was entertaining himself by trying to con, charm, and weasel personal info out of their newest hire. Chef Beck, first name unknown to anyone other than Gus, who'd presumably seen his paperwork, gave Win back the stone-faced, crossed-arms routine he gave everyone—but Jules thought she detected a slight softening around his eyes.

She sympathized. It was hard not to soften up around Winslow, who had the kind of infectious good humor that was so sorely lacking around here, these days. Even Phil hadn't been able to—Jules cut off the thoughts of her ex before they could begin.

"How long do you think they'll stick around if Dad can't make payroll?"

Jules jolted free of the endless circle of worries and fears and slanted Danny a glance. "Don't talk like that. We're not there."

Yet.

Danny gave her the look that meant he heard everything she wasn't saying, loud and clear, but he let it go.

Twisting his hands in the white cloth looped through his apron strings, Danny slumped against the kitchen door beside her, his head dropping forward so all she could see was the pale, vulnerable back of his neck. Danny always took so much on. Too much, and he refused to lean on anyone. Only Jules got to see the exhausted, careworn side of him—and that, only when he was too tired to hide it from her.

"Your dad has a plan," Jules reminded him brightly, ignoring her own misgivings.

Danny hissed out a sigh, lifting his head to bang it once against the door. "Judas priest. Don't remind me."

"The Rising Star Chef competition could be the answer to all our problems," Jules argued. "Every restaurant that's ever won it has turned into a huge sensation—reviews, publicity, and most of all, customers. Think about it, Danny. All the business we can handle, and then some!"

"You sound like Dad."

Jules bit the inside of her cheek for control. "I believe in Gus. Wherever he leads, I'm going to be right behind him. A hundred percent."

"Even if what he wants is for you to follow Max?"

Damn it. Danny knew her too well. Meeting his watchful gaze, Jules admitted, "Okay, maybe ninety percent. We don't need Max to win this thing."

He knocked his head against the door one more time in agreement, with a twist to his mouth that tugged at Jules's heart. "Mom's calling him today anyway, whether we like it or not. But hey, the good news is, he probably won't come home. How could home be more fun than backpacking around Asia, living by his wits and a wok? And Dad doesn't want Max to know about . . . how bad the restaurant's doing."

Danny's moment of hesitation was like flimsy aluminum foil covering a heavy pot full of boiling, seething,

steaming resentment, worry, love, and—worst of all—
fear. Jules knew, because she felt the same way.

It wasn't only the restaurant's dire straits Gus intended
to hide from his oldest son.

Facing forward and pretending to watch Winslow tease
Beck, she cleared her throat and said, "How's your dad
feeling? Better?"

"He insists he's fine," Danny murmured. "He doesn't
want to talk about it."

They lapsed into silence. Jules took in the demoralized
kitchen crew leaning against their cold, empty stations. She
thought about Gus and his hopes for the restaurant, and
Danny, trying desperately to hold everything together, the
weight of his own legacy bearing down on his shoulders.
She remembered that snowy night six years ago, and how
much she owed this family.

She'd do anything she could to save Lunden's Tavern,
up to and including working side by side with the guy
who'd occupied most of her teen fantasies.

How bad could it be, right? After all, she was completely over him. Over men, in general, after Phil. So there
was nothing to worry about. Not a thing.

Beck began to show signs of irritation with Winslow's
increasingly hyper bouncing. But as Jules moved in to
rescue him, glad of the distraction, she couldn't help but
notice that the shiver running down her spine at the thought
of Max wasn't all dread, or even resignation.

It was anticipation.

The streets of Tokyo were a blur of dizzying colors, sounds
too loud to understand, and smells that usually made Max
Lunden want to tackle the nearest vendor for a taste of
whatever mysterious meat on a stick was putting out that
rich, fragrant smoke.

Today, though, Max's normally ironclad stomach was

too jumpy to risk street food. Ducking out of the swift, relentless current of foot traffic into an arched stone doorway, he looked down at his cell phone for the hundredth time, making sure it was on, had full bars, was ready and waiting to receive the most important call of his life.

For the last hour, Max had been elbow-deep in dough struggling to learn how to cut perfectly straight, even ramen noodles, and sucking at it because all he could concentrate on was his silent phone.

Once he finally had gotten his hands free and clean, and apologized to a very grouchy Harukai-sensei for being so distracted during his lesson, Max took to the streets to try and walk off his frustration.

He kept his fingers wrapped around his phone inside his pocket, so he'd feel it the instant it started to vibrate.

Ring. Ring. Ring, for shit's sake!

As if by magic, he felt a buzz against his fingertips, followed by Steve Tyler's unmistakable, if tinny, voice singing about living on the edge.

Heart in his mouth, palms suddenly slick with sweat, Max got the phone free of his pocket with only one near-catastrophic fumble. Centering himself with a deep breath, Max hit the button and lifted the phone to his ear.

"Hello? Yes?"

Silence, punctuated by a bit of static and some breathing.

Cursing himself, Max cleared his throat. *"Si? Pronto."*

They were the magic words, unleashing a volley of rapid-fire Italian Max had to struggle to wade through.

"Si. Si. Si," he kept saying, feeling like a moron and not sure what he was agreeing to, until the gruff voice on the other end exhaled sharply.

"Italiano. You learn. Fast. I teach nothing until you understand my language."

Max's rib cage expanded with joy like phyllo pastry

puffed up with honey. For a moment, he was honestly afraid his chest would pop open and spill his heart onto the street.

"You'll teach me, then?" He had to clarify, had to be sure this wasn't a mistake or a misunderstanding.

A long pause. "When you came to see me, two summers before . . . you were not stupid. Not completely. I think you can learn." Vincenzo Cotto's thick, accented growl went even rougher and lower. "So long as you learn to speak . . . and more important, to listen, in *italiano*."

"I'll learn," Max promised. "I swear, I'll be fluent by the time I see you."

"Hmph. You have four weeks."

Calculating frantically, Max immediately started listing in his head all the things he'd have to do—finish his lessons with Harukai-sensei, pack up all his gear, find a place to stay in the tiny Italian village that housed Cotto's famed *macellaio*, the butcher shop where he sold his award-winning cured meats and sausages, and also occasionally took on an apprentice.

Very occasionally. Rarely, in fact, so rarely that Max could hardly believe his last two years of intermittent campaigning by letter and visit had finally paid off.

Once he'd learned what Cotto could teach him about prosciutto, pancetta, and fresh pasta, Max would be versed in the skills of every major cuisine. And a lot of the minor ones, too, since he tended to veer off course whenever curiosity beckoned. But this final piece of the puzzle?

Max had waited a long time to slot it into place.

"Four weeks," he repeated, like a vow. "I'll be in Le Marche in a month."

Cotto grunted again, sounding satisfied, and hung up, leaving Max to stare out at the rushing river of pedestrians, bicycles, mopeds, and buses that clogged the Tokyo street.

He was moving on again, onto the next new thing, the

next challenge—and maybe this time, it would be enough. Maybe he'd find the place where he could stop for a while, and feel at ho—

His phone rang again, almost vibrating itself right out of his hand.

Shit. Had Cotto changed his mind already?

Dread clutching at Max's heart, he thumbed the phone on and said, *"Pronto."*

"Max?"

The uncertain voice didn't belong to a mercurial Italian butcher-savant.

"Mom! I'm so glad it's you. I was just about to call, I've got amazing news."

"Do you?" The alarm in her voice sliced neatly through Max's euphoria. He frowned.

Something had wigged his normally unwiggable mother.

"Mom? What's up?"

"Nothing, honey, tell me your news." The clear nerves in her voice twisted Max's tension a notch higher.

"Mom, you're freaking me out, here. What's going on?"

"You need to come home."

The world stopped.

"Did something happen?" Max forced out through numb lips.

Nina's pause was enough to get Max's heart jackrabbitting in his chest, but she said, "No, of course not. I'm sorry, I didn't mean to scare you, honey."

Max's lungs jerked into motion again. Relief made his voice sharp. "If everybody at home is fine, then what's this all about?"

"Don't take that tone with me."

Max winced. Nina rarely busted out the steely grim, but when she did, no one was dumb enough to cross her.

"And you'd better not be saying the only way you'd come home is if someone's dead or in the hospital."

Max worked at smoothing out his tone. "No, of course not, Mom." Although that was kind of true, wasn't it? His conscience reared its ugly head, but Max sat on it. He'd left home for a reason, and he hadn't looked back.

"So you'll come home."

"Mom. Seriously. Do Dad and Danny even know you're calling me?"

"Of course!"

Her overly bright confidence set off Max's bullshit meter. "Oh yeah?"

Her huff of frustration was clearly audible, even over the somewhat crackly reception he got on his international cell phone. "Your father wants you home. Your brother's not thrilled about it, but deep down, he knows I'm right. We need you, Max."

Max sighed. It was entirely lame, but for one brief, glittering moment he'd actually allowed himself to contemplate the possibility of his family being ready to forgive and forget.

He'd talked to them since he left home—casual, careful conversations, chitchat. It was okay with Dad, if stilted. With Danny, though? Not so much. The kid knew how to hold a grudge. Every conversation was an emotional minefield.

"Sounds like nothing has changed," Max said, trying to keep his heart open and yielding, rather than bitter and shielded. It was harder than usual. "And I don't have time to come home—I have to be in Italy in a month."

Even in the midst of arguing with his mother, anticipation thrilled through him.

"What? Honey, that butcher you're always going on about? The one who never takes on an apprentice."

"Almost never," Max clarified, grinning into the phone. "I need a crash course in Italian, because I'm going back to Loro Piceno in four weeks. And this time, I'm staying until I learn everything Vincenzo Cotto has to show me."

"I'm proud of you. I know you've wanted this for a long time," Nina said, and she did sound happy for him. Her urgency had dimmed somewhat, giving Max hope he'd made his point.

"So you get it? I'd love to come visit, Mom, but I can't miss this opportunity. Vincenzo Cotto is the best in the world, and he picked me."

As if it could be that easy.

"A month is all we need." Nina rallied quickly. "You'll be back on the road before you know it."

"Mom—"

"Maxwell Gerard Lunden. You had better not be thinking about saying no to me."

Max hesitated. The note of steel had reentered his mother's sweet voice. Nina Lunden might look like a cream puff, but she was filled with sterner stuff than vanilla-flavored pastry cream, for sure.

"If I show up at the restaurant," he said, trying to be reasonable, "it's going to be a fight. You know I'm right."

"It's not okay for you and Danny to be at odds. You're brothers. It's past time to fix things between the two of you. And your father might surprise you. Besides, we don't need you to work at the restaurant—where we need you is on the team for the Rising Star Chef competition."

"What?" To Max's knowledge, Lunden's Tavern had never participated in any culinary competitions, let alone the largest, most prominent one in the United States.

"We've put together a team, and we could really use your competition experience. Your father's even willing to give you his spot on the team for the first leg of the competition—that's how serious he is about winning."

Max leaned back against the wall, trying to take it all

in. He'd been making his living for years by entering culinary challenges around the world, winning enough cash prizes to give him the freedom to apprentice himself to whatever master of the local cuisine could teach him the most. But those were single-competitor challenges in small cities and even villages, not a huge national competition like the RSC.

And the idea that his father could admit, even obliquely, that Max might be better at something . . . Max couldn't help the grin that spread over his face.

As if sensing a weakness, Nina immediately segued into wheedling. "Come on, honey. I'm sure after so many wins, you must have lots of tips and tricks you could share, strategies that could help your brother and the others!"

Max laughed. "You're laying it on a little thick," he told her.

He heard the smile in her voice. "Is it working?"

Sighing, Max knocked his head against the rough wall behind him. "Kind of," he admitted. "I'd do anything I could to help you, and the chance to make things right with Danny, with Dad—I won't lie. It's tempting. But—"

Nina wouldn't be reasoned with. "Things change, honey. People change."

"In our stubborn family? No. Not really." If Max knew anything, he knew that. He'd given up on hoping for more a long time ago.

"Fine, but situations change. If you don't join the team . . . Max, we can win. We have a good team, but they're green. It's imperative that we pass the initial qualifying rounds and get chosen to represent the East Coast. Once we're over that hurdle, I think we'll be okay, but to get there, we need your help. I'm pulling the mother card here, Max. Give me some credit; I haven't seen my oldest son at home in six years, but have I nagged you about visiting? No. I've flown out to see you when I could. But now

I'm not asking, I'm telling. Whatever it takes, whatever happens after you get here, we'll work it out. I just . . . you need to come home."

Max's throat tightened in defense against the almost undetectable quiver in his mother's voice. Not so steely, now, and he couldn't remember the last time he'd heard her sound like that. Maybe when his grandmother died. Something was up, something more than this sudden obsession with winning the Rising Star Chef competition. And whatever it was, it was bad enough to make the strongest woman Max had ever known sound like she was about to cry.

"Just for the qualifying round?" Max clarified, wanting to be sure he understood what she was asking. "I get you a spot in the competition, and then I'm on a plane to Italy."

"That's all I'm asking," she said, cautious happiness coloring her voice.

Gripping the phone tightly enough to make his fingertips go numb, Max breathed in the hot, wet air of Tokyo, heavy with the scents of fog and car exhaust, and said, "I'll be on the next flight out."

Chapter 2

Stepping off a plane and into the bustle of weekday New York City was like being tossed headfirst into raging white-water rapids.

Good thing he remembered how to swim, Max mused as he tossed the single, beat-up duffel that held all his worldly possessions into the backseat of a cab, and climbed in after it.

He'd been navigating the furious, thrilling, dangerous waters of Manhattan since he was old enough to sneak under the subway turnstiles and hop a train going wher-ever.

No matter how far he traveled, or how many exotic foreign cities he saw, nothing from London to Marrakech could compare with the sheer jolt of electric excitement straight to the nervous system that was New York.

God, he'd missed it.

The cabbie swerved to avoid being cut off by a bus as they merged onto the Long Island Expressway, swearing violently in Bengali.

Max grinned as the guy cursed the bus driver's ances-try, homeland, and manhood. "Bastard son of a motherless goat," Max agreed when his cabbie stopped to take a breath.

The guy's eyes in the rearview mirror lit up with surprise and pleasure to hear his native tongue from the random, scruffy white guy in the back of his cab. He launched into a stream of rapid Bengali, all liquid vowels and harsh consonants, that Max had no hope of following.

Holding up his hands in surrender, he said in English, "Sorry, man. I pretty much shot my wad with that one sentence."

Having worked in kitchens around the world, Max could order food—and curse a blue streak—in more than a dozen languages. His polite vocabulary, on the other hand, was decidedly lacking.

The cabbie didn't seem to mind. He switched to English, too, and they spent the last fifteen minutes of the cab ride comparing notes on the places they'd both been in Bangladesh, how beautiful it was, and how much they missed it.

It seemed to be Max's lot in life to always be missing the amazing places he'd lived. He almost wished, sometimes, that he could be happy staying in one place.

Almost.

Until he remembered that staying in one place meant expectations, responsibilities, and the inevitability of disappointment. Whether his, or someone who counted on him, Max would take a pass.

As long as he could make a good life for himself out of cooking his way around the world and winning the occasional culinary competition, he'd keep on rolling and gathering no moss.

Weird fucking phrase, anyway. He was never sure if gathering moss was supposed to be a good or a bad thing. But he'd always loved the Rolling Stones.

He was impressed when the cabbie got them through

the rabbit warren of narrow Greenwich Village streets to the corner of Barrow and Grove without needing any directions. The restaurant loomed in front of the windshield, as stolid and immutable as ever. Max felt everything inside him tensing up as if he were heading into a hotly contested war zone. Stuffing it down, he paid the cabbie and hefted his duffel onto one shoulder.

Enough stalling, Max.

He breathed out, long and slow, then inhaled another deep breath through his nose, imagining himself filling up with peace and serenity.

He had a feeling he was going to need it.

The restaurant dining room was empty of customers, but the place wasn't really open yet. The front-of-house staff was starting to get set up for lunch, going through the familiar dance of clean white tablecloths and gleaming glassware. Max didn't recognize any of them; not surprising, considering the high turnover rate among servers in Manhattan. They looked up curiously as he strode between the tables, but Max tipped them a nod and kept moving toward the kitchen.

He'd always found that a confident stride and a straightforward gaze kept people from questioning his right to be places he had no real business being.

Making it to the kitchen door with no hassling, Max blew out a breath and braced himself, then pushed it open.

Here goes nothing.

The kitchen wasn't as active as Max remembered—only a single lone chef doing prep. Max frowned. Was there a lunch service today? There ought to be at least three prep chefs busily chopping vegetables and making stock. Where was everyone?

Stepping farther into the kitchen, Max stared at the one guy over in the corner, who seemed to be working industriously enough for ten chefs. His head was down, only a hint of short brown hair peeking out from under the bill of his backward baseball cap. Max grinned at the familiar Yankees logo for a second before realizing with a start that he was looking at his younger brother.

Tension shot through him, but he plastered on a grin and repeated his mantra.

You gotta give love to get love.

"Danny! How long has it been, man?" Max dropped his duffel and walked over to drape an arm around his kid brother's shoulders.

Despite the mindfuck of being home for the first time in six years, despite the lingering hurt of knowing the kid hated him for leaving, Max found himself sincerely happy to see Danny.

"Too long," Danny said, barely sparing him a glance as he shrugged Max's arm off.

Apparently, the reverse wasn't true for baby bro. Okey-dokey, then.

Danny's hands hadn't paused in their machine-gun-fast knife work, the rat-a-tat-tat of his blade turning a few big pieces of candied ginger into a perfectly uniform pile of honey-amber cubes sticky with sugar. Max stepped back to watch, impressed by the kid's precision and concentration.

Although he really wasn't such a kid anymore, Max reminded himself. "Dude," he said, as easy and casual as could be, "I know it's been a while, but hey, the phone works at both ends."

Danny snorted, unimpressed.

"Or you could've come visit me when Mom did. You would've loved Morocco."

There it was, the flicker of an eye that told Max he had his brother's interest piqued. "Oh yeah? Better than Tokyo?"

"Different. The air is hotter, drier. Thick with spices.

And some of the desserts—you should've tasted them, they would've given you so many ideas . . ."

Whoops, wrong thing to say. Whatever headway he'd made in loosening Danny up was lost; the guy's shoulders tensed up practically to his ears, and his voice was rough with some suppressed emotion when he said, "I don't need new ideas. The desserts we make here were good enough for people like Frank Sinatra and Rudy Giuliani—I don't see any reason to change. Besides, there's only room for one person in this family to be a carefree world traveler, and it ain't me."

The slice of guilt was quick and deep, but Max muscled through it with the ease of practice.

"Well, Danny boy, you might not have missed me, but I sure missed the hell out of you."

He wrapped his arm back around his brother's shoulders and squeezed, but Danny stayed stiff and resistant, the distance between them a deep, silent chasm.

Taking in a cleansing breath of calm and serenity, Max started, "Look, Danny. I never really got a chance to say good-bye to you, but—"

"It's fine," Danny said, stepping away to grab the white plastic tub of granulated sugar. "Don't worry about it."

It very obviously wasn't fine, but Max had a feeling he wasn't going to get any further with his brother right then. Calling on the patience he'd worked so hard to hone and deepen, Max gestured around the mostly empty kitchen. There were a few guys working the line, but Max didn't recognize them. "Where is everyone?"

"Dad likes to give the team the day off when we're practicing for the competition at night."

"Sure, so they can't hand him any lame excuses about being tired from service." Max nodded, familiar with his father's wily ways of extracting peak performances out of his employees.

"Yup."

"But you, he cuts no slack, whether you work lunch or not. Am I right?"

Danny's shoulders went rigid as he hunched over his cutting board. "Don't start, Max. Forget what I said before, about the world travel and all that bullshit. I'm here because I want to be."

Max scowled. "Sure. Because your dreams have never extended beyond the confines of this one restaurant."

Instead of whirling to face him, Danny hunched over the board and sped up his knife cuts, turning a peeled apple into julienned strips so thin they looked like the translucent fringe on a Moulin Rouge dancer's costume. Max watched him for a long moment. "How much pastry you doing these days, anyway?"

"Plenty," Danny said, but the words were strangled, forced out through a clenched jaw. "Working on a gingered apple tart right now. And it's my position on the team, after all."

"Right, the team, the team." Max sighed. "I guess you'd better tell me the deal with that, since I'm supposed to be jumping in and leading it to victory."

Danny snorted. "If you want to lead, you might have a fight on your hands."

"Whoa," Max said, backing way the hell off. "I'm not Fearless Leader Guy—I only meant what Mom said, about handing out tips and tricks for dealing with competition. I've got no interest in calling the shots."

"Yeah, you've made that crystal clear." Danny didn't say anything else, but then, he didn't have to. They both knew what he meant.

Danny loved baking—since they were kids, he'd been doing stuff with chocolate that wasn't natural—so all he'd ever wanted was to take over as pastry chef at Lunden's Tavern. Whereas Max, the elder son, the all-around chef who loved coming up with new recipes and trying new techniques—he was supposed to be the executive chef after their dad retired, and carry on the family tradition of being boxed into the stifling, rigid prison of The Way Things Have Always Been Done.

It was why he left home. Max wouldn't give up his own dreams and ideas for the future—and Gus refused to accept it.

The Way Things *Could* Be Done. Max loved the thrill of risk and challenge that raced down his spine at the thought of shaking things up. Of taking his family's West Village institution of a restaurant and making it . . . new. Fresh. An exciting blend of tradition and innovation.

Neatly sidestepping the landmine, Max said, "So who's on this crackerjack team of culinary studs? Anyone I'd remember from the old days?"

Because he was a stand-up guy, Danny let him get away with it. "Maybe; depends how sharp your memory is. There are at least a couple of new guys, too."

"Yeah? They any good?"

"One of them is the best fish cook I've ever seen," Danny told him. "Brand-new guy, just hired a few weeks ago to replace . . ." A muscle ticked in Danny's jaw, and his eyes went flinty enough to raise the short hairs on the back of Max's neck.

"Replace who?"

"Not important. Anyway, Beck's a killer in the kitchen. Hell, maybe out of the kitchen, too—no one knows much about the guy, other than that when he's cooking, he runs his station like the fate of the planet hangs in the balance. He cuts no corners, accepts no shit off anyone, and takes no prisoners."

"Oh good." Max stuck his hands in his pockets and leaned against the counter beside Danny's pastry board. "My favoritest thing ever! A tough guy. Lay you dollars to doughnuts he's got a thick neck, a shaved head, and no sense of humor."

"Uncanny," Danny deadpanned. "How did you guess? Except for the part where you're totally wrong. He's a big guy, but his hair's longish. Longer than yours, Buzz Cut. And he doesn't crack wise too often, but when he does, it's extra hilarious. And speaking of hilarious, there's Winslow Jones. He's our prep chef."

Max snapped his fingers. "I think I know him! Did he stage in Provence?" He'd met a young black chef named Winslow Jones—and how many guys with that name could there be?—when he was in Avignon learning how to make perfect ratatouille from a tiny, white-haired lady who spoke no English.

Winslow was doing his stage, a sort of unpaid culinary apprenticeship, at the ratatouille lady's grandson's restaurant, and Max had instantly bonded with the short, quirky, smack-talking chef. Maybe it was the expat thing; there was something almost magical about reconnecting with another person from your own country when you were living among people who didn't speak your language. But Max couldn't actually picture anyone not liking the guy—he was funny as hell, and he kicked ass on the line the few times Max had invited himself over to the restaurant kitchen to watch them cook. What more could you ask for?

"Yeah, he mentioned having met you over there when Dad hired him."

Max snorted. "That was a tactical blunder. I'm surprised Dad didn't fire him on the spot."

A muscle ticked in Danny's jaw, but all he said was, "Win is solid. We're lucky to have him—but not as lucky as we got with Jules."

Max felt like a dog hearing a knock at the front door. All systems alert! Potential fun ahead!

"Jules. Jules. I seem to remember a Juliet hanging out with you, the two of you following me around, looking to get into trouble. Same girl? I bet it is. A chick on the team. Score. Come on, dish it up. Is she hot now? I bet she's hot."

Danny shook his head, amusement relaxing the tense line of his mouth. "Is that all you ever think about?"

"No! Sometimes I think about food. And beer. Scuba diving. Horse races. The color cyan. I'm a complex and multilayered flower, Danny."

"Well, Jules isn't for you." Danny swept the flat of his knife across the cutting board and scooped up his apple fringe, depositing it in a big rectangular plastic tub. "She's a damn fine chef, Mom and Dad adore her, and most importantly, we need her. The team can't win without her— we'll smoke the time challenges with Jules on board. You've never seen anything like this girl when it comes to knife work. Hand to God."

Max hopped up on the counter. "Sooo . . . you're saying hands off the merchandise? Keep my distance? No touchy, no feely?"

Danny rolled his eyes. "She also happens to be a friend of mine. A good one, so lay off, okay? You must've banged a billion girls, from Paris to Sydney. Aren't you done yet?"

"Never," Max declared. "And I resent your slurs against my chivalrous character. My heart burns for the pure, sweet love of this paragon of virtue, this goddess of sweetness and light and the perfect *brunoise,* this . . . what did you call her again?"

"Jules," said a husky, somehow familiar female voice from behind him.

Every hair on the back of Max's neck stood up as if someone were blowing a warm breath over his skin.

When he passed through Bangkok, he'd learned to take note of that feeling—a couple of times, it was all that saved

him from getting run down by one of the motorized rick-
shaws they called tuk-tuks.

That prickle saved him from getting his pocket picked
in Rome, from a snake bite in Sao Paolo, and from dancing with a yakuza's girlfriend in a Tokyo club.

So when he felt it now, in the middle of this nearly
empty kitchen in his family's restaurant, he was under-
standably wary. Sliding off the counter, he turned slowly,
hands loose and ready at his sides, pushing his weight
onto the balls of his feet.

Prepared for anything.

Anything except . . . her.

Chapter 3

It figured. Less than two months after swearing off men for good—and dating coworkers in particular—the hottest chef Jules had ever seen stood in her own damn kitchen.

Max Lunden. In the unbearably delicious, sinfully tempting flesh, and wasn't it a cleaver to the back of the neck that she even noticed how hot he was?

Not that it mattered. Whether she liked it or not, they were going to be working together, and that meant she couldn't afford to notice anything about Max Lunden beyond his cooking skills.

In the testosterone-laden world of professional restaurants, it was hard enough for a female executive chef to earn and keep the respect of the male chefs under her. Sleeping with them? Almost never a good tactic. If she'd learned nothing else from Phil the Phucktard, as Danny always called him, she'd learned that.

Max gave her a long, slow, sweeping glance like a head-to-toe caress. Not to be outdone or intimidated, Jules returned it.

God. She hated—hated!—the fact that he was still tall.

Still broad in the shoulder and lean through the hips, all scruffy along the jaw and still with that casual disarray to his light brown hair that made him look like he'd perpetually just stepped off a sailboat.

Her fingers twitched involuntarily, itching to run through the short cowlicks. Standing motionless and indoors, Max Lunden managed to look as if he had wind in his hair.

Because that's who he is, she reminded herself. *A guy in perpetual motion. Sure, he's back—but not for good. Keep him at a distance, get whatever competition tips out of him you can, remember your promise to Gus, and everything will be fine.*

She knew how to do this. She was a professional, damn it.

God knew, she'd always been better at that than at the personal stuff, anyway.

Jules let the dining room door swing shut behind her and hiked the nylon strap of her knife roll higher on her shoulder. She moved forward, hand outstretched, a determined smile on her face.

"Hi," she said, going for calm and easy. It came out more robotic and weird, but there was no help for it—this was an awkward moment, at best. At worst? He'd remember the gangly teen girl with stars in her eyes whenever she looked at him. "I'm Jules Cavanaugh. Sous chef here for the past year and a half."

Recognition lit Max's blue-gray eyes, almost surprising Jules into dropping her hand.

"Well, well. Little Juliet, all grown-up."

She tensed, getting ready for a smart-ass remark about her stupid, schoolgirl crush. "I go by Jules now."

"It's so nice to see you again." Max enfolded her proffered hand in both his large, warm palms, sending a strange shiver of electricity dancing up her arms. "Although, really. Nice doesn't begin to cover it. Danny, for shame, keeping this loveliness all to yourself."

Before Jules could overcome her confusion and jerk her hand back, he'd raised it to his mouth for a quick kiss. His stubble scratched the backs of her fingers, but his mouth was soft and hot. And when he glanced at her over their linked hands, that mouth was curved in a wicked smile that spoke volumes about the hot, sweaty, naked things he'd like to do with her.

Or maybe I'm just projecting, she thought dazedly as she snatched her hand away from him and put it behind her back. Because this bore a startling resemblance to the onset of one of her better teen fantasies, where they met as equals and she gave him the cold shoulder, forcing him to work hard to win her.

Except this was real life, not some fantasy, and in real life, letting guys get away with playing grabby hands never ended well.

Clearly she needed to keep her distance from Max physically. Which was maybe easier said than done when rubbing the backs of her fingers against the worn, ribbed cotton of her tank top couldn't scrub the memory of his touch out of her brain.

Max rocked back on his heels, shoving his hands into his pockets, and said, "So. Juliet Cavanaugh. I assume my parents have been talking your ear off for the last however many months, telling you how awesome I am, and filling your head full of stories of my impressive talents in the kitchen."

"Um. Not so much," Jules said, shooting a glance at Danny, who shook his head and went back to his prep work.

"No? I should take this opportunity to set the record straight, then." Max heaved a deep sigh. "It's all true."

"What?"

"Everything they should've told you about me," Max explained. "And I don't know why they didn't, because it's all true. No exaggeration or family bias plays into it at all—I am the best chef in the entire world."

Danny snorted in the manner of one who'd heard this line before. Jules narrowed her eyes at Max, who stared back innocently, an expression of pious truth on his face. She couldn't help it—she knew he was kidding, he was practically winking and inviting her into the joke—but somehow, it caught her on the raw edge of the conversation she'd had the night before with Gus and Nina when they'd broken the news that Max was definitely coming home.

Max is a good boy, with a good heart, Nina had said, her softly lined face lovely when creased with a smile of pure joy and anticipation of her son's return. *He can be a little careless, sometimes.* She'd shot a look at her husband, unusually subdued. *Max doesn't always think about how his actions will affect others.*

Jules had to agree. Max clearly didn't understand the effect he was having on her, right now.

"Best chef in the world, huh?"

"Yup. I've been all over the world to check it out myself, personally, and I'm here to tell you. No one can touch me in the kitchen." He propped one lean hip on the counter, throwing his long-muscled form into stark relief, and grinned at her. "Well. You can, if you want."

"No need," Jules said, working to keep her voice even. "You might be the best chef in Europe, or wherever, but just so we're clear, you're not the top dog around here."

His eyes went a little wide when she didn't pick up his flirtatious cues, but he shrugged. "Hey, no worries. I don't need to be on top." Pausing, he quirked one brow outrageously before continuing smoothly, "I like to be on the bottom every now and again."

Jules wondered if there were some sort of daily sexual innuendo quota he had to meet. The danger of being misheard, her words misinterpreted, sent a cool wash of fear over her skin. She bit out, "As long as you understand. I'm in charge."

Max's eyes brightened. "Oooh, kinky! I think I'm in love. Juliet, I'm yours forever."

Danny slapped his white kitchen towel down on his cutting board with a loud *thwap*. "Get a room, you two."

Heat flared in Max's eyes, warming the blue to the color of the summer sky. Desire mixed with laughter looked good on him, Jules thought nonsensically, even as she fought the scorching blush streaking up her neck.

It had been a while since a guy affected her this much, this quickly. She didn't like it.

But then, she had a history with Max's smile—that same smile the Lunden men all shared. And the way Max laughed with his whole body, a sharp, emphatic bark that sounded a little bit surprised. Even though he laughed a lot, more than almost anyone Jules had ever met.

Well, he could laugh himself all the way back to Thailand or wherever, for all she cared. This was Jules's house. Her home, her job, her life—and she wasn't jeopardizing that for any hot piece of kitchen ass, no matter how flirty. And charming. And tall.

"It's Jules," she reminded him, before turning away abruptly and facing Danny. "Where are your mom and dad? Is Gus going to make it to practice tonight?"

"They were gone when I got up this morning; not sure when they'll be back."

"Dad's not making it to all the practices?" Max interjected, frowning and glancing around. "Speaking of which, holy crap. It's nearly time to open for lunch and he isn't here. Wtf?"

Jules stiffened. Max's bewilderment brushed right up

against one of secrets she'd been asked to keep: the fact that the lunch "rush" at Lunden's, lately, was more of a "dawdle." They were all worried about it, but no one was more stressed over the restaurant's falling numbers than Gus.

And if there was one thing they were all agreed on, it was that Gus didn't need any more stress.

"He has a lot on his plate at the moment," Jules said carefully. "Between the restaurant and the competition, and everything. It's fine. We'll soldier on without him."

"Beck and Winslow should be rolling up in about an hour," Danny said, shooting her a grateful glance.

"I'm going to get the demi-glace going," Jules said, already heading to the sink to soap up, slinging her knives onto the corner of counter she'd staked out as hers when she first started working at Lunden's Tavern.

"How about you, hotshot?" Danny asked, shooting a glare at his brother. "You want to hop onto the line and help out?"

Max grinned, that easy, crooked smile that Jules had to come up with a way to ignore. "No need for that," she cut in sharply. She needed a little extra time to get her personal stuff under control, and bumping into Max in the narrow confines of the kitchen wasn't going to help anything.

Instead of looking offended, Max laughed again, lighting up his whole face as he scooped up his duffel and headed for the back stairs. "Hey, I'd love to hit you with an assist, Danny boy, but the lady says you don't need me, and I've got some studying to do. Catch you later!"

"Slacker," Danny yelled after him, but Max just flipped the bird over his shoulder and kept going.

The instant the door closed behind him, it was as if all the air rushed back into the room, but some joker had switched the oxygen for nitrous oxide—but without the fun euphoria.

Jules's head whirled, filled with nothing but the helter-skelter of relief at being able to breathe again . . . and a sharp stab of fear that the return of the prodigal son meant the life she'd carved out for herself was about to change forever.

Chapter 4

"No, no, no, not like that! You have to strain the sauce. Twice, but not more than that, because—"

Jules put on her most soothing voice and moved to intercept. "Twice makes it smooth, three times makes it watery, Beck knows, Gus. Are you feeling okay?"

Worry clutched at Jules's heart with a tight fist as she stood next to Beck, ostensibly overseeing his stirring of the port wine sauce, while watching a grumbling Gus out of the corner of her eye.

Beck was hard to read—okay, make that impossible to read—most of the time, but tonight, as Jules met his expressionless gaze over the pan of roasted duck stock thickened with a sticky syrup of reduced port and minced garlic, she was pretty sure she knew what he was thinking.

It had been a long, uneventful slog of a dinner service—but their head chef still looked exhausted, pinched around the eyes and mouth.

If the restaurant were booked to full capacity, they might've been in trouble. She never thought she'd be thankful for a slow night.

Although the lulls between orders gave them all way

too much time to contemplate the elephant in the kitchen—Max's homecoming.

"I'm fine," Gus said firmly. "It would take more than high blood pressure and a few twinges to slow me down."

Jules didn't want to argue, she really didn't, only—"Come on, Gus, it's not just the blood pressure thing. It hasn't been even two months since you collapsed! In the middle of dinner service! The doctor wants you to take it easy, and I'm—we're worried."

I couldn't bear it if anything happened to you, she thought, but didn't say.

"Well, I wish you'd all quit worrying," he said irritably, swiping his wild gray hair back from his blotchy, pale face. "It's not making this practice go any more smoothly."

"Maybe if the whole team were here," Danny muttered from the pastry station. "Where the hell is Max?"

Jules shot her oldest friend a narrow look. She knew Danny liked to pretend there was no love lost between him and Max, but that conversation earlier told a different story.

There was plenty of love. If there weren't, they wouldn't be able to get under each other's skin so quickly and easily.

"You know he's on his way." Winslow Jones jumped in. "I mean, there's been an actual confirmed sighting and everything, so our boy's surely around here someplace." Win dropped the bright tone to mutter out of the corner of his mouth to Jules, "You saw him, right? Confirmed sighting, for real?"

She barely managed a nod. This practice was kicking her ass. She was completely off her game, jumping at every sound—and it was a high-stress, fast-paced, timed kitchen challenge. There were a *lot* of sounds.

It would be easier, she mused, if Max were here, where he was supposed to be. Sure, his presence equaled its own kind of tension, but to have him missing was like seeing a rat scurrying across the subway tracks. It wasn't as if she wanted to get up close and personal with the thing, but once she saw it, she didn't like to lose sight of it. Who knew where it might go?

"I wish he'd just get here already." Danny unconsciously echoed Jules's thoughts.

"Maybe he's asleep," Win suggested, looking almost unbearably calm as he expertly trimmed a skirt steak and flashed her a brilliant smile that creased his freckled cheeks. "I mean, give the guy a break. He did just fly halfway around the globe. There's such a thing as jet lag, yo."

Danny snorted. "Max never gets jet lag. It's one of the many annoying things about him."

"Taking my name in vain again, Danny? Tsk, tsk, for shame."

Jules stiffened all over at the lazy drawl of Max's voice in the instant before the man himself sauntered into the kitchen, hands in his pockets and lean shoulders slouched as casually as if he'd just been hanging out in the dining room this whole time, waiting to make the perfect entrance.

"Max!" Gus's happiness at the sight of his son flashed over his face, sharp enough to hurt Jules's heart. "Welcome home, son."

Surprise widened Max's eyes for a second, and Jules held her breath as the tension of the moment coiled tight. Max started forward, a smile pulling up one corner of his mouth.

Jules grabbed a silver tasting spoon from the stack on the counter and dipped up some of Beck's sauce, but she couldn't concentrate on the flavor because she was too busy watching as Max grabbed his father for a bear hug that nearly lifted the shorter, stockier man off his feet.

"Dad," was all he said, face buried in Gus's neck, but it

was enough to make the fist around Jules's heart squeeze down hard.

"Nice of you to join us," Danny said, slamming his pizza dough down onto the pastry board with a loud wham.

Max set his father back on his feet and tilted his head at Danny, who looked angry but stubborn, and totally unlike himself. He was usually the peacemaker of the bunch, the one everyone came to with their problems—but today, he seemed intent on stirring up trouble.

"I would've been here in the kitchen all afternoon, but I had the distinct impression I wasn't wanted. And I'm sorry to be late, but no one mentioned what time, exactly, the practice started. Is that enough mea culpa-ing for you, or should we get into the real reasons you're acting so pissy?"

Danny made a frustrated noise. "This isn't some backwater kitchen in the jungle, where anything goes, Max. We've got real work to do here, and if you're not prepared to commit to it, you might as well leave again."

For the first time, Jules saw real anger in the twist of Max's mouth. "Hey, you just say the word, Danny boy. This wasn't my idea in the first place. I could be prepping for my new apprenticeship, finding an apartment in Le Marche, brushing up on my Italian. For instance, do you know what *vai e fottiti* means?"

"That's enough, boys," Gus growled.

Jules flinched at her boss's tone. She'd never heard him sound quite like that.

"Yeah, come on," Winslow said unhappily. "The first round of qualifiers is in two weeks. Gus is right, we got work to do, and we could sure as shit use your help, Max."

"Some help," Danny grumbled, but when Gus shot him a look, he subsided. "But since Mom insisted on calling you, I guess you might as well make yourself useful."

Jules stole a look at Max, who seemed to be caught on

the point of actually following through on his threat to leave. Her stomach knotted, but even Jules wasn't sure what outcome she was hoping for.

Sure, she maybe agreed with Danny that they didn't need Max's help—they were doing fine, and she could totally work harder and pick up any slack. But Gus wanted him there, and after that scare last week when he almost collapsed again, pretty much whatever Gus wanted, Gus got.

It had nothing to do with the fact that the way Max stood there like an island in the middle of the kitchen made her want to do something nutty like give him a hug. She didn't do hugs.

All the same, she knew what it was like to be told in no uncertain terms exactly where she stood. The memory of that harsh awakening made her speak up.

"Where's Nina? Were you with her, Max?"

As she'd hoped, the mention of his mother brought a softer smile to Max's hard face. "Yeah, she was helping me with my studying. It's hard to learn a language from a book! I do better by speaking it."

Jules focused on making the swirling pattern of her spoon through the sauce, knowing the moment when Max might storm out in a rage was past. For better or worse, the reminder of Nina was all it took to get him to stay put.

"Enough chitchat," Gus boomed, clapping his hands together the way he always did when he got excited, or wanted to make a point. "Max is home, for a while at least, and we've got to make good use of his time with us. Your timing's actually perfect—we're just finishing up a practice challenge, so I can introduce you around."

"Sure," Max said, making an obvious effort to shake off his mood. "So this is the team, huh?" He glanced around the kitchen. "The group of talented young things who are destined to win the coveted title of Rising Star Chef for the East Coast of these United States, thus showering our humble family restaurant with fortune and glory."

Danny scowled. "You don't have to sound so dubious about it."

"Boys."

Gus looked tired again, Danny was reaching peak irritation—Jules could tell by the way his eyebrows were climbing toward his hairline, and the increasing vigor of his hand gestures. And Max . . . he was shutting down.

Jules couldn't believe she remembered him well enough to read those signs.

Abruptly unable to bear the heavy, smothering fog of pressure hovering over the kitchen—even happy-go-lucky Winslow was hunkering down over his cutting board and holding his chef's knife as if he might have to fend off an attack—Jules spun the dial regulating the heat under her saucepan to low and wiped her hands on a towel.

"Why don't I do the honors?" she said loudly, striding forward to grab Max by the sleeve of his worn white linen shirt without waiting for an answer.

"Well, thank you kindly, pretty lady," Max said, twisting his mouth into a grin. It wasn't all that convincing, but Jules took it as a sign she'd done the right thing by stepping in. He blinked. "Wow, that came out creepier than I was expecting. Sorry about that."

"Don't sweat it," she replied, hauling him up the line. "I'm going to assume you're familiar with the layout here. Danny's at the pastry station in this corner. He's the source of everything sweet that our team puts out."

"Gotcha. Baby bro, in charge of being sweet as pie. Check."

Danny rolled his eyes at them as they sped by.

"This," Jules said, pointing at her prep station with the hand she wasn't currently using as a pincer around Max's hard bicep. "This is Winslow Jones; he's on prep, so it's his job to make sure every ingredient is perfectly prepared before he hands it off to the other chefs to cook."

"We're glad you're in, Max," Win said, bouncing a little. "You are in, aren't you? You're not just back to help with the restaurant, right?"

"Hey, man, excellent to see you again," Max said, holding out a hand to slap palms with Win, who turned it into one of those complicated patterns of fist bumping and hand wringing that had taken Jules a week to figure out. Max, she noticed, executed the routine as flawlessly as if he and Win had been practicing it for days. Not that she felt threatened, or anything.

"And no, I'm not planning to serve any time on the line during normal restaurant hours. I'm not interested in expediting steak-and-potato dinners to the good people of Manhattan. I was told I'm strictly a ringer, brought in to lead the team to greatness."

Jules gritted her teeth against the urge to protest, for the zillionth time, that the last thing the team needed was another leader.

Another minute shift of movement in the muscular man farther down the line distracted her, reminding Jules of the final member of the team. "Hey, one more guy to meet, Max."

"Your wish is my command," he said gallantly.

Jules towed him back to the corner where Beck liked to work. The muscular, imposing chef loomed silently over his pristine cutting board, every movement of his big, trim body swift and economical. He had dark brown hair, chin length, the long front strands pulled back from his stark face into a short tail. There was a forbidding cast to his large, deep-set brown eyes that always made Jules think twice about bothering him. He was a little scary. But in this case . . .

She shoved Max forward. "Beck, this is Max. Danny's brother."

Beck was silent for a long moment, his flat, cold gaze taking in every inch of Max, from the golden-brown spikes of his short hair to his hiking-boot-clad toes. Jules could practically see him cataloguing the easy, careless way Max held himself—it looked loose, thoughtless, but the way Beck's eyes narrowed made Jules take a second glance.

There was something battle-ready about Max's stance, she realized. Something awake and aware in every line of his spare frame—something the rest of his persona seemed perfectly calculated to hide.

The charmingly off-kilter twist to his sensually shaped mouth, the masculine beauty of his bone structure, the ever-present light of mischief in his cloudy–sky eyes—and above all, the devil-may-care attitude. All of it seemed deliberately designed to distract the observer from noticing that there might be more to this wandering chef than met the eye.

"Boss says it's good that you're here." Beck's voice was quiet and deep. He never shouted; he didn't have to.

Max rocked back on his heels, hands heading for his pockets again, as his gaze darted from Beck to Jules. "You're not buying it, though, huh?"

Beck shrugged. "Not up to me. I'm just the new guy."

The knotted muscles of Jules's shoulders ached with new tension at the reference to Beck's recent hire, and from the quirk of Max's brow, he noticed.

But when he replied, it was to Beck. "Well, considering I've been out of the picture for the last six years, and only just got back today, I think that makes me the new guy. Okay if I watch you to learn the ropes?"

For the first time since she'd met him, Jules saw surprise flash across Beck's face. He didn't do anything other than nod and go back to deveining a quivering lobe of foie gras for a mousse, but still.

Jules pulled Max aside. "How did you do that?"

"What?"

"Get Beck to like you! It takes him at least a week to warm up to people, usually."

Max glanced over his shoulder. "That was warm?"

"For him? That was positively toasty. He's been here three months, Max, and this is the first time I've introduced someone and not feared for their lives a little. Not that he'd ever really hurt anyone! I don't think. He's just taciturn."

"Is that what they're calling it these days?" Max smirked in a way that instantly had Jules palm itching to connect with his stubbled cheek. "I'm glad I got his stamp of approval, but Beck isn't the one I'm hoping warms up to me."

The core of her body heated up as if someone had just lit her pilot, and the shock of it was enough to render her actually speechless for a moment . . . a moment Max took advantage of to lean in close, until his breath fanned the strands of hair that had escaped from her ponytail to wisp around her ears.

"Who could've guessed little Juliet Cavanaugh would grow up into such a gorgeous woman?"

Jules jerked away from him, her blood going the temperature and consistency of boiling tomato paste.

"I'm going to show you the layout of the pantry."

"I've seen the pantry in my parents' restaurant. The kitchen I grew up in? Unless they moved it out onto the street, I'm almost positive I remember where the pantry is." The amusement was back in Max's tone, with a vengeance. Jules gritted her teeth and restrained herself from yanking him around the corner where the dry-storage closet was, a little apart from the rest of the workspace.

"Well, it might have changed since the last time you saw it," Jules ground out. "And being able to find and grab materials quickly is a major part of practicing for the timed challenges we'll face at the actual competition. Here, go in. Don't let the door shut all the way!"

"What?" Max said as the door swung shut behind her, enclosing them in pitch-darkness.

"The door," Jules said, hearing her voice hit a new register. "It sticks."

"Oh, for God's sake, Dad hasn't fixed that yet?"

"Not yet," she gritted. "Can you get the light? There's a cord dangling from the bulb—oh, never mind, move, I'll get it."

This isn't happening. Please, God, please let me have hit my head in the kitchen—maybe a Dutch oven fell off a shelf and now I'm concussed, and this is all just a nightmare.

As she prayed for a return to consciousness, her flailing hand finally made contact with the string connected to the light.

She pulled it, and squinted against the sudden glare.

Either this concussion is more like a coma and I'm going to be stuck in it for a while, or I'm actually awake and locked in a storage closet with the one man on the planet who makes me want to break my own rules.

Jules honestly didn't know which version of reality to hope for.

Chapter 5

Max's day was looking up.

"I approve," he told Juliet. "I mean, the accidentally-getting-locked-in-a-closet thing is a little amateur, and I might've saved it for when the whole prospective East Coast team for the Rising Star Chef competition, including my kid brother and my dad, weren't standing twenty feet away, but hey, whatever works. And this totally worked! Message received. I'm yours for the taking."

Those gorgeous brown eyes widened, giving the solemn oval of her pretty face an innocent cast. Surprise was a good look for her, he decided.

"You're unbelievable."

"Thank you."

"That wasn't a compliment!"

"I know you didn't mean it as one, Juliet, but when you think about it, what could be more glorious than to be too much, too out of the ordinary, to be believed?"

She blinked again. "Well, out of the ordinary is right. And will you stop with the fucking 'Juliet'!"

Max cocked his head, studying the way she had her arms crossed over her chest, slender fingers digging into her arms and a look of horror dawning over her pretty face as she replayed her own last words.

Should he? Naaah, too easy. "So why do you hate that name so much? I haven't even had a chance to break out the Romeo jokes yet!"

Some of the tension relaxed out of her shoulders when she realized Max wasn't leaping all over her little verbal stumble. "Oh yeah," she said, rolling her eyes. "You're definitely the first guy who ever made that connection."

"I bet I could come up with something you haven't heard before," Max said. "But you didn't answer my question. Why the switch to Jules?"

She shrugged, but couldn't quite pull off the casualness she was going for. "Suits me better. Juliet . . ." She made a face, sort of a sneer crossed with a wrinkled nose, to convey her disgust—Max was afraid to tell her how unutterably adorable it was.

"Juliet's all flowery romance and coy seduction and deathless tragic passion. I don't really go in for that stuff."

Max looked her up and down, at the long, toned length of her athletic body, the high, round curves of her breasts, the gentle swell of her hips—and admitted to himself that she wasn't quite the awkward girl of his memories. He couldn't believe this was the woman his mother had told him about, the perfect chef who was like a daughter to them, and who'd slid into Max's vacant spot in the restaurant as if she'd been born to it.

He'd heard all about Jules, but he hadn't expected to like her. And he definitely hadn't expected her to be so enticing.

Maybe this visit home didn't have to be all tension and stress and misunderstandings. Max didn't have quite the girl-in-every-port mentality that Danny had accused him of, but he wasn't against having a short-term fling with a cute brown-eyed blonde, either.

And the challenge of her? The way she didn't want to admit to the electric spark zapping back and forth between them? That lit Max up like nothing else.

He'd never been able to resist the lure of exploring new territory.

"Maybe you just haven't met your Romeo yet," he couldn't resist saying.

Jules opened her wide, generous mouth, but snapped it shut again. He liked the way her brown eyes flashed with gold, like sunlight through a glass of whiskey.

"Nope," she finally managed. "I've definitely heard that one before."

"I'm still getting warmed up," Max protested, taking a meandering circuit around the pantry that brought him ever closer to Jules's taut, tense form. He especially enjoyed the blush she couldn't seem to control. "I can do better."

She cleared her throat, alarm widening her whiskey eyes. "No! I mean, don't bother. Seriously. Not with the jokes, not with the flirting—just stop it all."

"Flirting?" Max pointed at his own chest and blinked innocently. "Moi?"

"All that crap about wanting me to warm up to you," Jules said. Tilting her chin aggressively, she pinned him with a fierce look. "Let's be clear on this—I have absolutely no interest in you. All I'm interested in is leading this team in the Rising Star Chef competition."

"Hmm," Max said, stalking his prey with slow, sure steps. "Is that what this is about? You think I'm trying to . . . what? Get in your pants to distract you so I can take your spot as leader of the team? Not a bad plan, as plans go, but no. Sorry to disappoint, but I'm not quite that Machiavellian."

The sound of her swallowing was loud in the close, silent pantry. "You're saying you'll be happy to follow my lead. Take orders, do the work, and not get in my way?"

"To tell you the truth, leading anyone's not really my style. I'm less of a dictator, more of a collaborator. I've got ideas, sure—man, sometimes it seems like I've got more than my brain can hold, stuff I want to try out, new ingredients I want to play with and techniques I want to try— but I'm open. I like to learn."

And of all the shit he'd said, all the wiles and tricks and winks and flirty looks he'd thrown her way, this one simple truth was what got to her.

Max saw it hit home, saw the way her chest rose and fell quickly as she absorbed the fact that he wasn't a threat.

Not to her career, anyway.

Driving the point a little deeper, he leaned in and said, "You want to be queen of the mountain, you take that crown and wear it with pride. It's gonna look great on you. Me? I'm more of a baseball cap kind of guy."

Her breath was hot and fast against his face, and when her gaze flicked down to his mouth for a split second, exultation spilled through Max's veins like the homemade hootch he'd had in the Ukraine, searing through him and stealing his balance.

He had her.

"Okay," she said, voice sounding strangled and husky. "Good. That's . . . good. My first order is for you to back the fuck off, Max. I mean it, this isn't happening."

She brought her hands up to his shoulders, but instead of pushing, she clutched at the fabric of his shirt, wrinkling it between her strong, slender fingers.

"No?" Max licked his lips, watching as she dropped her gaze again. "I hate to contradict my fearless leader and all, but it looks to me like this kind of is happening."

"Okay. Maybe I used to have a crush on you," she allowed, her fingers restless against his chest. "I guess that's no secret. But that was years ago. I've grown up a lot since then."

"Yes, I see that," he purred. He crowded her up against a stack of canvas sacks filled with flour. Her quick, short breaths pushed the slight, firm curves of her breasts against him. "Don't you ever miss those days when we were kids? When everything felt so intense, like the world might end if you didn't get that one . . . perfect . . . kiss . . ."

Her eyes flashed, her cheeks blazed with color, her luscious lips opened—no doubt to deliver some scathing retort—and Max thought, *To hell with it,* swooped down and took her mouth in a fast, devouring kiss.

The first touch of their lips was like the starting click sparking under a gas burner, and in the next breath, fire swept up and over both of them in a whoosh of crackling heat.

The taste of her exploded over his tongue, lemon drops and cool, clean water, drugging and addictive. He speared his hands into the tumbling fall of her long honey-blond hair, messing up her ponytail, and gripped gently to pull her head back and expose the slim column of her throat. Max couldn't resist diving down and tasting that, too, the warm, salty-sweet flesh so fragile over the beat of her pulse, the throb of her life under his lips and pounding into his head.

She gasped, her hands fluttering up to clutch at his biceps. He wasn't sure if she was pulling him closer or pushing him away—maybe she wasn't sure, either.

Max replaced his mouth with his hands, framing her neck loosely and rubbing his thumbs at the hinges of her sharp jaw. He had to take a moment to drink her in, red, kiss-swollen lips, flush riding high on her cheekbones, and her golden eyes half-lidded and dazed with pleasure.

"God, but you're gorgeous," he breathed. "If you kissed me back to prove how over me you are, I'm going to need a little more convincing."

Jules blinked, then those pretty eyes went wide and

aware, and Max stepped back regretfully the instant before she could push him away.

"Damn it," she said. "I *am* over you. What the hell am I doing?"

"You're going after what you want," Max said helpfully. "I don't see the problem here. Unless—are you married? Engaged? Seeing someone?"

"No," she ground out between gritted teeth. "We can't do this because I'm the sous chef at your parents' restaurant, and the head of the Rising Star Chef team, which is competing in the qualifying round in two weeks, when we have to work together and be at our best, and also, you're . . . crazy."

"Funnily enough, that's not the first time I've been accused of having mental problems." Max stuck his hands in his pockets so he wouldn't be tempted to reach for her again. She was oddly tempting while rejecting him. "I've noticed that people almost never mean that I should be institutionalized or heavily medicated—it's more like that I should set my sights lower. Do the boring, expected thing instead of whatever cool, new thing I want to try. But the way I look at it is, there are no guarantees in life except that it's gonna be nasty, brutish, and way too fucking short. It's up to you—up to me—to make something amazing out of it."

She stared across the pantry at him, and this time it was Max's turn to blink. He hadn't meant to say all that. "Pardon my philosophizing," he said smoothly. "I've been studying Buddhist parables; you get sort of used to breaking the world down into stories with lessons attached."

"Okay," she said slowly. "So long as the lesson you take away from this conversation is that this was a mistake. That kiss, just now . . . let's chalk it up to satisfying old curiosity, and let it go. It's over. I've moved on; you should do the same."

"I don't know. This doesn't seem like fate to you? I mean, I come home to help my parents enter some big cooking contest they've got their hearts set on, sure I'm going to be bored spitless the whole time I'm Stateside—come to find out, the 'Jules' my family's been gushing about for the last six years is you, all grown-up, and oh by the way, we're hotter than hell together. The way I see it, fate is definitely trying to get us naked. Preferably together."

Those pretty eyes narrowed. "I don't believe in fate. And you're the one who took off, as I recall, to Outer Mongolia or East Anglia or wherever. I've been right here the whole time, so it's hardly an epic coincidence that I'm still here when you finally decide to come back."

"Ah yes. You've been here all along, haven't you," Max said, his gut tightening at the reminder of how completely he'd been supplanted. Bitterness scalded his throat, making his voice uncomfortably hoarse. "How convenient—and economical! No expense and hassle of a wedding, and my parents gained a daughter! I guess the fact that they sort of *did* lose a son was irrelevant. So long as someone's there to keep Lunden's going, that's what counts."

Her face went kind of red and her chest heaved interestingly. "It wasn't convenient, or some cynical scheme to get a job. Your family has been wonderful to me, and if all you want to do is talk shit about them, then you might as well go back to the west end of nowhere and leave us alone!"

Emotion surged past any hope of Zen calm, uncontrollable and painful. "And you'd just love that, wouldn't you? Tell me the truth. Hearing that I was coming home was your worst nightmare."

Some of the color drained from her cheeks, leaving her looking kind of blotchy and worked up. It should have made her ugly, but it didn't. "Don't flatter yourself," she said. "You being here or not means nothing to me. Your parents think you can help us—and as long as you do, I've got no problems with you." Her eyes narrowed, and she stepped close enough to jab a finger into his chest. "But the minute you start spouting off about things you know nothing about, or fighting with Danny and upsetting your parents? You and me are going to have a big ass problem, Max Lunden."

If she were a hedgehog, she'd be all pointy right about now. That mental image poked a pin into the balloon of anger filling his chest, deflating it. What the hell was he trying to accomplish, anyway? He tried to imagine what his Zen master would say if he could see Max now, and utterly failed.

"I'm sorry," he said, making it as sincere as he could. "Obviously, I've got some issues to work out with my family, but none of this is your fault. And you really don't have anything to worry about, here—I'm not back for good, or anything. Just for the qualifiers. I already told my mom. And after that, you crazy kids are on your own, because I've got an Italian butcher genius to learn from."

She hesitated for a minute, clearly not sure that was good enough. Max let his arms hang loose at his sides, hands open and unthreatening, as if he were confronting a wild animal in the jungle.

Finally, she said, "Okay. So we understand one another. I'm the head of the RSC team, and you're merely here to consult."

He shrugged. "Sure, whatever."

Those whiskey-colored eyes narrowed to suspicious slits. "And there'll be no more weirdness between us, either. We're teammates, and that's it."

With the memory of that kiss still stinging his mouth, Max wasn't quite so willing to agree to that. "What? There's a rule about teammates getting together for . . .

fun? I can't believe that. These culinary competitions are usually pretty much an excuse for bacchanalian-style orgies scandalous enough to make a Roman emperor blush."

"It may not be an official rule in the RSC handbook, but it *is* my rule. And I'm not breaking it for anyone ever again."

Again, huh? Interesting.

Max wondered what it said about him that he found the stubborn jut of her jaw and the snap in her voice so appealing.

"Well, unofficially, I'm not giving up. A chance meeting like this, after all this time has passed—it means something, Juliet Cavanaugh. You may not believe in fate, but I don't believe in coincidence. The universe isn't random; it means something that you're here. And I'm going to find out what."

Chapter 6

That sounded like a threat. Jules couldn't help the fine shiver that ran through her whole body, even knowing that the way they were leaning together meant he might be able to feel it.

Hopefully he'd just attribute it to suppressed desire, rather than bone-rattling fear of making the same mistakes all over again.

Which he probably would, the arrogant ass, she thought, ignoring the tiny voice of truth whispering that fear certainly wasn't her one and only reaction to feeling that lean, hard-muscled form pressed tight to her body.

Face it, girl. It's been a while—and even if it hadn't, no guy's ever made you feel quite like Max Lunden.

Sucking in a deep, fortifying breath and trying not to notice how it smelled like cake flour, rolled oats, and the clean, complicated salt-musk of Max, Jules forced herself to meet his wicked, laughing gaze.

"It means nothing," she said, as firmly as she could. "We're teammates. I'm here to cook, to compete, to help some people who mean a lot to me—and most of all, I'm here to win. And no one and nothing is going to stop me . . . including you."

Max opened his mouth to reply, but before he could get a word out, there was a loud knock on the pantry door.

Winslow's voice was muffled and extremely welcome. "Y'all okay in there? Gus is starting to get his worried face on."

Oh God. The idea of Gus Lunden, who was more a father to her than any of the parade of losers her mother had dated throughout her childhood, standing around in the kitchen while Jules carried on with his son made her want to cringe. And after she'd promised him never to mix up her personal life with kitchen business again!

"Win," she called. "Can you get the door open from your side? It's stuck."

"Saved by the bell, huh?" Max sauntered over, sticking his hands in the pockets of his ripped, faded jeans.

Beck's voice, deep and sure. "You've got to jiggle the knob hard then bump with your hip."

A low cackle of laughter sounded from the other side of the door. "That's what he said. What? Hold on a sec. I got this."

Five seconds later, they were free. Jules gave Win a quick kiss on the cheek as a thank-you, smiled at Beck, then hurried back to her station, trying to pretend the flush she could feel heating her cheeks was nothing but embarrassment at getting stuck in the pantry.

Danny raised one eyebrow at her in a clear, if silent, statement that he wasn't buying it. From the rear of the kitchen, Beck snorted, which was as close as he usually got to a laugh.

Winslow, hot on Jules's heels, slipped back into his spot on the line next to her and slanted her a look—the one that, roughly translated, meant "Girl, you *will* be dishing some dirt later."

Jules scowled at him, which made him grin before turning piously to face the front of the kitchen where Gus was pacing.

The old man's faded blue eyes were fixed on something behind Jules, and she didn't need to turn around to know it was Max. Which didn't explain why she turned around anyway, but Max always seemed to have that effect on her. Whenever he was there, rationality went bye-bye.

Evidently in no hurry at all, Max sauntered up the line, hands in pockets and looking all sexy and rumpled, to prop one indolent hip on his brother's pastry board. Danny scooped a pile of pitted cherries out of the way with an irritable sigh, but Jules noticed he didn't actually shove his brother out of his space.

"If you're done reminding yourself where everything is in the kitchen you practically grew up in, maybe we could get back to our practice?"

Jules straightened her shoulders and grabbed her chef's knife, more than ready to take out her frustration and tension on some poor, unsuspecting ingredients.

"Sure thing, Danny boy. No need to get riled up. We're all here now and ready to work. Right, guys?"

Gus's knuckles stood out white against his red, weathered hands where he had them clenched on his hips. "Come on boys, stop that now. We don't have time for this squabbling! The qualifying round to decide what team will represent the East Coast is in less than two weeks. We have to prepare, drill, get Max up to speed on the recipes . . ." He broke off, lines of strain bracketing his mouth.

"Everything will work out. I promise," Max said softly, straightening away from the pastry board and starting toward his father.

"I'm fine," Gus said briskly, holding up a hand. Max stopped in his tracks, an indefinable spasm of emotion tightening his face for an instant before he fell back into his default expression of lazy interest. "Just didn't sleep all that well last night. Maybe . . . I should lie down for a while. Jules, you can take it from here, right?"

A chill roughed up the hair on the back of her neck as she nodded. She'd never seen Gus Lunden walk off the line before. Not for any reason.

"Good idea," Max said calmly, one hand clenching into a fist at his side, then slowly unfurling, finger by finger.

Jules watched him struggle to maintain his air of serenity and wondered what it would take to make him lose it completely.

Silence descended on the kitchen in the wake of Gus's slow departure. No one was making eye contact; it felt as if something momentous and awful had happened.

Max broke the silence by shaking out his hands and then clapping them together. "I've competed in cooking contests before, but not on this scale. And always as an individual, never as part of a team. Lay it out for me. How's it going to go down?"

"The qualifying round is rough—it's intended to weed out the teams who aren't serious or who don't have the skill level and experience to truly compete," Danny said.

"So it's a cooking challenge?" Max asked.

"Not exactly," Winslow said, grinning. "It's more like kitchen *Jeopardy*."

"Seriously? Like, trivia and buzzing in and stuff?"

"Exactly." Danny shook his head. "And the questions are crazy hard. More than one team of cocky cooks has been knocked out before the competition even gets started, based on their scores in the qualifier."

"Well, crap," Max said, rubbing the back of his neck. "I hate to tell you this, but I'm not sure how big a help I'm gonna be."

"Ain't no thang." Win slung an arm over Jules's shoulders. "We got our ace in the hole already. Jules, here, is our resident nerd."

She poked him in the side hard enough to make him twist away, squawking. "You're just saying that because you don't want to get blamed when we flame out early because you didn't study."

"You know that's right." Win laughed, unrepentant.

Beck stepped up to the group, his large, solid presence quelling even Winslow's antics.

"We all study," Beck said, his deep voice making it sound like an edict from on high. "We don't want any weak links on the team. Jules shouldn't have to carry us on her own."

"Thanks, Beck." Jules smiled at the big guy.

Out of the corner of her eye, she caught Max's fleeting frown, but all he said was, "I'm willing to study, but what kind of trivia are we talking about here?"

Danny gave his brother the kind of scathingly skeptical look only a younger brother could achieve. "I'll believe it when I see you actually hitting the books. And hauling off and punching them doesn't count."

"The type of trivia is where this gets tricky," Jules cut in, before the sibling spat could escalate. "All the questions will be cooking related, obviously, but the categories are really up to the judges. And we can't even begin to predict what the judges might focus on until we know who they are."

"We know one," Winslow pointed out, hitching his narrow hips up onto the high counter behind him and swinging his legs.

"Claire Durand," Danny agreed. "She's a given." Turning to Max, he started to explain, "Claire Durand is editor in chief—"

"Of *Délicieux* magazine, I know," Max interrupted,

then rolled his eyes at his brother's surprise. "Oh, come on. I've been out of the country, not dead. *Délicieux* is a huge deal, even internationally. Durand has quite the following in Thailand."

"Great," Danny sniped. "You can tell her all about it when you meet her. She'll definitely be one of the judges, because *Délicieux* cosponsors the RSC with the Jansen Hospitality Group."

"What the hell, Danny," Max said, laughing. "Did you swallow the brochure, or what?"

The tension in the room soared several hundred degrees, setting Jules's teeth on edge. How in the world were they supposed to work together as a team if they couldn't manage to get through a single practice without fighting?

"It doesn't hurt to know the rules before going into something," Danny shot back. "Just because you like to wing it—"

"Hey," Winslow said, his bright green gaze darting between the two brothers. "I heard Devon Sparks was on the short list."

"He'd be a good one." Jules rushed to follow Win's lead, steering the conversation back to the competition. "There's usually a celebrity chef on the panel, and I know he's got some new charity he's pushing, so he could probably use the publicity."

"I've watched tapes of past years," Danny said, turning pointedly away from Max. "And Claire Durand usually asks very precise, technical questions about obscure points of classical French cuisine. Devon Sparks—he used to be super experimental with his food, so we should brush up on our molecular gastronomy. And his new charity deal, that's what? Teaching kids to cook, or something? So maybe nutrition."

"That third slot, though . . . that's still up in the air," Beck reminded them.

"So we study everything," Jules ordered, which ended the confrontation for the moment, as everyone shuffled through their bags looking for reference books and comparing notes.

But as Jules observed the subtle angle of Danny's body away from his brother's, as if unconsciously excluding him from the group, she felt a chill down her spine. And when Max glanced up from a battered, food-stained copy of the *Larousse Gastronomique* and caught her gaze with a slow grin, that shiver of fear turned to a cascade of something much warmer, but no less unsettling.

And she'd already sent him about twenty mixed signals, let him flirt with her, and made out with him like a sailor on shore leave.

Damn it all to hell and back. This swearing off men thing was tougher than it sounded.

At least when Max Lunden was around.

Chapter 7

"All right, out with it. Who are you planning to saddle me with this year?" Claire demanded, glaring across her pristine glass desk at the bane of her existence.

The bane had the audacity to laugh, sleek black hair swinging against her angled jawbone. "It always cracks me up when you bust out the Americanisms."

"I've lived in your country for more than fifteen years," Claire said quellingly. "Approximately half your lifetime, little girl."

"Hmm. I also enjoy it when you try to pretend you're old. Come off it, *ma chérie*. You're . . . what? Thirty-five?"

"Enough of your flattery. It won't get you anywhere," Claire snapped. She couldn't quite stop a small, satisfied smile from giving her away, however. Ridiculous vanity, and she knew it, but there it was. She'd never relished the idea of becoming a *woman of a certain age*. "Besides, you're off by about seven years, on the wrong side of forty. And your French accent is atrocious."

Eva Jansen grinned, a surprisingly roguish look on her perfectly tanned, discreetly made-up face. "Tell it to Madamoiselle Mireille, the worst French tutor ever born.

Maybe if she'd spent more time making me conjugate verbs, and less time being conjugal with my father, I wouldn't embarrass myself in front of native French speakers."

"I'm from Paris," Claire reminded her. "We don't think anyone outside the city speaks the language properly, not even the rest of France. Now state your business and get out, some of us have real work to do."

Being editor in chief of an international lifestyle magazine meant Claire spent most of her time lambasting terrified underlings and directing a multimillion-dollar operation for which she held full, final responsibility. Some women in that position might enjoy the chance to converse with a peer, to have an interaction that was completely devoid of coercion or intimidation.

Claire Durand was not that woman.

She pushed her desk chair back and stood to pace across her office to the enormous glass wall overlooking the magazine's test kitchen on the floor below. The worker bees were testing recipes for the Fourth of July issue, and the rich, smoke-salty scent of Texas barbecue sauce wafted up through the vents, sharp with vinegar and caramel-sweet with brown sugar.

"Right," Eva drawled, tapping one manicured finger against the polished mahogany arm of Claire's best office guest chair. "Because running a top-rated hotel and restaurant group while organizing the biggest culinary competition in America is such a snap."

Claire waved a hand. "Your father still ran Jansen Hospitality, when last I checked. As for the competition . . . well. You're a spoiled little girl playing with dolls. Only in this case, your unfortunate Barbie is me."

So what if Eva had inherited her father's killer business sense along with her sizable trust fund? Claire was not impressed. Even if Eva also happened to mix a deadly martini and occasionally made Claire laugh hard enough to shake her chignon loose, none of that would save Eva from certain annihilation should the foolish girl attempt to replicate the fiasco of the last Rising Star Chef competition.

"Oh, Claire." Eva dismissed her friend's concerns with a flick of her poison-apple-red fingernails. "It won't be like last time. I've got fabulous judges lined up for you."

"You'd better have. I refuse to be the lone voice of reason in the wilderness of insanity again, Eva. Nor will I serve as au pair for your latest boy toy. Your father didn't found this competition merely to provide you with bedroom playmates."

"I know. That's just a side benefit. Ha! But don't worry, I won't be culling from the judging panel. As if I'd trust any man I'm interested in alone with a cougar like you."

Claire snorted. For the umpteenth time, she was glad she was French, and had learned at a very young age how to snort elegantly to show disdain. "Eva. I have a travel piece on Bali coming in, eleven versions of barbecue sauce to taste, problems with the layout for the photo slide show of the Milan Melon Festival on the Web site, and my new restaurant critic is an irretrievable idiot. I have no time for nonsense about large cats. Deliver your atrocious news and leave me to my frustrations."

"I'm getting to it! Claire, honestly. Where's your sense of drama?"

"You're confusing me with an Italian. We French value pragmatism above all else. Well, pragmatism and wine. I assume you didn't bring any of that along with you, either."

Eva clapped her hands together. "I was already looking forward to this conversation, but you're making it extra fun! It's almost like you know how hard I worked to make this happen."

A wave of foreboding enveloped Claire. "What do you mean?"

"This is going to be the best RSC ever! And all because of me."

Merde.

"What did you do?"

Eva beamed. "I got Devon Sparks to agree to be a judge!"

Claire allowed her shoulders to relax marginally. That wasn't so bad. "Well. It could be worse. He's an unmitigated ass, but at least he knows food."

"Not entirely true," Eva said. "I'd heard his assness had been mitigated recently by finding true love, or something ridiculous like that. Obviously, I discounted that story as the worst sort of slanderous gossip. And then it turned out to be an actual fact! Devon is off the market, stupid in love, and on our judging panel."

"Oh yes, I heard about his new bride. Well, it should make him easier to handle, at any rate. Who else?"

Eva's eyes gleamed with unholy joy. "This is the best part. Wait for it—"

"Eva!"

"Oh fine. Be that way." She pouted prettily for a bare instant before the urge to spill got the better of her. "I did it, Claire! I got Kane Slater to agree to be an RSC judge!"

Just like that, tension yanked Claire's shoulders back up around her ears. "You what? Eva—this had better be one of your oh-so-droll American witticisms. Ha. Ha."

"No! I know it seems too good to be true, but I promise you, I'm not kidding. Kane Slater, the hottest rock star ever to throw an eighteen-course banquet dinner party based on the last meal served aboard the *Titanic,* is our third judge!"

Claire grasped the back of Eva's chair and white-knuckled it before her knees could give out. "A rock star.

You could have asked anyone—a food historian, a famous chef, a well-known restaurant critic—and you ask a rock star."

"I had to!" Eva widened her eyes until she looked like a cartoon character. "We've got to sex up this competition, or die trying. It costs a lot of money to run this show, and Jansen Hospitality can't foot the entire bill. We need to attract bigger sponsors, with deeper pockets, if we want to pull off the best Rising Star Chef yet!"

"It's not a competition, Eva." Claire rolled her eyes when her friend smirked. "Enough, you know what I mean. Between you and your father—the RSC should not be the latest battleground on which to wage your ongoing campaign for Theo Jansen's approval."

Eva's red mouth hardened into a flat line. "Look, I know you never cared about having the competition televised, but it's the next step. I know it. Dad never managed to do it, and when I thought I'd be able to . . . but now the Cooking Channel execs are balking, saying they're not sure it's sexy enough, blah blah. Don't you see? Kane Slater is my magic fairy dust! Everything he touches turns to sex. It'll be the best panel ever. You'll have a blast. How much fun would some crusty old food historian have been, I ask you? Please. I can so see that increasing our market share. Right."

"But this is outrageous! You're risking the reputation of the entire competition by involving this person, who has no credentials and no knowledge—the sponsors might be happy, but what about the chefs who are competing? You ridiculous child, have you thought this through at all?"

Eva stood, turning on one black stiletto heel to face Claire. Her eyes flashed with something Claire had never seen there before, a determination that made her look older, more serious. "Just because you've known me since I was a child doesn't mean I still am one. My father put the

RSC completely in my hands for the first time this year, and I will. Not. Screw. This. Up. And you won't screw it up for me by acting all stodgy and conservative and horrified, when that isn't even who you are, anyway."

Staring at her young friend, Claire understood immediately that she was in a nonnegotiable situation. Eva had made up her mind and nothing would sway her now.

Which didn't mean that Claire was without recourse. She would simply need to bide her time.

"Fine. I'll do my best to keep your publicity stunt from doing anything gauche enough to cause irreparable damage to the competition. But you will owe me for dealing with this ludicrous situation—and believe me when I tell you, I will be collecting on that debt."

Relief smoothed Eva's face until she was the same pampered beauty she always appeared to be. Few ever glimpsed the shark skimming along beneath the surface—and usually by then it was too late. "You're the best. I knew I could count on you! Now I've got to dash, I have a lunch meeting at Market in ten, but I promise I'll give the chef a smooch for you if I see him! And maybe one for me, too. That Adam Temple, yummy. Why is everyone paired off, these days?"

Eva chattered as she gathered up her things, stuffing a purple silk scarf printed with the address of the original Hermès shop in Paris into her cavernous black-and-white Chanel tote.

Claire air-kissed her young friend good-bye, one kiss per smooth, powdered cheek, smiled pleasantly, and worried.

Chapter 8

Jules was in the zone. Every move she made—bend, open the lowboy, grab ingredients, swirl them into the pan, toss them over the leaping flame with a flick of her wrist— flowed naturally. Her mind was a perfect, beautiful blank, empty of everything but the next order, and the one after that, and the one after that, an endless line of rib eye, mid-well, no mushrooms in the garnish; Brussels sprouts side, heavy on the bacon; two lamb chops, normal; a porter-house, bloody . . .

She dipped and whirled, leaning up to grab a clean sauté pan to reheat the sprouts, and instinctively curved her body inward to avoid Winslow as he spun a set of dirty pans toward the dishwashing station on the back wall.

Flinging a handful of diced pancetta into the hot pan, she let the heat render some of the fat while she checked on her steaks. The big, heavy porterhouse was giving off enough red juice to let her know it was about done, but the rib eye needed another couple of minutes.

Spinning the porterhouse onto an individual serving platter spitting with hot butter, she put it up on the pass for a runner to grab and take up to the window, then turned back to her sizzling bacon.

Jules stirred the bits of salt-cured meat around, then added the baby Brussels sprouts. As she watched them dance in the molten spiced pork fat, she thought about how much she'd hated these vegetables when she was a kid. Her mom had sure never cooked sprouts this way.

Okay, granted—Victoria Cavanaugh pretty much never cooked at all, if she could talk a man into taking her out instead, but still. Jules was a connoisseur of public school lunches and diner specials, and none of them had made Brussels sprouts like this, either.

One of the first things Winslow did every day when he got to the restaurant and started to prep for dinner service was to crank the oven up high and roast a big batch of the tiny green orbs. When he spread them out on a hotel pan, they looked like miniature cabbages, their tightly furled leaves shiny with oil.

When he pulled them out of the oven half an hour later? They were shriveled and golden, the edges of the tender leaves curled and caramelized to a tasty, dark brown crispness.

He let them cool on the racks, then put them in a container, and when Jules came in to set up her mise en place for the night, she always made sure to keep the sprouts close at hand. They were one of the restaurant's specialties, and she could count on putting out at least twenty orders of sprouts on a busy night like tonight.

Thank God for Friday, indeed. It was the one night they could count on doing at least one full turn, fifty covers, and sometimes even more once the posttheater crowd had a chance to make it from Times Square down to Greenwich Village.

Seasoning the roasted sprouts with salt and pepper, Jules savored the nutty, rich scent rising from the pan as they warmed through. While they got hot, she checked her vinaigrette—a little low—and swiftly added a generous glug of balsamic vinegar and a steady stream of olive oil, whisking like crazy. A sprinkle of chopped fresh herbs from her stash of bowls at the corner of her station, and her stock of vinaigrette was replenished.

Scraping the sprouts and crispy pancetta into a bowl, Jules drizzled them with the vinaigrette and shook the bowl to make them jump. Since she'd done new vinaigrette for this order, she grabbed a clean tasting spoon and popped one of the sprouts into her mouth.

The sharp sweetness of the balsamic vinegar burst across her tongue, and as she crunched into the sprout, she took a second to marvel at the way the little vegetable retained its deep caramel flavor and pleasingly burned edges. A warm sauce would've turned them into the limp, soggy sprouts of her youth, uninspired and unappetizing. This bright vinaigrette elevated them to another level.

A quick dash of salt, a few more turns of the pepper grinder, and the sprouts were done.

"Sprouts up," she called, shoving the bowl onto the rack, where Emilio, one of the runners, was waiting to carry it up to the front of the kitchen.

Jules spun around and checked her rib eye again, the noise of the kitchen a soothing background music to her thoughts.

The kitchen was a living, breathing organism during the rush of dinner service, especially when it was busy like this. Every chef, runner, and dishwasher was a major, life-sustaining organ, all working together to power the beast through the frenetic couple of hours between seven-thirty and nine-thirty, when everyone in Manhattan seemed to get hungry for steak at exactly the same time.

Jules barely noticed the sweat sticking her shirt to her

back and stinging the shallow knife scrape on her knuckles. She was only peripherally aware of Nina bringing tickets up to the pass and handing them to Gus, who called out the orders in the sharp, no-nonsense bark he'd perfected long before Jules ever thought of becoming a chef. She danced with Winslow and Beck as they maneuvered their way around the narrow, heated confines of the kitchen, and she only surfaced long enough to slap Danny a high five when Gus called out, "Last ticket cleared! Danny, they want two crèmes brûlées, and we're done."

The fog of war was slow to clear from Jules's head; she missed it the instant it was gone.

Jules found a lot of comfort in the buzz of adrenaline and strain of muscles it took to get through dinner service. Once it was over, all that was left was her life—and she'd rather think about meat temperatures and oil-to-vinegar ratios any day of the week.

She sighed loudly enough to make Danny raise his brows at her. "What are you mad about? You don't have to make the last desserts."

"Neither do you," she pointed out as he snagged a couple of white porcelain ovals off the speed rack next to his station.

"Au contraire," he replied, waggling his handheld butane torch and flicking the button to make it spark. "The crème might be done, but that sugar topping isn't going to brûlée itself."

With a flourish, he scattered a layer of sugar crystals over the top of the cold vanilla bean custard and bent to direct the blue heat of his torch flame over it in sweeping arcs. Jules watched the white sugar brown and start to bubble, forming a hard, shiny crust that made her itch to grab a spoon and tap hard enough to crack it. She loved crème brûlée; since the first time Danny made it for her, to celebrate turning eighteen and getting hired at Lunden's for real instead of under the table, she'd asked for it on every birthday.

Glancing up at her, Danny waved the torch menacingly. "Back off, Cavanaugh. These aren't for you!"

"But if I steal one, then dinner service isn't over," she said.

Danny's eyebrows shot up one more time. "Don't get greedy, Jules. We had a good night! We should savor those. Or wait—is this about avoiding practice later?"

Jules made a face, annoyed with herself. Danny handed off the desserts to Emilio, waiting until the runner was halfway to the window before continuing in a low voice. "This is about Max."

If it were anyone else, she'd stiffen up, blank her face, shrug her shoulders, and deny everything. But that stuff never worked with Danny; they'd known each other way too long.

"It's just a little stressful," she admitted, "the way your dad hopes Max will be the magic ticket to success, but they never talk about why Max left in the first place. And the look on Gus's face when you and Max fight. I know there's some bad blood and hurt feelings on all sides, but you need to suck it up and put it aside. For the good of the team."

Wiping down his station with a white side towel, Danny scrubbed harder than necessary at a patch of something sticky and red. "I know," he said without looking up, "I'm fucking this up for everyone."

Guilt scored down Jules's spine. Danny had a tendency to shoulder burdens that shouldn't be his to carry alone. "No you're not. You were hurt when he left, and I remember how hard it was to deal with your parents being so upset about it all the time. I was there."

Those first few weeks after she'd moved in with the Lundens had been so strange. Surreal, like a dream where Jules got to live someone else's life, where she felt safe and cared for and happy and *safe,* but everyone around her was living under this awful, aching cloud of sadness.

There was a Max-shaped void in the Lunden family, from that very first night, and Jules had never been able to fill it.

"It sucked." Danny's feeling tone made her want to grin.

"Big time," Jules agreed. "But you know, he did come back. When your mom called and said she needed him, he dropped everything and came home. That has to mean something."

"Yeah. That Nina Lunden is a force of nature."

Jules nodded. "And I bet she's been on your ass about getting along with your brother, too. It means a lot to her, and to your dad. So maybe you could just, I don't know, fake it until he leaves again?"

Danny frowned. "I hate that, too. Weird, huh? It's hard, so hard to have him home and around all the time. But I hate that he's not staying."

As always when she and Danny did that weird best-friends-forever, same-wavelength thing, Jules got a chill. "I know."

"And it sucks to know that he'd probably stick around, if he knew what was up with Dad!" Danny was getting frustrated, running his hands through his hair the way he always did, leaving streaks of sticky cream custard clumping the golden brown tufts together.

"Yep, sucks," Jules acknowledged, hardening her heart against the misgivings that arose every time she thought about the secrets they were all keeping from Max. "But it's for his own good. He's got that amazing opportunity in Italy. Your dad couldn't stand to be the reason Max misses out on that."

"Well, I could." Danny set his jaw stubbornly. "I don't care if that makes me selfish."

Warm affection surged through Jules. She tilted her head. "You care. Maybe more than anyone I've ever met. And that's why I love you."

Danny gave her that smile, the one that meant friendship and home and family. Slapping him on the back, Jules turned back to the kitchen to oversee the exhausted team as they broke down the dinner service stations and got ready for their nightly RSC practice.

Jules managed to lose herself in cleaning for a while, but once her station was pristine enough to satisfy the most critical health inspector in Manhattan, she looked up to discover that the entire team was gathered, prepped, and ready to get to work.

Everyone except Max.

She caught Gus's eye, sending him a questioning glance. His mouth was tight, and that vein over his forehead was popping out a little.

"Damn it, Max," Danny muttered, starting for the stairs, and Jules caught Gus's instinctive wince.

Jules wadded up the dirty towel in her hand and chucked it toward the laundry bags in the corner.

"Don't worry about it, Danny," she said briskly. "I'll go get him and tell him it's time."

Time to put aside all this petty bullshit and grow the hell up, she added silently as she headed for the door up to the apartment.

Deep breath in . . . hold it for one heartbeat . . . then out again in a slow stream. Gather all the stress and emotion inside yourself into the breath, Max thought, *then push it out with the exhalation. Let it go. Just let . . . it . . . go . . .*

Something in his back pocket was digging into his left butt cheek, and his nose itched. Max suppressed a sigh in favor of regulating his breath and doing his damnedest to let it all just fucking go, but it wasn't working.

None of the strategies he'd learned for allowing the distractions and tensions of daily life to pass through him were working today. In fact, Max realized, disgusted, he hadn't been able to get through a single meditation session since he got back to New York.

Harukai-sensei would beat his ass if he could see Max now.

A knock on the door startled him out of the lotus position, but his numb right foot caught on his other leg and sent him sprawling to his back on the floor. Smooth.

His voice hoarse from disuse, Max called out, "Come in." How long had he been sitting here, failing to surrender to the nothingness of being?

The door opened to reveal the slim, lightly toned form of the woman who was responsible for a large part of Max's meditation-blocking distraction.

"You're late," Jules said, staring down at him with her dark blond eyebrows crinkled in confusion. "And you're on the floor. What are you doing?"

"Meditating."

"Is that what the kids are calling it these days?"

"No, really," Max protested, then frowned. "Or, not really, because my meditation attempt was pretty failtastic. Couldn't focus. Too much on my mind."

She crossed her arms over her chest. "Like what?"

The hint of belligerence in her tone made him want to smile. She was expecting him to flirt, to say all he could think about were her sweet lips and firm, luscious curves or something unimaginative like that. And she wasn't entirely wrong, but it went against everything in Max to do the expected thing.

"Like Italy," he sighed, stretching his arms over his head and watching as her gaze tracked the hem of his shirt pulling up over his stomach. "The little village in Le

Marche where Vincenzo Cotto's studio is—it's one of the most beautiful places on earth. I can't wait to go back."

Jules dropped her arms, a spark of interest lighting her eyes. "You've been there before? I thought a rambling man like you was always wanting to see new places, have new experiences."

He laughed. "Well, it's not like I've taken a vow of wandering, or something. I've gone back to lots of places, to visit the friends I made or check in on projects I started while I was there. But the thing with Cotto is different. When I went two years ago, I didn't stay long, hardly got to explore the town at all. I was trying to get him to see me—to agree to let me study with him."

"Two years." There was an odd quality to her voice, something he couldn't place. "That's how long you've been waiting for the chance to learn from Cotto?"

"Yep. I've been working toward this opportunity for a long time."

"Why is it so important to you?"

The question hovered in the air between them, unexpectedly personal and strangely hard to answer. Unsure what to say, Max let his gaze slide to the side. "I'm interested in Italian food—the culture of the cuisine is so much about comfort and simplicity, making the most of simple, pure ingredients, letting them shine. People think that means it's easy, but it's not. There's as much technique to it as any other cuisine. It's not just about throwing tomato sauce over boiled pasta—the Italians have a million ways to build deep, layered, complex flavors. I want to learn them all."

"And you couldn't learn from a book. Or from any old random Italian cooking teacher."

Max shrugged sheepishly, his shoulders scratching against the woolly fibers of the rug. "As you may have noticed, I'm not a big book guy. More of a doer than a reader. Things don't make sense to me until I have my hands in them. And Cotto's the best. I try to only learn from the best—saves having to unlearn bad techniques later on."

"There's a pretty extensive Italian-American community in New York," Jules observed, carefully neutral.

"Yeah. But Jules, there's nothing like immersing yourself in the culture you're studying—living and breathing it, every day and every night. The language, the architecture, the incredible faces of the old people in the marketplace, doing their regular shopping and living their regular lives. Everything is specific to the place, and every place has its own magic. But Italy . . ."

Max breathed in deeply and closed his eyes, imagining the sweetly pungent tang of roasted garlic and tomatoes, the mouthwatering sour fruit of the bold, unlabeled local wine, the softness of the breezes rolling down the Sibillini Mountains and into the valley where Vincenzo Cotto's studio nestled like an egg in a basket.

"You love it there."

Jules's quiet comment opened Max's eyes. He looked up at her and smiled. "I haven't spent enough time to really be sure," he hedged, "but I think I might."

She was silent for a long moment, her face unreadable as she scrutinized him. Then, with a light kick to his ankle, she said, "Come on, get off your ass, we've got practice."

"I'd love to," Max told her, flexing the foot she'd tapped, "but, sadly, I seem to be paralyzed from the knee down." Folding one arm up to cushion his head, Max sent her his most disarming smile. "Want to come keep me company while I wait for the pins and needles to stop poking me?"

She glanced behind her as if his brother were standing in the hall, arms crossed disapprovingly.

God. Danny. The thick, scratchy cloak of betrayal and

anger he'd wrapped around himself when Max left was another major meditation buster. It wasn't like Max hadn't been aware of Danny's resentment, and he tried to accept it, but being face-to-face with it every single day was wearing him down until each muttered aside and disgruntled look scraped over Max's raw nerves like the flat of a knife scraping the seeds from a hot pepper.

Jules always took Danny's side, Max had noticed.

"Just get up," she said. "Everyone's waiting."

"Don't you want to inspect my room?" Max said, knowing he was being a shit but unable to stop while he had her all to himself. "Who knows, it might give you some fodder for mocking."

"I'm familiar with the room already," she murmured, taking a few hesitant steps inside. Max's gaze followed the high, round swell of her ass, the long tail of hair twitching just above it.

She stopped a few steps into the room and turned, almost catching him in the act of ogling.

Startled, Max rapidly replayed the last few seconds of conversation in his head. "Wait. What?"

Chapter 9

Jules regarded him silently for a moment, and the lack of expression on her face could only be on purpose. "When I was about seventeen, I had to leave home. Your dad offered me a job, and this room to stay in until I could find my own place. I thought they would've mentioned it—I lived here for about six months, right after you left, until I turned eighteen and got my own place."

"You're kidding." That was . . . bizarre. Max wasn't sure how he felt about Jules having full access to his childhood stuff. And his adolescenthood stuff, cripes. His mind immediately zoomed to the stash of dog-eared skin mags hidden under the box spring.

Then something else she'd said filtered through the red tide of embarrassment, making him frown. "What happened that made you leave home?"

Her eyes went kind of shifty. "It's a long, very boring story, and we need to get back to the kitchen. Get up, your leg's fine."

Whatever happened back then, she clearly didn't want to talk about it with him. Interesting. And also okay, because Max had more questions about this woman who'd taken over his old life, like some kind of hot, blond identity thief. "You said my dad offered you the place to stay?"

In his family, Nina Lunden was indisputably the hospitable one. It was Nina who met a nice young man who helped her with her groceries in exchange for a couple bucks, and brought him home to sleep on the couch while he sorted himself out. It was Nina who invited the entire kitchen crew for holiday dinners, knowing their families were in other countries and they'd otherwise be alone.

It was always his mother whose open heart and sharp eye for the goodness inside others prompted her to bring home strays. Never his dad.

But Jules confirmed it. With a defiant toss of her head, no less, as if she expected him to accuse her of lying.

"Yes. Your dad was closing up the restaurant one night, and I wandered in. I was looking for Danny, but he wasn't home. And Gus and I got to talking, and when he found out I needed somewhere to stay, things just sort of . . . fell into place."

There was way more to this story, Max knew. But he wouldn't push it right now, he decided. She was skittish enough without forcing her to spill all her secrets out onto the scuffed hardwood floor next to his childhood bed.

"Cool," he said, giving her a smile to let her know he was backing off. "I'm not complaining, okay? I'm happy you're here."

"Oh, stop it."

Max frowned. "Stop what?"

She threw up her hands. "Stop acting like there's something between us! We work together, that's all. And even that's only temporary. As soon as this phase of the competition is over, you'll be in the wind again."

There was something in her voice, something Max couldn't place. Relief? Regret? He didn't know, but he wanted to find out.

Testing his tingling foot, Max thought he could stand on it. He pushed off the floor and straightened, looming over her for an instant before she scowled and stood, too. She went toe to toe with him immediately, and Max felt his blood quicken. Was that anger? Or something else?

The first step to letting go of your emotion is to allow yourself to feel the emotion. Harukai-sensei's soft voice floated through Max's head. *Know what it is you feel, acknowledge it, then release it on a breath.*

That was his problem, right there. Max never knew what the hell he was feeling these days.

Losing himself in the whiskey-gold depths of her eyes, he said, "Aw, that's sweet. You saying you want me to stick around?"

"Of course not. I didn't think it was necessary for Nina to call you home in the first place," Jules replied.

Her words said "No, no, no," but the way she leaned in toward him, the pulse jumping in her neck, the heated flash of awareness in her amber eyes—that all said "Yes, yes, yes!"

Max was so intrigued, he could hardly stand it. Feeling his way along, he said, "Well, you're here now, and so am I. Who knows? Maybe it *was* fate. Or my dad. I guess I owe him a thank-you. I know it wasn't Danny who convinced him to call me."

"Would you shut up about Gus and Danny?" Jules spat suddenly, chest heaving with the force of her breath. Her hands were clenched in fists at her sides; she looked ready to deliver a serious beat-down.

Max felt as if she'd already slapped him, the mixed-up desire of moments before resolving itself into simple anger. He backed away from her, muscles jumping. He needed to move, so he paced. "Are you kidding me? You can't honestly think all the friction between my family and me is entirely my fault."

She shook her head. "Not the point."

"Oh? Then what is?"

"The point is, not everything is about you," she growled. "Your father's had a lot on his mind the last few weeks. Hell, the last few years! It's been hard on Danny. And where were you?"

Everything in Max's head went pure red for an instant. "I was anywhere but here," he said through clenched teeth. "Which you know perfectly well, since apparently you were on the spot the whole time, keeping it warm for me."

Her mouth trembled. "Every day I stayed in this room, I kept expecting you to show up and kick me out. But you didn't. After six years of phone calls and e-mails, the least you could do is cut everyone some slack." She turned away, giving him that perfect profile again. "Do you even know how lucky you are?"

Guilt scoured Max's throat with a taste like bitter orange peel, making his voice rough and grating. "I love my family. But we can't coexist, Jules. Since I was a teenager and started having my own ideas about what kind of restaurant Lunden's should be—it's been one long fight, punctuated by periods where we don't talk. At all. Dad on one side, me on the other, and poor Danny and Mom stuck in the middle." He swallowed hard against the knot that rose from his chest and jammed his hands into his back pockets, staring at his feet. "I don't know, maybe you're right. Maybe the fighting is better than nothing, and I should've been here, duking it out every night over dinner."

He risked a look up at Jules, who was watching him with her arms wrapped around herself, as if she felt a chill. Max forced himself to continue. "I would've stayed, but it was killing Mom. And it wasn't that much fun for the rest of us, either, if you want the truth."

Understanding softened the line of her mouth, turning it upside down into an unhappy curve.

"Nothing's simple when it comes to family," she said finally. "I get that."

She didn't look ready to slug him anymore, but she sure didn't look much happier. Max found himself in the odd position of wanting to hug her, comfort her—not that it was odd that he should want to touch her, since he'd wanted that since the moment he walked back into his old life and saw her again.

But he wasn't used to feeling so many competing, conflicting emotions, along with desire for a woman. Then again, Jules Cavanaugh wasn't a bored waitress at a falafel shop or a grad student backpacking across the Pyrenees. She wasn't someone who would flit in and out of his life, brushing up against the outer edges of him and never getting any deeper. Jules was someone his family loved. She had a place here—more of a place than Max did, really.

He looked at her now, though, and he didn't see his father's disappointed hopes for his eldest son to run the restaurant, or his brother's resentment that Danny, who'd rather devote his time to pastry, might be forced to step up.

Max saw a woman who'd been hurt, who'd chosen to be strong, who gave her heart with fierce loyalty . . . a woman who made him want to go deeper. Max took a step closer to her, then another.

Jules watched his approach with the stillness of a wild creature in the woods, eyes dark and wide, chest heaving a little with the force of her breaths.

Max reached out his hand and gently clasped her shoulder, angling her body in to face his. They were lined up, hips and belly and chest, and he loved that she was only an inch or so shorter.

It made it so easy, effortless, to dip his head and cover that sweet, pink mouth with his.

He wasn't holding her except with one hand on her shoulder, and he half expected the shock of the kiss to break the moment; he thought she'd stiffen against him and pull away.

Instead, she surged into him, her body moving hard against his and knocking him back a step before he caught his balance and wrapped his arms around her back.

And suddenly, his emotions were as clear to him as the crystal lake water beside the mountain temple where he'd first learned his meditation techniques.

He wanted her. Badly.

Prickles of heat washed up and down her spine, racing along her nerve endings and puckering her nipples into hard points pressed tight to his chest.

It felt amazing. Also amazing? Max's mouth.

That honey-smooth, wickedly grinning mouth devouring hers, licking into the depths of her as if he'd never get tired of the taste.

Dimly, Jules remembered that she wasn't supposed to touch him. Wasn't supposed to look at him, flirt with him, give him the wrong idea . . .

But was it the wrong idea? Being in this room again, where she'd thought about him so often, imagined so many things—and then talking to him, yelling at him, which made her want to cringe now, but the way he talked back . . . the openness of him.

Jules was so used to guarding her heart; she'd forgotten what it was like to be around someone who had no shame, no fear about what he wanted.

And Max wanted her. She could feel it in every sweep of his tongue along the roof of her mouth, tickling and making her squirm closer to him. She could feel it when he pulled her closer so he could get his hands on her hips and dig his fingers in just enough to let her know how desperate he was.

She could feel it most of all in the thick, hard length of

his erection, hot even through all their clothes, notched high against the vee of her thighs.

With the strength of every night she'd lain in this room, thinking about Max and wondering where he was, Jules wanted to rip open his pants, sink to her knees, and swallow him down.

The very urgency of that desire was what shocked her out of the dream of heat and push and thrust and clench, and back into the world of reality, where their teammates were waiting for them downstairs, and they had a competition to qualify for—one that would prove to the Lundens, once and for all, that Jules was the best choice to run Lunden's Tavern when Gus retired.

And the one person standing in the way of all that currently had his tongue in her mouth.

Jules had to be smart about this. She couldn't afford to be like her mother, allowing her sex drive to steer her entire life.

Sex was dangerous. It blinded you to the truth, made you do awful things . . . She had to be stronger than this. She had to control this.

Jules let her weight fall back onto her heels with a thump and untangled her fingers from his short, silky hair.

It was harder to let go than she'd anticipated; she had to slump over and rest her forehead on his collarbone for a minute, just a second, so she could catch her breath.

"Hey," he whispered above her head. "You good, sweetness?"

His arms were still around her, pressed flat to her shoulder blades, so comforting and strong and warm. She let her face fall against his chest, let him cuddle her close, even though she knew it was asking for trouble down the road.

"I'm good," she whispered back, aching deep in her throat. "But we can't stay up here much longer; someone's going to come looking for us."

His chuckle reverberated through his chest and into her cheekbone. "Yeah, you're right. And I really don't want that someone to be my dad. Ew, or my brother. Yikes."

They separated slowly. Jules thought Max was as reluctant to pull away as she was to let him go, but eventually they managed.

Okay. So that didn't go quite the way I imagined it.

In Jules's experience, getting up close and spit-swappy with a guy was a surefire way of letting that guy know he didn't have to respect her or care about her anymore.

One look in Max Lunden's bright, open eyes, however, and Jules felt the truth like a ball of raw dough expanding in her stomach.

Max wasn't like other guys. He wouldn't mean to hurt her . . . but he would. By leaving in a month, if nothing else. The way he talked about Italy—so much longing and desire for a country, it was enough to make Jules jealous. And sad, because she knew she couldn't compete. Didn't even want to, if it would mean standing in the way of Max's dream.

So it was up to Jules to protect her heart. No one else was going to do it for her.

Chapter 10

Once they'd finally managed to get downstairs, and waded through the obligatory commentary about how long it took and what they might have been doing up there, complete with grossed-out faces from Danny and total glee from Winslow, Max retreated to the station he'd set up for himself in the corner and started playing with the set of chopsticks he liked to use instead of a whisk.

Jules sent Gus a pleading look. *Please, let's get on with this. I can't take too much more joking about what a cute couple we make.*

As always, Gus caught her drift without a word passing between them. "All right, kids, settle down. We've got plenty of trivia prep to do, but before we get started, I asked Jules to investigate this new judge."

"Kane Slater," Win said, with a smirk. "Smokin' hot foodie rock star . . . and this competition just got a whole lot sexier."

Gus's cheeks went brick red. He cleared his throat uncomfortably, and this time he was the one turning on the pleading look. "Jules, you want to tell us what you found out?"

"Well, basically, Win's right," she said. "Kane Slater got his start singing in clubs in Austin, near where his mother lives. He's into food in a big way."

"And he's smokin' hot. Don't forget that part," Win put in. He blinked into the pause, then quirked a brow at her. "I know you're not even going to play like you didn't notice."

"Okay," Jules admitted, feeling the tips of her ears get hot. "Yes, it's kind of hard to miss. But down, boy—there are strict rules against fraternization between judges and chef contestants."

Win sighed. "Sadly, I'm pretty sure he doesn't bat for my team. But hey, if you and Max really aren't bucking for Cutest Couple on the Manhattan Restaurant Scene, maybe you can make a jump for Kane."

A loud crack shocked Jules stiff, and she looked over to see Max sheepishly dropping the chopstick he'd been playing with, snapped into two pieces.

"Or not," Winslow said, eyes wide.

"Getting back to the subject at hand," Beck said, crossing his arms over his massive chest. "And leaving out the gossip-magazine stuff, what do we know?"

Jules crouched to retrieve her Moleskin notebook from her backpack. Flipping through the pages, she read, 'He was born in a small town in the Texas hill country, but moved to Austin when he was about eighteen, and he still lives there some of the year. The rest of his time he's on tour, or recording in his studio in L.A.'

"Apparently, he's one of those musical people who can pick up any instrument, mess around with it for a second, and then play a song. His music is fast, irreverent, with influences from punk to hip-hop to reggae; it's hard to pin down. And he writes his own lyrics, most of which seem to be about living life to the fullest. For instance—" She checked her notebook again. "The refrain from his latest hit starts: 'Let's suck the marrow from the bones of our days.'"

"A food reference," Danny observed.

Jules nodded. "You got it. And it's not the only one. His songs are full of cooking metaphors, kitchen wisdom, food imagery . . . the guy clearly thinks of himself as a major gourmet. Have any of you heard his music?"

Unsurprisingly, Winslow's hand shot up, and after a beat, Beck shocked everyone by raising his, too.

"What?" Beck scowled, shifting defensively. "I like music."

"Ooookay, moving on," Danny said, eyebrows at his hairline. "Jules, you're up. Whaddaya know?"

"Well, for starters . . . you know that phrase 'larger than life'? It could've been coined for this guy. Everything he does is big: he pulls life-threatening stunts, throws insanely lavish, star-studded dinner parties—where he actually does a lot of the cooking himself, according to rumor—and he's adventurous." She flipped forward a couple of pages in her notebook until she found the quote she wanted. "He said in a *Rolling Stone* interview, 'I'll try anything once. And if it doesn't kill me, I'll probably do it again, only blindfolded and naked.'"

"I wonder if that sense of adventure extends to his palate," Gus said, stroking his jaw.

Jules nodded. "Apparently so. He likes to push his own boundaries, and the likelier something is to fold, spindle, and/or mutilate him, the better."

"So maybe we should expect some questions about dangerous food items. Like . . . huh. Well, there's that Japanese puffer fish, I know. What else can kill you?"

"You're thinking of fugu, Dad," Max put in. "Other dangerous stuff I've run across . . . hmm, bitter almonds, full of cyanide. Unripe ackee fruit, which is weird-looking stuff, let me tell you. Oh, and in Korea, they serve baby octopus raw, still squirming all over the plate. Those aren't poisonous, but sometimes the suckers attach themselves on the way down and choke people."

"Wow," Jules said, impressed and slightly nauseated. "So. You're in charge when it comes to strange, disgusting, potentially lethal food questions."

Looking unhappy to be put in charge of anything, Max said, "Hey, *sannakji hoe* aren't disgusting, and they're not really dangerous as long as you give 'em a good long chew."

"Meanwhile," she went on, giving Max a suppressing look. "I'm going to brush up on the history of Texas, especially anything about Southwestern and Mexican foodways. Also, Slater's got this thing about famous historical meals—"

"Oooh, like Czarfest 2010!" Win said, light green eyes wide, excitement darkening his cheeks until his sprinkling of freckles disappeared. "Last year, Kane Slater threw this huge bash at his house, all decorated to look like an imperial ball, and the guests had to come dressed as Russian nobility. He re-created the Romanovs' last banquet. You know, before everything went to shit for them."

The entire team turned to look at Winslow, who shrugged, utterly unabashed. "What can I say? I'm a fan. Plus, TMZ had pictures and oh em gee, let me tell you— you haven't lived until you've seen Britney Spears in a tiara, falling down drunk and tangled in a mile of silver tulle."

Jules exchanged an amused glance with Danny, then said, "Win, it sounds like you're the perfect person to research Slater's dinner parties."

Winslow clasped his hands in front of him. "Can I? Can I really, and call it work and get paid for it and everything?"

"Yup," Gus said. "Just like it'll be work for Danny to go through Devon Sparks's old menus, and for Beck to read through back issues of *Délicieux* from when Claire Durand was still doing restaurant reviews, before she became editor in chief. So let's get to it."

Everybody nodded and hopped to it as soon as they received their orders—everybody except, predictably, Max.

He leaned back against his makeshift station, more of a movable butcher block on wheels than actual counter space, eyes on his father as Gus started making the rounds of the other chefs, dispensing advice and patting backs.

Hoping to forestall another fight, Jules went over to Max. "What's the problem?"

He raised a brow at Jules. "I can't believe this is what they called me home for. Celebrity gossip and food magazines? They don't need me for this. I could be learning to speak Italian right now, figuring out where I'm going to hang my hat in Le Marche. Something useful."

Jules struggled with her temper. Apparently, sharing a hot kiss wasn't like getting a booster shot immunizing her against any future aggravation with Max.

Keep it cool, she told herself. *There's enough heat in this kitchen already.* "Maybe this isn't the part where you can help out the most. But the trivia is only the beginning. We get points for every correct answer, and the more points we have, the better position we're in going into the finals, which is a full-on cooking challenge, the kind we'd get if we made it to the actual Rising Star Chef competition. And even if we win the finals and are named the East Coast team, we'll still have to compete against the South, Midwest, Southwest, and West Coast teams for the ultimate title. There's a long road ahead of us, Max. This is only the first step."

He studied her face, head cocked to one side as if that would help him see deeper inside of her. "You really care about this, don't you?"

"You sound surprised," Jules said. "You shouldn't be. After what your parents have done for me? I'd do anything to help them."

"Sheesh." Max ducked his head, palming the back of his neck. "Way to make me feel like a tool."

But Jules wasn't finished. "Of course I want to win, Max. This competition might not mean anything to you and your career as a professional wanderer, but it's a big deal to those of us hoping to make a name for ourselves in the legit restaurant industry. With something like this on my résumé, I could work anywhere. I could run a kitchen."

His gaze sharpened on her face like a freshly steeled knife. "Like this one, for instance."

It took everything Jules had not to freeze in place. She managed a casual shrug. "We'll see. I've got options, but the point is, winning the RSC would give me more."

Max was still scrutinizing her far too closely. "Yeah, see, that's what I don't understand. My parents already own their own restaurant, and run their own kitchen. What do they stand to gain if they win this competition?"

Jules glanced over her shoulder to where Gus was standing by Danny's station, drawing the pastry chef's attention to a line in a thick cookbook. She couldn't believe she was about to do this.

"Look, I'm not supposed to say anything, but if it'll help you understand . . ." She stopped and bit her lip, torn between her promise to Gus and her need to make Max see how important this was.

"Tell me," he said, concern shading his eyes to a stormy blue-gray. "I need to know."

"The restaurant's been slipping," she said, keeping her voice low and her eyes on his, so he'd know she was serious. "A lot. Quality of food is the same, the menu hasn't changed in twenty years, and yet—the number of customers keeps going down and down and down. No big names come here anymore—with so many new hot spots opening in the city every year, old classics like this place are a harder sell, and the Village isn't the most fashionable part of town. But Gus knows if Lunden's Tavern supplies the team that wins the Rising Star Chef competition, that'll put us back on the map. In fact, we'll be bigger than ever."

Max blew out the breath he'd been holding. "Shit. I knew this was coming. I always expected to feel smug when I heard it—God knows, I warned Dad about it—but . . . I'm not." He pressed a hand to the flat belly Jules knew from recent experience was ridged with muscle. "I feel sick."

"I know. But now do you get it? All of this, the stress it's putting on your dad, how tense Danny is, everything—it's all about this. Because they're terrified of losing this place."

A bitter twist she'd never seen before took Max's mouth. "Believe me, I know exactly how much this place means to my dad."

There was a deep hurt there, Jules recognized. Gentling her voice, she said, "If you think Lunden's Tavern means more to Gus than his actual sons, you're dead wrong. He's afraid of losing the restaurant because it's your heritage. Your birthright, and his responsibility to pass it down to the next generation, the way it was passed down to him."

Max paused, a new light coming into his eyes. "Huh. I never really thought about it that way before. Maybe you're right. God, Jules. What did we ever do around here without you?"

"Don't worry. I'm not going anywhere." Then her mouth got the better of her brain. "That's more your department, anyway."

From the way Max's face tightened, that was a direct hit. But his only response was a rueful laugh. "You got me there. I like to go and see and do and experience. I can't believe I ever thought running this place would be enough for me."

"Max, I'm sorry, I shouldn't have said—"

"No, it's fine," he interrupted, eyes shifting away. "Really. Not like it isn't true. Anyway, shouldn't we both be getting to work? I've got some lethal toxins to look up. And you've got the great state of Texas to research."

Okay, this time I really am taking my own advice and letting it go.

Jules nodded, still a little worried by the dark undercurrents running through Max's normally sunny mood. "Yeah, you're right. We only have a few days left before the qualifiers. Not a lot of time to learn everything there is to know about another human being, even if he is famous."

"A famous dickwad, is what he sounds like," Max muttered, turning away from her to reach up to the shelf above his butcher block for the stack of reference books he'd stashed there.

Jules moved back to her station. "I don't care what he's like in person; all I care about is knowing what kinds of questions he's likely to throw at us."

Beside her, Winslow poked her with a discreet elbow. "Not to spin your stress-o-meter into High Freakout Mode, but from what I know about Kane Slater? The only thing we can reasonably expect is the unexpected."

That was exactly what Jules was afraid of. She glanced over at Max, who rolled his eyes and hauled a copy of Harold McGee's scientific treatise *On Food and Cooking* toward him. He caught her eye and mouthed something that looked like "only for you" and bent to his task.

She caught her breath and turned back to her own work,

lingering unease about Max and his father and the restaurant and the competition all swirling together in her belly.

Kane Slater better not throw her any curve balls—and that went for the other judges, too. Jules had about all the unexpected she could take in her life, right now.

Chapter 11

Max behaved himself for five long, boring days.

Five days of showing up to practice on time, dutifully leafing through reference books, helping Jules keep the peace in the kitchen, and not throwing any more woo Jules's way.

It was harder to be good than it should've been.

Maybe if he believed Jules really didn't want him, every bit as much as he wanted her, Max reflected as he pulled on his freshly laundered chef's whites. There were benefits to living at home again, it turned out—the Mom Laundry Service being one of them.

It wasn't that Max didn't get where Jules was coming from. Two people, small kitchen, same team, already complicated family dynamics—it could get worse than messy, really damn fast.

But from the way she kept watching him, with heat in her eyes and a flush on her cheeks, and still managed to keep her hands to herself, Max was pretty sure he was fighting more than logic, reason, and practicality. Something beyond rational thought was holding Jules back. The mystery of it hooked into Max's overactive curiosity and tugged relentlessly.

Curiosity was Max's number one favorite vice.

Jules Cavanaugh was fascinating, like a new knife trick or an innovative technique for layering flavors in dashi. Max had never met another woman who made him want to pull back her layers and learn every inch of her, inside and out, with the same hunger that drove him from city to city, continent to continent, in search of culinary adventure.

If he'd known about her, he might've come home a lot sooner.

Not that Max fooled himself into thinking he'd stay. Even without Italy beckoning him, he'd get tired of standing still, bored with the routine and the sameness of everyday life all in one place. He always had before, and there was no reason to believe this time would be any different.

Home was a concept that didn't really apply to Max anymore.

But just because he knew he'd be leaving in a few weeks didn't mean he and Jules couldn't have something special.

It was the night before the qualifying round, and Gus had called one final practice session for the team members who weren't working dinner service at Lunden's.

To keep out of the way of the actual restaurant business, he'd asked them to meet in the kitchen of the apartment upstairs, but when Max sauntered out of his room five minutes after the appointed hour (okay, so he was mostly on time—nobody was perfect) the only person in the kitchen was Jules.

She was slumped over the scarred wooden table shoved into the corner of the kitchen, but when he came in, she straightened up and gave him a tired smile. "Hey. I thought maybe you forgot."

"A date with you?" Max said. "Never."

Her gorgeous wide mouth twitched, as if she wanted to laugh but held herself back. She did that a lot, Max had noticed. Held back. It made him hungry to know what it would take to shake her loose.

"I realize that women have always been tragically easy when it comes to you, myself included, but you might want to rethink your understanding of the term 'date.'"

Max looked around the empty kitchen. "You. Me. Alone. A whole night ahead of us to do whatever we want together? I'd say that sounds like a date. And for the record, you've never been what I'd call 'easy.'"

Her eyes flashed with interest, but then her mouth got that stubborn set that he liked so much. "We don't have the whole night, and we should work. That's what this practice is for."

"You call it a 'practice,'" Max said, making big, ostentatious air quotes. "But I don't see the rest of the team anywhere around."

"Beck, Danny, and Winslow all ended up working tonight because the second-string hot line chefs got food poisoning or something. And your dad had an appointment that ran late. He called a few minutes ago; he and your mom are both there."

Max frowned. "What kind of appointment?"

Something like alarm flickered across Jules's face, but she shrugged and said, "Don't know, they didn't say. But I guess we'll just have to wait for everyone else."

The full ramifications of the situation sank into Max's consciousness. Giving a silent nod to his old pal, Fate, he felt a slow smile crease his cheeks. "So," he said. "We really *are* alone."

"Yeah," she said, then her eyes widened comically. "Hey, no—stay over there. What are you doing? Personal space!"

Max laughed as he prowled closer, one hand bracing

his weight against the back of her chair so he could lean in and get a breath of that sugar-lemon scent wafting up from her hair. God, he loved that.

"We're supposed to be practicing," he purred, drunk on the closeness of her. "So let's practice."

He could hear her swallow. "What . . . what sort of culinary challenge do you think this applies to?"

Curling his hands over her shoulders, he smoothed them down over the wings of her shoulder blades, pressing his fingers in to urge her to her feet. She stood shakily, the front of her body brushing his, inch by inch, teasing them both.

"Let's see. There could be a challenge about working closely together," he said, low and soft, his lips skimming her ear. "Maybe in . . . tight spaces."

"Oh," she said, her hands coming up to rest against his chest, lightly, as if she weren't sure whether to pull him closer or push him away. "That actually . . . they've done that. A few competitions ago, they put the teams on a sailboat and made them cook a five-course gourmet meal in a tiny galley kitchen."

"See? We're totally practicing."

"This isn't fair," Jules moaned as Max trailed his hands up her neck to palm the shape of her skull. He pulled the elastic band out of her hair and let it tumble over his fingers in a citrusy wave, soft strands catching on his scarred knuckles.

"What's not fair?" he asked, rubbing her head in soothing little circles.

"Oh . . . you. This. No flirting for almost a week—I let my guard down! Now here you are."

"Here we are," he agreed, pulling her unresisting body even closer. They were almost eye to eye, except hers were closed, gold-tipped lashes fanning across her flushed cheeks.

How far would she let this go? he wondered as he tilted her head gently and laid his mouth across hers, dipping deep at once in search of that delicious Jules flavor.

"This is so unbelievably stupid," she moaned, and the hands that had been resting against his chest rose to his shoulders and gripped, hard. Evidently, she'd made up her mind not to push him away, because the kiss flashed from sweet to sultry in the blink of an eye. She got her fists into his shirt and tugged so hard he stumbled into her.

Knocked off balance, Jules fell back but kept her ferocious grip on his shirt, yanking Max with her. And once he got his feet under him again, he decided she was on to something, because with a few more steps she'd be up against the wall and they wouldn't have to worry so much about equilibrium.

He maneuvered them past the table and pressed her back to the lovely, solid wall, letting one leg slide between her thighs to pin her there.

Not that she was struggling—at least, not to get away. If anything, Jules seemed to be trying to climb through him to get to the other side, and her frantic, clutching fingers and soft, throaty noises were driving Max out of his mind.

"So be stupid, for once," he gasped against her neck. "Quit thinking and live."

Her breathing was harsh and erratic, puffing into the hair at his temple. "Once," she echoed. "Just this once."

She hooked one long leg around his hips, tilting her pelvis that extra, perfect, amazing, magical little bit—and suddenly his aching erection was notched tight against her softest place.

He couldn't resist grinding into it, and even through the heavy denim of their pants, it felt insane. The inseam of his jeans rubbed him in a way that was almost painful, sending electric bolts of sensation straight up his spine.

Jules tilted her head against the wall, eyelids fluttering,

and Max slipped his hands under the hem of her shirt. They both gasped when his fingertips found the warm satin of her skin, and Max thought, *What the hell,* and pulled the shirt off over her head.

Blinking dazedly, Jules emerged from the fabric with her hair a tousled honey-blond crackle of static around her head. Max took in the long smooth lines of her torso, his hands mapping the lean muscle at her waist, strong from all the bending and turning and lifting that came with being a chef.

Keeping up the calm, slow petting at her sides, Max let himself enjoy the sight of her, arched against the wall and bare to his gaze, the swells of her pretty, round breasts peeping golden and succulent over the top of her white cotton bra. Glancing up to meet her hooded gaze, he said, "You're gorgeous."

He'd never meant anything so much in his life.

She blushed a darker shade of red, the color washing from her cheeks all the way down her neck, and looked away.

"You don't like hearing that?"

Her laugh was short and choked off. "It's usually a warning sign that a guy's about to ask for something I don't want to give."

A dark undercurrent throbbed through her voice, pressed into his shoulders in half-moons of pain from her unconsciously tight fingernails, and Max frowned.

Someone had hurt her. The knowledge crashed over him in a wave of shockingly violent anger. Max tried to breathe through it, tried to keep his heart going in the wake of the sudden understanding of his own limits when it came to peace, Zen, and avenging Jules Cavanaugh.

"Max?" She sounded uncertain. Max immediately leaned forward and pressed his mouth to the flushed skin of her neck. It was hot enough to make his lips tingle.

"Max," she repeated, in this small, throbbing voice that just about killed him. Her hands opened and closed on his shoulders, and she gave one tiny, abortive squirm with her hips that was enough to make him grunt and shift her leg higher around his waist.

"I want you," he told her. "I don't think I've ever wanted anything as much. But if you don't want this, say the word, and I'll never bother you again. Because it's no good if we're not both in it."

An emotion came and went, flitting across her mobile features in the amount of time between one gasped breath and the next. "I want you, too," she said, her voice raspy with desire. "I guess it would be kind of ridiculous to deny it, at this point."

"I don't know. You could be standing on one leg because you're part flamingo, and I just happen to be in the way."

Her laugh did crazy things to Max's insides. "Right. And I'm not wearing a shirt because I'm practicing cooking topless, in case the judges give us that as a challenge."

He ran his palm along her uplifted thigh, cupping the shapely curve of her hip before gliding onto her inner thigh and nudging the heel of his hand into the moist heat at the notch of her legs.

Her eyes flickered shut again, and her hips hitched when Max moved his hand in tight little circles. "And you're all hot and bothered because . . ."

"Because . . . because . . ." She rolled her head against the wall, pretty mouth going slack.

"Because you want me," he whispered triumphantly into the soft, bitable skin of her neck.

"Because you're touching me," she countered weakly, clutching at him and wobbling. "Oh, touching me. Keep touching me, Max . . ."

Forever, he wanted to say, which was weird enough to

almost make him pull up short in the middle of some of the hottest sex he'd ever had in his life.

To distract himself, Max opened his mouth and bit down gently on the slope where Jules's neck met her shoulder. Jules made a high-pitched keening noise and Max just about broke a finger trying to get the button of her jeans undone.

He had to shift back to get her pants open and pulled down enough to fit his hand inside, and the way she looked—utterly luscious and abandoned, better than the best porn he'd ever imagined—made Max squint against a sudden fear that if he kept looking at her, he'd shoot before he even got his dick out of his pants.

Unacceptable. Max got back down to the business of working his hand under the elastic leg of her underwear.

Because the only thing he wanted more than to come with her hand on his cock was to make her shiver, writhe, and fall apart on the tips of his fingers.

Was it possible to surrender her body while protecting her heart?

Jules moved and shuddered against Max, his skillful fingers easily manipulating her responses and sending flashes of pure pleasure to cloud her already whirling mind.

This wasn't how she'd planned to spend her evening. She could only thank whatever god looked out for women who couldn't be bothered to listen to their own very sound advice that she was wearing matching, if boring, bra and underwear.

Every tiny shift of his fingers sent an overload of sensation to her brain, confusing messages that were half blinding pleasure, half jumpy pain from being so swollen and sensitive. Max did something fast and dexterous that her brain was too awash in lust to figure out, and suddenly there was lovely, firm pressure right where she needed it, while two of his strong, rough-knuckled fingers slid into her aching opening.

"Oh there," she stuttered out, her inner thigh muscles twitching with the need to clamp down on his maddening, teasing hand. Tension coiled tight at the base of her spine, and when he bent forward to bite at her neck again, shivers wrapped around her entire body and suddenly she was coming, hot and shaky, bursts of color exploding in the darkness behind her closed eyes.

He groaned against her throat, the sound of a man in torment, and said something vehement in a language she couldn't place. From the tone of voice, she'd bet it was a swear word.

"You are so damn sexy," he said thickly, withdrawing his hand from her oversensitized flesh and petting her gently. "Like no one else, in the whole fucking world. Please. Tell me I can have you."

Still lost in the aftershocks of pleasure, Jules barely registered it when his hand left her and moved to fumble at the fly of his jeans. The sound of the zipper shocked her back into her head, though, and her eyes popped open.

Do I really want to do this?

"Wait." She put out a hand instinctively and encountered gaping denim, the cotton boxer-covered push of his thick cock spearing up from between the flaps.

He dropped his head to her shoulder, breathing hard. "Waiting," he gasped. "It's killing me, but I'm waiting."

Jules's brain stumbled into action. This was it. If she did this, she couldn't take it back.

She wasn't really worried about keeping Max's respect in the kitchen—he'd made it clear he didn't want to take her place as team leader, and his behavior over the last week proved his point. Unlike Phil the Phucktard after they'd started dating, Max didn't undermine her authority, didn't contradict her, didn't act like somehow the fact that he had testicles made him a better chef.

He pushed her, prodded her, challenged her—but when she started to crack, he didn't try to break her. He stopped and made sure she was okay.

No guy had ever done that for Jules before. Ever. And it was dangerous, so dangerous, because it made her want to trust him with everything.

But when Max left in a few weeks, she'd be here. Alone. With nothing but the memory of his touch to keep her warm at night.

Would one hot memory be enough to compensate for the lingering chill of missing Max Lunden?

Trying to buy a little time, she let her fingers wander up and down the throbbing column of flesh. It felt good under her hand, even with his underwear dulling the heat of his skin. Apparently, it felt good to Max, too, because he pressed an openmouthed kiss to her shoulder, licking the patch of sore, tingly skin he'd bitten before, and said, "Okay, I could wait a little longer, if we spend the time like this."

Max nuzzled into her, his body covering her protectively as if he were shielding her from the world, and Jules melted a little.

Enough thinking. Enough worrying about the future. Max leaving again was going to suck, whether she took this moment with him or not.

At least this way, she'd have the memory.

Chapter 12

Summoning all the strength her delicious orgasm had drained from her limbs, she pushed away from the wall and spun them so that Max stood, blinking in surprise, with his back braced against the white plaster.

"What are you— Oh, sweet fancy Mary on a cracker."

Jules sank to her knees in front of him, wincing at the cold, hard linoleum. She looked all the way up his body to where his eyes were nearly popping out of his head, and told him the truth. "I've been wanting to do this ever since you came back. Let me?"

His Adam's apple bobbed and he made a quick gesture with one hand. "Uh, yeah. Sure. You know, knock yourself out."

She kept her gaze locked with his, and the way he avidly ate up every slight move she made started to rekindle the heat in her belly. Reaching up, she carefully freed his erection from his boxers, pulling them and his jeans down below the lean cut of his hips.

His cock sprang out at her, eager and flushed red at the tip, where a bead of moisture welled temptingly into his slit. Jules licked her lips, flicking her stare back up to Max's eyes when he growled.

"You look good like that," he rasped hoarsely.

Jules shivered at the compliment, a mix of her usual discomfort and a new, swelling sense of her body as an instrument of pleasure. She leaned in to draw her tongue up the underside of his penis, swirling over the head to capture the salt-smoke taste of that one clear droplet. When he was done gasping, she said, "You taste good like this."

His head knocked back against the wall, rapping hard enough to almost make her worry for his brains. Staring at the ceiling, he said, "I'd really like to last longer than fifteen seconds. But you're not making it easy."

"That's my job, though, right?" She licked him again, enjoying the silky skin under her tongue, and the way his belly muscles jumped and quivered. "To make it hard."

Max made a strange noise, half grunt, half snort. "Don't make me laugh when my bits are that close to your teeth."

"Don't worry," she told him. "I'll be gentle with you."

And with that, she took him all the way into her mouth.

She played with the head at first, sucking lightly, then harder, hollowing her cheeks to make him moan. When she scooted forward to let him drive deeper, Max's hips bucked uncontrollably. Jules reached up, curving her palms over the jut of his hipbones, and pressed him back into the wall.

"Sorry," he gasped. "Sorry, sorry . . ."

Jules let him know it was okay by going down farther until the head of his cock tickled the back of her throat, then pulling up, sucking strongly. They fell into a rhythm, in, out, lick, suck, push, pull, and every move seemed to tug at things low in Jules's body, the parts of her that were still thrumming with arousal.

Max's hot eyes staring down at her, the hardness filling

her mouth, the slick, salty taste of him. Even the sharp throb of pain in her knees somehow added to the heat of the moment.

She could feel it building, sweeping higher like a bank of storm clouds rolling in to cover the sky and turn everything dark and electric. Taking one hand off his hip, she twisted it around the base of Max's erection and bobbed her head down to meet it, sucking furiously. She wanted everything he would give her, and she did her best to pull it out of him.

"I'm close," he gasped out after a moment, his hands moving to her head to try and gently dislodge her.

Jules pulled off his cock with a wet pop, and shook her head. "Go ahead," she said, her voice raw. "I want it." Then she dove back down.

His eyes widened, pupils dilating until only a slim ring of silvery blue showed, and he shuddered, pulsing over her tongue. Jules swallowed him down and felt the moment stretch taut between them, connected and alive.

She kept sucking, drawing it out, until he made a high, thin noise and put his hands back on her head. Letting him slip from her mouth, she rested her head against his thigh to catch her breath and try to make sense of the emotion welling up in her chest.

Dangerous, she thought again. Because maybe Max didn't look at all the places where she was cracked and broken, and pick up a hammer to finish the job—but that didn't mean he wasn't going to shatter her, all the same.

But here, now, in this moment, with him panting and writhing under her mouth and this deep, glowing connection arcing back and forth between them like a current of electricity, Jules couldn't make herself care.

She'd lost the self-preservation instincts that had been an integral part of her since she was seventeen years old, cold and shivering and hoofing it away from her mother's apartment.

It was official. She was fucked.

Max stopped the rising tide of panic by hooking his hands under her arms and pulling her up to lean against his chest. He mouthed softly at her chin, little shivery nips and licks that had Jules tilting her head for more. She sighed into the kiss and wound her arms around his neck.

"You're incredible," he said into her mouth. "Seriously, I think you sucked my brains out."

She snickered, breaking the kiss. "Is that what that was?"

Max laughed and bent down to pick up her discarded T-shirt when she shivered, suddenly aware of the fact that she was half naked in his parents' kitchen.

Grabbing her shirt, she struggled into it so quickly she almost fell over. "I can't believe we didn't even make it to your bedroom. Your parents could've walked in anytime!"

"The possibility of discovery gives everything a little extra spice," Max said, tucking himself away and doing up his jeans with lazy fingers.

She snorted. "I'm not thinking we needed too much extra spice." Jules tried to smooth her hair down; a hopeless task without a mirror or a hairbrush. Whatever happened to her ponytail holder?

His eyes glittered with remembered pleasure. "Yeah," he sighed. "We were in danger of getting over-spiced there, if anything. But spice is always hottest when it's a surprise."

He was looking at her far too closely. "I don't see what's so surprising about it," she bluffed. "You've been after me since you got home. Now you've had me. We can get back to normal." Jules ignored the way her heart clenched at the thought. Stupid heart.

"Normal. Huh." His voice sounded carefully neutral, and he'd ducked his head so she couldn't see the look in his expressive eyes.

"Yeah," she said, ruthlessly suppressing the urge to lean on him. "We got it out of our systems, so now we can work together. Keep it strictly professional."

He angled his head to gaze up at her from under the sweep of his dark lashes. "I can't speak for you," he said slowly, "but I can already say for sure . . . that one taste of you isn't going to be enough. Not for me."

She caught her breath at the banked fire in his eyes.

"So if you find that your . . . system"—he quirked a grin—"isn't quite as squeaky clean as you hoped, feel free to jump my bones. I'm up for it. Anytime."

Heart scrabbling at her rib cage like a lobster trying to escape from a boiling pot, Jules hardly knew what to say.

This wasn't going to end well. There were so many reasons why this should never have happened—or, at least, why it should be a one-time thing.

"One taste wasn't enough for me, either," she heard her own voice say. Thready and shocked, but recognizable. She blinked.

His grin widened into a look of pure happiness. "Yeah? Cool. Because I think there's something here."

Jules reared back, suddenly nervous. "Right," she said, "scorching hot chemistry. Your body likes my body, and vice versa."

A stubborn look darkened his tanned face. "Okay, sure, but there's more to it than that."

She backed up a step, holding her hands in front of her, palms out.

"Hey hey hey, let's not get ahead of ourselves, here. We've got something good going on here." Jules gestured between their obviously compatible bodies. "There's no reason to muck it up with a lot of emotion and relationship

talk and whatnot, if that's where you were headed with
that. We've got enough on our plates already, with the
competition and everything. Please. Can't we just play it
simple?"

She tried to keep things light and calm, but she was
very much afraid that there was a clear plea in her voice.

Jules could do this. She could get involved, she could
get close, she could live in the moment with Max—but
only if she kept her heart separate. Fair was fair. When he
took off again, she wouldn't survive if he took her heart
with him.

A muscle tightened in Max's jaw, but he smiled as he
said, "You want simple? I can do that. Hell, I'm the king
of that."

Jules let her shoulders relax, feeling a pang in the
muscles as she did so. She must've been really clenched.
"Okay, good. We agree, then. Simple. Like a stress-relief
thing."

He arched a brow, finally seeming to unclench a little,
himself. "Better than ashiatsu," he said. When she shrugged,
he explained, "That barefoot massage they do in Japan,
where the masseuse walks on your back. It's awesome. Almost as good as Thai massage, where they stretch you all
over, pull on your arms and legs like you're made out of
taffy."

Jules laughed, relief bubbling up inside her like a pan of
hot broth coming up to the boil. "Come on," she said, grabbing his hand and pulling him over to stand by his parents'
ancient gas range. "Show me a new trick. I heard you telling Danny about that technique you learned for crisping
the skin of a whole fish without cooking the meat."

"Sure," Max said, heading for the sink to wash his
hands.

Jules went to the fridge to see what Gus had left for
them to practice with. Pulling open the door and letting

the cool interior of the refrigerator chill her still-warm cheeks, she said, "While we're kind of on the topic of keeping it simple . . . this thing we've got going on—our stress-relief program? It's just between us, right?"

She held her breath, one hand frozen on a flat paper-wrapped parcel with "snapper" scribbled in pencil on the side. There was a long pause.

"Right," Max said, his voice quiet and a little muffled from behind her. "No need to tell the whole world about it. Since it doesn't mean anything."

Jules's hand twitched, nearly ripping the paper. But that was ridiculous, there was no reason to flinch at the flat way he said it. The important thing was, they were on the same page.

"Great," she said brightly, straightening up and holding out the parcel. "Look what I found! Gus must've been down to the fish market this morning."

Max took it from her, brushing the back of her hand with his fingers. "Great," he echoed, and he smiled at her, but it didn't quite reach his eyes.

Simple. Right, Jules thought, and shivered.

Chapter 13

The morning of the qualifying round dawned hot and muggy, with the kind of sharp, glaring sunlight at nine o'clock that forecast an inevitable citywide meltdown. The Javits Center air-conditioning was no match for it, especially since it was already overtaxed by the hundreds of tense, excited human beings milling around the showroom floor. The qualifiers wouldn't begin for another hour and a half, but teams of hopeful chef contestants were already staking out their territory on the floor, huddling together and drilling each other with last-minute trivia practice.

Claire stood ten paces back from the raised dais serving as their stage, and watched with a critical eye as two unlucky Javits Center employees attempted to hang a banner across the back wall.

"That's nowhere near straight, I hope you realize," she said. "The left corner is at least five centimeters lower than the right."

"Oh, Claire," said a low, feminine voice over her shoulder. Eva, smiling like the cat who got the cream, and looking stunning as usual in a red sheath dress. "Don't you have an assistant to take care of this kind of thing?"

"Not all of us travel with an entourage, Eva." Although Claire was well aware that she was likely the only one of the three Rising Star Chef judges who didn't. Hmm. Clearly, she was in the wrong line of work.

"Why don't you let my assistant take over, then? Drew, you can sort this out, right, love?"

A studious-looking young man with dark hair and black glasses stepped up. "Of course, Eva." Striding forward while pushing his glasses up the bridge of his nose, Drew called out, "No, guys, look. That's too far down, it needs to come back up an inch or so."

"There, he has that in hand," Eva said, triumph gleaming in her eyes as she took in the names of the sponsors on the banner. Claire braced herself for a moment of gloating, but Eva didn't mention the addition of the Cooking Channel to the list of RSC sponsors, instead saying, "Drew's a treasure, I hope he sticks it out longer than most of my assistants do."

Claire allowed herself to be led away by the elbow, casting no more than one or two looks over her shoulder to track the progress of the banner. "You know your assistants all call you Eva the Diva, don't you? There's a reason you have such a high rate of turnover."

"I'm preparing them for real life," Eva protested. "Which can be demanding, unreasonable, and mercurial. Just like me. I'm like a crash course in how to deal with the world."

"Speaking of mercurial, where are the other two judges? They know they're required to be here today, yes?"

"Don't fret, darling. They'll be here." Eva twinkled at her. "I even had Drew give them a call time about an hour before we actually need them, so they could be here any minute!"

"Or, when they're both late, as they undoubtedly will

be, perhaps they'll arrive at something approaching the correct time." Claire was unwillingly impressed.

"It's a gift." Eva shrugged modestly. "Deep calling to deep—I know how to deal with sensitive, high-strung artistic types."

"I know you're not talking about me." The light, amused voice wasn't like anything Claire had ever heard before. The only word she could think of to describe it was "musical," but it was completely masculine, and rough enough to be interesting. "I might be an artistic type, if you squint, but I'm one of the loosest mofo's you'll ever meet, and you know it."

Eva swung Claire carelessly around by the elbow, one of her rare genuine smiles breaking over her beautiful face like the flash of a photographer's camera. "Kane! You made it."

Claire stared at the young man grinning lazily back at them with his hands tucked into the front pocket of one of those awful zippered sweatshirt things. The hood was up over his head, pulled taut by the weight of his hands, but even the shadow of black cotton couldn't dim the brilliance of his wavy blond hair.

Younger than Claire by at least fifteen years, if not more, Kane Slater, with his baby-blue eyes, full, laughing mouth, and casual, thrown-together attire, made Claire suddenly wish she'd dressed a little less formally than her perfectly tailored navy suit. Pencil skirt and lacy lavender camisole shell or not, she felt every one of her forty-two years standing so close to the youthful exuberance of Eva bouncing over to give the handsome musician a quick, smacking kiss to the cheek.

Stop being ridiculous, Claire lectured herself. *No one cares what you're wearing, and if they did, you look perfectly professional—severe enough to be taken seriously, while remaining elegant and feminine.*

It was a fine line, one she'd danced on successfully for the last twenty years or so.

In her decades covering the largely male-dominated world of fine dining, Claire had also learned to keep any slight flicker of interest in someone of the opposite sex to herself.

That training came in handy now, as Eva and Kane finished their playful salutations, which seemed to involve a lot of poking one another in the ribs, and turned back to her.

By the time their attention was back on Claire, she'd pulled out her iPhone and started checking her e-mails, grateful as never before for the advanced technology that had finally given nonsmokers something to do with their hands in awkward social situations. Besides, if she had her eyes on the tiny, backlit screen of her phone, she wouldn't be telegraphing any stunned, humiliating flickers of interest at the famous musician, half her age, standing in front of her.

Not half my age, her vanity protested. *Two thirds, at worst.*

Merde. Claire barely restrained an eyeroll at her own expense. Was this what it felt like to be starstruck? She'd broken bread with and interviewed enough famous chefs to have supposed herself immune.

Perhaps it was different with rock stars—a new strain of the virus, and if her reaction to this Kane Slater was any indication, a virulent one.

Kane smiled and moved forward to shake her hand, his muscles carrying him with smooth, almost liquid grace despite his slouchy American posture.

He was certainly young enough, Claire decided, to make her layer an extra sheet of frost over her normal chilly politesse as she clasped his slender, blunt fingers briefly and said, "Good morning. Our mutual acquaintance is too much of a social heathen to do her duty, so I suppose we must fend for ourselves. I'm Claire Durand, editor in chief of *Délicieux* magazine, and head judge of the Rising Star Chef competition." She made sure to enunciate that last part, wanting no confusion later over whose opinion counted most in these proceedings.

"Believe me, I know who you are," Kane said, that voice catching at Claire again—so expressive, rich with laughter and a warmth her vanity desperately wanted to read as sexual awareness.

"Oh dear," Claire said, forcing herself to drop his hand and take a step back. He really was a bit mesmerizing; his meteoric rise to fame didn't surprise her, now that she'd met him. "I hope little Eva hasn't been telling tales. She ought to remember how long I've known her, and how very many more embarrassing stories, starring teenaged Eva Jansen, I have in my arsenal than she could possibly dream."

"I haven't!" Eva pouted prettily, eyes dancing. "I've been a perfect angel, tell her, Kane."

"Eva is a perfect angel," Kane parroted. "Actually, she did tell me you'd be on the judging panel—that's pretty much why I agreed to do it."

Firmly quashing the idiotic flutter of her womanly feelings, Claire lifted one eyebrow into a perfect arch. "Oh? A fan of *Délicieux,* are you?"

His handsome—*young!*—face went serious and intent, which only made him appear even more boyish. "Only for about the last year and a half. Since you took over."

Taken aback, Claire noticed she was fidgeting with her phone, flipping it over and over in her hands, and returned it to her purse as smoothly as she could. "Really. You see a difference in the magazine already?"

"More and more every month," he said, lighting up enthusiastically. "It's rad. I mean, I know when you first took charge you were still working with just putting out whatever articles were already lined up, right? But even then, I could sense a difference, like the whole magazine was pulling just slightly off center into coolness."

Claire blinked. He wasn't wrong; the magazine tended to work about a year out from the month each issue would hit newsstands. "That's quite an in-depth analysis of our little publication, Mr. Slater. I didn't realize your hectic touring and recording schedule left you much time for reading."

He laughed as if he hadn't even heard the implied insult. "Hey, crammed on a bus with four other guys and a tour manager, driving seven hours between venues, there's pretty much nothing to do *but* read. I bribe one of the sound techs to stockpile *Délicieux* for when we hit those long stretches of road, then I gobble 'em up like candy."

Trying not to allow the hot rush of satisfaction washing through her chest to flush up her neck and into her face, Claire inclined her head with all the dignity she could muster. "Thank you. I'll convey your regards to my editorial board. Some of them are fans of yours, I'm sure."

"Not you, though, huh?" Kane looked crestfallen for a long enough moment to make Claire actually consider feeling guilty for hurting his feelings. But in the next instant, he brightened again. "That's okay. I'll get you yet! I'm persistent like that. One day you've never heard of me, the next you've got *Come to the Table* playing on endless repeat."

"I love it!" Eva clapped her hands like a delighted child. "For once, Kane's not the one getting fawned over—he's the one doing the fawning. Buck up, sweetie, it's good practice for when you get a girlfriend."

"Aw, Eves. You're the best big pseudosister ever. Always looking out for me." Kane hooked an arm around Eva's neck and kissed the top of her head while Claire hoped fervently that she wasn't being groomed for the role of "pseudomother" in the drama of Kane's life.

As maternal as she felt toward Eva, at times, Claire didn't think she could quite bear for Kane Slater to look at her that way.

Cursing herself as twelve kinds of idiot, Claire deliberately glanced away as Kane and Eva started talking about some Los Angeles party they'd both been to the previous weekend. Ignoring the way things low down in her body tightened every time she felt Kane's gaze drift back to her as if he wanted to pull her back into their conversation, Claire scanned the room around them.

It looked as though the last few days of round-the-clock stress, during which Claire had had nothing more to sustain her than several liters of stale coffee and at least five tongue-lashings of slow-moving employees, had paid off. Everything was ready for the first event of this year's Rising Star Chef competition.

Well, everything except the fact that they were still down one judge.

Just then, she heard a susurrus of excited voices near the doors, which swung open to reveal a preternaturally good-looking man with dark hair, blue eyes, and the widest, most blindingly white smile Claire had ever seen.

The whispers continued as the man made his way through the crowd toward the other judges, stopping every so often to slap someone on the back here and shake a hand there.

"Devon Sparks," Claire said, feeling unreasonably fond of the man all of a sudden. "Finally, some adult conversation."

Here, at least, was someone she didn't need to worry about being attracted to. A celebrity chef who'd catapulted to stardom with a hit show on the Cooking Channel, Sparks also had a new wife, a young son, and a well-deserved reputation for losing his temper in the kitchen. And with reviewers, as well—he'd detonated like a bomb when *Délicieux's* restaurant critic lambasted his Vegas outpost a couple of years ago.

And no matter how much said wife and son had turned Devon's life around, Claire wasn't worried. Married men were out of bounds, even for her sometimes quirky and unreliable libido. Which probably indicated she'd been living away from France for far too long, but *c'est la vie*.

"Claire, how nice to see you again," Devon said, giving an infinitesimal bow over her hand. It was the kind of gesture that should've seemed silly and overdone, but on Devon, it worked. Despite herself, Claire was charmed.

He was good, she'd give him that.

Turning the glare of his personality on Eva and Kane, Devon introduced himself while Claire looked on. She wondered if it bruised Kane's ego that Devon's entrance—and the man certainly knew how to make one—had caused a bigger splash with the crowd here than the presence of a multiplatinum recording artist.

From the sheer joy on the younger man's face, it didn't appear so. He looked like a kindergartener meeting Mickey Mouse for the first time.

Devon accepted Kane's and Eva's adulation as his due, with regal head nodding and a bit of preening. Still, watching him, Claire could see that he wasn't as camera ready and fake as he used to be. His flashes of brilliant white teeth appeared genuine, and his voice was warm with sincerity when he thanked Kane for the compliments, and returned them by claiming to love his music.

Before Kane could keel over with glee, Claire cleared her throat and stepped purposefully into the middle. "Now that we are all fast friends, I think we'd better go down to the judges' box and let Eva get the event started. Gentlemen, if you'll follow me?"

Without looking to see if they did as she ordered, Claire marched back in the direction of the stage, already ticking things off in her head.

Three judges, present and accounted for? Check. Banner announcing Délicieux, *the Jansen Hospitality Group, and the Cooking Channel as sponsors of the Rising Star Chef competition, hung straight and proud across the back of the stage? Check. Judges' box well supplied with bottled water, paper, and pens? Check.*

She glanced over to where Eva was conferring with her assistant before mounting the steps at the side of the stage and heading for the microphone situated in the center.

"Good morning, chefs!" Eva's voice rang out over the crowd like a happy bell, calling everyone toward the stage. "In just a few short hours, we'll know which four teams will continue on to the cooking challenge in two weeks. Out of the hundreds of you gathered here today, only four groups will get the chance to seduce us with your culinary skills into allowing you to represent the entire East Coast in this year's Rising Star Chef competition. Are you ready to get started?"

One beautiful, articulate woman to host the festivities and keep things moving? Check.

A cheer went up as Claire and the other judges took their seats. After a moment of hesitation over who should sit where, Claire lifted her chin and yanked out the chair on the far left. She was the head judge, damn it. She could sit where she wanted. And she wanted to get into a position where it wouldn't be impossible to ignore both of the male judges, if she had a mind to.

Quick as a pan of milk boiling over, Kane Slater slipped past Devon and snagged the middle seat, giving Claire a slight grin as he sat down and proving, yet again, why

Claire would need every advantage possible if she were to block the presence of the other judges from her mind.

One horrifically ill-timed, ill-conceived, ill-fated attraction to a completely unsuitable, much younger man?

Claire sighed.

Double check.

Chapter 14

Max was honestly starting to worry that if someone didn't sit on Winslow, the kid was going to jitter right out of his basketball sneakers.

"For serious now, man. Take a deep breath in through your nose, let it out through your mouth. We really can't afford any medical mishaps. If you stroke out, we're sunk."

"I'm all good," Win gasped, eyes wide and fingers clenched around the opposite elbows. His gaze skittered around the packed floor of the convention center, never landing on any one sight for longer than a second. "I mean it, I'm cool. I'm just getting my head together."

Max raised a skeptical brow and left him to his head gathering. The rest of the team wasn't looking much better. It was the first large-scale competition for most of them, and everyone except Beck looked vaguely nauseated.

An air of forced, brittle calm hovered around Jules, as if she'd shatter if anyone so much as spoke to her. Not wanting to push his luck any further than he already had, Max turned to his brother. Danny had his grimmest face on, as if he were about to be stripped naked and rubbed with fish guts before being tossed to the lions, rather than answer a few questions about food.

Gus hurried up just as Max was about to try distracting Danny from the crowds of people. "Okay, we're all registered and ready to go. We got lucky, our slot is in a couple of hours, so we'll have plenty of time to watch and get a feel for the judges and the other competitors."

"Where's Mom?" Max asked, looking over his father's shoulder.

"She's back in the stands with the camera, going to try and get a good group shot when you boys go up on stage." As official team coach, Gus was allowed to stay on the floor with the contestants, but there were bleachers set up at the back of the room for the few people in the audience who weren't there to compete.

"Maybe you should go sit with her," Danny said. Max caught his brother's worried stare over their father's balding head, which was already flushing pink with heat and excitement. He did look a little tired.

"And miss all the fun? No way!" Gus bounced on the balls of his feet a couple of times. "I only wish I could go up on stage with you."

Max knocked his fist against Gus's shoulder. "We're going to be fine, Dad. I'll get everyone centered, maybe go through some deep breathing exercises, before we go on. Hey!" Max smiled as if he'd just thought of something. "I bet it would help if you did those with us, make everyone feel like you're really rooting for us."

"That's not a bad idea, Maxwell," Gus said, scrutinizing the pale, sweaty faces of his crew with a critical eye. "Come get me when you're ready. In the meantime, I'm going to see if Jules turned up anything new on that Kane Slater guy."

"Thanks," Danny said reluctantly, as they watched their father stride over to Jules and nearly shock her into collapsing with an unexpected slap on the back. "It's good to get him to stay calm. He's been off the charts, lately."

"Yeah," Max said with a rueful laugh. "I don't know why Mom called me back here, really; all I've ever done is get Dad worked up by fighting with you."

"That's not true."

Max stared, startled by his brother's ferocity, no less intense for how quiet he was. As if realizing how he sounded, Danny flushed a little and glanced away. "You being here . . . it helps, Max."

It was the first time Danny had even hinted that he was glad to have Max back home and on the team. The past couple of weeks had been too frenetic and busy for Max to worry much about it, but he'd found himself, in odd moments, wondering if he'd ever be able to repair all the damage he'd done when he took off and left his family behind.

He and Danny used to be so close. And to have his brother acknowledge that now, even in a small way, gave Max hope for the future. He rubbed his stupidly burning eyes and swallowed hard against the tightness in his throat. "Thanks, man. I'm trying. Falling short a lot, that's for fucking sure, but I am trying."

"I know," Danny said, shaking it off and giving Max a small grin and a thump on the shoulder. "Now, if we're done with our bromance moment, let's go watch the competition. I want to see what we're up against."

Jules's hand was cramping. She hissed a little, shaking it out, then clenched her pen in her fist and kept filling her composition book with lines of cramped, scrawled notes.

She'd been sitting to the left of the stage and studying the competition for the past two hours, and she'd learned a lot.

Two teams at a time faced off across the stage from each other, lined up behind tables equipped with actual buzzers. The judges asked three questions each, in rotating order. At the end of the match, the team with the most points moved on to the next round, up against a fresh new batch of five hopeful chef contestants. Major bonus points were awarded if every member of a team answered a question.

Jules stuck the end of the pen in her mouth and bit down on it, thinking furiously.

"Mmm, a woman with an oral fixation." Max sprawled down beside her, his long legs kicking out in front and crossing at the ankles.

She spat out the pen. "Shut up. It helps me think."

He did a quick double eyebrow raise. Together with the smirk he had going on, it was lethal. "Honey, I like the way you think."

She cracked, letting out a tiny snort of laughter before she could muffle it. "God. Doesn't anything get to you? Have you heard some of the questions the other teams have been asked? We're going to get creamed!"

"No way." Max leaned back on his elbows and rolled his head toward her. "We'll smoke 'em."

Jules closed her eyes briefly. "Just tell me you studied up on toxic foods."

"I looked over a few books, made a few notes," Max said, tilting his head lazily until the sun-bronzed tips of his buzzed–short brown hair kissed the floor. The tilt of his chin made the harsh overhead light find the threads of red and gold in his stubble. "No sweat."

Jules didn't want to think about exactly how much sweat, of the cold, clammy variety, was currently trickling down the small of her back. She wanted to scream, "If you're not going to freak out with me, then get the hell away from me!" But at the same time, she couldn't help taking comfort in the long, solid line of his body stretched out next to her.

His olive cargo pants were worn thin, almost see-through in places, and they molded to his legs so lovingly, her palms itched to smooth down the fabric and chase the warmth of his skin underneath. He was wearing his white chef's coat, per regulations, but he hadn't buttoned it. The white poly-blend flapped open over a red ringer shirt sporting three cans of Suntory beer across Max's muscular chest.

The chest she'd seen, touched, kissed her way down, in a hurried assignation behind the towering sacks of flour in the pantry. They hadn't had time to do much more than they'd managed in their first encounter, until yesterday morning in the pantry.

She'd sunk to her knees, her cheek against the crisp silk of the hair arrowing down into his pants, and he'd husked out, "Stop."

Jules had looked up, confused, until he'd gripped her arms and hauled her up his body, spinning her until her back was against the wire racks of shelving.

"This time it's my turn," he'd told her, in that deep, shattered voice that scraped over her nerves like the edge of a knife over a cutting board. And then he'd proceeded to drop to his knees and turn her whole entire world into fire and melting and little explosions of breath that she muffled with both hands.

Sadly, the liquid relaxation she'd experienced after that encounter only lasted about an hour. Not a trace of it was left in her wire-strung body at the moment.

It wasn't fair. She was a ball of stress, vibrating with tension and worry and nerves and expectations—and Max reclined on the floor like a pasha waiting for some harem girl to feed him a peeled grape.

"I can't believe you're not more nervous," she said.

Max laughed. "It sounds like you wish I were sitting here wringing my hands and rending my garments."

"Is that too much to ask?" Jules knew she sounded grumpy, but she couldn't help it.

The gentle bump of Max's knee against hers made Jules suck in a quick breath. "Hey," he said softly. "I bet I can make you forget your nerves."

"Stop that," she hissed, looking over her shoulder. "Your parents are around here somewhere."

"So what?" Max said, sitting up. Now he looked grumpy. "I mean, not that I have a yen to make out right in front of them, but seriously. Let 'em see. I don't care if they know something's up with us, Jules. I wouldn't mind."

The tip of her pencil pressed so hard into her notebook that it snapped. She blinked. "What?"

Max's scowl smoothed into a softer expression, a hint of vulnerability sneaking into his eyes. "That is, I guess—if you agree that something's up with us."

Jules breathed in, the whole, crowded room fading away, but before she could say anything, Max swiveled to face her. "Look, I admit when this thing between us started out . . . I wasn't exactly thinking it would be anything serious. And I know you've got your own issues about that, and I respect them, Jules, I do. But then there's the fact that I really like you. As in, the whole you. Not just the outside parts, which I'm admittedly most familiar with." He smiled, but it was a quick, fleeting thing followed by a shrug. "What can I say? I always seem to want more from people than they want to give me."

Blinking rapidly, Jules tried frantically to sort through the mess of emotions called up by Max's declaration. It was tough not to focus on the part that scared her spitless— the part where he could look at her and see that she had "issues."

She didn't want him to ever know about all that crap. It was over and done with, she'd put it behind her and moved on. Even thinking about it cut off the flow of warmth from the rest of his words, reducing it to a thin trickle that couldn't reach the cold, deep inside her.

Because as tempting as he was, as much as she wanted to throw caution under the bus and really be with Max for however long they had together—she couldn't escape the past. Shouldn't escape it—because she owed too much to the people who'd helped her. And, deep down, she knew there was another reason.

She didn't want to end up like her mother, at the whim of her so-called love for some man.

Feeling numb all the way to her fingertips, Jules stared for a long moment, taking in the lean, perfect lines of his body and the open brightness of his heart shining out from his eyes.

God, she wanted him. But could she really have him? Maybe it would be better to end this now. She'd already let him in too far.

Even though part of her knew she was taking the coward's way out, Jules turned a pleading look on Max. "Do we really need to have this conversation now? Like, right now, only minutes before we go on stage to compete in a high-stakes challenge?"

Disappointment flashed over his face for a bare instant before he laughed and looked down, scrubbing a hand across the back of his neck. "Sorry. This whole relationship thing is kind of new to me. I've never really been in one place long enough before, you know? I'll try to get it together."

And wasn't that the perfect reminder of why she had to keep him at a distance? Jules said gently, "And in a few more weeks, you'll be gone again. So what's the point of pretending this is some big, forever thing in front of your family and the guys on the team? Our timing is just a little—off. I need to focus, and you . . . God, Max. You're pretty much the biggest distraction I could possibly imagine."

Glancing up at her from beneath his lashes, Max pulled his mouth into a lopsided parody of his usual bright grin. "Yeah?"

Jules shook her head. "Oh, you like that, don't you?"

"Hey, I've been called worse things than a distraction. And for the record? I'm holding back. A lot."

She raised her eyebrows. "This is you holding back?"

"Considering what I really want is to drag you off to a nice secluded custodial closet or something and get you naked and horizontal? Or, actually—vertical works for us, too, doesn't it? Yeah. This is me holding back."

His words conjured an immediate picture in her mind's eye, and Jules shuddered with the shaft of heat that went through her like a hot knife through butter. "Okay. I think that's my cue to get up from here and go find everyone else," she said, shaking free of the sex haze.

Max stood up in a fluid move, then reached down a hand to help her to her feet. Jules wobbled embarrassingly. She told herself it was because she'd been sitting on the floor for so long, but one glance at Max's heated, knowing stare and she knew they were both aware of just what it was that made her weak in the knees.

Swallowing hard, Jules turned to walk back to the bleachers, but Max still had her hand captive, and he used it to tug her to a stop.

"I'll work on my timing," he said, his voice serious and low. "Because this is real, Jules. It's good. It makes me feel the same way a brand-new stretch of open highway does, or a shaded alley winding between buildings in a city where I don't speak the language. When I look at you, I get that same rush. And I want to see where it goes."

This time, the shudder down her spine was mostly fear, with a pinch of despair thrown in. She stared at Max, the openness of his expression, and knew she was already in way over her head.

But how am I supposed to resist this?

Pulling at her hand, she broke free of Max's grip. "They're going to be calling us any minute. We have to go."

Turning blindly, Jules made her way to the bleachers where the rest of the team stood clustered around Gus and Nina.

"There you are," Gus said with relief as she walked up. "Our number's almost up. Where's Max?"

"Right behind me," Jules promised without looking back. "Are we ready, gang?"

The chorus of "hell, yeahs" was enthusiastic enough to almost make Jules smile. She looked at Gus, his handsome, lined face alight with all the excitement of a kid at Christmas, and at Nina, dispensing last-minute good-luck hugs. Danny submitted to his with a good-natured eye roll, Winslow with an answering smacking kiss on the cheek. Beck, though . . . he let Nina enfold him, bending down from his great height to make it easier on her, his dark hair swinging forward to hide his face.

Tears clogged Jules's throat. This was her family. They were the ones who'd still be there for her when Max was long gone. She couldn't let them down.

Gus stepped down a bleacher to wrap one long arm around her shoulders. She sniffed back the emotion making her mouth tremble and her eyes sting, knowing it was too late. Gus saw her—he always had.

"You ready to rock and roll, little girl?" His voice was kind, soft in that way Gus mostly only used when he talked to Nina. Sometimes when he talked about Max and Danny, too—a blend of pride, bone-deep affection, and worry.

"I'm good," she started to say, but she couldn't stop her voice from breaking, her shoulders from tensing under Gus's arm, when Max stepped up to the group.

And as Max swept his mother into a hug tight enough to lift her feet off the ground, Gus scowled and turned to Jules, putting both hands on her shoulders and making her face him. "What did he say to you?" Gus said.

"Nothing," Jules said, too quickly. God, she didn't want to be the cause of any more friction between Max and his family.

Gus's eyes narrowed on her face. "Is there something I should know about?"

Jules mustered up a smile and a wink. "No, I'm fine. What about you? Promise me you'll sit down and keep calm while we're up there. Watching you collapse in the audience would really ruin our chances!"

"Oh, for the love of . . . I'm perfectly healthy! Nothing a little steak and red wine can't cure." Gus made a face. "You kids better win—I'm counting on the victory celebration to con Nina into letting me off the spinach and oatmeal regimen."

"No steak for you, not until your numbers improve," Jules warned.

"Who's having steak?" Max's voice came from behind her, and it took everything Jules had not to jump like she'd been stung by a wasp.

"Max," she said helplessly, trying not to sound as freaked as she felt.

"Weren't you going to lead the team in some kind of Buddhist prayer circle or something?" Gus said smoothly. "If you still want to, you'd better get on it."

"Right, meditation circle, gotcha," Max said, backing off with a questioning glint in his eye. "You guys coming?"

"Be right there," Jules promised.

Heart in her throat, she watched him bound off to tackle

Winslow. And when she finally glanced back, Gus was studying her, bushy eyebrows raised.

"I don't like lying to him." The words burst out of her, fervent and choked.

Gus's watery blue eyes softened. "I know. But he's got a life out there, opportunities to learn and grow beyond what his mother and I could give him. All we can do is not stand in his way. And if Max knew about my heart thing . . ." He shook his head.

"He'd stay here." Jules couldn't help the longing in her voice, the layers of yearning that gave her away so neatly, Gus's gaze snapped up.

"So that's it."

She swallowed and nearly gagged. "What?"

"Something's up with you two."

Struggling with her breathing, Jules forced her voice steady. "Okay, maybe. But it's brand-new, and I wouldn't even want to call it a 'thing.' Especially since it's not going anywhere."

Gus pursed his lips. "Looked like a 'thing' to me," he said. "And not a casual thing, either. Jules. Is it serious?"

Only if you consider falling ass over stupid, idiotic heart "serious."

The busy conference center faded away, Jules's vision graying at the edges. It was the question she didn't want to answer, above all others, and here Gus was, standing in front of her with hope bright in his eyes.

Before she could gather her shattered thoughts to figure out how to respond, like a miracle, their number was being called over the loudspeaker.

Everyone erupted into a flurry of movement, last-minute advice, and hurried toward the stage.

They massed at the steps on the left, waiting for the cue to mount the stage, and Jules ended up next to Danny. He leaned over and mouthed, "Are you okay? You seem a little out of it or something." He tensed, shooting a glare at his brother. "Shit, what did Max do?"

Jules shook her head, breath coming too fast in and out of her lungs. Everything was unraveling, the life she'd painstakingly carved out for herself here breaking apart like an overheated sauce, and she couldn't go off somewhere and cry about it. She had to get up on stage in front of hundreds of people and answer questions. It suddenly seemed like an insurmountable task.

Too late for nerves, though, and too late for the emotional breakdown she could feel looming over her head like an ugly summer storm.

It was too late to do anything but square her shoulders, lift her chin, and move forward into the hot glare of the spotlights.

Chapter 15

The first few questions passed in a blur while Max was still riding the high of having finally done it. He'd told Jules what he wanted—and she hadn't run away. This was going to work, and it was going to be amazing, and he couldn't wait for this stupid competition to be over so he could get her alone and— Ow!

Danny elbowed him sharply in the ribs, glaring. Max blinked and realized he'd blanked out of the competition completely, like some kid chasing butterflies in the outfield.

Pathetic, Lunden.

He straightened his shoulders, taking in the scene in front of him. Enemy team across the stage, looking fierce and focused and ready as hell to defend their spot. Max glanced toward the front of the stage. Most of the audience disappeared into a noisy, dark mass behind the bright shine of the lights, but the judges' box was close enough to the stage for him to be able to make them out.

Claire Durand was instantly recognizable from the head shot they ran beside her Letter from the Editor feature in every issue of *Délicieux*. She was magnetic in person, all cool and elegant, but with dark, snapping eyes that gave away the intelligence that had propelled her to the helm of an internationally renowned magazine.

On her right sat Devon Sparks, looking carved out of cream cheese, as always, with his photo-shoot smile and six-hundred-dollar haircut.

And in the middle . . . huh, that must be the rock star. Kane Slater. He looked more like a surfer than a musician, to Max, but whatever sold records, he guessed.

It was Slater's turn to ask a question, apparently. He rocked back in his chair, tilting it until the front legs left the floor, and wobbled there precariously.

"Okay, I've got a good one," he said, his voice a thick drawl that clashed with his tanned SoCal blondness and made Max think about cowboys. The surfer-cowboy-rocker seemed not to be consulting any notes. Max frowned. Both of the other judges had stacks of papers and books in front of them, passages marked with Post-its. And this guy, this nonchef nobody, was asking questions off the top of his head?

Well, this ought to be excellent.

Max checked the scoreboard. Shit. While he'd been having his emo moment, the other team had snaked the first two points!

Okay, Max had just made a declaration of . . . whatever . . . to the woman he was having intensely delicious sex with. What the hell was the rest of his team's excuse?

Steeling himself for the lurch in his chest, Max leaned forward far enough to see down the table to where Jules stood, as stiff and lifeless as a mannequin modeling chefwear.

Something was off.

Instead of the laser focus she'd exhibited at every trivia practice for the last two weeks, Jules looked dazed. Her pretty mouth was a thin, bloodless line, not a muscle in her forehead or cheeks moved—but her eyes were swimming with fear.

Max felt a chill that had nothing to do with nerves ripple down his spine.

He'd wanted to get to her . . . and apparently, he really had. But instead of being able to savor the victory, all Max could feel was regret.

Movement from the judges' table caught Max's eye as Kane Slater let all four legs of his chair hit the ground with a loud bump.

"So. If you go to Central Texas, alongside all the barbecue and Tex-Mex, you'll see a lot of signs advertising kolaches. Who can tell me what that is?"

Max relaxed a little. Okay, that was something Jules should definitely be able to answer. He knew she'd been studying Southwestern food culture, Texas in particular, for a week, and this sounded like a dish she definitely would've run across.

He looked down the table, expecting her hand to shoot out and whap the buzzer any second . . . but it didn't.

She was stuck. He could see her mind working frantically behind the glassy amber of her eyes, but nothing was happening.

The other team conferred furiously behind their hands, clearly without an answer, but the way they were eyeing their buzzer, Max could tell they were going to jump on it and at least give a guess soon.

The tension of the moment coiled tighter and tighter, as if some giant hand were cranking an old-fashioned metal citrus press, squeezing and squeezing until Max thought he'd turn inside out.

Out of the corner of his eye, Max saw the lead chef of the other team reach for their buzzer, and he snapped. Without a single thought in his head other than beating the other guys, he whipped out his hand and smashed it down.

The loud, harsh, unending buzz shocked Max back to reality, where he glanced down at his own hand still mashing the buzzer and realized that he didn't have the first idea what the answer might be. Kolackees? It sounded Native American. Was that a clue?

A long pause, broken by the smooth, cultured voice of the announcer lady whose name Max didn't remember, a chic, sort of feline woman who said, "And the team from Lunden's Tavern makes their first play. Answer?"

Max's tongue was abruptly filled with sawdust. He unstuck it from the roof of his mouth and said, "Um . . ."

Winslow shot him a horrified look. "Oh no, you did *not* buzz in without knowing the answer."

Max met his gaze helplessly. "Oops?"

Next to him, Danny went stiff-legged like a junkyard dog about to start a brawl. "*Oops?* Are you shitting me?"

"We're going to need an answer sometime this year," the catty announcer said. Her tone was full of amusement, but Max had honestly never in his life felt less like laughing.

He could feel every eye in the convention center like a separate needle gouging into his skin. And his dad—God.

Dad's out there, watching me blow this for him, for Danny, for Jules . . . oh God, oh fuck . . .

"Anybody have any ideas?" Max whispered out of the corner of his mouth.

They all looked at Jules, whose agonized eyes filled with tears. She opened her mouth, but nothing came out.

"He said Central Texas," Winslow reminded him desperately. "I don't know, maybe it's something with a tortilla?"

"Come up with a guess," Beck advised calmly from the other end of the table. "Take your shot; it won't make or break our chances. We need to move past this."

The guy might have chilled cucumber water in his

veins, but he was right. Max faced the judges' table. Slater wasn't smirking or doing anything obnoxious, but Max stared down and hated the little fucker anyway.

Kolackees. No, that was wrong. Kolache? That sounded less Native American, and didn't sound like Spanish at all. Shit, he was so screwed.

"Kolache," Max said, hoping he had the pronunciation right, at least. "It's a Native American dish featuring cold smoked fish and sweet corn."

A spasm of what looked like genuine regret twisted Slater's mouth. "Aw, man. I'm sorry, but no." He glanced over to the other team. "Any guesses?"

The muscles in Max's shoulders clenched at the smug smile on the opposing team leader's face. "A kolache is a pastry—semisweet yeast dough baked around fillings, which can be sweet, like the traditional poppyseed variety, or savory with spicy sausage or jalapeños."

"Correct!" crowed Slater. "Weirdly enough, Central Texas has one of the largest populations of Czech people outside of the Czech Republic. And I, for one, am grateful for that because I love me some kolaches. Although, technically, it should be noted that 'kolaches' is a total Americanization of the actual Czech, since 'kolach' is already plural. And authentic kolach would never have jalapeños in them. But still, another point for you guys."

Well, fuck. That puts the score at three to nothing. Max could feel the tension vibrating through his team.

"Wow," Max said, trying like hell to lighten the mood, get his team relaxed and centered again. "Heart attack on a plate. I bet it's wicked addictive."

"You know it," Slater agreed, leaning back in his chair again. "The hangover food of the gods, my friend."

Danny snorted a little, and Max felt the team start to breathe again.

"All right, settle down. And step it up, Lunden's," Devon Sparks interrupted. "You've got a lot of catching up to do. And I'm not taking it easy on you with my question. Here it is: every good chef should be able to do recipe conversions in his or her head, to be able to quickly triple a recipe on the spot." He grinned, and Max was alarmed to see the hint of wickedness in that smirk.

"But what if you were cooking for a huge crowd of people, all showing up at the same time? Let's do something simple—cream of tomato soup. The base recipe is—maybe you want to write this down?—three ounces of oil, one pound of mirepoix, two minced garlic cloves, half a cup of flour, twelve cups of chicken stock, two pounds of chopped plum tomatoes, twenty-four ounces of tomato puree, and two cups of heavy cream. It makes a gallon of soup, which serves eight as a meal with grilled cheese. Convert that recipe to serve eight hundred. Go."

Max stared down at his scribbled notes without really seeing them. If this was for real what it took to get in on the RSC competition, maybe he deserved to get cut, because there was no way in hell he was getting these calculations done anytime in the next half hour.

Staring down his own table, he saw Win and Danny writing frantically, and he was happy to see Jules was back in the game, at last, bent so close to her notes that her nose almost brushed the paper. The only one not even trying was Beck, who stood staring off into the distance with a slight scowl, arms crossed over his chest.

Big fucking help you are. Max attempted to telegraph the message directly into Beck's brain, but it didn't seem to have any effect.

A quick glance across the stage told Max the other team wasn't harboring any secret math geniuses—maybe he had time to figure this out after all.

But just as he put his pencil to the paper, a large, square-palmed hand shot out and clapped the buzzer twice, in quick, precise bursts.

Max felt the beginnings of a grin tugging at his mouth. It was Beck.

"Go for it," Devon Sparks said, glancing down at the legal pad in his hand. "I've got the answer right in front of me."

"For eight hundred two-cup servings," Beck said calmly, "you'd need a hundred gallons of soup. That's thirty-seven and a half cups of vegetable oil, a hundred pounds of mirepoix, two hundred minced garlic cloves, and fifty cups of flour, which is probably gonna be easier to measure by weight: about eleven pounds."

It was at this point that every eyebrow in the room shot straight up, Max's included. Turned out, his team was the one harboring a math genius. Who knew?

"Okay, you're halfway there," Devon said, nonplussed but clearly fascinated. Max was pretty sure he'd intended to stump the room with that one, or at least have the time run out before anyone could come up with an answer. "What's next?"

"Well, the chicken stock is easy, that's seventy-five gallons. We'd need two hundred pounds of chopped plum tomatoes, I'm thinking canned for a job like this, plus you get more consistent flavor for a big batch of soup. Seventy-five quarts of tomato puree, fifty quarts of heavy cream, plus enough salt and ground pepper to bring out the other flavors. And personally, I'd add in about a dozen pounds of diced bacon, for that nice, smoky flavor, but maybe that's just me."

"Um, it's not just you," Kane Slater said. "Bacon makes everything better."

Shooting his fellow judge an amused glance, Devon

said, "Correct on every point. You adjusted some of the measurements to metric, though—can I ask why?"

Beck shrugged. "It's how I learned to do big conversions. It's easier to visualize. And a lot of product is labeled that way these days, so that makes it easier, too."

Interesting. So Beck has actually cooked for huge groups of people, Max mused. It was the kind of revelation that made him realize he knew next to nothing about the big, silent guy who'd staked out his territory at the back of the Lunden's Tavern kitchen.

Shit. I don't even know the guy's first name. Which made Max feel like a grade-A dick.

"Seriously, good job, man," he told Beck, leaning on the table to offer him a fist to bump. "Talk about bacon—you saved ours."

Beck gave him a small smile, and it transformed his hard, stony face. Max grinned back.

"Yes, yes. If we've finished with the male bonding ritual," Claire Durand said, "May we continue? I believe it falls to me to ask the next question."

"By all means," Slater said, his blue eyes vivid with laughter. "It's been way too long since our last helping of vitriol. I'm sure the cheftestants are as starved for it as I am."

Max was unwillingly impressed. It would take balls of solid carbon steel to tweak a woman like Claire Durand. Slater either had an uncontrollable libido or no sense of self-preservation. Maybe both.

Or maybe the guy just flirts with anyone of the feminine persuasion who comes within fifteen feet of him, Max amended with a frown, watching the way Slater's gaze darted to Jules. The rock star gave her an encouraging thumbs-up coupled with a goofy face, as if he could tell just how unnerved she was and wanted to make her laugh.

With a sidelong glare at her cojudge, Claire raised her stern, clear voice. "What are the three primary reasons to sift dry ingredients before baking?"

Max felt his brother jolt next to him. "Oh," Danny said, and slammed his fist down on the buzzer. "Well, to blend them together, obviously. Also to get rid of lumps and whatever impurities made it into that bag of flour or whatever. And you want to aerate them, so they can mix into the wet ingredients more evenly."

Claire Durand bestowed one of her rare smiles on Danny, who flushed and straightened his shoulders. "Well done," she told him. "Clearly, unlike most chefs, you know your pastry."

Max glanced at the rest of the team, whose faces registered a spectrum from delight (Winslow) to quiet pride (Beck). Even Jules appeared to have gotten control of her emotions and was giving Danny a one-armed hug.

"The score is now three to two—you're catching up, Lunden's!" The announcer woman strolled over to their side of the stage and leaned on the end of the table, right next to Danny. She tilted the microphone away from her mouth and leaned in, her voice soft enough that only Max could probably hear what she said in Danny's ear. "Not that it matters," she cooed, "but I'm rooting for you. I've got a bit of a sweet tooth, you see, and it's been a while since I had a pastry chef."

Electricity arced between them, hot enough to singe Max, a foot away and minding his own business.

Yowza.

Danny looked right at her and said, without even blinking, "I'm not as sweet as I look, dollface."

Max bit the inside of his cheek to keep from giving Danny an obnoxious, older-brotherly slap on the back.

Sure, it was a little ick-making to be even accidentally privy to his kid brother getting prejiggy, but he was proud of Danny, too.

This Eva Jansen chick was hot enough to scorch grill marks across his ass, and she wasn't playing around, either. She had a sharp, predatory look about her, from the smooth, blunt swing of her dark hair against her jawbone to the way her mouth seemed to naturally curl up at the corners in a secretive smile.

"Eva, we'd like to move on, if you please." Claire Durand's voice cracked across the stage, making half the contestants jump like beans in a hot, dry pan.

Eva Jansen didn't jump. She gave Danny one last languid smile, and when she caught Max watching out of the corner of his eye, she winked at him for good measure. Then she uncoiled herself from the table in a sinuous rush, moving back to center stage.

"Of course. Contestants, are you ready? I believe it's Mr. Slater's turn to ask another question."

"This one's for the fans," he said. "Or, you know, anyone who's been stuck in the grocery store checkout line long enough to see the gossip rags. So, it was widely reported that I threw a *Titanic*-themed dinner party—the actual historical ship, not the movie. Although Kate came, and once I got her liquored up, we did a ten-minute speed-through of the entire story that nearly killed half the guests with laughter. Apparently, I'm no Leo DiCaprio."

"I assume there's a question included somewhere in this press release," Claire said without looking up from the notes she was making.

"Yeah, of course," Kane said, sinking down in his chair a little. "Anyway, there were lots of stories and pictures on the costumes people wore, and some of the more outrageous stunts we pulled . . . but not one reporter mentioned the menu I slaved over for three weeks. So I figure this is my chance to tell the world about the feast I cooked. What did I serve?"

Winslow nearly knocked Max over as he lunged for the buzzer. "Oh, I have so got this one bagged," he announced brightly. "Hi, Kane. Loved the last album."

That earned him a thumbs-up and a "Cheers!" from Kane, and a glower from Claire Durand. Clearing his throat, Win said, "Okay. Tragically, I wasn't at the party, myself, but word on the street is you replicated the final meal served aboard the doomed ship *Titanic,* down to the last detail. Which means you served oysters for the first course, followed by consommé Olga and cream of barley soup. The third course was . . . fish, right? So, poached salmon with a mousseline sauce and cucumbers. After fish comes meat, so that was filet mignon Lili, sautéed chicken à la lyonnaise, and vegetables with marrow sauce. Fifth course: lamb with mint sauce, roast duckling with apples, beef sirloin with Château potatoes . . . and this is where I always mess up. Peas? Yeah. Green peas, creamed carrots, boiled rice, and potatoes both boiled and parmentier. Now!" Win did half of an aborted touchdown dance, body jerking like a rag doll.

"This is awesome," Slater said, grinning. "Keep going! You're halfway there."

"Right, five courses down, five to go. Damn. Okay, after all that meat must have come the . . ." He screwed his face up in concentration. "Palate cleanser! In this case, Punch Romaine, which, I looked that up, and it sounds like the definition of awesome."

"Highly recommended," Slater agreed, nodding.

"Course seven, roasted squab and watercress; course eight, cold asparagus vinaigrette; course nine, pâté de foie gras and celery," Win continued, getting into a rhythm and bobbing his upper body along with the menu recitation. "And last but not least, dessert. Oh Lord, let's see if I can remember."

The crowd, which had been fairly quiet up until now, gave an encouraging round of applause punctuated by loud clanging. Max shaded his eyes to peer beyond the floodlights and saw that several groups of hopefuls had brought big pots and wooden spoons to bang on them with.

Obviously energized by the surge of excitement from the crowd, Win said all in a rush, "Waldorf pudding, peaches in Chartreuse jelly, chocolate and vanilla éclairs, and, and, and . . ."

Come on, come on, Max thought, clenching his fists tight at his sides.

"And French ice cream!" Win concluded triumphantly, a rush of blood turning his cheeks the color of milk chocolate.

"That's right!" Slater added his enthusiastic clapping to the roar of the crowd while the rest of the team took turns squeezing the breath out of Win.

The score is tied. Max realized with a spurt of joy. *Just gotta keep it up and get into the lead . . .*

He didn't stop to wonder when he'd started caring about winning this thing.

Chapter 16

Jules could only think of one single day in her life that had been worse than today. And that one had involved her mother tossing Jules out on her ass in the snow.

To know that she was the one her team relied on for this challenge—and to freeze up . . . it was hideous. It felt like a panic attack, only worse, because it was endless, but low-key enough that she wasn't about to pass out.

At this point, passing out would be a relief.

Get it together, she lectured herself as Winslow made his spectacular response to Kane Slater's *Titanic* question. *So what if your personal life is a hot mess? This is business. This is the culinary competition you've been working toward for months. This is war!*

"You're the comeback kids," Devon Sparks observed. "Let's see if you can keep it going. As some of you may know, I recently started an after-school program to teach kids how to cook. Yeah, we talk about making healthy food choices, how to read nutritional labels, all that jazz, but what everyone really likes are the days we get into the kitchen and get our hands dirty. Those are the days I'm peppered with all sorts of interesting questions—no one comes up with better stumpers than an eight-year-old. Like this one! What makes an apple smell like an apple?"

Jules snapped to attention. She knew that!

She reached for the buzzer but before she could make contact, the other team buzzed in.

As the officious-looking team leader answered with a long-winded explanation of ester chemicals, and how they were a combination of acid and alcohol molecules like ethyl acetate, the one that gives apples their characteristic tart, sweet scent, Jules struggled not to deflate.

Beside her, Danny jostled hard into her, then suddenly he was gone, and Max was standing in his place and Danny was swearing under his breath on Max's other side.

Quirking his mouth into a smile only slightly more strained than usual, Max said, "Don't sweat it! You're back in the game, that's what counts. You'll get the next one, for sure."

Despite everything, all the dangerous hopes and unrestrained vulnerabilities between them—Jules actually felt better just having him beside her.

I'm so screwed.

"Another point to the team from Ristorante D'Este," announced Eva Jansen to the crowd. "Which means they've pulled back into the lead. This one might be a photo finish, folks. Anything could happen!" She cast a sidelong glance across the stage to someone at Jules's table. "Who thought the qualifiers would be such a thrill a minute?"

"Thank you for that status update, Eva," Claire Durand said briskly. "My next question is concerning sauces. Specifically *le fond brun*, the brown sauce, what we call in France a mother sauce because it is the foundation for so many more. I would like you to take us through the standard preparation of a basic brown sauce, then name three classical variations on the sauce, and what they entail."

Jules and Max reached for the buzzer at the same time,

their hands colliding on top of it and mashing it down for a long, loud moment.

Blinking, she turned to him, heart pounding. "I know this one."

"So do I. For real, this time," Max promised. "Let me take it. We've got one last question after this, and it's Slater's. There's no way I'll get that right, but you studied him. You answer that one and then we'll get the extra point for having each member of the team answer at least one question."

Fear turned Jules's knees to gelatin. "But I know *this* one," she whispered frantically. "What if I freeze up again?"

His hand was still covering hers on the buzzer, and he twined their fingers together, squeezing warmly. "You won't," he said, confidence spilling from his pores. "You'll know the answer to Slater's question. You're our last, best hope for winning this thing, Jules. There's no way you'll let us down."

She stared straight into his calm gray eyes, her breath caught in her chest.

Is there anything on earth more seductive than a man who believes in you?

Jules closed her eyes and tried to be the woman he thought she was. "Go for it. I'll get the next one, and we'll win."

Max's eyes flashed bright blue with approval for one instant before he turned to face the judges.

"Brown sauce," he said. "You take bones and trimmings, veal is best, and roast them until they're all golden and caramelly. Drizzle them with oil and sauté them with mirepoix. Um . . . that's diced carrots, onion, and celery. Which I'm sure you knew, but now you know that I know, too. Um. Where was I?"

Maybe he wasn't as confident as he seemed. "Breathe,"

Jules whispered out of the side of her mouth. "You're doing great."

Max shot her a grateful look and reached for her hand under the table. Jules grasped his sweaty fingers and held on tight, the familiar zing of attraction almost subsumed in the rush of adrenaline from the competition.

Almost.

"Okay. Let the mirepoix and bones get good and brown, adding in some tomato paste right before they caramelize. And don't burn the tomato paste, because you need it for color and depth of flavor. Deglaze the pan with stock and scrape up all the good, crusty bits from the bottom. Then you want to simmer it for a long time, two to four hours, skimming every now and then to get the gross stuff off the surface of the sauce, which is way easier if you offset the pot a little bit. Makes all the nasty come up on one side, so it's a snap to scoop."

Max paused for another breath, and Jules checked the judges' table. Claire Durand had the look of a woman who'd ordered a shrimp cocktail and been served a raw bar full of oysters, clams, and crab legs.

Perfect. Jules bet even the crankiest judge was unlikely to downgrade them for being too detailed.

"You can add a little pouch of herbs tied up in cheesecloth or whatnot, if you want. I go by taste, usually, see what it needs more of. Strain out the chunky bits, then you can thicken it with a roux of flour and butter for sauce espagnole, or with plain old cornstarch for a jus lié, just keep simmering until it's all thick and glossy. And that's it."

"That was . . . very comprehensive," Claire said, eyebrows high. "Full marks for your explanation. Now for the rest of the question?"

"Oh right!" Max looked surprised for a moment, as if he'd forgotten the second half of the answer he'd signed on for.

Jules didn't even have time to get worried, though, before he was rattling off, "Let's see, I guess I'll say sauce robert, which is brown sauce with butter, white wine, and onions, finished with a pinch of sugar and a little mustard. If you add thin strips of cornichon pickles to that robert, you get sauce charcutière." His eyes gleamed. "I gotta give it up for sauce zingara, though. Brown sauce with minced shallots, fresh breadcrumbs, and butter, brightened up with a dash of lemon juice and a handful of chopped parsley. That's my favorite; plus, come on. It's got way the best name."

Claire Durand doled out a small, approving smile. "Well done. And your team has once more caught up with Ristorante D'Este. The final question will decide who moves on to the next round. And I believe you're close to receiving the extra bonus point for this round, if the last member of your team who has yet to field a question is the one to provide the correct answer this time."

"Remember, folks," Eva Jansen interrupted, speaking to the crowd. "It's not the last two teams standing today—we've got room for four in the finals to see which team will represent the East Coast in this year's RSC. The longer you stay on the stage today, the more points you rack up. And at the end of the day, that's what will decide who goes to the finals. So really make an effort to spread the questions out over your whole team; it could make the difference between continuing on in this competition, or going back to your restaurant and watching the RSC on TV."

"Also," Devon Sparks added, "making every chef contestant answer at least one question proves to us judges that you're a well-rounded team, and that every member deserves to be there and will contribute equally."

"And thus endeth the public service announcement," Kane Slater intoned solemnly.

Even from up on the stage under the hottest lights known to man, Jules felt the freeze of Claire's glare.

"If you're so eager to be done with this round," the female judge said, "then why don't you ask your last question?"

Shooting her a sunny smile, Kane said, "I think I will, thanks."

Jules felt her lungs starting to work overtime. There was a warm squeeze around her fingers, and she realized she and Max were still holding hands under the table. Well, not really holding. At least on her part, "clutching" would be a better term. She tried to ease up on her grip, but he moved even closer to her so she could feel him all along her side, and twined their fingers together tightly.

"You're our resident geek," he reminded her softly. "Go get it, girl."

Bolstered by Max's encouragement, she zeroed in on Kane, watching his lips move and trying to anticipate what he was about to say.

"Final question. Let's make it a good one." He paused for a long moment, as if thinking, and Jules would have sworn he made eye contact with her before saying, "You all know what the *Michelin Guide* is. Love it or hate it, agree with it or not, it's been awarding stars for fine dining restaurants since the turn of the last century. And nearly all the chefs who've been lucky enough to rate the maximum number of stars—three—have something in common. They're men."

Claire's head whipped around to laser a narrow-eyed stare at her fellow judge, but Kane Slater ignored her. "The first two women were awarded three stars in 1933, then almost twenty years later, another one made the cut. And then? About fifty years go by, the pages of the little red guidebook filled with dude after dude after dude. Until

2007—one lone woman appears. The next year? The total number of Michelin-starred women chefs doubles. So who can name the trailblazing female chef and the restaurant that broke the seal in 2007?"

Jules blinked. This was definitely not in her thick manila folder of info on Kane Slater, rock star and amateur gourmet. Which didn't mean she didn't know the answer, she realized with a start.

As quick as a breath, she buzzed in. "It was Chef Anne-Sophie Pic of Maison Pic in Valence, in southeastern France."

"Ding ding ding," Kane said, standing up so fast his chair fell over. "We have a winner!"

Instantly, Jules was surrounded by the rest of her team, the center of a knot of embracing arms and cheering voices.

Good thing, too—without four big men anchoring her to the floor, she might just have floated straight up to the Javits Center ceiling like an escaped helium balloon. Euphoria streaked through her in a golden rush, clearing the cobwebs out of her brain and sharpening every sense, so that even over the din of celebration and the applause of the audience, she heard him.

Max.

He put his mouth right next to her ear, close enough to tickle, and said, "I knew you could do it."

With shivers of delight cascading down her spine, Jules straightened her shoulders and stepped back up to the table.

"All right," she said as the opposing team left the stage scowling, and a new group of chefs in white jackets trooped on to take their place. "I'm ready for the next question."

They lasted a record eleven rounds.

Jules was unstoppable, on fire, and Max could only

watch her with a mixture of pride, admiration, and nearly uncontrollable lust.

Smart chicks are hot. Damn.

The rest of the team did their part; even Max managed to contribute a few more answers to obscure questions about stuff like fishing practices in the South China Sea and the ingredients of harissa, the hot chili sauce he'd gotten addicted to in northern Africa.

But mostly it was Jules, whiskey-brown eyes blazing with intelligence and confidence, who kept them going.

When they finally tapped out after two full hours on the stage, Max thought it was probably due more to dehydration and exhaustion than because Jules ran out of answers.

As they dragged themselves off the stage, she said, "Sorry, guys. I just couldn't get to the buzzer fast enough."

"Hey." Danny muscled Max aside and slung an arm over her shoulders. "Do not sweat it, girl. You were incredible up there."

While the rest of the team echoed that sentiment, Max did his best to drill a hole through the back of his brother's skull with the force of his glare. It didn't work.

Max wondered when the green-eyed monster had gotten its teeth into him. He couldn't remember ever being jealous over a chick before, especially when he knew she'd been best friends with Danny since the dawn of time.

Now? He kind of wanted to bend his baby brother's fingers back until the kid squealed like a pig, just because those fingers had touched Jules. Weird.

Hell, Max had even felt a flash of jealousy at the way that blond rocker judge smiled at Jules! Which was ridiculous, he told himself, watching her throw her head back to laugh at something Danny said.

Getting bent out of shape over a simple smile, when I'm the one who's allowed to touch her, kiss her, and make

*her smile all the time. She knows how I feel now. And I
know she feels something, too, even if she's not ready to
admit it.*

The crowd in front of them parted to let an exuberant
Gus through, his arms waving with dangerous abandon,
nearly clocking a hapless bystander in the head.

"My little band of geniuses!" he chortled. "You were
magnificent. Stupendous. Outstanding! I only wish I
could've been up there with you, in the thick of things."

"We could've used you," she said, making a face. "Especially at the beginning, when I nearly choked."

Never one to dwell on the past, Gus waved that away.
"You finished strong, and that's what counts. With the
number of points you kids racked up, there's no way we
won't make it into the finals."

"For heaven's sake, don't jinx it," Nina said, walking up
to hug first Danny, then Max. "They're announcing the
teams who get to move on once everyone finishes competing, but I just talked to a very nice young man named Drew,
who I think is Eva Jansen's assistant, and he said the
announcement probably won't happen until late tonight,
after all the teams get their chance and they can tally up
the results."

"Any reason we need to stick around?" Max asked, already imagining dragging Jules off somewhere private
and secluded, so they could finish what they'd started that
morning.

Gus looked torn. "You don't want to size up the competition?"

"We are the competition," Max said, giving his father
a grin.

Gus liked that. His eyes gleamed as he said, "Yeah,
you're right. And you're all probably sick of this place.
Plenty of time to study up on the enemy teams once we
know who's in the finals with us. All right, all right, don't

fret, woman! I won't say it again until we get the final word. I promise. Now. Drinks are on me at Chapel!"

Beck, Winslow, and Danny all cheered—to be expected, no chef worth his salt ever passed up free booze. But it was Jules's wide smile and flushed cheeks that made Max want to groan.

As the whole pack of them moved toward the exit doors, excitedly recounting the entire suspenseful event, Max lengthened his stride to catch up to Jules.

"There's really not a chance in hell of convincing you to ditch this party and invite me back to your apartment for a private party of our own. Is there?"

She glanced around once, quickly, as if to make sure no one had heard. Then she smiled up at him. "Not a chance, no. Your dad deserves to share this with us, and this is the only way he can right now. Besides. I don't know about you, but I could really use a beer."

Resigning himself to the still very enchanting sight of Jules with her clothes on, at least for a few more hours, Max laughed. "I love that you drink beer."

"The cheaper, the better," she affirmed. "Although I admit to a fondness for Asian beers. Sapporo is my favorite, if I had to pick one."

Max slowed his pace slightly, allowed them to fall to the back of the group, then reached for her hand. She tensed for a moment, but when he curled his fingers around hers, she squeezed back. "Maybe one day we can drink Sapporo together in Tokyo. I'd love to show you the city, introduce you to the guy who taught me everything I know about Japanese food. I think Harukai-sensei would actually like you—and he doesn't like anyone."

A shadow passed over her face like a cloud scudding across a blue sky, but it was gone before he could interpret it. "That would be incredible."

But as they made their way out to the street, and

followed the group toward the A-C-E stop at Thirty-fourth Street, Max couldn't help feeling like she meant the most literal definition of "incredible"—as in, something impossible to believe in.

If I were truly Zen, I'd pull back. Try to want less, let her come to me, be happy with what I have.

He sighed as they caught up to his family and Jules casually disengaged their fingers.

Too bad he seemed to have lost his knack for Zen.

Chapter 17

The interior of Chapel, the after-hours bar of choice for many of Manhattan's hardworking chefs (along with an assortment of avant-garde actors, performance artists, off-duty cops, exhausted nurses, and punk rock aficionados) seethed with illegal cigarette smoke, flashing lights from the platform stage in the corner, and the heaving bodies of people thrashing to the music pouring from the speakers.

Some local band was on tonight; Jules thought she'd seen them at Chapel before. The neon-haired lead singer threw herself around the stage like a pinball, careening into her lanky bass player and getting a manic grin and shove back to center stage for her trouble.

Jules could relate. Her whole life felt like a game of pinball lately, bouncing from joy to fear and back again. It was nice to be on one of the highs at the moment, she reflected, taking another drink from the ice-cold bottle of beer in her hand and leaning her elbows back on the bar.

She was pleasantly warm and fuzzy, the frenetic energy of the bar passing through her in waves, keeping her from having to think or talk or do anything other than exist in the moment.

Very Eastern philosophy, she decided. *Max would approve.*

Where was he, anyway?

He hadn't been glued to her side all night, but he was keeping tabs on her, Jules knew. Every now and then, she'd feel someone's gaze like a warm palm trailing over the back of her neck, and without even needing to look up, she'd know it was Max, checking in. She got the same glow of happiness every time they made eye contact. It was nice, to feel like someone cared if she was having a good time.

Ah, there he was. She finally located him at the other end of the bar, in the midst of what looked like a very involved discussion with Beck. The large, taciturn chef was more animated than Jules had ever seen him, his face alight with interest.

Jules shook her head slowly, the move unbalancing her enough to make her glad she was braced against something as solid as the scarred wooden bar that ran the length of Chapel's main room.

"What's up?" Danny appeared beside her, clinking his glass to her bottle and leaning back companionably.

"Nothing," she said. "Your brother."

"What about him?"

Danny's voice was neutral, but in a studied way, as if he had to work at it. "Only Max," she said, tilting her glass in his direction as if toasting him. "He's got Beck eating out of his hand."

Affection mixed with exasperation crept into Danny's tone. "He's always been that way," he said, sipping at his beer. "Like he's got his own gravitational pull. People flock to him, they like him, they want to tell him their troubles. And the sick part is, he likes them back! It's genuine. And I don't just mean the chicks, either, although he's never had any problems in that area, the bastard."

"No, I'm sure he hasn't."

She thought she'd managed to keep her voice as neutral as Danny's, but he shot her a pointed look. It was too much to hope Danny wouldn't remember the die-hard crush he'd teased her about all through high school. "Not that Max's a dog," he said grudgingly. "He doesn't screw around."

Jules shrugged, squinting in the other direction and ignoring the heat in her cheeks. Hopefully it was too dark in here for Danny to make it out, anyway.

"Come on, Jules," he sighed. "I know something's going on with you two."

"So what if there is?" she said, suddenly fed up with the inquisition. "First Gus, now you! Okay, so Max and I are maybe, possibly, thinking about talking about having some fun together while he's home. Why does it have to be a big deal? Can't we just figure it out on our own and then let the rest of you in on it?"

"Whoa!" Danny held up his hands in alarm, his glass of Guinness tilting dangerously. "Cool your jets. I was only wondering. And maybe worrying a little about the effect a thing between you could have on the team, not to mention how you'll feel when he fucks off to Italy and his next bright, shiny adventure."

That was totally valid. Which only ticked her off more.

"Well, stop worrying," Jules said, downing the last of her beer in one decisive gulp.

"Look, Jules. My brother's a great guy in a lot of ways, but steadiness? Dependability? Those qualities don't really make the list."

Her stomach muscles tightened as if she'd taken a hit. "I know Max well enough to know you're right about that. But he's been more than honest about his intentions to leave after the qualifiers, and I'm not some starry-eyed girl looking for love and forever. I don't even believe in those things. I'll be fine. The team will be fine."

Danny tightened his mouth, a muscle in his jaw ticking. "You deserve more than that, Jules. I know that thing with Phil the Phucktard messed you up, but that doesn't mean—"

"Hey, come on. I was messed up way before the Phucktard got to me," Jules broke in, flashing a smile.

But Danny refused to let her lighten the mood. "Not every guy is like Phil. Or Joe, or Mitchell, or whoever it was that first convinced you that who you are isn't good enough. You're better than good enough, Jules. And if Max weren't such an oblivious asshole, with all his Zen master bullshit and fortune cookie sayings, he'd see that."

"So . . . what? I should hope Max sticks around long enough to figure out my inherent awesomeness? Because I'm not holding my breath on that one."

Danny shook his head. "I'm just saying . . . be careful. Because it's been a long time since I've seen you like this, and normally I'd be stoked about it, all gung ho, thumbs-up, rah-rah—but Max leaves. It's what he does. And when he goes, he won't look back. I don't want you to be hurt."

The solemn look on Danny's familiar face melted Jules's insides like butter in a hot pan. "I have no illusions about how this is going to go," she said softly, picking at the blue and gold label on her beer bottle. "I'm not counting on Max. I like him. And he likes me, and none of that is going to stop him from leaving when this is all over. None of it's going to stop me from letting him go. And sure, maybe it'll suck—but I'm a grown ass woman, and Max is sure as hell a man. We can make our own choices about what we want and live with the consequences."

Right now—and for as long as she could have him—Jules wanted Max.

Leaving Danny staring after her, she made her way over to where Max and Beck had commandeered a small, round table. She was pleased with the steadiness of her progress, and moving around, dodging flailing dancers and moshing head bangers, actually cleared her mind of some of the alcohol haze.

"Hey, gorgeous." Max smiled up at her, lazy and relaxed as he reclined in his seat, one arm hooked over the back of his chair and long legs sprawled out to trip unwary dancers.

"Jules," Beck said, nodding. He had a glass of whiskey in front of him; Jules was pretty sure he'd been nursing that one drink all night.

"Hi, guys," she said. There were no more chairs at the table, but Max patted his thighs and gave her a cheerful leer.

"I got a seat for you right here, babycakes," he said in this smarmy, awful lounge-lizard voice, the kind of suggestive talk that would normally send her running.

Lifting her chin, Jules said, "Perfect." And plopped herself right down in his lap.

"Oof," said Max, his arms coming up to circle her waist. "Well, hello there, little lady."

Enjoying the surprise in his voice, she tilted her head back to see his face. "Thanks for the seat," she said blandly.

"Anytime," he told her. "And I mean that. Any. Time."

"Has Gus heard anything?" Beck asked, glancing at his watch. Jules felt a little bad—had they embarrassed him?—but she was still buzzed enough to not quite care.

"No," she said. "At least, I assume he hasn't, or we would've all heard about it by now."

"Uh-oh, heads up," Max said, pointing across the bar at the stage.

The band was taking a break, unslinging guitars from their necks and jumping down from the stage, and there, ready to step into the empty spotlight, was Gus Lunden.

"I think we're about to hear something, one way or the other," Beck said.

Max's thighs went rock hard with tension under hers, and the rest of the alcohol in her bloodstream was drowned out by a surge of adrenaline.

This was it.

Gus stepped up to the microphone, tapping at it. "Is this thing on? Hello?" He winced along with the rest of the room at the loud shriek of feedback, then laughed giddily. "I guess so. Heh. Well, good, because I have an announcement to make."

He paused dramatically, long enough to be sure he commanded the attention of every soul in the bar. For the first time all night, silence blanketed the room.

"I just got a call from Eva Jansen's assistant—the Lunden's Tavern team is going to the finals! We've got a shot at being the next East Coast team in the Rising Star Chef competition!"

The whole bar erupted in cheers. Every line cook, dishwasher, and chef in the place yelled and stomped his or her feet, and slapped the nearest Lunden's chef on the back. Beck leaped out of his chair with a loud whoop that sounded like "oo-rah" and Max's arms contracted around Jules hard enough to compress her ribs around her lungs.

She twisted in his embrace, squirming until she could get her arms around his neck and lock her legs around his waist. And right there, in full view of half the chefs she knew, including the ones she worked with and the ones she considered family, she kissed Max Lunden on the mouth.

He tasted like laughter and smoke, his tongue bitter with the dark ale he'd been drinking. She licked into his mouth, flexed her fingers in his hair, and tried to hold on to her spiraling joy long enough to get out of the bar and find someplace they could be alone.

"My place," she husked against his lips. "Now."

It took way longer than Max wanted to extricate them from Chapel. From the electrifying moment of Jules's hot little demand to the sudden chill of night air cooling their sweaty faces, it must have been at least two eternities. Maybe three.

First they had to drag Gus down off the stage, where he was giving a maudlin toast to his wife and his team, and deliver him to said wife, who seemed more concerned than touched by the declaration. Maybe because Gus didn't drink that often, and when he did, he tended to make up for lost time.

It took the entire team, with Danny and Win pulling and Beck pushing, to help Max and Jules get his arguing parents into a cab and on their way home. Danny was determined to deposit them on their actual doorstep, so he got into the cab with them. The last they saw of him was his grim expression, hunched between his parents, as the cab pulled away from the curb.

After that, the party seemed to break up naturally. Win went back into Chapel to finish his drink and the conversation he'd been in the middle of with the bartender. Beck nodded good night and trudged off down the street in the direction of the subway that would take him back to his Brooklyn apartment.

Max stood in the cool night breeze and stared at Jules. She had a wholesome, all-American, athletic strength about her that made Max want to spread her long hair out on a pillow and kiss her until her lips were swollen and debauched looking. But under the soft, shifting glow of the city lights all around them, she seemed ethereal—

almost fragile. Which wasn't a word he would normally associate with Jules Cavanaugh.

"So . . ." he said, shoving his hands in his pockets and rocking back onto his heels. "You come here often?"

Picking up on his mood with the lightning quickness that had won them a space in the finals, Jules flirted right back. "Pretty often. But you must be new. I'm sure I'd remember if I'd seen you here before, hot stuff."

That made him grin and saunter closer, close enough to reach out and smooth a lock of dark gold hair behind her ear. "What do you say we blow this joint? There are things I want to do to you that would shock even this wild crowd."

Standing so close, he could feel the shiver that took her body. "Maybe some privacy would be good," she agreed. The breathless quality of her voice went through Max like a shot of sake.

He cocked a brow and manfully took the next cliché. "Your place or mine?"

She broke finally, bending over to bark out a real laugh. "Well, considering your place is full of your bickering family at the moment, I think you'd better come home with me."

Max shrugged. "I had to ask. I don't know your kinks—maybe shouting and recriminations turn you on."

"I'm not that adventurous," she said, taking his hand and stepping off the curb. She looked over her shoulder at him, a wicked glint dispelling the brief fragility he'd seen in her face. "Also not that patient." Throwing her free arm up, she had a cab pulling over in seconds flat.

They piled in like a couple of puppies, shoving and giggling and sprawling over each other. Max got a pair of fingers into her ribs and tickled her mercilessly until he realized she couldn't give her address if she was panting and shrieking with laughter.

"Where to?" the cabbie asked, bored gaze in the rearview mirror making it clear that this was far from the craziest scene he'd witnessed that night.

"Stop it," Jules hissed. "Oh, my God. We're going to the corner of Fourteenth and Third."

"That's like ten blocks," Max chortled. "We could have walked it!"

"It's twelve blocks," she said, raising her eyebrows at him. Her cheeks were flushed, eyes sparkling. She'd never looked more gorgeous. "Ten minutes. Did you really want to wait that long?"

His cock twitched, cramped and half hard in his jeans, and started to thicken. "No," he said, mouth dry. "You're right. I bow to your authority, one hundred percent. The faster we get to your apartment, the better."

Just as Max was wondering if Jules was still tipsy enough to let him get away with kissing her in the back of this taxi, the cabbie glared into the rearview again and said, "If you stain the seats, it's an extra twenty. For cleaning."

Jules made a face. "Okay, yuck. Max, keep your hands to yourself."

Grumbling, Max pushed himself into the opposite corner and contented himself with watching the play of light across her creamy white skin. It was an enjoyable way to pass the four-minute cab ride, and by the time Max shelled out the cab fare, he was in a good enough mood to tip the guy. Not twenty bucks—the seats were still pristine, after all—but a couple.

Jules's building was a narrow, five-story brick with a Korean deli on the street level. She tugged him under the tattered scarlet awning with HEART & SEOUL MARKET in faded black letters, and fit her key to the door on the side of the building that led up to the apartments above.

"Is the deli any good? I haven't had decent Korean since I got back."

"They actually don't have a lot of Korean stuff," she

said as they tramped up the dingy stairs. "It's more organic produce, fresh flowers, that kind of thing. They sell great kimchee, though, if you're in the mood for pickled cabbage spicy enough to shear off the first three layers of taste buds on your tongue."

"I think I'm okay for right now," Max said. "Maybe for breakfast tomorrow. Kimchee eggs, mmmm. . . ."

"Oh ho! So you think you'll still be here for breakfast?"

"I think you're going to have a hard time kicking me out before the hot and spicy eggs, since I plan to be doing hot and spicy things to your body all night long."

"You're incredible."

"Thank you."

"It wasn't a compliment."

"Haven't we discussed this before?"

Jules huffed out a breath as they finally hit the fifth-floor landing. "What I actually meant was, where do you come up with these lines? All I can assume is that they're bad English translations of something smooth you heard in Russia or somewhere."

"I'm shocked and appalled that you would dare to suggest I might not be completely original and unique in every way. I'll have you know that I'm a very special snowflake, Ms. Cavanaugh. There's no one like me anywhere in the world. I know, because I checked."

"I believe you," she said feelingly, stopping in front of a door at the end of the narrow hall. "The universe has a sick sense of humor, sometimes, but two of you? That would just be cruel."

Max clutched at his heart and staggered into the door frame while she jiggled her key in the lock and bumped the door open with her hip. "Abuse! Abuse! Isn't there some hotline I can call to report this kind of thing?"

Jules grabbed his wrist, her face bright with laughter.

"Shut it, you! Or I'll give you something to report. Come on, I've got neighbors."

He waggled his eyebrows at her and twisted his wrist, just to feel her grip tighten on him. "Your neighbors aren't used to you carousing in the corridors with gentleman callers at all hours, huh? Good to know."

She tugged him into the apartment with her, shutting the door behind them and spinning him until his back was up against the solid wood.

"My neighbors are a nice little old lady who gives me rugelach every time she makes a batch, and a lesbian couple who run a design consulting firm out of their apartment. They get up early to walk their daughter to school. Do you know what time it is?"

Max savored the way she leaned into him, matched hip to hip, belly to belly, chest to chest, for a long moment before sliding one long arm around her waist. "It's time to step away from the door and find someplace soft and cushiony, so I can make love to you the way you deserve. I like wall sex as much as the next guy—more, maybe—but right now? I want to lay you out and take my time with you."

Her breath sped up, rib cage jumping against his. Someone's heart was banging hard against Max's chest, but he wasn't sure if it was hers or his.

She still had his wrist trapped in her fingers, and without taking her eyes off him, she pressed that wrist back against the door beside Max's head and stretched up the last inch to touch her mouth to his. Something about the gentle restraint of her grasp revved Max up like a Formula One racing engine, and the instant she opened her lips to him, he thrust his way inside and tried to devour her.

Gasping together, they stayed pressed against the door for long, lovely minutes, bodies rubbing slowly, lips and tongues stroking, teasing, playing. Max kept his arm around her slender waist, his hand flexing against the small of her back, and didn't try to shake loose of her hot grip on his other hand.

In a way, he liked the security of it; if she had his hand, if she kept him where she wanted him, he didn't have to worry about pushing her too hard and scaring her off. She was still a flight risk, he knew—something deep inside her didn't trust him all the way. And that was okay, he could work with that. Trust could be earned. But not without patience, and patience was a thing Max hadn't struggled this hard for in a long, long time.

So he let her keep him pinned when his instincts told him to reverse their positions and ravish her against the door. And he lifted his head from her soft, sweet mouth and said, "This is your show. Your house, your rules."

Chapter 18

As always, Max's kiss told her something new about him. He didn't kiss like other guys, who all seemed to want to take charge and establish dominance immediately, as if losing control of the kiss would mean they were weak.

Not Max. Even when he was voracious, like now, with his tongue tracing patterns of pure fire across the roof of her mouth, it felt like genuine hunger—not a battle for supremacy. And when Jules melted into him, he backed off, his lips going soft and searching, trading control back and forth between them as easily as tossing a softball.

Then he said it.

This is your show. Your house, your rules.

Jules felt his words all through her, like the blast of searing heat from opening a hot oven.

The very idea of it soothed something inside her, something that had been there so long, she hardly remembered a time when she hadn't felt the thin, cold trickle of helplessness. No matter how strong she got, how independent and in control of her life, there was part of Jules that had always associated sex with danger, fear, and struggle. She hadn't let it rule her life, but she'd never exactly healed the damage, either.

But this. What Max offered her now? Was a whole new way to think about sex.

There was something indescribably empowering about the way Max was staring at her, his eyes burning with desire, but his body loose, relaxed—almost yielding against hers.

"Do you mean that?" she said, lust rushing through her in an overwhelming wave.

He tensed and released every muscle at once before nodding. His gaze never left her face. "Whatever you want," he said. "As long as it ends with you and me together, naked and exhausted, I'm good."

She had to swallow hard to speak past the picture that popped into her head. "I could go for that," she said, before letting her heels touch the floor so she could step away from the support of his lean, hard body.

He made a sad noise. "Nooo . . ."

Jules couldn't help smirking a little. "Wow, you need a quick lesson in how to take direction."

"Hey, I reserve the right to comment on the proceedings," he said quickly. "But you're not wrong. I don't do this often. Or ever." He ducked his head for an instant, long enough to tell Jules how true his next words were. "I'm not really big on taking orders. It's kind of a thing."

Her heart went as gooey as sticky toffee pudding, while other parts of her got even hotter. His honesty was like a hook in her guts, pulling hard and demanding the same in return.

"I love that you're giving me this," she told him, rubbing her fingers in a loose circle around the wrist she'd captured out in the hallway. "It makes me want to give you anything. Everything."

She heard the click of his throat as he swallowed. "So what are we waiting for?"

Her apartment wasn't a studio, but it was close enough. Her bed was in a separate room from the living/dining/ kitchen area, but the bedroom was small enough that once she opened the door, they only had to take one, single step over the threshold before they could fall onto the queen- sized mattress.

As drunk with freedom and touch and body heat as she was, Jules's brain still managed to send up enough signal flares to warn her to glance around the bedroom, make sure everything was put away, nothing incriminating or embarrassing was lying around. Nope, it was as bare bones and utilitarian as ever. She only used the apartment to sleep in, really, so why spend a bunch of money on décor she'd never see?

One quick glance around was all she could spare be- fore Max loomed over her, blocking out the rest of the room, the rest of the world, with his broad, wiry body.

She felt herself opening to him, her legs and arms falling lax and inviting him down to lie in the cradle of her body. Never one to pass up an opportunity, Max fitted himself against her, all muscles and hardness and vibrating ten- sion against the softer lines of her liquidly passionate body.

Smoothing the hair off her forehead, Max looked des- perately tender—or maybe just desperate. "Tell me what you want," he urged her.

Without meaning to, Jules bucked against him, their hips sliding in an achingly good rhythm for a moment. He groaned and closed his eyes tightly.

The possibilities were endlessly tantalizing—she could ask to be on top, riding his thighs and splayed open above him. Or she could try something she'd never done before, with him behind her, both of them on their knees.

Everything low in her body pulled tight and wet at the images that raced through her mind, every one like a hit of an illegal substance, sending reality, the past, the future, whirling away into the void of the all-consuming present.

And in the present, she was on her back in the comfort and security of her own bed, her familiar pillows and cotton sheets under her, and Max over her, gentle and demanding by turns, his strong body like a barrier keeping everything bad away.

Jules smiled, filled with certainty and a sense of rightness.

"This," she whispered, reaching up to feel the solid planes of his back stretched taut with his effort to keep his weight from crushing down on her. "I want this, you there and me here and both of us exactly like this."

His eyes darkened, pupils expanding and eating up the blue of his gaze until there was nothing but smoky black want looking back at her. "Can we be . . ." He paused, swallowed. "I need you naked. Now."

"Yeah," she said, getting a grip on his shirt and skimming it up and over his head. "Skin on skin. I want that, too."

Max reared up on his knees, making short work of removing his shirt and tossing it into a corner. He helped Jules lean up on her elbows and worked her shirt off, too. He hesitated, but she reached around behind and snagged her bra closure, fiddled it open, and sent the scrap of cotton and lace after their shirts. "Pants, too," she said, then gave him a challenging grin. "Bet I get bare faster than you."

"Oh, it's on now," Max said, laughing and going for his button fly. There was a mad scramble around the bed, jeans and underwear flying into the air and smacking into walls, and then there they were. Both bare and exposed, kneeling on the bed facing each other.

Jules shivered. They were really going to do this.

"God," he said, reaching out one finger to trace the line of her collarbone, then straight down over her sternum, in a hot line all the way to her belly button. "You're so much more beautiful than I imagined. And I've imagined this pretty often."

In a dim way, she knew she'd usually feel embarrassed by that, or that it would make her tense up and wonder if he was using a line on her. But those fears seemed to belong to someone else. To Jules, who fretted and worried and was afraid to live.

I'm not that girl anymore. I don't have to keep feeding her fears.

Reaching out a finger of her own, she mirrored Max's move, enjoying the satin warmth of his skin, the hardness of bone under her fingers giving way to the different hardness of tense abdominal muscles.

His flat belly tensed under her light touch, making her want to press harder, feel the muscles jump and quiver under her hand. At the same time, she was utterly distracted by the tickling trace of his fingers around the shallow indentation of her navel.

Max looked at her from underneath his lashes, a long, seductive glance that had her hand changing direction and heading south to where his erection speared up between them, thick and insistent. Jules clasped the base and gasped, knees weakening, as Max followed her lead and plunged his long, agile fingers between her thighs.

Collapsing forward to rest her forehead against his hard shoulder, Jules panted and tried to keep her hand moving while Max did wicked things to the most sensitive part of her body. He shifted against her, free hand coming up to wander her back, sliding down the ladder of her spine. "Come on," he whispered in her ear. "I won't break."

Jules firmed her grip, and pulled up, hard, saying, "Neither will I. Ah!"

All oxygen was sucked out of the room when Max took her at her word and twisted his fingers up and into her, giving her pressure and fullness where she needed it most. Her hand on his cock faltered again, and Jules swayed, but this time she let gravity take her down onto her back amid the pillows.

"On me," she said, reaching up to him.

Max looked down at her, his eyes hot and bright in the dimness of her room. "God, you're so gorgeous like this. I never thought . . . this is better than anything I could've dreamed up."

His words rushed through her in a flush of heat, and Jules was abruptly done with talking. She wasn't as good at it as Max. She'd learned early on to keep her words safe inside, where they couldn't get her into trouble. But she could show Max how she felt.

Pulling him down over her, she arched up into the muscled heat of him, the roughness of his body hair sensitizing her skin, his weight a solid, welcome reminder of how very not alone she was. They fell into a rhythm, writhing and pushing, his erection a burning brand against her thigh.

The room felt like a sauna, her bed sheets warm and damp against her heated flesh. Jules threw her head back, looking for a breath of cool air, her body strung tighter than steel cable. "In me," she said. "Please." Max shuddered and shook atop her, his hips stuttering out of rhythm for a moment.

"God, don't beg. You don't ever have to beg me. Plus, I really can't take the overwhelming sexiness of it right now," he said.

Jules's head felt like it was filled with hot terry-cloth towels, and Max was still putting together sentences like that? He had some serious catching up to do.

Hooking one leg behind his thigh, she dragged him in

closer and got her teeth into the taut muscle at the side of his neck. He made a strangled noise like a cross between a groan and a growl, deep in his throat, and Jules smiled against his skin.

"God, you're so . . . Okay, that's it. You're in for it now."

He kissed her before pulling out of her arms, and the bed dipped as he left it. Jules whimpered a little, the cold air blowing over her sweat-damp skin making her feel chilled. Hugging herself, her arms brushed against the high, tight buds of her nipples, which felt pretty good. She rubbed more purposefully—felt even better—and un-crossed her arms to palm her own breasts. Heat rose in her belly again; it hadn't receded very far, after all. She could feel the beat of her heart pulsing between her legs, the wet flesh there aching and empty.

Twitching her legs against the sheets, Jules covered herself with the fingers of her right hand, touching gently. It was nothing like when Max did it, but it eased the ache a little, and when Max reappeared beside the bed, he made that choking sound again.

"Jesus. What did I just tell you about the overwhelming sexiness, woman?"

"You left," she pointed out. Any shame she might ever have felt at being caught touching herself had burned it-self out in the crucible of her body's heat and her desire for Max.

"Well, I'm back now," he said, crawling onto the bed and looming over her once more. "All suited up and ready to go."

"Come on," she said, straining up to nip at his lower lip. "I need you."

Max would have dared any guy he'd ever met to resist Jules Cavanaugh at this moment. And that included Zen masters, Buddhist monks, and Vatican priests.

She was on fire, burning up from the inside, and Max could hardly wait to plunge into the hottest part of the flames.

It took everything he had to go slowly when all he wanted was to fall on her and touch every part of her, all at once, with every part of himself. He settled for stretching out on top of her, the way she'd asked, their legs and arms tangling and moving as they shuddered into perfect alignment.

His dick found the notch between her thighs as if drawn there by a magnet, and when she bucked up against him, he felt his latex-covered erection slide against the slippery wetness of her silky folds.

"Now, now, now," she whimpered, the mindless murmur of her voice and the dazed heat in her eyes pulling Max over the edge of rational thought and into a place where all that existed was the slip of their bodies against one another, and the pounding of blood through his veins.

"Now," he told her, framing her face in his palms. He thrust home at the same moment as he took her mouth, swallowing her cry of delight greedily.

God, she was fist-tight, and hotter than anything he'd ever felt, even through the condom. He stared down into her lust-blown eyes and rocked his hips, nudging deeper into her and feeling her clench around him.

He wished for a moment that he could feel her with nothing between them, but he'd never in his life had sex without gloving up, and anyway, it barely mattered. She was so slick and open, so abandoned and responsive, Max was already fighting for the last of his self-control.

"More," she said, bringing her legs up to wind around his hips.

The shift changed the angle of his penetration just slightly, just enough that on his next thrust in, he went even deeper, and they both moaned. Max felt something inside him straining to connect with something inside her, as if their bodies weren't meant to be separate and he wouldn't be happy until they were one.

He thrust harder, making her gasp and tighten with every stroke, his blood pounding out a feral beat his hips couldn't help following.

And then she blinked those beautiful brown eyes open and said, "Max. I think I'm—"

Before she could finish the sentence, she threw her head back on a wail of pleasure, and her silky sheath clamped down around Max's prick, pulling the orgasm out of him in an explosion of force.

Max collapsed against her, lungs seizing and body shaking with aftershocks. He couldn't get his elbows to work right, so he rolled to the side to avoid crushing her. In the process, he slipped free of her body, and they both inhaled at the strange sensation of disconnecting.

Groaning, he hauled his ass out of bed to dispose of the condom. The room was a lot colder now that he wasn't in a sex fever, and he stubbed his toe on the way to the bathroom. Shit, this place was tiny.

"Stay," she said, her voice fucked out and raw, sending shivers down Max's spine. He'd done that, made her sound so exhausted and satisfied.

"I'm not going anywhere," he promised, clicking out the bathroom light and burrowing under the covers. In that moment, he meant it completely.

He pulled her into his arms, heart thumping at the way she pushed her head into the curve of his neck, her breath warm and sweet against his skin.

Counting the slowing beats of her heart lulled Max into a sleepy contentment. And the last thought he had before he closed his eyes was that he'd stay forever, if she asked him to.

Chapter 19

Jules stretched, feeling twinges of pleasant soreness in places that made her frown in confusion for a long moment before she opened her eyes and remembered.

The large furnace of a masculine body lying next to her in the bed was a major memory jogger.

Holding her breath, she sat up very slowly, trying not to jostle him. She didn't want to wake him up, not until she got a minute to think, now that her head was more or less clear. Not that she could blame last night on the alcohol—no, it usually took way more booze than that to lacquer over her bad memories and allow her to let go.

Everything was different with Max, though . . . and that was the problem. She wasn't drunk on beer last night. She was drunk on Max.

Even now, with the harsh morning light streaming in through the open curtains—because who had the presence of mind to close the blinds when getting the daylights kissed out of them?—she still shivered at the memory of what she and Max had done together.

The way he'd let her take the lead . . . nothing in her life had ever been quite so devastatingly seductive. To have all the charm, vibrant life, and deep-running waters that made up Max Lunden stretched out on her bed, spread and yielding under her hand—it had been a revelation. Heat rushed into her belly, her skin prickling with awareness, and Jules tore her gaze away from Max's long, lean form to raise her eyes to his face.

She caught the hint of a smile curling up one corner of his mouth, and the quick flutter of his lashes.

"Busted," she said, unable to curtail her own smile. "I know you're awake."

Max sighed, his eyes still innocently closed, and turned over in the bed. He nestled his face deeper into the pillow and threw his near arm out, catching Jules around the waist.

She squeaked as he pulled her in tight, snuggling her like a teddy bear. "Max! Come on. You're not fooling anyone."

"Shhh . . ." He exhaled a sleepy whisper. "S'nighttime. Sleepy."

Jules lost the fight against melting and allowed herself to be nuzzled, Max's deep breaths warm and even against her temple.

Judging by the angle of the sunlight turning the dust motes by the window into sparkling flecks of gold, Jules decided it couldn't be later than seven o'clock. They probably could afford another hour of sleep; before they left the bar last night, Gus had called a meeting for nine at the restaurant to go over the next challenge.

But despite the beguiling warmth and safety of Max's hard arm clamped around her, Jules lay blinking up at the ceiling, more awake than she could ever remember being.

Max groaned, the vibration carrying through his chest and into hers. "I can hear you thinking," he said accusingly. "Stop that."

"Can't," Jules whispered, watching the gold dust shift

and dance on the currents of air from her window-mounted air-conditioning unit.

They'd had sex. And he was still here. Worse, she wanted him here.

Without opening his eyes, Max lifted his hand and petted blindly at her hair. "Wanna talk about it?"

"Not especially."

That seemed to wake him up a little. He raised his head an inch or so off the pillow; Jules could feel his gaze, sleepy and intent, on the side of her face.

"No. You never want to talk, do you? I'm thinking maybe I shouldn't let you get away with that anymore."

Jules felt herself begin to stiffen, and deliberately relaxed. "Don't worry about it," she said. "Go back to sleep. We've got time."

"Hmm. Let me think. Time for me to snooze while you think over what happened last night and wind yourself into knots I'll just have to untangle later . . . or time to finally get to the bottom of what's keeping you from being happy here with me, in this really freaking rare, nearly perfect moment."

"Is that a choice for me?" Jules asked grumpily. "Or have you already decided?"

"Now, now. It was your turn to do the choosing last night. This morning, I get to be the bossy one. And I say we talk. For once and finally, let's get it all out there." He sat up, mauling the pillows behind him until they were plumped to his satisfaction. Leaning back against the wooden slats of her simple headboard, he gave her a wide-eyed, earnest look. "You can tell me anything; this is a judgment-free zone."

Still flat on her back, Jules debated pulling the covers over her head and hiding. That probably wouldn't do much good. Max had his determined face on.

"Jules," he said softly, pushing one big hand through

the tangled snarls of her unbraided hair. "Let me in. Just a little bit. I swear it won't hurt."

The tenderness in his touch released a valve in her chest, and an aching torrent of emotion flowed in. She had to tell him.

"You can't promise that." Not wanting to be lying down for this conversation, Jules hauled herself up and turned to face him, pulling her knees to her chest and wrapping her arms around them. The AC wasn't spectacularly effective against the muggy heat of a New York City summer, and the room was warm enough that her nakedness didn't matter. Except that it made her feel more vulnerable, but with a sudden surge of determination, Jules welcomed it.

Max deserved this. After how open and real he'd been with her, the least she could do was bare herself, body and soul, and let him decide what to do once he knew it all.

"What do you mean?" Concern darkened his eyes.

"Pain is part of life," she said. "You can't escape it, so it's pointless to make promises about it."

He didn't exactly frown, but by the way his brows drew down a little, she could tell he wanted to. "Now you sound like Harukai-sensei. He used to say 'Life is suffering, Maxwell-kun. All Buddhist know this.'"

Jules felt her mouth twist. "All Buddhists know it, and so do all the women in my family."

Now Max did scowl. "I didn't like it when Harukai-sensei said it, but I like it even less from you." He paused, his voice going careful and quiet. "Is this about your mom?"

She tensed. "I guess you could say that. But really, I was talking about the sex thing. And, you know. Relationships." She couldn't help it; her mouth sneered a little without her even meaning to.

And of course, Max caught it. His gaze sharp on her face, he said, "I know I'm not exactly the poster boy for the r-word. But somehow . . . I'm getting the feeling this is about more than just me."

Uncomfortable, Jules shifted her weight, hunching forward to rest her chin on her crossed arms. "Look. You don't have to let me down easily or anything. I know how this stuff works; I'm not an idiot."

"No you're not." His voice was quiet, and she shot him a swift glance. "But that doesn't mean you know how this works. As far as I can tell, you don't have a clue."

"Fuck you," she told him, lips tight.

Max breathed in through his nose, as deeply and slowly as he could, and pushed the air out again. Calm, he had to stay calm and relaxed here against the headboard, because he could tell by looking at her that Jules was poised to leap off the bed at the first sudden movement.

He didn't want that, not now, when his gut told him if he could just be patient, she'd open up to him.

Moderating his tone, he said, "Come on, Jules. Give me something."

Her head came up as if he'd goosed her. "I'm trying," she gritted out, her fingers clenching so hard he could see the half-moon indentations her nails marked into her elbows.

Max frowned. They were both trying, so hard, and yet sometimes it seemed that for every step forward (and he'd tend to categorize the glorious clashing heat of the night before as more of a giant leap than a step) they skidded to a halt, danced sideways, then fell back. It was beyond frustrating.

Calling on all his meditation techniques, Max willed calm acceptance to flow into his lungs with his next mouthful of air.

"I can see that you're trying," he said. "But I can't help it; I'm greedy. I want more of you than I've had yet, and it's not really in my nature to sit around twiddling my thumbs and hoping."

"You don't like to wait," she said, with the ghost of a smile. "You like to make things happen."

It was no more than the truth—his truth, and one that had gotten him in plenty of trouble throughout his life. "Not fun to be on the receiving end, I'm told."

She shrugged again, her honey-blond hair a shiny silken veil whispering over her shoulders and back. "I can think of worse things than being pushed by you."

Her tiny smile made it abruptly easier to fill his lungs with serene, easy breaths. "So talk to me, gorgeous. Tell me what you think you know about how this is going to go."

She sighed, digging her toes into the bedding. Cute little pink toes, and Max was momentarily distracted by the urge to nibble on them to see if they were as delicious as the rest of her, but then she started talking.

"I don't mean to act like I think you're going to screw me over. I've known from the start, this is a temporary thing. You've never promised me forever, and that's important. It makes a difference. Because too many people think nothing of swearing eternal devotion one minute, and running out on everything the next."

And there went his serene calm. He twisted his fingers in the sheets to stop himself from making fists. "Someone ran out on you. Shit, Jules. You deserve better."

She shook her head, but before he could protest that, hell, yeah, she deserved better, she said, "No. I mean, it wasn't really me they ran out on."

Max subsided, confusion sucking him under like a whirlpool. "Then who—"

Biting her lip until the plump flesh reddened painfully, she said, "I don't mean to be so mysterious. It's just hard to talk about it."

"Hard to talk about what?" It exploded out of him before he could stop it.

She hugged her knees tightly to her chest, but her face was cool and composed when she replied, "My mother."

Trying to fit the puzzle pieces together, he said, "Your mother . . . she had bad luck with guys?"

Jules laughed, but it came out more like a sigh. "I don't think you could call it luck, but it was certainly bad. Her judgment maybe? I don't know. All I know is that from the time I was old enough to walk to the day I left home, I must have had a hundred new 'dads.' According to Mom, every new guy was 'the one,' her true love at last. Which was funny, because not a single guy lasted longer than three months."

"Jesus." Max wasn't sure how to absorb this new piece of information, how to make it fit in with the puzzle that was Jules. "And you met all of these men?"

"Met them? I adored them." She didn't look happy at the memory, though. The look on her face was scornful at best. "At least at first. My mother's boyfriends . . . they made her so happy. For a few weeks, anyway, and I loved that. She'd sing in the shower, and we'd all go to the park together, or out to dinner. The guy would move in, and there'd be all this excitement, this sense of potential. Possibilities. But it was all a lie, a fairy tale my mother told herself."

"And you," Max said, aching for the little girl she'd been, who'd found out way too early that not all fairy tales ended with happily ever after. Where the hell had her father been while this was going on?

"And me," she agreed. "But after a while, I stopped believing her when she'd tell me this time, this guy—he was going to go the distance. Mom, though. She never stopped believing it, no matter how many times her heart got stomped on."

The puzzle pieces slotted into place, flawlessly, as if

they'd always been there. "You don't want to be like her," Max said, pushing away from the headboard and prowling toward Jules.

She tensed at his approach, but didn't run. Max decided to count that as a win. "I'm nothing like her," Jules swore, eyes flashing. "I don't want the same things she wanted from life—some man to come along and make everything perfect for me, take care of me. Thanks, but no thanks."

Max knelt beside her huddled form and lifted a slow, cautious hand to the tangled silk of her hair. "I don't know what drove your mother," he said, "but it doesn't make you guilty of her same mistakes if you admit to wanting something for yourself."

"Like what?" she asked suspiciously, even as she leaned into his gentle touch.

Max hid a smile. "Like friendship. Hot sex. A guy who'd die before he let you down."

Like love.

The thought came to him unbidden, and once it was in his mind, he couldn't unthink it. Blinking rapidly, he pushed through the earthquake of his emotions and continued. "You know, regular relationship stuff. Good ones do exist; my parents are proof of that."

The line of her shoulders, which had tensed for a moment, relaxed at that. She turned her face into his palm, the skin of her cheek warm and satiny against his fingers. "Your parents. I've never met anyone like them. The way they took me in . . ." She trailed off, shoulders folding in again, and Max frowned. They needed to get past this.

Sitting down and pulling her unresisting body to rest against his chest, between his spread legs, Max gave himself one heartbeat to enjoy the trusting way she flowed into him before he started talking.

"I went to Japan to learn about ramen. They're nuts for noodles over there, and I'd eaten so many amazing bowls

of ramen that I couldn't wait to find out how to make it."
He laughed a little, remembering. "Turns out, ramen isn't
so much a dish as it is a way of life, intimately tied to the
Japanese culture. Most of the masters I spoke to laughed
in my face—they thought it was hilarious that a Westerner
would even attempt to learn the ways of ramen. Then finally, at a tiny noodle shop in Tokyo, I found a man willing to teach me his art. I've lived there for eight months,
and Harukai-sensei taught me as much about life as he did
about noodles. He's a Zen master."

Jules stirred against his chest. "I love hearing about
your adventures abroad," she said. "But I'm not getting
the connection . . ."

"Yeah. See, the thing about Zen is, it's all about the now.
Being truly present in the moment, living that moment as if
you'll never get another one—and as if it's the first you've
ever had. When I got to Harukai-sensei's shop almost a
year ago, I was still carrying around so much anger and
bitterness, it was like a second backpack clinging to my
shoulders, stuffed with bricks and cement instead of spare
jeans and a toothbrush." Max swallowed. She knew some
of this already, so why should it be this hard to say it now?
"I'd fought with my father, you see. After graduation. I
wanted more responsibility at Lunden's, more say in what
we served and more opportunities to test out my newly
minted culinary credentials. But Dad wasn't into that, and
I—well, you know what I did. I took off."

She pulled away, making his heart clench hard in his
chest, but it was only so she could turn enough to face
him. Her eyes were serious, deep pools of aged Scotch. "I
understand why you left. And I know it wasn't easy for
you. We don't have to talk about this again, if you don't
want."

"No, I need to explain," Max said, gratitude for her
understanding rushing through him. "Because all that re-

sentment and anger I was dragging behind me, it was warping me. Changing me into someone I didn't even recognize. And Harukai-sensei, a complete stranger, saw that. He refused to teach me about ramen until I learned about Zen. Once I knew enough to be able to accept the suffering of the past and live in the moment, that's when the lessons started."

Max tilted his head back, the taste of the hot, salty dashi, redolent of sea brine and rich with melted pork fat, as real in his mouth as his teeth and tongue. "God, that first bowl of ramen I made with my own hands," he whispered. "It was incredible. Not because it was so perfect—it wasn't, the noodles clumped and I overcooked the strips of pork in the broth—but it tasted like freedom. For the first time since I left home, I found what I'd been looking for. And it wasn't freedom from my dad and his stubborn insistence on clinging to the old ways. It was freedom from myself, from my own anger at him."

Jules moved back into his arms, throwing her legs over his to wrap around his hips. "And now that you're home again?"

Max laughed. The back of his head itched where Harukai-sensei used to thwap him with a wooden spoon to get his attention. "Being home—it may have strained my Zen poise a bit. I'm working on that, and I wasn't finished with my training when Mom called me back here. That's part of what made it so tough to leave Japan. But Harukai-sensei was all for it—he wanted me to go home. Anyway, that's not the point. The point of all this is—"

"Live in the now," Jules interrupted, her eyes shining as she touched her nose to his and twined her arms around his neck. "Enjoy the present."

Max sucked in a breath at the way her soft, round breasts swayed against his chest, the tight buds of her nipples drawing up hard and pointed.

"Experience the moment fully," he said thickly, gripping the curve of her hips and pulling her even closer.

"And to do that, you have to let go of the past . . . and the future," Jules said, determination firming her mouth into a rosebud he just had to kiss.

She opened for him at once, slick and sweet and fresh as spring water. The last thing Max remembered thinking before desire tugged him down and had its way with him was that Jules was beautiful when she'd made up her mind to be happy.

Chapter 20

Let go of the past, forget about the future.

It could be her new mantra, Jules decided as she and Max strolled up Barrow Street toward Lunden's Tavern.

Easier said than done, maybe, but she was highly motivated.

No more waffling, no more internal debate. And if she could swing it, she'd be giving the fear and self-doubt a pass from now on, too, because Max was right. The past was gone. The future was unknown. The present was all the mattered, all she could count on.

And maybe that was the true lesson she should've learned at her mother's knee. Because no matter how many times Victoria Cavanaugh's love affairs flamed out in a burning explosion of recriminations, when she met a new man? Her mother was one of the happiest people Jules had ever known.

Maybe Jules wanted more than her mother's brief flings and bitter regrets, but she wasn't going to get it by taking herself out of the game and letting life rush past her in a glittering river of wasted potential.

Max was whistling through his teeth, a jaunty tune that

for a moment sounded like the exotic strains of some Indian love song, until it resolved itself into a melody Jules abruptly recognized.

"Hey! That's one of Kane Slater's songs!"

The whistle died as if someone had punched Max in the solar plexus. He turned to her, dismay clear on his handsome face. "Oh God. I've been infected. It's the rock sensation that's sweeping the nation, the Texas Hill Country invasion, the—"

"I can't wait to tell Winslow," Jules said, rubbing her hands gleefully and quickening her steps.

"No!" Max wailed behind her.

She had one hand on the restaurant door when he grabbed for her, his strong hands gentle on her waist as he yanked her back against him. "You can't do that, I'll never live it down."

"Maybe I'll get you a subscription to *Teen People*," she gasped through her giggles. "For your next birthday."

If you're even still around then. The thought floated into her head, freezing her in place for a painful instant.

Hmm. Apparently letting go of the past was easier than ditching her worries about the future.

Max growled and tugged her in close, stealing one last kiss before they went inside. Jules gave herself up to it, welcoming the hot slide and thrust of his tongue, the solid, undeniable strength of his body against hers. It was a handy distraction from her thoughts.

Live in this moment, she reminded herself, kissing him back with everything she had.

A long, low wolf whistle pulled them apart. Jules caught her breath, already feeling her cheeks heating, as she turned to confront the unabashedly amused face of her youngest teammate.

Winslow wiggled his fingers at them, hitching his knife

roll higher on his shoulder. "Well, well. Looks like some-one's having a very good morning, indeed."

Jules tensed—the habit of hiding was hard to break, and these people had all been around for her last stupid kitchen fling—but Max reached out one big paw and did that complicated fist-bumping, palm-slapping greeting with Win, as cool as anything.

"Hey, man," he said easily. "How was your night? You get home from Chapel okay?"

"Hmm, yes," Win said, his bright green gaze darting back and forth between them. "I managed to secure an escort home. One can't be too careful, out wandering the streets alone at night."

Jules forced herself to relax. The familiar comfort of Win's teasing about his sexual escapades helped. "So can we assume you had a good morning, too?"

"Well." He smiled smugly. "A good night, anyway."

"Good enough to make you almost as late as us," Max said. "Come on, we'd better get inside before Danny's head explodes."

He held the door open, ushering Jules and Winslow in ahead of him. Win curled his arm into the crook of her el-bow and leaned close enough to whisper, "Oh girl. Please tell me you're going to be dishing up the good stuff, be-cause I have got to know what's up with you and our boy."

"I'll give you the whole scoop, with a cherry on top," she muttered back, grateful for Win's simple, jubi-lant acceptance. She had a feeling things wouldn't be so uncomplicated with Danny. "But later. I promise. Maybe after the meeting . . ."

"Nope, sorry," Max said, coming up behind them to wrap his arms around her shoulders. "You're gonna be busy later. Win, she'll call you. Maybe next week sometime."

Jules could hear the grin in his voice, although most of

her attention was taken up with the feel of his hard body pressed to her back.

"Damn, stud," Win laughed. "Where can I find me one of you?"

"Well, I've got a brother," Max said contemplatively. "But something tells me he's not what you're looking for."

"Or vice versa," Win agreed with a heartfelt sigh.

"Are you talking about me?" Danny looked up from the pastry board, suspicion written clearly across his face.

"Just bemoaning your tragic heterosexuality," Win sighed, slinging his knives down on the prep station.

"Oh," Danny said, blinking. "Well. Sorry about that, but there's not much I can do about it."

Win waved that away. "No big. I'm not that into work-place romance, myself."

"Unlike some people, apparently," Danny replied, eyes narrowing on Max's arms, still slung around Jules.

She stilled, paralyzed by the sudden silence. Winslow gave her an encouraging smile, while Beck stepped back from his station far enough to be able to check out the commotion at the front of the kitchen.

Gus was over by the ovens, bouncing on the soles of his feet, obviously impatient to get the meeting started. But at Danny's comment, he paused.

This was it. The moment where Jules got to decide whether to keep to the shadows, or step into the light. Meeting the worried gaze of the man who was more of a father to her than anyone her mother had ever brought home, Jules tilted her head and gave Max a very deliberate kiss on the cheek.

She could feel him dimple up under her lips, and he hugged her tighter for a second before she shrugged him off and shooed him over to his corner.

Head buzzing with the nervy thrill of staking her claim on Max Lunden in front of half his family and all the people they worked with—oh God—Jules lifted her chin and crossed her arms over her chest.

She'd made her choice; she'd live with the consequences.

Which, for the moment, included Gus clearing his throat uncomfortably and shifting his weight from side to side. "Um," he said. "Well. So we're all here now. That's . . . good."

"Here, and ready to work, Dad." Max unrolled his canvas bag and removed the knife Jules knew was his favorite, a short, Japanese-style cleaver called a *chuka bochu*. The sound of him running the sharp edge of the knife along a honing steel rang through the short silence that followed.

Gus shook his shoulders back, the slight bewilderment clearing from his expression, and Jules relaxed.

"Right. That's good, because we've got our work cut out for us. As I said last night, I couldn't be more proud of you—all of you—for getting through the qualifying round. I know it wasn't easy. But the fact is, it's only going to get tougher from here on out. The pressure's really on."

He paused, glancing from chef to chef. Jules straightened her spine when his gaze landed on her. It felt like that first day of working at Lunden's Tavern all over again, that spike of warmth and affection, nearly sharp enough to slice through her need to prove herself.

Nearly, but not quite.

"We got the word this morning," Gus continued. "The final round to choose the East Coast team, the lucky sons of bitches who get to compete in this year's Rising Star Chef competition, is all about being local."

"What does that mean?" Danny asked, frowning.

"It means we gotta prove we know this area better than anybody else, and we gotta cook our hearts out to do it. Listen, here's the deal. The four finalist teams are going to face off in a cooking challenge—a five-course meal made from ingredients sourced exclusively from the Essex Street Market. We've got tonight to plan, then two days to prep and cook, serving the judges the day after tomorrow."

"Cutting it close," Beck observed. His gruff tone somehow conveyed the certainty that there was another twist coming, and Jules felt a tingle of anxiety skitter down her spine.

"Oh, but wait! That's not all!" Everybody blinked, heads swiveling from Gus to Winslow, who had piped up before their boss could get another word out. "I mean . . . tell them what I mean, Chef."

"Okay, leaving aside the mystery of how exactly Winslow knows the content of the challenge, when the team sponsors were only contacted this morning," Gus said, quirking one bushy brow, "he's not wrong."

Jules sent her station mate an arched eyebrow. "Sounds like I'm not the only one who needs to dish," she murmured.

Sometime in his short, eventful life, Winslow Jones had perfected the art of winking without moving a single muscle in his face other than the one eyelid. "Remember my gallant escort home last night?"

Jules nodded quickly.

"Let's just say, he may have an inside scoop on the RSC. Because he may or may not be the assistant to a member of the culinary council. Whose name may or may not rhyme with Beeva Smansen. And that's all I'm going to say."

Jules suppressed the laugh that wanted to snort out through her nose. "You're the soul of discretion," she said.

"Ahem." Gus beetled his bushy brows at them. "Before this entire conversation devolves into yet another discussion of Winslow's love life, maybe you'd like to hear the details of the challenge? Hmm? Unless that's boring. I could just go take a nap instead."

"We're listening, Dad." Danny could be very soothing when he wanted to be, Jules reflected. "Go ahead."

Puffing out his chest, Gus assumed his teaching stance. "What can you kids tell me about the Essex Street Market?"

"Umm . . . it's an indoor market on the Lower East Side?" Win offered apologetically.

"Right. What else?"

Max drummed his fingers on the stainless steel counter. "It's been around a long time," he said. "Since the forties, I think. And it's gone through a lot of incarnations, but at the moment, it's the permanent home of some of the city's best produce, meat, and fish vendors."

Pride gleamed in Gus's quick smile. "That's right. It used to be two buildings, but when the city took it over and started trying to revitalize it after the glut of supermarkets hit in the seventies, they consolidated all the vendors into a single building. Take a look at this map."

Unrolling a large sheet of paper, Gus beckoned them all to gather around the butcher block as he spread it out. Jules leaned over to get a better view, every inch of her aware of the fact that Max had stepped up behind her and was looking over her shoulder.

"The judges couriered this over about an hour ago," Gus said. "It's a map of the Essex Street Market. Notice anything in particular about it?"

Her pulse jumped when Max's hands settled large and warm on her hips. Shifting her weight back, she brought her heel down on Max's toes, bare and vulnerable since he was wearing scuffed leather flip-flops. Max made a noise like a chicken laying an egg, but when he backed off, he pinched the undercurve of Jules's ass.

She squeaked, glared, and pointedly moved around to the other side of the table to stand next to Beck, who was studying the market map as if it were the diagnostics of a bomb he had to disarm in the next thirty seconds.

"Well?" Gus said, bouncing on the balls of his feet. "What do you see?"

Beck reached one long arm to point out the four corners of the map. "Access here, here, and there. The perimeter appears to house most of the specialty product—I see a chocolatier, a couple of cheese shops—while the main vendors are in the center."

He drew invisible lines around the four large squares down the middle of the map. Jules scrutinized the layout closely. Each square was divided between two vendors, one with fruits and vegetables, and one selling proteins like meat or fish.

"If I had to make a guess," Beck said, "I'd say the judges plan to divvy up the market between the four teams; give each of us one of the center squares, along with the specialty shops in that same area."

"Good guess," Winslow crowed. "You're a master tactician, my man, because that is exactly what . . . I mean." He faltered under Gus's glare, wilting like a head of butter lettuce on a hot day.

"Yes," Gus growled. "They're slicing the market into four equal pieces, and everything we cook for our five-course meal has to come from our specific area."

"So which is our quadrant?" Max asked, peering down at the names of the vendors. Gus raised his eyebrows at Winslow, who looked up at the ceiling and pretended not to notice. "I was told we'd be sourcing our meal from section number three, right here."

They all leaned in.

"Viva Fruits and Vegetables, New Star Fish Market," Danny read aloud. Then he whooped with joy, pumping a fist into the air and startling the whole team. "Yes! We got the chocolate shop. Roni-Sue's chocolate rocks. I can do a lot with that."

"Which brings us to the next point," Gus said, wiping

at his forehead. Jules watched him, a bolt of concern shooting through her when she saw how pale he was. "Each chef on the team will be responsible for a single dish, but the meal has to be cohesive and make some kind of sense, because we'll be judged as a team. Obviously Danny's on dessert, but we need to brainstorm the menu and figure out who wants to make what. We've got tonight to plan, tomorrow to shop and prep, then cook and serve the following day."

"Maybe we should take a quick field trip," Max suggested. "Check this market out; it's been years since I was there. See what product we're going to be working with so we know exactly what our options are."

"Waste of time," Gus said dismissively as he rolled the map back up. "We've only got one day to plan this meal; we don't have time to go running all over the city. We need to focus."

Jules frowned. That didn't sound like Gus; he was usually so detail oriented, and hated cutting corners. "Chef? Are you feeling okay?"

"I'm fine," he said irritably. "Except for being sick to death of people asking me that."

"Don't worry," Max said, sauntering back to his station with his hands in his pockets. His short brown hair was still roughed up on one side, making him look like an angry hedgehog. "Dad's perfectly all right. He just won't take the suggestion because it came from me." He hitched one hip onto the counter behind him, all idle grace and mockery. "Wouldn't want to encourage me to think I had an actual say in things around here, would we?"

Tension settled over the kitchen like a cloud of smoke billowing from a hot oven. Win hunched his shoulders, Beck stared off into the middle distance, and Jules fought the urge to shuffle her feet. Danny looked ready to haul off and smack someone.

"Oh, for the love of . . . I can't believe you're bringing this up again!" Gus threw up his hands. "Grow up, Maxwell."

Max's face flushed. "The fact that I won't fall in line and do things the way you think they should be done doesn't mean I'm some snot-nosed kid, rebelling against authority. We need to see what's available, let ourselves be inspired by the ingredients."

"Inspired." Gus sneered. There went that vein in his forehead. "What, you gonna do some kind of interpretive dance around the kitchen? Maybe write some poetry? Sing us a song? Or you could maybe just settle the hell down and be a damn chef. Besides, we already know what we're going to base the meal on. Steak, because that's what we do best, and we want to highlight Lunden's Tavern."

"Steak! Of course, that's what you want to make. So fucking predictable—"

"Cut it out, Max," Danny said, shifting angrily. "We don't have time for this. Let's just make a plan and go with it."

Max put his hands on his hips, his jaw like granite. "Fine. I say we go down to the Essex Street Market and look around for an hour before coming back up here to plan. All in favor?"

Jules stiffened. She couldn't believe it was coming down to this. They'd been doing so well, ignoring the tension and the lingering hurt feelings over why Max left in the first place. She should've known, though.

Jules understood, better than most, that not talking or thinking about your crappy past didn't mean you were over it.

But she hadn't been prepared to ever have to choose between Max and his father. No matter which way she turned, she'd be letting down someone she cared about.

Max looked at Danny, who cast a quick glance at his

father before looking down at his black leather kitchen clogs. "I know what Roni-Sue usually offers; I'm probably okay to plan without checking it out in person."

"Good boy," Gus said approvingly.

Max absorbed the blow with his lips folded together tightly, a watchful stillness falling over him like a white linen tablecloth settling over a four-top.

Beck, who'd watched the whole argument with his arms impassively crossed over his massive chest, calmly raised one hand. "I want to see what they've got fresh down there before I come up with my dish."

Scrunching his face up so tightly that his freckles stood out like sprinkles of cinnamon on his café au lait skin, Winslow said, "I'm good, either way. Um, maybe more time to plan wouldn't be a bad thing. I don't know."

So it was a tie.

A fierce light of hope glinted in Max's eyes when he turned to Jules, burning bright enough to make her want to look away. But that was no good, because if she shifted her gaze, she saw Gus standing alone at the front of the kitchen, the weight of his expectations heavier than a stockpot filled with boiling water.

"Jules."

That was all Gus said, just her name, but she heard everything he wasn't saying. She heard the affection and pride he felt in her; she heard the unshakable faith in her loyalty. And she wanted nothing more than to prove him right . . . but the problem was, she didn't think he was right.

Not about this.

"Come on, Jules." Max's voice was low, intense. "You don't have to follow along just because Danny always falls in line. You're the team leader. We'll go with whatever you decide."

She looked at him helplessly, her shoulders hunching

up in an instinctive defensive move that must have looked
like a shrug, because his gaze went flat and opaque.

Gus said, "I taught Jules to be a team player, Max. Too
bad you never learned that lesson."

The satisfaction in his voice made Jules cringe a little.
"I'm sorry," she said, feeling ripped down the middle like
a page torn out of a cookbook. "But I agree with Max. We
need to know exactly what we're dealing with, or our
choices for what to make for the judges are way too lim-
ited."

She couldn't look him in the eye, so she turned back to
Max. Triumph mixed with joy blazed across his face,
making his eyes glow like moonstones.

"Okay, gang, let's head out. I want to get this done in
one hour so we have plenty of time to plot."

It was a sad commentary on the state of things in the
kitchen, Jules thought, that the oppressively wet heat of
New York City in July was preferable to the atmosphere
at Lunden's. But everyone leaped at the chance to escape
the thickening friction of the kitchen, gathering their
things and heading outside, even Danny.

Everyone except Gus. Jules paused in the act of following Max through the dining room doors.

The executive chef of Lunden's Tavern stood alone in
his kitchen, looking somehow depleted. Smaller. It hurt
her heart to see him that way.

"Chef? Aren't you coming with us?"

Gus kept his gaze on the map of Essex Street Market,
still clutched in his hand. "No need," he said. "I trust you
to report back to me, Jules. Besides." He smiled faintly.
"Someone's got to hold down the fort and start prepping
for lunch service."

Guilt scoured her nerves. "I could stay with you and
help out," she offered, moving to put her bag back under

her station. "The others can fill me in on what's available at Essex Street."

"No, no, you go ahead," he said, snagging a clean apron off a hook on the wall. "I'm just going to butcher some steaks; kind of a one-man job, and I could do it in my sleep. Thanks, though. You're a trouper, Jules."

She nodded, turning to follow the others, but before she'd made it two steps, Gus's low voice stopped her.

"You're a good girl, too, and you've come to mean . . . well, you're like family, Jules. And that's why I've got to say this, as much as it pains me—but you need to stay away from my son."

Chapter 21

Jules tried to breathe through the sucker punch.

I knew it, this was a mistake. The Lundens could never accept me as a real part of the family, I don't even know what "family" means, or how to be part of one— Stop it! With an effort, she got a grip on her galloping emotions.

"I know it could be bad for the team," she managed.

"No, no," Gus protested. "Well, actually, yeah. It could really throw things out of whack when it all goes kablooey. Like when we had to fire Phil because he stopped following your orders in the kitchen! What a mess that was. But we got Beck out of it, so all's well that ends well. My main point is, Jules—with Max, kablooey isn't a maybe. It's a definite."

"What?"

Shaking his head, Gus said, "I love my son, but he's no good for you. No good for anyone, at least not until he figures himself out and learns how to spend more than a month under one roof. He's not going to stick around once we get picked as the East Coast team—that was the deal all along. He's got the chance to learn the art of butchery from one of the greatest living masters, and he's going to take it. Hell, if I were his age, I'd probably take it, too! But I hate that it means you could get hurt, kiddo."

Jules blinked. Gus wasn't objecting to her as a significant other for Max. It was the other way around.

This must be what it felt like to have a protective father, watching out for you and worrying about you. She smiled, because the other alternative was bursting into humiliating sobs. "Gus. Thank you. It means . . . more than I can say, that you care enough to warn me about Max. But believe me, I've got my eyes wide open. I see your son clearly, and you know what? I like what I see. He's a good man, better than you give him credit for."

Gus's expression closed down, locking her out. "You think so? I know my son like I know myself, and the way you're looking at him lately, I'm pretty sure he's not ready for that."

Embarrassment scorched red hot down the back of Jules's neck. She wasn't used to being obvious. "Gus, we're just starting this thing, whatever it is," she choked out. "We're paddling around in the shallow end, I promise. I'm not about to drown."

"Bullshit," he said bluntly. "You think I didn't see you at the qualifiers? This 'whatever' with Max had you so turned around, you could barely talk. And the expression on your face . . ." He shook his head, pressing his lips into a hard line. "I haven't seen you look like that since the first night I made you hot chocolate."

Jules's lungs knotted up like a tangle of overdone pasta. Through the pounding in her ears, she became aware of movement behind her, a slight shift of the dining room door that sent her pulse into overdrive.

Oblivious to Jules's struggle to breathe, Gus went on. "You had the exact same look of fear behind those pretty brown eyes that you had up there on that stage yesterday. It's the same fear I see every time you look at Max—and it sends me right back to that night when you wandered in here out of the cold and snow, alone, exhausted . . . and with the beginnings of the worst shiner I ever saw in my life."

Max froze in place, his father's voice going through him like a thrust from a samurai sword, so sharp he didn't feel the pain for several seconds.

Stay away from my son.

His own father. God, he knew they had their problems, but for his dad to try to actually undermine the first real relationship Max had ever fought for—it hurt.

Max immediately wanted to burst into the kitchen and confront the man, demand to know how he could say something like that, but . . . what could he really argue? The pride in Gus's voice as he reminded Jules of the apprenticeship in Le Marche warmed something deep in Max's chest, even as the implications he'd managed to ignore for so long sank in.

He was leaving. Jules knew it, had known it from the start. She'd tried her best not to get involved, but Max, relentless as ever once he'd set his sights on a goal, had ignored her reservations. He'd pushed and prodded and cajoled and seduced—and now he had to face the fact that he'd done all of that for a relationship that could only last a few short weeks.

He'd convinced himself, believed down to his bones, that it didn't take a promise of years together to create something meaningful between two people. That the connection he and Jules felt was good and right, even if it wasn't destined to be forever.

Had he been fooling himself?

The conversation went on and Max paused, one fist pressed to his stomach. And when Jules defended him . . . a knot Max didn't know he'd been carrying around in his chest loosened, and a flood of emotion surged into his heart.

His father's next words ratcheted Max's runaway emotions up to a new level.

What? Someone gave Jules a black eye?

"That was a long time ago," she was saying. "Not everything in my life is about that anymore."

"So I noticed," Gus said, his voice tight with something that sounded like pain. "Since you went against me, after everything I taught you and did for you, to side with your boyfriend."

Jules sounded almost as short of breath as Gus when she answered. "I sided with Max because he was right, not because we're . . . involved. And if you weren't such a stubborn old ass, you'd be able to admit that you know it, too. I love you, Gus, but you're wrong."

The sound of footsteps nearing the doors had Max sidling back through the dining room and out onto the street mere seconds before Jules emerged.

She looked unbearably young, eyes snapping with darts of pain, dark gold hair streaming out behind her. He'd distracted her from braiding it back this morning, with a strategic openmouthed kiss to the side of her neck, and when she came to a stop beside him, her silky hair brushed his bare arm below the sleeve of his threadbare HELLO, KITTY T-shirt.

"Let's go," she said, all terse and commanding.

Max searched her face, trying to imagine how she'd look with bruises and fear marring her clear, perfect skin.

"Okay, gang," Winslow cried, bounding forward. "Looks like we're off to see the wizard!"

He led the crew down the block toward the West Fourth Street subway station. Jules dropped back to say a few quiet words to Danny, but within minutes, she'd reappeared at Max's side.

He glanced over at her, noting the lines of stress bracketing her wide, mobile mouth. "You okay, sweetness?"

She did a quick, full-body shiver, like a duck shaking
water off its back, and Max felt slim, strong fingers twin-
ing with his. He looked down at their joined hands in surprise.

"I am now," she said, a slow smile chasing the shadows
from her eyes.

Max did a quick inventory. Humidity thick enough to
remind him of Saigon and make the thin material of his
shirt stick to his back. A five-course meal to plan that
would make or break their chances to compete. The worst
fight he'd had with his father since he left home six years
ago.

Jules's hand in his, her quiet presence a reassurance
that, for once, someone had sided with Max.

He grinned and swung their hands in a high arc as
they swarmed down the concrete steps with the rest of the
commuters, entering the dim, oppressively hot confines
of the subway station.

Max couldn't remember ever being happier, even with
the specter of his trip to Italy looming over his head. He
should take his own advice and celebrate every precious
second with Jules.

Now if he could just get her to open up and tell him
exactly what happened the night she turned up at his parents' house, and ended up as part of the family.

It took the entire hot, crowded subway ride for Jules to
calm down from her confrontation with Gus.

The air-conditioning wasn't working, which turned
their subway car into a bullet-shaped oven, broiler going
full blast. Jules's fingers slipped on the metal pole as they
swayed around a curve in the tunnel, and Max was right
there to brace her.

When she leaned back, trusting some of her weight to

his steady, spread-legged stance, Max couldn't help but smile. Even in a heat that reminded him of the noonday Marrakech marketplace, he wanted nothing more than to press Jules close to his sticky, sweaty skin and feel her breathing against him.

The noise of the subway car rattling along the tracks made it hard to hear the conversation of the other chefs around them. It was almost as if Max and Jules were enclosed in their own isolated bubble. Private.

Somehow, that made it easier for Max to put his mouth next to her ear and say, "Thanks for what you said back there."

"You were right," she told him.

"Still. I know it wasn't easy for you to go against Dad like that."

She wriggled, and Max reluctantly loosened his hold to allow her to brace her back against the pole running through the middle of the subway car.

"No, it wasn't," she said, looking Max in the eye. He could see exactly how much she meant every word she said. "Because your father is pretty much the only father I've ever known, and his opinion means a lot to me. A whole hell of a lot."

Max nodded. A spasm tightened the muscles in his jaw into a painful, molar-grinding knot. "Jules . . . you don't have to tell me, but I know your mother had a lot of . . . male friends. Was your biological father around at all?"

The train lurched to the right, nearly sending them all toppling. By the time Jules righted herself, she'd covered the instant flare of pain Max had caught in her eyes when he asked the question.

Max regained his footing and hauled her up against him, steadying her as she replied, "Nope. Never met the guy. He left before I was born. Told my mom he had itchy feet, and wandered off for parts unknown, searching for something. Maybe the cure for athlete's foot. Who knows? Anyway, he wasn't around."

He felt the impact of that description all the way down to his toes. Voice catching, he managed to say, "That must have sucked."

She shrugged, a quick twitch of the shoulders that made him notice the tension in his own neck. "It is what it is. Not like I'm crying into my pillow every night for some loser who couldn't be bothered to stick around long enough to see his kid born."

Feeling his way, Max ventured, "It would be okay if you . . . I don't know. Missed him. Or felt sad about it."

Jules gazed at him, her whiskey-gold eyes as ancient and worn as an antique coin. "People leave. That's life. All crying about it will get you is bunch of wet tissues and a headache."

Max stared back at her, everything in his body suspended like a shipwreck survivor clinging to a life raft. He was afraid to blink, afraid to break the tremulous safety of their surface conversation and dive down into the depths of what they were really talking about.

"Anyway," Jules said. Her smile wasn't the least bit convincing, but he had to give it to her. She stuck with it. "Who has time to worry about ancient history? We should be coming up with ideas on this five-course meal we're supposed to create."

Max seized on the change of subject with a gasp of relief, as if he'd been holding his breath for the last five minutes. "I've got about a zillion ideas. That's kind of the problem, narrowing it down . . ."

But even as he relaxed into the familiar excitement of brainstorming a menu and planning what exciting techniques he could showcase, Max couldn't keep his mind from drowning in the knowledge that when his four weeks were up and his post in Italy came available, Max would be doing to Jules exactly what her father had.

He'd leave. Like he always did.

And for once in his life, Max wished, with a fervent passion that felt like fiery hot peppers burning through his chest, that he'd worried a little more about the future.

Maybe a life lived with only a thought for the present wasn't enough anymore.

Chapter 22

Claire Durand absently smoothed a hand over the knife-edge crease down the front of her crisp white slacks and very deliberately did not think about the fact that she'd chosen to dress casually for the judges' meeting she'd called that morning.

Bon. She shrugged. Casually for her, at least.

Very possibly, her cojudges wouldn't find linen pants and a red and blue striped bateau-neck top to be terribly casual. Kane Slater probably thought ripped denims and scuffed cowboy boots were appropriate dinner wear.

She pursed her lips, annoyed at herself. Kane Slater had been popping into her thoughts with alarming frequency since she'd met him. It was unacceptable, and more than a little embarrassing, to find herself unable to control her wayward thoughts of the golden young man.

Straightening in her seat, Claire crossed her legs and checked her watch. If Monsieur Cartier was to be believed, her cojudges were both late.

Even as she rearranged her brows—their tardiness, while aggravating, was no reason to suffer the indignity of wrinkles—she spotted the object of her recent musings making his slow, slouchy way across the crowded café toward her table.

Yawning hugely, Kane Slater dropped into the chair opposite Claire and gave her a sleepy smile. His golden hair stuck up in improbable tufts all over his head, except for the left side, where it was mashed flat.

She blinked. Either she was not as au courant as she thought when it came to style, or he'd neglected to prepare for this meeting in any way other than to roll out of bed and throw on the rattiest pair of madras-patterned shorts he could find. Paired, naturally, with the same black sweatshirt he'd worn the day before. This time he'd left the hood down, however, perhaps to better display his impressive bed head.

There was no logical reason why the sight of those messy blond tangles should make Claire's lower body swim with warm desire, but then, who could claim to be purely rational when it came to attraction?

Evidently not Claire Durand.

"Morning," the boy slurred, the music of his voice gone rough and deep, like the throbbing tones of a double bass.

"It's one o'clock," she informed him frostily, emphasizing the word "one." She'd called the meeting for twelve-thirty.

"Man. No wonder I need coffee so bad," he groaned, twisting in his chair and holding up a hand to call over the waitress.

They were at Café Noir, Claire's favorite coffee shop on the Upper East Side, a short walk from the Délicieux offices. She liked it because it reminded her of the places she used to go in Paris, with lots of little round tables crammed together, brisk, no-nonsense wait staff, and bracingly strong espresso.

Claire was distracted from watching the way Slater's wide, dimpled grin charmed a grudging smile out of a waitress who'd never even nodded hello at Claire in all the years she'd frequented the establishment, by the trilling of her cell phone.

Thumbing it on, she scanned the text message from Devon Sparks's wife and newly appointed keeper, Lilah, and pursed her mouth in annoyance.

So sorry for sched mixup, DS doing live interview w/ NY1, can't make meeting. DS says sorry, promises to dock my pay. :)

Well, perhaps it was for the best. Claire had wanted a chance to speak to Kane Slater alone.

Alone? Mais oui, her inner seductress purred, but Claire cut the ridiculous thought short in time to blink innocently at Slater when he turned back to the table, having secured a double-shot cappuccino with extra foam, a croissant, and the undying devotion of the waitress. And quite possibly her panties, as well; Claire hadn't been watching closely enough to know for certain.

At least I'm not the only woman of a certain age to find him inconveniently appealing.

"Where's Devon?" Slater asked.

"Giving an interview to the local television station that covers New York City metro news. Which reminds me . . ."

She whipped out her phone and texted Lilah back.

Tell your truant husband he'd better mention the RSC competition, if he knows what's good for him. So long as he works in a reference to Délicieux *sponsoring it, all is forgiven.*

It took time to thumb-type the whole message, but Claire refused to employ the ridiculous abbreviations most people used.

Another sign that you're getting old and set in your ways, the voice in her head snarked.

"So it's the two of us," Slater remarked, leaning back in his chair. His lids were heavy over the ridiculously clear ocean blue of his eyes, giving him the look of a man who'd just risen from his bed, and would happily fall back into it at a moment's notice.

Claire swallowed a mental picture of a particular woman accompanying Slater back to his bed . . . a woman who happened to have long, chestnut hair just beginning to show threads of silver.

"In fact, that's exactly what I wish to speak to you about," she told him, forcing steel into her words and gaze. "This ridiculous flirtation . . . it must stop, Mr. Slater."

"You sound like my high school history teacher when you call me that."

Suppressing a pang of horror at the comparison, Claire replied, "I can only imagine she wished to convey, as I do, the appropriate distance that should exist between people in our position."

He blinked slowly, like a cat in sunlight. "Wow. You sound so . . . American."

Claire stiffened. "I can't think what you mean."

Slater tore a piece off the end of his croissant, flaking buttery bits of pastry all over the table. "Prim. Proper. Puritanical. And possibly other alliterative terms I can't think of until I finish the first cup of coffee."

Genuinely insulted, Claire snapped back, "How typical to assume my attitude has nothing to do with the subject matter—namely, you."

"Baloney," Slater said bluntly, after swallowing his mouthful of croissant.

At least he doesn't speak with his mouth full.

"If it were only about me coming on to you," Slater continued, pointing the pastry at her, "then you wouldn't have gotten annoyed when I smiled at that woman chef from Lunden's."

"And that's another thing!" Claire leaped on the chance to redirect the conversation. "You cannot flirt with the chef contestants. Absolutely no. It is strictly forbidden, and for very good and obvious reasons."

"I haven't flirted with any contestants," he protested, shredding more croissant in his agitation. At this rate, there would be nothing left for him to eat.

"Please," she scoffed. "That question you asked, about female chefs and the Michelin stars. You targeted it directly to that Lunden's Tavern woman, don't pretend to me that you did not!"

"Okay, fine," Slater conceded, abandoning his ragged croissant to blow the steam from the surface of his coffee. "I hoped she'd know the answer; she was struggling, and I felt bad for her. But it was a totally legit question. Anyone, from either team, could've picked it up. I didn't feed her the answer, and you know it. Quit dodging the issue."

"What issue?" Claire picked up her own coffee mug, pleased at the steadiness of her hand.

Kane Slater let all four legs of his chair touch down so he could lean both elbows on the table. "The issue is that we're attracted to each other. You don't want to be, but that doesn't change the fact that you are. And so am I. And it's against my philosophy to keep pretending I'm not."

It was suddenly difficult to catch her breath. "You are . . . very direct, Mr. Slater."

"Kane," he said, tilting his head insistently, his eyes intent on her face.

She filled her lungs with air. "Kane," she agreed without looking away. "All right. You make your point, and I won't disagree. Yes, I find you attractive, as do most women you encounter, I'm sure. It changes nothing."

"Are you nuts? It changes everything!" His voice had warmed and smoothed while they talked, his vocal chords waking up as the shots of espresso coursed through his body. Claire shivered. "Even if we never act on it, there will always be this electric charge between us, this knowledge, this potential. Inevitably, it will change things."

"You accused me of sounding American," Claire said, hiding behind her coffee mug once more. "But you're the one who fits that description, I think. American men, in my experience, are never content to allow life to take its course. They have always to be pushing. America is a very pushy nation, as a whole."

Truth be told, she loved that about her adopted country. Claire, herself, preferred to do rather than to sit idly by and comment ironically on the doings of others.

In romance, however . . . well. It wasn't as if she had energy or desire to devote herself to attending to someone else's fragile ego in her spare time. She did enough of that at work. No one could match a celebrity chef for ego, either in towering height or eggshell frailty.

Not that Slater was offering romance, exactly. Claire narrowed her eyes on the actual subject of her inner debate, who gave her a lazy grin. "So you're saying, if I bide my time and let the river flow across the rocks for a while, I'll eventually wear you down? Like the Grand Canyon."

Claire reached into the dark green Gucci purse that had been her first gift to herself upon being promoted to editor in chief of *Délicieux,* and pulled out her wallet. Tossing a twenty onto the table, she pushed back her chair and stood, intentionally positioning herself above him.

"What I say is that while I don't consider myself sexually inhibited, and I certainly don't think there's anything wrong with sex, it doesn't mean I make myself available to every man who catches my eye. You're attractive, certainly. I don't dispute this." She shrugged; it was more of an effort than usual to give the lift of her shoulders that perfectly casual, Gallic air. "But am I likely to lose all control of my body and my senses over you? No."

"No one has complete control of their senses," Slater

said, tipping his head back to gaze up at her. "That's what makes life such a kick."

He seemed perfectly at ease looking up at her, and Claire had the uncomfortable feeling that even leaning back in his seat, legs kicked out in front of him and arms curled up behind his head, Slater still managed to command the entire room. There was no denying his presence.

"Perhaps you've never dealt with an adult, experienced woman before," she said, "but I assure you, the choice is mine as to what I do with my desires, and I do not choose lightly." Drawn closer as if by the gravitational pull a planet had on one of its moons, Claire leaned in, placing one hand on the table for balance. "And I choose not to indulge myself with you. Do we understand one another, Mr. Slater?"

This close to him, she could see the glint of red in the short blond stubble sandpapering his cheeks. He was almost too pretty to be real—that lush mouth!—but the hardness of his jaw and the strength of his high, intelligent brow saved the masculinity of his face, giving him a rough-and-tumble look Claire never would've imagined could appeal to her.

"I understand," he said. "That you're worried about how it might look. So I'll swear to be the picture of decorum in public . . . if you promise to call me Kane from now on."

"Done," Claire said swiftly, holding out her hand to shake on the deal. She'd worry about the rest of his interpretation of her concerns later.

Slater—Kane—took her hand, but instead of shaking it or bending to kiss it as Devon Sparks had done, he turned it so that her palm was facing up. He traced one long, callus-tipped finger down the center of her palm, and smiled to himself. "A fire hand," he murmured. "Why am I not surprised?"

"Excuse me?" Claire said frigidly. Her hand was ablaze with tingling sensation everywhere he'd touched it, and her fingers twitched spasmodically, desperate to curl around her buzzing palm. But she held perfectly still, determined not to get into some sort of ridiculous tug-of-war over her own limb.

"A fire hand," he explained, still studying her palm. "Long palm, firm, warm skin . . . hm, very warm." He looked up at her, and his blue eyes seemed to gaze right into the center of her. "You're ambitious and creative—you see the world around you in all its beauty, and you want to conquer it and bend it to your will. To do that, you've repressed your true passionate nature, forcing the river of your desires into neat, tidy channels of pragmatism and practicality. You've denied your inner danger junkie way too long . . . and that's why you're attracted to me. I'm everything you think you shouldn't want and can't have."

Claire swayed on her feet, transfixed. His voice was like the beat of her own heart, pounding in her ears, drumlike and entrancing.

"But I'm telling you, Claire Durand," Kane said, letting go of her hand, "you can have me."

She blinked and the world rushed back in a cacophony of coffee orders, clattering china, and customers chatting. The strange spell was broken the instant he stopped touching her, and without hesitating, Claire scooped up her purse and made her escape.

"It's sort of like Grand Central Station," Winslow marveled, "but with fewer trains and more yummy free samples. Why, yes, ma'am, I would absolutely love to try your house-cured duck sausage!"

While Winslow chowed down, Max looked around to see if he could spot the rest of their crew.

The sea of people surging around in the high-ceilinged

warehouse space made Max nostalgic for the open-air markets of Asia, where he almost always stood head and shoulders above the crowd.

There! He caught a glimpse of Beck, the other tall member of the team, over by the huge case of cheese in front of Formaggio Essex. The dark head, hair half pulled back from his face in a short ponytail, bent down, presumably to examine some interesting brie more closely, and Max lost sight of him.

But with a whistle and a head jerk to Winslow, Max was already on the move.

They'd split up on entering the Essex Street Market, scattering in different directions like sparks from the fireworks on Chinese New Year. There was a lot to see and explore down the aisles of food vendors—cheeses from around the world as well as specimens from local dairies; organically grown peaches and tomatoes from farms in upstate New York nestled side by side with cassava melons and yucca roots flown in from Mexico.

Every aisle was crammed with shoppers, who were as eclectic a bunch as the produce they haggled over.

Max dodged a guy with a toxic green mohawk and skinny black jeans just in time to push through a crowd of squat, gray-haired women with pushcarts and loud voices. On the other side of their chatter—was that Portuguese?—Max finally found his quarry.

Behind a pallet heaped with handfuls of glossy red cherries, Jules was in deep consultation with a broadchested man in a weathered green baseball cap. When Max got closer, he could see that the cap read WILDMAN FARMS in darker green lettering.

Sneaking up behind her, Max dared to sling an arm casually over her shoulders as he said, "What's up?"

He wondered what it said about their relationship that it made him so freaking gleeful when she didn't tense up, just glanced over at him with her eyes shining deep amber.

"Zach thinks he's going to have plums tomorrow. We could really do something cool with that, don't you think?"

Max's brain spun with the possibilities. "Wow, yeah," he said. "Are you sure, man? I haven't seen any around today at any of the other stalls."

Zach shrugged. "They weren't ready yet this morning, my brother said." He gave a quick smile, blindingly white against the deep tan of his face. "Jon's the farmer—he was born with a whole green hand, and part of his arm, too, maybe. If he says they'll be ready tomorrow, they'll be ready."

"Shit, that's exciting," Max said, rocking on his heels. "We could do a plum gastrique, or there's a tart with plums and honeyed crème fraîche that I learned how to make in Avignon . . ." He wanted to jump up and down like a little kid, the fever of the competition heating his blood like a dip in a hot spring pool. "Good detective work, Jules."

"Know your purveyors," she said as they waved good-bye to Zach Wildman and started moving toward Beck and the cheese counter. "It was one of the first things Gus taught me."

Max felt a pang at the downward curve of her mouth. "I'm sorry about all this," he said. "I shouldn't have pushed you to choose between us—that was unfair."

"Was it?" Jules hooked her thumbs under the straps of the backpack she used instead of a purse. "We never would've been able to plan on those plums if we hadn't come down here. I didn't even know Wildman Farms had a stall here; I'm used to seeing them at the Union Square Greenmarket."

Inside Max's chest, it felt as if a bowl of warm clarified butter that he'd been holding on to very tightly with both hands suddenly tipped, spilling a big splash of rich, buttery happiness all through him. "That's good, then," he said, hoping the general din of the market would mask the way his voice scratched out of his constricted throat. "Guess my work here is done."

"Not so fast, stud," Winslow said, catching up to them. His shaved head was shiny, green eyes bright, and he was clearly juiced on about twenty-five different varieties of cured meat. "We've still got to come up with a whole menu with a dish for each of us, and then, you know, cook it. For the judges. One of whom is the God of Rock, Kane freaking Slater!"

Max lifted his brows. "Win. Man, you know you squeaked a little there, right?"

Raising his voice to be heard over Jules's laughter, Winslow said, "Oh sure. Mock me for my beliefs. How would you feel if it were the Dalai Lama judging our food, and I was all, 'Oh, Max. He's only the embodiment of the Buddha on earth, or whatever. Be cool.'"

They were still laughing, all of them, excited and energized and nearly running down the street on their way back to the restaurant, when they turned the corner of Barrow and Grove . . . and saw the ambulance parked directly in front of his parents' building.

Chapter 23

Max wasn't aware he was running until he felt the slap of his feet on the pavement, the vibrations shuddering up his legs as he pounded forward as fast as he could push himself.

A million scenarios flashed through Max's head, jumbled and jerky like a horror movie reel on fast-forward, images of everything from a pregnant lunch guest going into labor in the middle of the dining room to awful, stomach-roiling thoughts of his mother losing her balance and hitting her head on the hostess stand.

But even with all those fevered imaginings, he wasn't prepared for the sight that greeted him when he burst through the Lunden's Tavern door, the rest of the kitchen crew hard on his heels.

His mother stood at the back of the dining room beside the kitchen door, white as salt and covering her mouth with both hands. She didn't even see Max until he was right next to her, putting his hands on her shoulders to feel the tremors working through her.

The moment he touched her, all the steel went out of her spine and knees, and she crumpled in his arms.

"Mom," Max said, aware of the others gathering around them, helping him to support her weight. "What's going on? Are you okay?"

She shook her head, but said nothing, her breath starting to come in quick gasps punctuated by coughing sobs that sounded painful enough to make Max's chest twinge in sympathy.

"It's not her." Jules's voice was odd, almost distant. Max lifted his head and looked for her. She stood by the swinging metal door that led into the kitchen, peering through the oval glass window at something inside.

Sick fear clamped down on Max's gut, but when Beck laid a big hand on Nina's shoulder, Max transferred her to the larger chef as gently as could. He had to force himself to step over to Jules, some part of him knowing already what he was about to see.

Danny was at his side, a silent, bolstering presence, as they pushed open the kitchen door.

Dad.

Two paramedics were working over him, swift and efficient and frighteningly calm as they strapped Max's father to a collapsible stretcher. Gus's face was partially obscured by an oxygen mask, but beneath it, Max could see that his father's skin was papery and pale. His eyes were closed, and tufts of gray hair stuck out oddly around the rubber strings holding the mask to his nose and mouth.

When did his hair go gray? Max wondered.

"What happened?" Danny's voice made Max flinch. It was too loud, grating and rough, like trucks grinding their gears as they barreled down the dirt mountain roads in South America.

One of the paramedics spared them a brief glance, fingers never ceasing their quick, methodical movements. "Severe chest pains, dizziness, loss of consciousness," she said, removing the stethoscope from her ears and draping it around her neck.

"It's his heart," Jules murmured in a low, shocked voice.

Danny made a harsh noise in his throat; Max wrapped an arm around his shoulders and leaned into him. They could help each other stay on their feet.

"If you're going to freak out, do it somewhere else," the paramedic said tersely, reaching underneath the stretcher to elongate the legs so they could roll Gus out to the waiting ambulance. Danny started forward at once, following the stretcher, but Max's feet were nailed to the floor.

Oh my God. They're rolling my father out of here on a stretcher.

Max felt his balance go an instant before he wavered, but all it took was the pressure of a slim, strong hand on his back to steady him.

"He's going to be okay," she said, resting her forehead on his shoulder and encircling him with her leanly muscled arms. Encompassed by her warmth, her support, Max regained his equilibrium.

"Of course he will. Stubborn old bastard—no lousy heart attack is enough to keep him down."

"He'll be okay," she repeated. "He has to be."

Max heard the catch in her voice, the way it broke on the word "okay," and turned to give Jules a brief, hard hug that comforted him as much as her.

After that, Max made it through the rest of the day by stopping every ten minutes to breathe, center himself, and allow the crashing waves of fear and guilt—why had he fought with his father that afternoon? Why hadn't he noticed how tired he looked? Were there other signs he'd missed?—to break over him and then pass through him like water through a sieve.

The next hour was an interminable blur of calming his

mother down and negotiating how they'd all get to the hospital, a too-bright waiting room with uncomfortable chairs and a coffee vending machine that produced nothing but hot chocolate, no matter what button was pushed.

When Max brought Jules one of the paper cups of extremely mediocre, not-all-that-hot chocolate, he was surprised when she reared back and away from it as if it were a steaming cup of yak butter tea.

"No," was all she said, though. "No, thanks, I'm fine."

Max was pretty sure she wasn't fine—he hadn't gotten more than ten words at a time out of her since they'd arrived at the hospital. She was silent and still, her eyes wide and somehow bruised looking, as if she'd been awake for two days straight.

Not that she complained, or cried—in fact, she was the one who got up and went to Danny when he found them all in the waiting room. He'd been the one to ride along in the ambulance, and the look on his face when he walked in and said the doctors were prepping Dad for surgery was one Max hoped he'd never have to see again.

Jules hugged him tight, let him bury his face in her shoulder, and all the time, Max could read the mute suffering in her eyes as clearly as if she were weeping and rending her garments. But she never broke down.

When they'd been waiting with no word for three hours, she and Winslow went to the hospital cafeteria and brought back food that no one wanted to eat. Beck had already gone over to the restaurant to deal with the locking up and closing down everyone had been too upset to do earlier. And a little while later, Winslow needed to run home to his apartment to let his dog out. Both had extracted solemn promises of updates the minute there was any news.

When Nina started to pace and fret, Jules went and quietly asked the nurses if they knew when the doctor would be coming back to tell them something. Anything.

And when a slight, trim man in rumpled green scrubs finally came out and asked to speak to Gus Lunden's family, Max held out his hand to Jules, and she took it and let him crush the life out of it while they listened to what the doctor had to say.

The words washed over Max, strung together like waves on the shore, and almost as hard to follow. Stable angina progressed to severe—didn't respond to beta blockers—surgical option—stent—intensive care—

"Oh, thank God. Thank you, thank you, God," Nina breathed, her eyes shining with unshed tears, and that was when it finally made sense to Max.

His dad was going to be okay.

"Of course we hoped to avoid all this, after the collapse in May," the doctor continued, "but sometimes a reduction in stress and a change of dietary habits aren't enough. And in this case, the second collapse may have been a blessing in disguise, because putting in the stent should help to keep the artery from narrowing down again. Barring complications, Gus should be back on his feet, nearly as good as new, very quickly."

Max's mind went blank and still, a frozen tundra buried under a whiteout blizzard.

Second collapse?

"Can we see him?" Danny asked eagerly.

"He's still pretty out of it," the doctor warned. "But he's been moved out of Recovery and into ICU, so you're welcome to go back. Family only, of course."

Clinging to Danny's arm, Nina let the doctor lead her down the hall. It made his breath stop, but Max let them go. He wanted to keep them right next to him with a deep, frantic need that he knew was at least partly based on his brand-new fear of letting anyone he cared about out of his sight for a second, but he had to talk to Jules first.

He looked down to find his fingers crushed too tightly

around Jules's more slender hand. She didn't complain, though, simply looked back at him with her wide golden-brown eyes, red-rimmed but dry.

"What was the doctor talking about?" Max demanded, barely recognizing his own voice under the growl of fear and pain.

Jules closed her eyes for a brief instant, and when she blinked them back open, Max could see the mirror of everything he was feeling. But her voice barely wavered, steady and soft, as she began to explain.

"A few months ago, your father passed out during dinner service. We all thought it was just exhaustion, or heat—you know how it gets in the kitchen, like being trapped inside a pressure cooker—but it was more than that."

"His heart." Max felt every beat of his own heart like an accusation, a slap, a punishment.

You should have known. You should have been here. You should have helped.

Jules nodded. "High blood pressure, mostly, but high enough that the docs were concerned, made him promise to slow down, eat better, cut out as much stress as he could."

"The competition," Max realized. "That's why they called me back to take his place. Not for my expertise, but because Dad's heart couldn't withstand it."

"That was your mother's argument," Jules said.

Guilt and anger made for an ugly combination, roiling in his belly. "And what was her argument against telling me exactly what the fuck was going on? Or maybe I didn't deserve the truth, since I apparently forfeited my place in this family to you."

Jules flinched, her pale, waxy skin acquiring a red stain across her high cheekbones. "For what it's worth," she said in a low voice, "I thought you should know."

Sick rage churned through him as he began to under-

stand the extent of the deception. Everyone had known—
his mother and brother, of course, but all the kitchen
workers, the servers. The team.

Jules.

They all knew more about his father's failing health
than Max did. And not a single damn one of them had the
balls to tell him the truth.

For one blazing instant, he hated them, all of them, for
letting this happen. For shutting him out and blindsiding
him with the most agonizingly frightening experience of
his life.

But not all of them were right there, in front of him.
Only Jules. The woman who'd kissed him, held him, allowed him into her body—all without knowing Max well
enough to understand how much this secret would devas-
tate him.

Or maybe she'd known, but just hadn't cared.

"You thought I should know," he echoed, swallowing
down the rising bile of terror, shame, and betrayal. "But
you still kept it from me."

He watched her recoil from the vicious fury in his voice,
from the snap of his angry stare, and winced as a new
layer of guilt spread thinly over the throbbing pain of *bad
son, bad brother, they didn't tell you because they knew
they couldn't count on you.*

"I'm sorry," she whispered, and he could see that she
was. It didn't actually make him feel any better. "The
important thing is that Gus is going to be okay."

"You're right," Max said, reaching for his Zen calm
and feeling it drip between his grasping fingers like water.
"Come on, let's go see how he's feeling."

She tried out a smile, but it didn't stick. "Go ahead. I'll
call the others and let them know Gus is out of the woods."

He hesitated. Angry as he was, he knew how much Jules
loved Gus Lunden. And vice versa.

"It's fine," she said, as if sensing Max's reluctance. That same sad excuse for a smile twisted her mouth. "Immediate family only, remember? They wouldn't let me in, anyway, and someone has to let Beck and Win in on the good news."

Max looked away, staring down the hall at the brisk nurses and patients with wheelchairs and walkers and IV stands. It wasn't pretty, but it was easier than standing there, feeling how the good, bright thing between him and Jules was broken, sharp and pointed and slashing into him with every breath like a cracked rib.

"Okay. I'll tell Dad you were here."

Her throat worked for a second, making an audible clicking, before she said, "Thanks."

She walked away, head down and shoulders slumped, and in spite of it all, Max wanted to go after her more than he'd ever wanted anything.

But a tug to his elbow had him glancing down at a short, plump nurse with kind, tired eyes.

"Mr. Lunden? Your father is asking for you. Come on, I'll show you where his room is."

And when Max looked up again, Jules was gone.

Jules walked out of the hospital feeling as if her heart were tearing itself in half, wanting to stay there, in the impersonal, concrete-slab building that held the family and future she'd always wanted.

But she wasn't allowed—wasn't family—and it was better this way.

Better for Max, who'd hardly been able to stand the sight of her once he'd realized the truth they'd all been hiding from him for weeks.

Shoving her hands in the pockets of her cargo pants, she fumbled her cell phone open and dialed Beck and

Winslow on automatic pilot, relaying the news and feeling like a total imposter the whole time.

They were so happy, their joy as uncomplicated and pure as Jules's was shadowed by guilt and regret. She made an effort to sound normal, though, and they didn't notice anything off. Jules had always been good at that. It was an old skill, but it turned out to be like any other often-repeated action—the same way she'd never forget how to turn an artichoke heart, she'd always be able to fake normalcy even when everything inside her was screaming.

Screaming, "It's over. It's over. He hates you for lying to him. It's over."

Not that she hadn't known it would end, she reminded herself. But she'd been counting on the next few weeks to store up a lifetime's worth of memories before Max left for Italy.

Now she wouldn't even have that.

Halfway down the stairs to the downtown train, she hesitated. The downtown train would take her back to her apartment.

Her apartment that Max had been to, knew how to find, and might take it into his head to visit tonight so he could make it one hundred percent clear that they were over.

No. Even the possibility . . . she couldn't bear it. She chewed her lower lip until it was sore.

After the hospital, and Max's anger burning over her skin like spatters of hot oil, she needed a few hours to regroup. To rebuild her walls so that whatever happened after, Jules would be able to survive it.

But where else could she go? She'd run out of the restaurant today without her backpack; hadn't even realized it until she'd had to get Win to spot her for the pile of stale cellophane-wrapped sandwiches at the hospital cafeteria.

Her Metro card was in her pants pocket, as always, but that was all she had.

Everyone she could go to for help was either at the hospital or would want to talk about what happened at the hospital.

Everyone . . . except one person.

Shoulders sagging, Jules turned around and trudged back up the stairs and across the street to the uptown train, pulling her phone back out as she went.

Before descending into the dark, heated mouth of the subway station, she flipped open her phone and punched in a number.

"Mom?"

Chapter 24

"But where else would she go?"

Max was starting to feel a little frantic. It didn't help that he hadn't slept all night. He'd sat up with his mother in the hospital waiting room after she'd refused to go home, and at this point, he hadn't showered in so long that his scalp actually itched.

Gross. The life of a wandering mystic who slept by the side of the road may have been an enlightened one, Max mused, but hot, running water was starting to sound like a true religious experience.

Danny shook his head. He looked about as wiped out as Max felt—there were deep purple smudges under his gray-blue eyes, and his brown hair stood up in funny tufts all over where he'd gripped it. "I don't know, Max. She hasn't checked in with anybody, she's not answering her phone, and you said Winslow told you she wasn't at her apartment when he dropped by this morning?"

"And Win's all worked up now, too." Apparently, Winslow had Jules's extra key, so when she hadn't responded to the doorbell, he'd gone in to check on her. He'd told Max it looked as if Jules hadn't been there all night.

"I'm sure she's fine," Danny said, darting a look at the bed in the corner of the hospital room.

Gus was asleep, finally, after a long night of interruptions and checks by the brisk, attentive nursing staff. Danny had persuaded Nina to run home for a shower and some clean clothes by promising to stay in Gus's room and make sure he slept until she got back. Barring some sort of medical emergency, he was supposed to keep everybody out.

"Well, I'm not sure," Max declared in a low undertone, chest tightening.

Danny gave him a narrow look. "Why?"

Max didn't know what his tell was, but something tipped his kid brother off because Danny's eyes got big and accusing. "Max! What did you do?"

"Okay, we had a fight," Max said. "I was so pissed when I found out you'd all lied to me about Dad's health. I laid into her."

"What did you say?" Danny's voice was low and angry.

"The same stuff I said to you, basically." Max had pulled his brother aside a couple of hours into their bedside vigil, but by that time, he'd had a chance to calm down. To get both his lungs and his brain working again. And when Danny shrugged and told him it was their father's decision—his health, his heart, his choice—Max hadn't been able to argue.

Cursing under his breath, Max paced the length of the small, private room that was starting to feel as airless and confining as a prison. "I shouldn't have let her go. I was pissed, but I should've listened to her."

"Yeah, you should've." The voice was weak and rough, but unmistakably his father's.

Max stopped his pacing and went to the bedside. "Hey, Dad. Go back to sleep, or Mom'll kick our asses when she gets back here."

"I'm tired of sleeping," Gus said, irritably hitching himself higher on his flat hospital pillow. "I feel like I've been asleep for a week. And besides, you boys clearly need a kick in the pants to get you going. What the hell are you both doing sitting around here? We've got a culinary challenge to win! And, more importantly, a missing member of the team."

Exchanging a glance with Danny, Max couldn't help but grin at the overwhelming burst of relief. After hours of seeing his father pale and passed out in that bed, hooked up to tubes and bleeping machines, Max was ecstatic to see Gus's blue eyes open and aware and full of his old fire.

"Mom said we have to stay here," Danny protested. The corner of his mouth twitched, and Max knew his brother was hiding a smirk.

"I don't need a goddamn babysitter," Gus growled. "Let alone two of them. What I need is to know that Jules is all right, and that you boys aren't going to squander all the hard work she put into getting us this far in the RSC."

"What do you want us to do?" Max asked.

Gus raised his bushy brows. "I want you to get your head out of your ass and realize that the only reason we didn't tell you about my stupid heart problems was that apprenticeship in Italy. I know how much it means to you, what a great opportunity it is. Once in a lifetime. And I will be damned before I'm the one standing in your way."

"Dad." Max's throat felt swollen and achy, like he'd eaten too many Thai chiles, but he couldn't step grinning at the return of Gus's normal levels of piss and vinegar.

Gus coughed, then grimaced. "Damn. I can't wait to be out of this hospital. Thank God for modern medicine. Did you hear the nurse? She said I'd be up and about in a matter of days!"

"Doing physical therapy," Danny reminded him. "Not running a marathon."

Gus waved that away as a trifling detail. "Point is, I'm going to be fine by the time the next phase of the RSC rolls around."

Max blinked. It hadn't even crossed his mind, what would happen if Gus weren't able to join the team as planned. Without thinking about it, Max assumed he would've stayed on, helped out—and missed the chance of a lifetime to study under one of the world's living culinary giants.

Fighting a weird mixture of relief and disappointment, Max said, "Until then, I guess you'll just have to run things from here."

Brightening at the thought, Gus hitched himself higher on the bed. "The way I see it, we've got to come up with a plan for the RSC meal, then shop and prep for it. We also need to track Jules down, and you need to make up with her, because that girl shouldn't have to be your scapegoat. Did that trip to Essex Street give you any ideas?"

Max's stomach clenched at the mention of that trip to the market. "Dad," he said slowly. "About the way we argued yesterday—the things I said—"

Gus waved a hand and scowled at the IVs attached to it. "Don't worry about it. I was out of line," he said, all gruff and not meeting Max's eyes. "I wasn't feeling too well . . . and I guess it's obvious now why that was. But I shouldn't have tried to stop everyone else from going. It was stupid of me. I guess I just didn't want anyone to think I was slowing down, getting old and weak."

"That *was* stupid," Danny agreed. "None of us would've thought that—we know better."

Clearing his throat, Gus blinked a few times and said, "So. What did you find at Essex Street?"

Max launched into a comprehensive list of the specialty products they'd investigated the day before, from Jules's plums to Winslow's house-cured charcuterie. Danny detailed the chocolate offerings for them, making Max's mouth water.

"I think what we need is a theme to build the meal around," Max said, watching his father carefully. "Something loose enough to allow each of us to play to our strengths and cook the dish we want . . . but structured enough to be sure the meal makes sense from course to course."

"That could work," Gus said, staring at the ceiling thoughtfully. "The standard five courses are soup, fish, meat, salad, dessert."

This was exactly the sort of thing he and his father had been unable to agree on, all those years ago before Max left home. Gus loved the old-fashioned stuff, the classics—and in his younger days, Max had found all of it unbearably dull and boring. But now, he thought he could come up with a way to blend their two styles.

"Exactly," he said. "I was thinking we'd keep the classic course structure, with the whole meal as a salute to New York City, the world's greatest melting pot of different cuisines and styles."

Max held his breath, watching for Gus's reaction. He couldn't even look at Danny, knew if he did, he'd crack.

They could both see the decision play out on Gus's weary face. He frowned, at the idea of mixing cuisines and trying new techniques, Max was sure. But then the lined brow smoothed, and a smile started at the corners of Gus's mouth. "You know," he said. "I think I like that. And I bet the judges will, too—it's the perfect answer to the challenge about being local! Okay, Danny, get the others on the horn and start gathering their ideas. You'll have to make the run to Essex Street to buy your ingredients in the next few hours, so you have the afternoon to prep."

"You got it." Clapping his brother on the shoulder, Danny picked up the room phone and started dialing out.

"He can take care of mobilizing the troops and coordinating the shopping," Gus told Max. "Or actually, he'll call Beck, and Beck will do it. In the meantime, I've got another job for you. An essential mission, of critical importance."

Max clenched his hands into fists, then forced each finger to release its tension. He hated to do this, but . . . "Dad, I'm sorry. I'm about to prove everything you ever thought about how unreliable and irresponsible I am, but I can't do anything more with the competition until I know Jules is okay. I have to find her, Dad."

His gut roiled with tension—he felt like he'd just gotten a second chance to start working on a better relationship with his father and here he was, already fucking it up.

Max darted a nervous look at the heart rate monitor. The absolute last thing he wanted to do was enrage Gus enough to set off another heart attack.

Except Gus wasn't going red with rage; in fact, he was rolling his eyes and smiling. "You shouldn't interrupt your elders," he said. "It's rude. Also, you miss important stuff, like the fact that what I was going to say was, your mission, and you better choose to accept it, is to find Jules and bring her back. Nothing matters as much as that, not the competition, or the restaurant, or anything."

Max's lips stretched in a smile so wide, his cheeks actually hurt. "I accept the mission," he said gravely. "And I think I know where to start looking."

Gus's smile faded to an expression more open and serious than Max could remember ever seeing on his father's mercurial face.

"Don't let us down, son."

As Max jogged down the steps outside the hospital, he realized that for once, the knowledge that someone was counting on him didn't feel like a dog collar choked tight around his neck. Instead, he felt as light and full of energy as if he'd spent the last two hours in an extended massage and meditation session.

It's a whole new world, he thought as he hailed a cab and gave the driver the address he'd gotten from Danny.

The feeling of euphoria lasted until the taxi pulled up in front of a smart midtown high-rise apartment building, shiny with glass and chrome.

Despite his confidence in front of his father, Max wasn't at all sure he was on the right track with this idea. After all, from everything Jules had told him about her childhood—admittedly, not much—her mother hadn't exactly come off as the safe shelter type. Then again, maybe Jules had been upset enough to go looking for any port in a storm.

A lackadaisical doorman, wearing a uniform about two sizes too big for his stooped, skinny frame, leaned on a podium inside the sliding glass doors. When Max said he was there to visit apartment nine "N" the doorman flipped a binder toward Max, pointed to an empty line and said, "Sign in here."

Great security, Max thought as he stepped around the slumped doorman and over to the bank of elevators. *Wonder how much extra you pay to have that guy standing guard out front?*

Nerves skittered under his skin and tightened his throat as the elevator doors slid open at the ninth floor. He hoped his instincts about where Jules might be hiding were on the mark—but at the same time, if she was here? He wasn't sure he liked what that said about her state of mind. It smacked of Jules punishing herself, and Max's fists clenched at the idea that he'd driven her to this with his blame and accusations and anger.

This was the woman who'd shaped Jules's childhood, and her entire worldview—the woman who'd warped

Jules's heart with too many broken promises and shattered expectations.

Anger simmered in Max's belly, hotter and more painful than a hit of wasabi, and Max closed his eyes and just breathed for a moment before continuing down the hall to the door marked "9N" in ornate black numerals.

Calm. I'm calm. I am a reed on the shore. I am a willow branch, bending in the wind.

Lifting one loosely curled fist, Max rapped twice on the door. Not too hard—he didn't want to pound. But the crack of his knock reverberated through his knuckles and echoed down the hall like a couple of gunshots.

I am . . . seriously pissed off.

It was easier to let go of his own petty hurt and frustrations, Max discovered, than the deep-seated, sympathetic anger he felt on Jules's behalf. He heard movement in the apartment, and put on his most innocent, harmless, I-am-not-a-mass-murderer face, in case someone was peering at him through the peephole set into the door.

A moment later, the door opened to reveal a tall, svelte woman who looked to be in her late fifties. She had blond hair, several bottle shades lighter than Jules's, which made the contrast of her brown eyes even more striking.

The smile she gave Max made him shift his weight from one foot to the other—there was quite a bit of Mrs. Robinson in that intent expression.

"Well, hello there," she purred. "And what can I do for you?"

"Mrs. Cavanaugh?" he asked.

A fleeting look of disgust swept across her attractive face, although the expression was hampered by the fact that the muscles in her forehead seemed to be frozen solid. But she shook her head in denial, trilling a little laugh. "Oh no," she said. "Not for a long time. And I happen to be between husbands at the moment, so I've gone back to the trusty old maiden name. Victoria Clarke, at your service, handsome. But you can call me Tori."

Max wasn't sure what to say to that. "Ah. Well, I'm actually looking for your daughter. Is Jules here?"

He had the sense that if she could've raised her eyebrows at that, she would've. "Juliet? Really? Well. Isn't that interesting."

His heartbeat sped up a bit. "She's here, isn't she?"

Jules's mother pushed the door open wider. "I suppose you'd better come in."

Chapter 25

Entering the interior of the apartment was like stepping into a snow globe. Max blinked, then squinted. Everything was white, from the walls to the sleek, leather couches and the velvety-looking tracksuit Tori wore. There was even a thick, white shag carpet to muffle their footsteps on the white marble floor.

Late morning sunlight streamed in between the hanging blinds, glinting harshly off the glass coffee table and casting shadows like prison bars across the empty living room.

Max tried to imagine growing up in this pristine showplace of a room, and failed. No doubt the furniture was all Italian and cost enough money to feed a village in India for a month, but it wasn't exactly what Max thought of as "homey." It certainly couldn't have been more different from Max's parents' house.

Or from Jules's place, he realized, remembering her spare, sturdy décor. It had been minimal in a whole different way from her mother's übermodern apartment—sort of Early American Broke-Ass Grad Student.

"She's asleep," Tori said, crossing her arms over her

ample, improbably perky chest. "Since about fifteen minutes after she got here last night. Barely said two words to me before she shut herself in the guest room and passed out on the bed." Her mouth twisted in a way that suggested annoyance. "She didn't even take off those mannish boots she insists on wearing. I'm going to have to get the duvet dry-cleaned now."

Max glanced down the hall in the direction Tori had indicated, wondering for a split second if he should go wake Jules up.

Wait a minute. Of course he should wake her up! They had a competition to win. "It's nine o'clock," he said. "I can't believe she hasn't woken up on her own."

"I know! Twelve hours," Tori said, looking surprised. Or maybe her eyebrows were just stuck that way. "But it's been a while since she came by. I didn't want to tick her off by shaking her out of bed. She can be so difficult, sometimes. I even missed my morning Pilates session waiting for her."

How selfless, Max thought, but he made sure to keep any sarcasm out of his voice when he said, "I'm sure you were glad to see her last night. Maybe she didn't have a chance to tell you, but her boss—my dad? He had a heart attack yesterday afternoon."

"Oh, that's terrible!" To her credit, Tori seemed genuinely upset by the news. She sank into one of the chairs that was made up of strips of white leather stretched across a chrome framework, and pulled the edges of her zippered sweatshirt tight around her torso. "Is there anything I can do?"

"It was kind of a shock for all of us, but he's doing much better. They say he'll make a full recovery." Surprise at her reaction had Max taking the chair across from her. He found himself wanting to know more about Victoria Cavanaugh. He'd been expecting someone very different in the role of Evil Mother Who Kicked Her Daughter Out. Certainly he hadn't expected her to be so clearly undone by bad news about the man who'd taken her daughter in.

She breathed an audible sigh. "That's such a relief. Your father . . . I'm sure you already know this, but he's a wonderful man. I'd hate to think of anything happening to him."

Max only hesitated for a brief moment of internal struggle before he said, "I'm sorry, this is sort of rude . . . but how do you know my father well enough to care about his health?"

She stiffened, the leather straps of her chair squeaking in protest. "Gus Lunden has done a lot for us, giving Juliet that job and all. Of course I'm grateful."

Max nodded, never taking his eyes off her, and allowed a full minute of silence to tick past, loaded with expectation.

She cracked. "Look, when Juliet . . . left and moved in with your parents, I tried to talk to her, to get her to come back home."

He must have made some involuntary movement or gesture, because she clenched her fists on the arms of her chair and her voice got loud and strident. Which was a particularly odd effect, since her facial expression barely changed.

"I did! I called her, I went to see her—but she wouldn't talk to me. I was beside myself. Of course. What mother wouldn't be?"

Max nodded, keeping a bland, interested look on his face. He hadn't missed the fact that it was all about Tori. "That must have been awful for you."

Whoops. Let a little bit of an edge creep in, there.

He winced inwardly, but luckily, Tori was oblivious to subtext. "It was. And your father understood that. He called me, when she first showed up and spent the night. And then, when she wouldn't talk to me, he'd call every few weeks to let me know how she was doing. It was . . . it meant a lot."

Max shifted in his chair, making the leather creak. Tori shot him a look. "I had certain . . . issues going on in my life at the time that complicated everything, and you know, it was always just me and Juliet, really. Being a single mom . . . it was rough." She sighed, the hard mounds of her chest straining the white tank top under her hoodie. Max worked hard not to let his eyebrows shoot to his hairline.

Maybe I should pretend my forehead's been Botoxed into submission.

It was important not to slip up and say anything that would keep Tori from finishing this little narrative. Max's heart rate sped, making him light-headed with the antici- pation of finding out more about Juliet's father . . . and the night she left home. A touch of subtle steering of the conversation might be in order.

He leaned forward, balancing precariously in his styl- ish Italian death trap. "So why did Jules leave home? If you don't mind me asking."

Screw subtle. It was lost on Tori anyway.

Waking up in her childhood bedroom always gave Jules vertigo. Not that it looked remotely the way it had when she was growing up; her mother had long since wallpapered over the pink and green Laura Ashley print, and exchanged the New Kids on the Block poster for a strangely mono- chromatic colorblock painting involving two squares and a diagonal line.

Which was fine, really—the Laura Ashley and NKOTB décor hadn't really suited Jules in the first place. This room had always been more a reflection of her mother's wishes than her own.

This was Juliet's room.

No, it was more the sense of having betrayed herself, somehow, that gave Jules the spins. Why was she back here again? Why did she keep doing this to herself? When would she ever learn?

She blinked fully awake and stretched her arms and legs out to the corners of the bed.

Wait. Why am I still dressed? And on top of the covers?

Her body twinged and ached, as if she were coming to after a bar fight instead of a good night's sleep.

What the hell time was it? She craned her neck to get a look at the tiny gray clock on the nightstand, and nearly levitated off the bed in a panic as the previous day came rushing back.

She stumbled out of the bedroom and down the hall, tensing as she registered the sound of two voices from the living room.

I hope to God I'm not about to walk in on Mom canoodling with her latest boyfriend.

Jules wasn't at all prepared for the sight of her mother in an apparently deep and intimate conversation with the man Jules, herself, had lately been canoodling with.

Almost as big and unpleasant a shock was the subject matter of that conversation.

"So why did Jules leave home? If you don't mind me asking," she heard, in Max's deep, calm voice.

"Hey," Jules said, temper flushing hot up her neck and into her cheeks. "I mind you asking. Ever think of that?"

Max gave a guilty start at her sharp tone. "Jules! I was worried about you."

"Morning, honey," Mom said, with that trembly, uncertain smile she always wore around Jules, these days. "I let you sleep; you seemed so exhausted."

Forcing her tone smooth, Jules said, "Thanks. I wish I'd set an alarm for myself, though. I needed to get going this morning." Trying not to notice the way her mother's face fell, or her own pang of guilt, she turned to Max. "I'm sorry you had to come all the way over here."

He shook his head. "It wasn't a problem. I mean, yeah, it freaked us out, not knowing where you were, but it was nice to get to meet your mom."

Jules fought the urge to wrap her arms around herself. "Sorry," she said again. Would it ever be possible to apologize enough? "I just needed some time. I didn't mean to take quite this much time, though, so we'd better get going."

She couldn't believe she'd come all the way over to her mother's place specifically to give herself a breather from Max—and he'd found her, anyway. He seemed to be over the worst of yesterday's anger, but Jules caught herself watching him warily from the corner of her eye.

Being back in this apartment always reminded Jules how fast things could slip from okay to shitastic.

Max struggled out of the hammock of white leather strips. "The guys are already at Essex Street—we need to call them with your shopping list. We've got a menu theme: I Love New York."

Goose bumps popped up along Jules's arms and legs. "Oh, that is *good,*" she said, ignoring the slight catch at her heart that she hadn't been around to help come up with it.

There was no time to worry about that now, no time for regrets. As she headed for the door, tunneling her mind down to the ingredients she'd seen the day before, and what she might be able to do with them, all she could feel was relief.

"Mom, thanks for letting me crash here," she said, one hand on the sleek chrome doorknob.

Something flickered in Tori's eyes, almost too quick to catch, and her pink-lipsticked mouth stretched into that unconvincing smile again. "Sure, baby. You know you're always welcome here."

Jules flinched. She couldn't help it. But there was no time for that, either, and she'd heard it all before, anyway. She just couldn't trust it.

"I'll call you," she told her mother, then made her escape.

Come on, come on, she mouthed as she jammed her finger on the elevator call button. Glancing back down the hall, she noticed that Max lingered at the doorway with her mother for a long moment before following Jules to her stance in front of the insanely slow elevator.

Before she could ask what that was all about, he said, "Listen, I'm sorry about before. The things I said to you yesterday. I was surprised, and hurt, and I took it out on you."

A tiny, tender green shoot of hope poked its head up, but Jules squashed it ruthlessly. "You don't need to apologize for that. I would've been upset, too."

"And I shouldn't have asked your mom about your past, that was wrong. Bad Max! But in my defense, asking you usually produces little to no result."

Unwilling to be charmed, and already anticipating a need for higher, thicker walls around her stupidly vulnerable heart, Jules said, "It's fine."

"Clearly, it's not fine." Max touched her shoulder with his big, warm hand, the heat of it seeping through her shirt and skin, warming her all the way to the bone.

Shrugging it off was the hardest thing she'd ever done. "Let it go, Max," she said, staring straight ahead. "I need to focus on what dish I'm going to prepare, and what I need to ask the boys to buy for me."

"Jules," he started, but the elevator dinged and the doors swooshed open.

She stepped on and hit the button for the lobby. "Are you coming?" she asked.

Max sighed and got on the elevator, and the rest of their conversation on the ride down to the first floor was all about the food.

That wave of relief rolled over Jules again. There'd be plenty of time to sort out all this messy emotional stuff later.

For now, there was only the cooking.

Chapter 26

"Hail the conquering hero," was Winslow's greeting as Max ushered Jules into the Lunden's Tavern kitchen. "Or, in the words of my people, you the man!"

Max mustered up a grin, but it felt tight. Everything felt tight—his shoulders, the line between Jules's brows, the timing on this competition, his worry for his father . . . they needed to do something to loosen up, or all their food was going to taste as overworked and stressed out as they all were.

Jules hadn't been able to come up with a complete dish in the cab ride over to Lunden's, but she'd managed to scrape together a list of ingredients that sounded pretty good. Max wasn't worried—he was nearly positive she'd pull off something fantastic—but he could tell she was far from convinced.

And there was still something very much up with her. She'd actually requested to do the appetizer course, leaving the two larger, centerpiece courses to Beck and Max. Now, Max didn't mind working on the meat course. Beck wanted fish, and that was fine—the dude had the magic touch when it came to seafood. But Max just couldn't believe Jules would give up the main courses without a fight.

Not that the app course wasn't important—it was. Hell, its whole purpose was to sharpen the diners' appetites and set the tone for the entire meal. And not that Jules was Big Mama Ego, or anything, either.

But there was definitely a competitive edge to her personality. Especially when it came to cooking, the RSC, and Max. So he couldn't help feeling like it was yet another indicator that Jules was . . . he couldn't think of a better way to describe it than "punishing herself."

For what, he wasn't sure. But he knew he wanted it to stop.

Max stole another look at her as she bustled to her station and started unpacking the boxes the guys had brought her from Essex Street. Her dark blond hair was up in a messy ponytail that slipped over the front of her shoulder when she bent down, exposing the sweet, vulnerable nape of her neck. Max remembered kissing her there, setting the edge of his teeth to the sensitive skin, but gently. So gently, just to feel her shiver.

She stood up, her hair swung back to cover the spot, and Max felt as cut off at the knees as he had the moment she walked in on him pumping her mother for information.

Every time she glanced at him now, there was a distinct chill. Not coldness, exactly, but more like a lack of warmth. Of connection. It was as if, when she left the hospital alone the night before, she'd slipped away from all of them, completely. Somewhere they couldn't reach her.

In fact, everyone in the kitchen was a little distant, as if each station, from prep to grill to dessert, was on its own mountaintop, swathed in clouds and silence and the oppressive weight of empty air. Winslow's smile was a couple hundred watts dimmer than usual. The movements of Danny's hands were disjointed and jerky, completely lacking their characteristic grace. And Beck wasn't saying a word—which wasn't weird—but he was also starting like a scalded cat at every bang of a pan or chop of a knife.

Max looked back at Jules, but she was ignoring everyone, concentrating on the components of the appetizer course she'd assigned herself. She reached for the carton of fresh plums, her fingers hesitating in midair as her mouth shaped a curse word. She scowled down at the fruit as if they'd offended her in some way, locked in combat with the problem of what dish she should make that would wow the judges and start their meal off on the perfect note.

If he spoke up now, if he said anything to the team, there was a distinct possibility she'd take it as confirmation that he was cutting her out of her leadership role, taking over. She'd either retreat further behind her wall of ice . . . or she'd fight.

Max knew which he preferred, and he knew what he had to do.

Don't let me down, son.

With his father's words ringing in his ears, Max said, "Guys, before we get too entrenched, can we huddle up for a second?"

Jules stiffened, but when she turned to join the others, who'd moved more quickly to group around Max at the front of the kitchen, her face was calm and expressionless.

Biting back a sigh, Max looked around the circle of chefs. He forced himself to meet each one's eyes, to stand tall and straight like the leader his father had always wanted him to be.

"We're all different," Max said. "We bring different things to the table, and that's good."

Max cocked his head. "I haven't been around, so I don't know you as well as my father does. But sometimes a fresh perspective can show you things that familiarity would miss. For instance, take Win."

Winslow blinked, then smiled that strangely innocent smile of his. It almost reached his eyes. "Win, here, has been through some shit in his life, I happen to know. But somehow, it never seemed to rub off on him. You're as clean as if you'd just been born, man. And I could like you for that alone, but when you add in your extra superpowers like being able to make any vegetable taste amazing and the ability to lift the spirits of your moodier teammates with a single joke, well. I'm glad as hell you're with us."

That smile went all the way now, brightening Win's eyes to the color of the light green jade Max had seen adorning a temple shrine in Shanghai. Max smiled back, and slid his glance over to Danny, standing next to him.

Max had been there for most of the shit Danny'd been through. At least for the kid stuff, and the messy teenage years. But he'd missed a lot, too—the past six years, when his shy, quiet baby brother made the leap from boy to man—and Max, who didn't believe in regrets, knew he'd do almost anything to get that time back again. But it was gone forever.

"You're my brother," Max said, feeling his throat thicken stupidly. "And I love you. But even if you weren't, and I didn't, I'd still be in fucking awe of what you can do with a square of chocolate, a cup of cream, a stick of butter, and some flour. I've been all over the world, and I'm telling you right now—you're the best pastry chef I've ever seen."

"Thanks, man." Good, Danny's voice was cracking, too. At least Max wasn't alone in his emotional idiocy.

Turning to Beck with some relief, Max said, "Now, you're a tougher coconut to crack—which I guess is the way you like it. When I first got back, I thought maybe you'd been in prison for a bit. And that question you answered at the qualifiers, about making a meal for hundreds of people at a time, that made me think I was on the right track."

Beck looked back at him, thick arms crossed over his chest, outwardly as impassive and unmoved as the Great Wall. But there was a flicker of something in his flat stare, a flash of denial, and Max suddenly knew.

"But I was wrong, wasn't I?"

Beck hadn't been in prison. He wasn't an ex-con. He was ex-military.

Every chef's head swiveled to stare at Beck, whose face betrayed nothing. His arms, though, tightened where they crossed over his torso until veins stood out along the roped muscles. Beck narrowed his gaze on Max, but said nothing.

Clearly, he didn't want to talk about it. And maybe that's what was important here—he didn't have to.

Max cleared his throat in the short silence that followed. "The point is, it doesn't matter. Nothing in your past matters as much as what you do here, in this kitchen, with us. Because even if we know nothing about you—shit, Beck, I don't even know your first name—we know all we need to. We know you'll work until your back breaks and never complain, and that you'll turn out some of the most beautiful, refined food I've ever seen. Whatever else you are or have been, you're a great chef. And a great teammate."

Beck continued the Great Wall of China impression for several heartbeats, which gave Max time to wonder if he was about to get his ass stomped. But then the big man dropped his arms, flexing his fingers as if he'd held them stiff and tensed for too long.

"Henry," he said.

Max blinked. "What?"

"My first name," Beck said. "It's Henry. Nice to meet you."

And then he smiled, and Max blinked again, because it changed the guy's whole face. "Nice to meet you, too,"

Max said, sticking out his hand and letting Beck grab and shake it.

"What about Jules?" Win piped up, waggling his eyebrows.

Max looked at her, but she shook her head. "I don't need the pep talk," she said. "Max is right. The past doesn't matter. All that matters is the next few hours, and tomorrow, when we cook our hearts out for those judges. You're great chefs—I know exactly what you're capable of, and I expect that and more tomorrow." Her voice caught in her throat, but her eyes were fierce as she nailed each of them with a look. "It's for Gus. All right? So enough talking. Let's cook!"

They all cheered, the atmosphere in the room exploding like a fireworks display in a shower of renewed energy. Sleeves were rolled up, knives were sharpened, and everyone got to work.

On his way to his station, Jules caught Max's arm and pulled him away from the others. For one heady second, when she dragged him around the corner toward the pantry closet and pushed him up against the wall by the door, all he could think about was their first kiss.

The way her lashes fluttered as her gaze dropped to his mouth made him think she was remembering it, too.

Everything in his body woke up and strained toward her, but her hands on his shoulders were firm. He waited to see what she'd do.

When she looked back into his eyes, he could see her there, more than he had since this morning. His heart did a slow somersault in his chest.

"Thanks," she said, voice rough. "For what you said back there, for pulling the team together. They needed it, and I . . . well, I was too wrapped up in my own stuff to do it."

The contempt in her tone grated over him like a citrus zester in the instant before he realized it was all directed at herself. He shook his head, confused.

"You take too much on your own head," he said. "Not everything has to be your fault, Jules. You don't always have to be perfect."

Her mouth twisted, darkness lowering over her face like a cloud. "Don't I?"

"No, you don't," he insisted, stoking the fire in her eyes. He'd rather be kissing than fighting, but anything was better than that cold, empty nothingness from before. "Besides, perfection isn't always what you think it is."

"God. Is that another Zen saying? Am I supposed to know what that means?"

"There's a story of a young priest," Max said, watching the way she rolled her eyes, but still settled back on her heels to listen. "Whose pride and joy was also his job— he was to tend the Zen temple garden, and no one could fault his devotion to his duty. No one except the old man who lived next door, who frowned as he watched the young man at his work.

"But the priest ignored the old man, and kept everything as meticulous and beautiful as he could. One day, he was told that a great Zen master would be visiting the temple, and the priest was overjoyed to have the chance to show off his perfect garden. He pulled all the weeds, pruned the trees and shrubs, and spent hours raking the leaves into neat, tidy mounds away from the paths. He even combed the moss! When he was done, he went to greet the Zen master."

"I bet I know who the Zen master turns out to be," Jules said.

Max gave her the glower Harukai-sensei would've given him. "You're lucky I don't have my teacher's propensity for smacking cheeky students with a wooden spoon," he told her. "But yes, spoiler alert, the visiting Zen master didn't have far to travel, because he was none other than the old man who lived next door! And as he wandered into the immaculate garden, the young priest couldn't help but anxiously inquire, 'Isn't it perfect?'

"The old master walked up to the largest tree, and shook its branches until it showered the ground with red, gold, and yellow leaves. 'There,' he said, smiling as he looked around the garden. 'Now it's perfect!' "

Jules searched his face for a long moment, as if she could read the meaning behind the story in his eyes. Max waited, because he remembered how he'd felt every time Harukai-sensei busted out one of these little tales.

"My life isn't some story," she finally said, her voice painful and raw. "I don't know what I'm supposed to do with that."

"Just think about it," he urged her, as gently as he could. "And try not to worry so much."

Shuddering in a huge breath, she squeezed her eyes shut, her fingers digging into his shoulders. "That's asking a lot," she said. "Considering your father's in the hospital, we have to cook the best meal of our lives tomorrow for people who will decide if we're good enough to continue on in the competition, and I have no freaking clue what dish I'm going to make."

"I don't know exactly what I'm making, either," he pointed out, deciding to ignore her choice of course for the moment. "But you don't see me stressing. And I've got to deal with the main course! The one the whole meal centers around! Oh my God, you're right, this is a catastrophe—quick, someone hold me up, my knees are going . . ."

"Oh, shut it, you," she said, but her eyes were open and she was actually smiling now. "Why do I even bother coming to you with this stuff? You're like some freaking Buddha statue."

"Is that a remark?" Max put on an affronted face. "Are you calling me fat?"

"I meant the fact that you could smile your way through a shit storm and come out the other side smelling like roses."

"Graphic."

She shrugged. "Not all of us went to Zen school to learn the Art of Romantic Poetry and Deeply Meaningful Fables."

This was as close as Jules got to flirting, and Max loved it.

Her hands slipped from his shoulders, brushing down the center of his chest and over his belly. His abs went rock solid under her touch, with almost no thought from Max, and she traced the outline of his muscles with a single finger.

"Okay," she said, sounding dazed. "Definitely not fat. Holy cats, Max, is that some Zen thing, too? Do all Buddhist monks do a hundred crunches every morning?"

Mission a-fucking-ccomplished, he thought, as smug satisfaction spread out from her smirk like rays of warmth from the sun. She definitely wasn't worrying about anything at the moment.

He hated to break the moment, he really did, but . . . "As much as I'd love to discuss Zen and the Art of Six-pack Abs with you, the RSC rep is going to be here in—" Max checked his watch. "Four hours, to watch us pack up our prepped stuff and cart it over to the competition kitchen, where we'll be cooking tomorrow."

The reminder made Jules take a step back, which Max hated, but he'd been prepared for it. So that was okay.

What he wasn't prepared for was the way her gold-green eyes went round and her wide mouth stretched into a happy O. She blinked at him, then surged forward and pressed her smiling lips to his in a fast, hard kiss.

"What was that for?" Max was having a hard time getting his breath back.

She beamed. "Believe it or not, that story of yours gave me an idea for a first course that will knock the judges right off their seats!"

"I believe it," Max said. "I'm very inspiring, you know."

"You are," she agreed, seriousness creeping back into her expression. "I can see why your parents were so desperate to get you back here in time for the competition. I thought we didn't need you . . . but I was wrong."

The acknowledgment was like cooling aloe on a burn he hadn't even realized he had. "Thanks. And I'm glad I could help, but Jules—the team needs you, too. You're not a placeholder. You're vital."

She flashed him a quick smile as they rounded the corner and walked back into the thick of the other chefs' preparations, but Max couldn't tell if she believed him or not.

"Hey." He caught her arm. "What, exactly, did I say that gave you your inspiration? I could use a little shot of that, myself."

Regarding him thoughtfully, she said, "Actually, it was more a thought I had while you were telling me that whole, long story about the garden. It sort of works as a moral of that story, too, I guess, but really, all I could think was, We're making this so much more complicated than it needs to be."

It was as if she'd whacked him on the head with one of the plucked whole ducks on her station's cutting board.

"Simplify. Cook from the heart. I like it," he said, the glimmer of an idea surfacing in his stunned brain. "Very Zen, Jules-chan. What are you going to make?"

She gestured at the duck, her eyes gleaming as brightly as the edge of the knife she honed against a sharpening steel. "I'm going to confit those duck legs, and pickle the plums. You?"

Max thought of the hundreds of dinner services his family had churned through, searing and serving thousands of perfect steaks at each meal. He thought of every fight he'd ever had with his father, right in this very kitchen, about how unchanging and boring the menu was, how steeped in tradition and imprisoned by people's expectations.

And he grinned. "I'm doing steak."

Chapter 27

There was truly nothing in the world more luscious than duck fat, Jules mused as she poured the creamy golden renderings over the duck legs she'd marinated in spices and sweet wine the entire night.

Settling the legs in their rich bath of melted fat, Jules bent to check the flame under the wide cast-iron braiser. It had to be hot enough to slowly poach the duck legs over the next few hours, but never so hot that the fat actually boiled around the meat.

She moved back over to her cutting board, resolved to keep an eye on the braiser. In an unfamiliar kitchen, with untested equipment, she wouldn't be comfortable until she'd examined and inspected everything.

Not that it wasn't a nice kitchen. In fact, the Rising Star Chef competition kitchen was probably the most luxurious, state-of-the-art kitchen she'd ever cooked in. The ranges and ovens had all been donated by top-of-the-line professional appliance companies, presumably for the exposure they'd get in *Délicieux* magazine, and the drawers of the movable stainless-steel countertops were filled with every conceivable culinary device.

And it was enormous. More spacious than most restaurant kitchens, that was for damn sure, which was lucky, since all four teams had to share it. Each group of five chefs had a corner of the room set up with two long prep tables, two gas ranges, and two ovens. The middle of the room was taken up by a huge grill, open on all four sides, with a giant hood hanging over it to suck up the smoke, and they all had to share that, too.

Calling it pandemonium in there would be understating things. It reminded Jules of the chaotic fighting and running and throwing things on the playground back at P.S. 721, only instead of elementary school kids banging around and bumping into each other, they were adult-sized people holding sharp knives and hot pans.

And the stakes were just a little higher than who got picked last for four square.

"Garlic press wishes and potato masher dreams," Danny said, whistling. He liked to read her mind sometimes, just to prove he still could. "This place has everything."

"For serious," Winslow agreed, racing by with his bowl of vegetables. "We get to keep all this high-tech stuff when the competition's over, right? Like a consolation prize?"

"I have a feeling Claire Durand would have something to say about that." In the midst of halving her beautiful, perfectly ripe Wildman Farms plums, Jules still made time to watch the head judge as she moved through the kitchen, checking in with each team.

"Besides, we won't need the consolation prize," Danny said with a manic grin. "We're going to win!"

His hair was sticking up as if he'd just pulled a sweater off over his head, and there was a smudge of flour lining one sharp cheekbone. He was so familiar and dear, for a moment it was all Jules could do to keep from going over and giving him a squeeze.

"We *are* going to win," Beck put in calmly, his fast-dicing hands never slowing their quicksilver motion. "For Gus."

"Any word from the hospital?" Win wanted to know. "How long do they think it'll be before Gus is back to normal?"

Jules swallowed, hard, and kept her gaze on the growing pile of plums. If Gus couldn't compete in the next round of the RSC, what did that mean for all of them when Max left for Italy?

Danny shot a glance at Max, sharing the adjacent table with Winslow. He'd ducked away for a second when his phone rang, presumably trying to find a place where he could hear over the din of people shouting and pots clanging on the metal cooking range, but he was back now.

"Dad's doing great," Max informed them all, his hands already fondling that fillet of beef. "The stent relieved a lot of the pressure and pain in his chest, and with this kind of surgery, they usually get a pretty quick recovery. He'll be back on his feet and hassling the hell out of us before you know it."

Out of the corner of her eye, Jules saw an upright form in an impeccable tan skirt suit approaching. A flash of silvery blue camisole peeked from under her crisp jacket, somehow picking up and emphasizing the chic, dignified threads of silver running through reddish-brown hair, loose and curling around slim shoulders.

Claire Durand.

Instantly on high alert, Jules put on her best, brightest smile and said, "Good morning, Ms. Durand."

"Good morning, chefs," she replied in her lightly accented voice, before turning to Max and Danny. "I was very sorry to hear about your father," she said, everything about her softening slightly, from her tone to the set of her mouth. "I hope that he is improving, and will be back with us soon."

"Merci beaucoup," Max said. "I just spoke with him, and he's so eager to resume his coaching duties, the nurses are threatening to tie him to the hospital bed."

Claire, who'd widened her eyes at Max's perfect French, now narrowed them in speculation. "And who is leading the team, may I ask, with your father out of commission?"

Max didn't hesitate. "Jules Cavanaugh is my father's right hand. We take our cues from her."

Pride burst like a bubble of champagne in Jules's chest, and she ducked her head. Beside her, Danny threw an arm over her shoulders, and she leaned into the support gratefully. "It's a group effort," she finally said, glancing up to meet Max's steady gaze and bumping her hip against Danny. "I lean on them, they lean on me . . . it's a whole leaning thing."

Claire smiled, the thin smile of someone who knows more than she should. *"Bien.* It looks as if you're doing an admirable job of propping one another up, so I won't keep you from your work any longer. I look forward to tasting your dishes later; I hope you'll let me or one of the other officials know if there's anything you need."

She wandered off to scare the life out of the team from the Red Orchid Bistro, and with a harried glance at the countdown clock hanging on the wall, Jules motioned the others back to work.

Very interesting, Claire mused as she took one final look around the busy kitchen.

All the teams appeared to be working well within the parameters of the strict time schedule she'd worked out.

To avoid forcing the judges to sit down to a table laden

with four separate five-course meals at once, Claire and Eva had decided to stagger the teams throughout the day, giving each a different start time to begin cooking. All of them would have the same total number of hours to prepare their dishes.

The first team had been cooking since six o'clock that morning, and would be serving at ten.

"Four hours to cook, plate everything up, and serve it?" Kane's voice had betrayed his disbelief over the phone lines. "That's some rough stuff right there."

Claire pursed her lips for an instant, displeased to be questioned, then forced her expression smooth again. "When Theo Jansen founded this competition twenty years ago, his aim was to elevate the craft of cooking to the highest level by testing the skills of chefs against one another. He never intended it to be a popularity contest, or a celebrity exhibition match, and I certainly agree. This competition is meant to separate the weak from the strong, Mr. Sl— Kane."

She corrected herself before he could do it for her, surprised and flustered by the heat in her cheeks, and thanked heaven that he couldn't see her blush over the phone.

"I get it, I get it," he said. "Guess that means I'd better have a light supper tonight, and nothing at all tomorrow morning."

Claire cleared her throat. "That would, perhaps, be wise. Do not starve yourself, however. That would give the first team too great an advantage."

His low, rough laugh sent a shiver straight down her spine. "Hunger is the best sauce."

"Indeed. That proverb exists in many languages for a reason."

"What is it in French?"

"À la faim, il n'y a pas de mauvais pain." And why

speaking her native tongue to him should prolong her blush, Claire didn't know. Perhaps she was coming down with something.

Better a fever than a severe case of ridiculousness.

"Wait, isn't *pain* bread?"

"The literal translation is 'to hunger, there is no such thing as bad bread.' And when you consider how picky we French are about bread . . ."

"Say it again," Kane requested, his voice deeper all of a sudden.

"Why?" Claire shifted. Her office chair wasn't terribly comfortable, but it wasn't usually this difficult to keep still.

"Because I like the sound of it."

And because she liked the sound of Kane when he dipped into that lower, seductive register, Claire had to sit up straight in her uncomfortable chair and remind him of their agreement about the flirting.

He hadn't been terribly repentant, and the whole thing had only reinforced her determination to be the one to check in with the Lunden's Tavern team, the night before the final challenge.

Kane hadn't seemed to mind being sent off to oversee the packing up of the Ristorante D'Este team, although Eva had pouted upon being assigned the Red Orchid group.

Just as well. Claire hadn't missed the byplay between Eva Jansen and that pastry chef from Lunden's Tavern, the younger brother, either. Yet another trouble spot to watch.

So Claire had done her duty, trundling all the way downtown to verify that the Lunden's team finished their prep at the appointed hour and packed all their items onto speed racks, wrapped them in clear plastic, and loaded them onto a truck to be delivered to the RSC kitchen, thereby saving both Eva and Kane from the temptation of getting into trouble with the all-too-attractive Greenwich Village team.

She was doing a much better job of removing temptation from the paths of her fellow RSC officials than she was for herself.

It had been interesting, however. Last night's observations, coupled with what she'd overheard this morning, seemed to indicate that if Kane Slater broke his word, and all the rules, by trying something with that female Lunden's chef, he'd be disappointed. The young woman in question appeared to have quite enough male attention on her hands already, from both of the Lunden boys. Which quite possibly spelled disappointment for Eva, too, which was just as well.

Good, she thought firmly. *We can all be alone, frustrated, and disappointed together.*

At least there was the food to look forward to.

Chapter 28

It was down to the wire.

Of course it was; in every competition Max had ever entered, it always came down to those final few seconds and the ability to power through the panic and get his dish done.

The difference was that in every other competition, he'd been on his own.

In some ways, that had been easier. At least when he was alone, he only had to worry about disappointing himself with his own fuck-ups.

But when a chef from another team crashed into Danny and made him drop his pan of melted chocolate, spattering everyone around him and wasting a good half hour of work, Max didn't have time to decide if it was an ideal time to let his tenderloin rest and marinate—he ran to the rescue.

Luckily, the meat was fine when he got back to it after helping his brother crush what felt like seven hundred bars of bittersweet chocolate. In fact, the time away from his cutting board had brought the steak up closer to room temperature, which would help it cook more evenly, and had allowed the miso, soy, and yuzu marinade to sink in even further.

Standing over his cutting board, Max nearly swooned as he inhaled the clean, earthy scent. The complex saltiness of the miso and the delicate citrus of the yuzu took him straight back to Japan, while the underlying smell of the beautifully butchered, bright red, high-quality raw beef was the scent of his childhood.

He closed his eyes and took a moment to wish Gus Lunden could be there to see and taste this dish.

I think you'd actually like what I've done with your old recipe, Dad.

The celery root puree he intended as the base for the steak was straight out of the Lunden's Tavern playbook, too, only Max had bumped up the richness and tang of the flavor with roasted, pureed artichoke hearts. And for color, he planned to serve a very pretty salad of organic yellow wax beans and green beans with gingered orange peel and toasted hazelnuts.

Of course, as the clock ticked down the final minutes of their allotted cooking time, it was the fucking side dishes that tripped him up.

His tenderloin had been grilled to the perfect temperature using his father's famous techniques, and brushed with the miso glaze until it glistened. Once it came off the grill, the timing was precise. It needed to rest for ten minutes, so it would retain its delicious juices when he sliced it, but not longer than that, or it would be cold.

The first three courses had already gone out—Jules's incredibly tantalizing duck confit with pickled balsamic plums, Winslow's updated matzo ball soup, and Beck's homage to the classic bagel and shmear.

Max was up next. The judges were waiting. His puree was down on the plates, waiting to have the thinly sliced beef fanned over it. Everything in him was clamoring that it was time, the beef needed to be sliced and sent out before it was ruined—but the fucking green beans would not cooperate.

Max stared down at the handful of hazelnuts, their papery, dark brown skins clinging to them so tenaciously, he despaired of ever getting them clean and pristine. He stole a glance at the clock.

Three minutes. His hands started to shake.

All of a sudden, there was a brown, agile hand gently moving him out of the way and scooping the toasted hazelnuts into a clean dish towel.

"I know a quicker way," Winslow said, winking.

"The gingered peel goes on the beans, too, right?" Beck confirmed, grabbing a knife and getting to work mincing the pile of sticky orange peel.

Max blinked until Jules gave him a shove toward the resting meat. "Get slicing," she ordered. "Unless your hands aren't steady enough."

He looked at his teammates, his friends, busily saving his butt, and picked up his favorite, perfectly honed chef's knife.

"Steady as a surgeon," he told her.

Now came the moment of truth. No matter how perfect your timing, how accurate your thermometer, or how refined and experienced your eye, there was really no way to be sure the tenderloin was grilled to perfection until you sliced into it.

Holding his breath, Max sent up a quick prayer and let the sharp edge of his knife sink down through the meat in a clean cut.

As the slice toppled gently to the cutting board, it revealed a gorgeously pink, juicy interior, still steaming slightly. Max let out a whoop of relief, slicing the rest as quickly and carefully as he could.

There was a bit of last-minute scurrying, but somehow, and with the help of every person on the Lunden's Tavern team, he managed to send three perfect plates of food out to the judges.

Slumping to the floor, Max threw his head back and stared up at Danny. His brother's course, dessert, was last.

"Need help?" Max asked.

"It's chocolate cheesecake," Danny reminded him smugly. "It's been finished and in the cooler for an hour."

"I hate you," Max said. "No, wait, I love you, because that means I'm done."

Ten minutes of tasting and exclaiming over his teammates' dishes later, Max had managed to catch his breath, only to lose it again when Danny sent out his plates and Jules turned to them, eyes tired and cheeks flushed, and said, "Now all we can do is wait."

The waiting was the worst part.

At least, that's what he thought until he remembered that once the judges finished tasting the food, he and the rest of the team would have to go out on stage, in front of the judges and a whole audience of people, and talk about their menu.

Normally? Not such a big deal. But as Max leaned against the wall of the kitchen, letting the insanity of the teams still cooking flow around him like a raging river, he could actually feel himself crashing.

At least he had the comfort of knowing, down to his bones, that they'd sent out a kick-ass lineup of dishes. If the judges didn't like them, or scored someone else higher, they were insane and this whole competition was stupid and pointless, and Max would be sure to tell them so.

Just as soon as he slept for twenty hours straight.

"You okay?" Jules slid down the wall next to him, her hip and shoulder settling companionably against him.

Even with his thirty-six straight hours of wakey-wakey time catching up with him, the lean warmth of her body still made him shiver.

"Tired," he said, yawning. "Was working on pure adrenaline, which sadly doesn't last forever. And once it's gone, there's not going to be a whole lot keeping me upright."

Jules sent him a hesitant, sidelong look. "I bet I could get you up."

And just like that, he was back. "Hey there," he said, dropping the hand he'd propped on his knees to tickle at the side of her hip, making her squirm and laugh. "How long do you think we have before they call us out there?"

A shadow fell over them. "Not long enough," Danny said, amusement curling his mouth. "Also? Get a room. Something a little more private than the dry-goods storage closet would be my recommendation."

Winslow bounced over on the balls of his feet, clearly not experiencing any sort of crash. "Aren't you guys nervous? I'm nervous as all hell."

"There's nothing to be nervous about," Beck said, joining them. "Nerves are only useful when they can spur you on to work harder, faster, better. Once the work is done, they become pointless."

"Wow." Max blinked up at the tall chef. "That's actually very Zen."

"Sounds like common sense to me," Jules said.

"Whatever," Winslow snorted. "The first team that got judged, from the Italian place on East Thirty-sixth? They came back in here looking like whipped dogs. Come on, I know I'm not the only one here about to wet myself."

There was a short pause while they all looked at Win, and the way he was sort of dancing in place.

"Dude," Danny said finally. "Maybe you just need to pee."

He opened his mouth to argue, but a smooth, cultured voice cut him off. "So sorry, your bodily functions will have to wait."

Eva Jansen beckoned to them from the door of the kitchen, looking unfairly cool and elegant. The blunt cut of her dark hair swing against her chin as she took in their ragtag little group. Brow winging up like a black bird taking off, she said, "The judges are ready for you now."

Max hoisted himself up from the floor, his muscles trembling with exhaustion. He held out a hand to help Jules up, pulling just hard enough to ensure that she fell against him as she straightened her legs.

"There," he said into her ear. "That'll keep me awake better than any adrenaline."

She was strung tighter than a wire cheese slicer, her slender shoulders and back vibrating in his embrace. Zen and common sense or not, Jules was clearly terrified.

But when he gave her a smile, she found one for him, too, and before he set her back on her own two feet, she said, "See? Told you I'd get you up."

That was the moment. Right there.

The moment when Max Lunden realized he was in love.

Jules focused on the warmth that spread through her midsection every time Max looked at her with that smile, that spark, and did her best to ignore the fact that there were hundreds of eyes on her at that very moment.

The setup was similar to the qualifying round, a big room with bleachers at the back, a banner proclaiming the name of the competition in terrifyingly huge letters, and a raised stage under hideously bright lights.

Somehow, it wasn't any easier to deal with the second time around.

In some ways, it was far worse. Because instead of

facing the opposing team across the expanse of the stage, they were standing directly in front of the judges, who were seated at a long table covered in a white tablecloth. On her feet, in line with her teammates, Jules felt as if she were facing a firing squad.

The next few moments would decide their fate.

"First of all, thank you for a delicious meal," Claire Durand began briskly. Jules's heart pounded, but the judges probably said that to every team. It didn't necessarily mean anything.

"We'd like to hear from each of you, now," Claire continued, glancing down at her notes. "Explain a little bit about your dish, the inspiration behind it, and so on."

Crap. This was one thing Jules hadn't considered when she'd said she'd make the appetizer. All she'd been thinking was that Max had earned the right to make the main course. But now she had to be the first one to talk to the judges.

Swallowing felt like trying to choke down a wad of uncooked bread dough, but she managed it.

"The theme of our menu was 'I heart New York City,'" she said, proud of the steadiness of her voice. "So that's really where we took our inspiration—the dishes and the ingredients that make this one of the greatest food cities on earth."

That got a cheer from the crowd—who were mainly, Jules imagined, other New York chefs, so it wasn't surprising they liked that. Grinning, she relaxed a little.

"So I had the first course," she said, "and I wanted to showcase a couple of my favorite ingredients—gorgeous, free-range Hudson Valley duck, and perfectly ripe Wildman Farms plums. I confited the duck legs with cinnamon, nutmeg, star anise, and Chinese five-spice, for a little kick, and I paired it with fresh plums pickled in aged balsamic vinegar and pure maple syrup from Smokey Hollow."

"There was a round of brioche toast under the duck," Devon Sparks said, peering at her. "Did you bake the bread yourself, or buy it?"

Jules felt a fine sweat prickle at her hairline. "Ah no, I'm not much of a baker. But Danny, our resident baking expert, helped me out."

"So it was produced by your team," Kane Slater clarified, looking pleased.

Jules nodded, shoulders inching up toward her ears as she waited for the verdict. "You deserve high praise for that dish," Claire said. "I enjoyed it very much. The balance of sweet and savory was masterful. However, the flavor of the maple was, for me, not so good. Too assertive."

Jules's heart seized in her chest. All she could hear was that damning French accent saying "not so good."

"I disagree, I liked the maple. Liked the whole thing, actually. Definitely whetted my appetite for the rest of the dishes," Kane said. "In the sense that I would've been happier with about twice as much of the duck and plums."

Jules felt as if her brain were the last horse in a race, totally unable to keep up. Before she knew what was happening, the judges had moved on to Winslow's soup.

The moment the intense glare of the limelight faded a bit, Jules found herself able to breathe again. Although still completely unaware of what it might all mean for the team.

She couldn't help feeling that she'd let them down, let them all down—but no, the judges had comments on Winslow's matzo ball soup, too, some good and some "not so good," and Jules had tasted his dish herself. It was superb, a lovely homage to one of the homeliest, most comforting traditional dishes in the world, but refined. Delicate.

And speaking of delicate. It was Beck's turn to talk about his fish course.

"As I'm sure you guessed," he said, "my dish was a play

on my favorite New York City staple—a bagel with lox and cream cheese. Only I baked fresh bialys, my salmon was gravlax that I cured in salt, sugar, lemon peel, and Pernod, and I used crème fraîche in place of cream cheese."

Jules licked her lips, remembering her one bite of the dish. It had been so pretty. The curing process darkened the salmon to a deep coral pink, the thin slices artfully arranged across the miniature bialy, a cousin of the bagel with the same dense, chewy texture but a softer crust.

"I never had a bialy before," Kane Slater said, causing both of the other judges to raise their eyebrows at him. "What? I'm from Austin!"

"I'm from Paris," Claire Durand said, sounding scandalized. "And I've had bialys. Enough of them"—she turned back to Beck—"to know that yours was a supremely well executed version, Chef Beck. And you were clever to use them—the caramelized onion and poppy seed mixture in the center of the bialy was an intelligent way to replace the onions on the traditional lox bagel. There were, perhaps, too many poppy seeds."

"I agree," Devon Sparks said. "I'm going to have to floss twice tonight. But I enjoyed how well you'd clearly conceptualized the dish, and the way the combination of flavors was familiar, but you brought it to a whole new level."

"Thank you." Beck nodded his head once, impassive as always, but Jules caught a flicker of satisfaction in his dark gaze.

The judges weren't going easy on them—they were coming up with a lot of nitpicky details—but overall, it seemed to be going well. Well enough to beat the other teams? Jules had no way of knowing, and the uncertainty was like ants under her skin.

The fear of being judged, and found lacking—jeez, it was like the worst parts of her childhood in a single, harrowing half hour, only this time, played out in public for the amusement of an audience. And she'd signed up for this voluntarily?

As the judges turned their attention to Max and his miso-glazed tenderloin, Jules squinted into the bright lights, searching the audience for Nina Lunden's kind, familiar face.

There, six rows back . . . and wait, was that Gus beside her? Everything in Jules's body and brain went supernova from joy and relief that he was well enough to leave the hospital.

Jules squeezed her eyes shut, just to make sure she wasn't having a stress-induced hallucination, and when she opened them again and blinked against the spots dancing through her vision, she caught sight of the woman sitting on Gus's other side, and her brain stopped working at all.

The woman wearing a low-cut, figure-hugging dress that threatened to spill boobs all over the recovering heart attack survivor next to her was Jules's mother.

Chapter 29

Max faced the judges with his head held high. They weren't giving anything away with their expressions, but the fact that they'd paused so long between their raptures over Beck's gravlax—well deserved, Max had tasted that ethereally scrumptious fish—and his tenderloin wasn't promising.

Fuck it. Even if they didn't get it, he knew he'd put out an excellent dish.

"Who came up with the theme for this menu?" Devon Sparks asked.

Blinking, Max said, "I did, actually, with the help of my father, who's been coaching us."

"Interesting. All of the dishes so far have very clearly fit in with the I Love New York motif, and of course, it's easy to see where your brother's cheesecake idea came from—but I have to say, your dish confused me."

Well, crap. Max tried to smile. "Confusion wasn't exactly what I was going for."

"I would imagine not," Claire Durand put in. "Nevertheless, I enjoyed the flavors very much—again, the play of dark, intense miso and spicy ginger, with that hint of sour from the yuzu, was quite harmonious and lovely. But I agree with Devon, it was difficult to see where it fit in."

"Yeah, I was expecting, like, an updated corned beef and pastrami on rye, or something," Devon said. "Maybe something with a pizza or a hot dog. Not that the steak wasn't good, it was. And the green bean salad wasn't just pretty, it packed a punch of its own."

Crapcrapcrap.

"Uh, guys? Maybe we can give the chef a chance to tell us what he was thinking?"

Max shot Kane Slater a grateful glance. Double crap, this probably meant he'd have to revise his opinion of the guy.

"Look, you all know my parents' restaurant, Lunden's Tavern. It set the standard of the Manhattan restaurant scene as far back as the forties, and my family has cooked for everyone from Old Blue Eyes to ex-presidents. We've been doing steaks there the exact same way for decades, and there's a reason for that—they're damn good. And as much as Chicago is steak central, New York City has a pretty fierce steakhouse rep of its own." Clearing his throat, he forced himself to keep it steady. "It was important to me to honor that."

"Well, sure," Devon said skeptically. "But the Asian influence . . ."

"It's not the usual pairing, I'll admit," Max said, talking quickly. "But one of the things I love most about New York City is that it's not about 'usual.' There's a place for innovation in the culinary community here, an openness to new techniques, new flavors, that is unrivaled anywhere. New York may not be the birthplace of fusion cuisine, but we certainly embrace it here. And that's something else that's important to me."

Claire was nodding thoughtfully, which gave Max hope.

"I've traveled a bit in Asia," he continued, "which is

where I came across the philosophy that the only way to properly honor your culinary tradition is to never let it stagnate. To take what you know from the way a dish has been prepared in the past, and build on that, expand on it, take risks with it, try to perfect it."

He glanced down the line at Jules, who was watching him with wide, unblinking eyes. "Knowing all the while that perfection is not only unattainable, it might not turn out to be what you think it is, anyway," he finished softly.

"Bravo, Chef Lunden," Claire Durand said. "You've convinced me that your very excellent dish belonged as part of this menu."

"Ditto," said Devon, sitting back in his chair.

"You know what?" Kane said, grinning up at him. "It was so damn tasty, I didn't even really care why you made it. I'm just glad I got to eat it."

Okay, fine. So maybe the guy was a little likable.

Or maybe Max was just giddy that he'd been able to make his case, to finally articulate his thought process behind the dish. It felt as if he'd been carrying those ideas around like a sack of rocks on his back, and unloading them here on this stage left him floating a few feet above the floor.

He barely registered the judges' unrestrained adoration for Danny's bittersweet chocolate cheesecake—Max had tasted it, so he hadn't been worried about how it was going to go over—and then they were trooping off the stage to wait for the other teams to finish cooking and be judged.

Eva Jansen's assistant, a young guy with spiky extra-black hair, pale skin, and chunky glasses that reminded Max of Elvis Costello, ushered them out of the hotel ballroom they were using for judging and asked if they wanted to go back to the competition kitchen, or to wait for their families in one of the hotel suites reserved by the competition.

Max looked around, noticing his surroundings for the first time all day. He knew, intellectually, that the Gala Hotel had donated the use of its facilities in exchange for RSC publicity. And that they were somewhere in midtown. What he hadn't realized before was how gorgeous the place was, in an old-world, gilt-encrusted opulence kind of way.

Curious to see what one of the suites would look like—and if, perchance, said suite would come complete with a bed on which to crash—Max was about to enthusiastically accept for all of them when he caught the stricken look on Jules's face.

Shit. He hadn't even noticed if Tori Cavanaugh, or whatever the hell she called herself, had managed to show up. Was it better if she had, or if she hadn't? Max couldn't begin to sort it out.

Before Max could force his tired brain to decide, one way or the other, Winslow piped up. "We'll take Door Number Two, the suite. I don't know about these jokers, but some minibar action is sounding pretty baller to me, right about now. Lead me to it, baby."

And that was that. Win looped one long arm over the shoulder of their spiky-haired guide, and the rest of them followed after.

Jules dropped back to walk with Max. "Your father was in the audience," she said. "I wasn't sure if you knew."

Suddenly, it was as if all the nerves he'd denied himself in front of the judges came swarming into his stomach at once, shortening his breath and drying out his mouth. "Yeah?"

Weird that he cared more about what his father thought than all three illustrious judges combined.

She nodded, not looking at him. "My mom, too. Thanks for that, by the way."

"Hey, I'm not taking the rap for that one," he protested. "She asked me, I told her. I'm not feeling too high on the keeping of secrets, these days—besides, it's been advertised all over the place. Don't you think it's kind of, I don't know, nice that she wanted to come?"

Jules pressed her lips together, clearly struggling with something. "It is," she finally said. "And part of me is ecstatic that she was there, that she got to see me in my element, doing what I love."

"So what's holding you back from just being happy about it?"

"It's complicated," she said, refusing to meet his eyes. "You don't know the whole story, which, I realize—that's on me, because I haven't told you. But trust me, it's not as simple as it seems."

Max thought it kind of was, but he kept quiet, contenting himself with saying, "Well, if it sucks to deal with her, you've always got my family to back you up." He paused. "Wait. That's a cop-out."

With a glance at the rest of the team getting farther ahead of them, Jules stopped walking, too. Max didn't understand why she suddenly looked afraid, but he hoped what he had to say would make her feel better.

"I mean, yeah, you've got my family," he said, impatient with himself. "But Jules. You've got me. And I swear, I'll try my hardest to make sure nothing bad happens to you."

The fear in her eyes transformed to a look of wonder, and she lifted a hand to brush his cheek. It was a tentative touch, but it still managed to set Max on fire.

"It's been a long time since I needed a protector," Jules said, her voice as gentle as her fingertips on his skin. "But just knowing you're here right now, that you're on my side—it means a lot, Max."

They had to walk quickly to catch up to the others, but Max couldn't help thinking about the way she phrased that—"on her side," as if Jules's whole life were a battle of some kind.

Max had never been much of a fighter. He preferred to go with the flow, change people's minds by wearing them down over time rather than with his fists.

But when he thought about anyone hurting Jules—he suddenly understood the urge to fight.

Max and Danny both looked like they were about to keel over. If Jules hadn't already been feeling like a total shit for oversleeping and nearly missing prep the day before, the way they fell onto the sofa in the hotel suite would've clinched it.

"What a day," Danny moaned.

"What a week," Max agreed, tilting over sideways until his face smushed into the pillow at the arm of the sofa.

Danny reached around him for the pillow, snatching it out from under him and making Max's head bounce off the hard cushions. Max squawked, Danny laughed, and the brothers fell off the sofa, wrestling and pushing at each other.

"No shit," Winslow said, letting himself into the room from where he'd been saying good-bye to their erstwhile guide, Drew, in the hallway. Jules studied him for a moment, enjoying the slight glaze over his sea-green gaze. "What a ride! You must be stoked your stint here's almost up, Max. Bet peppering pork for pancetta in some tiny Italian village will be like a total vacation."

Danny's chortling laughter cut off as abruptly as if someone had put a hand over his mouth. Max paused with one arm bent around his brother's neck, the smile dropping from his flushed face. His eyes darted to Jules, who couldn't conceal her flinch.

There it was. The tiny little piece of information she'd

been trying her damnedest not to let herself think about while she and Max fumbled their way past the fact that she'd kept his father's secrets.

Why had she even bothered? One way or another, once they found out the team's fate, Max was gone.

A knock on the door shocked Jules out of the strange moment of suspended disbelief—how could she have let herself forget, even for a moment?—and she hurried to answer it, glad of the distraction.

Glad, that was, until she opened the door to find Gus and Nina in the hallway . . . and right behind them was her mother.

Jules's emotions clashed horribly, yo-yoing between joy at seeing Gus, up close and in (pale, disconcertingly frail) person, and the chaotic blend of disappointment, bitterness, and helpless love the sight of her mother always produced.

"Gus." Jules was almost afraid to hug him, he looked so gray and tired, but he held his arms out and she more or less fell into them. "You look great," she lied.

"Pfft. Come on, Jules, I raised you better than that," he said fondly, then froze, as if he'd realized at the same time Jules did that the woman who'd actually raised her was about a foot away. Maybe Tori hadn't heard the comment?

Jules pulled away awkwardly to glance at her mother. Tori's nude-brown lipsticked mouth was pressed in a tight line. She'd definitely heard. Crap. Could this get any more awkward?

"Come on in, everyone," Jules said, forcing a bright, happy tone. "The more the merrier. Who wants a drink? I know I do. Beck?"

"On it," was his terse answer as he moved to the miniature fridge set under the wet bar on the far side of the room. It was a really nice suite, spacious and elegant.

Although it felt considerably less spacious with two sets of parental figures lingering just inside the door.

"Looks like we've got just about anything you could want, in airline-bottle sizes," Beck said, dangling a collection of miniature liquor bottles from his big hands. "Or there's a couple beers, and some wine."

"Go on and sit down with the others while I find a bottle opener," Jules volunteered, moving quickly to the bar. "Anybody else want a drink? We don't have a lot of mixers, but I can crack open one of these bottles of wine. Danny? Max? Win?"

Aware that she was talking too fast, but unable to stop herself, Jules took refuge in her search for the corkscrew.

Behind her, she could hear conversation, happy exclamations from Gus and Nina about how well they'd done, and rehashing of every single one of the judges' comments.

Without warning, a soft, white hand tipped with lethally long, sharp nails coated in candy pink reached into the drawer under the wet bar sink, and came out holding a corkscrew.

Cursing the thick-piled carpet that had masked the click of her mother's stiletto heels, Jules straightened up with a smile.

"Thanks, Mom. You want me to—"

"Goodness, yes." Tori laughed. "I've never been able to manage one of those."

Jules managed to uncork the bottle of wine without commenting on how glad she was to be the kind of woman who could pour her own damn drink without waiting for some man to come along and do it for her. That was progress, she thought.

Crap. When did I become so judgmental?

Determined to try harder, Jules smiled at her mother before bending to unearth the lone pair of wine glasses from the shelves beside the fridge. "I'm glad you came to the finals today. It means a lot to me."

"Oh honey." Tori's familiar hazel eyes filled with tears. "Of course I came. It was my first chance to see you in action! I just wish they would've let us into the kitchen to watch you actually cook. But the judging was fun, too."

Pouring out a generous helping of cabernet into each of the two glasses, Jules handed them both to her mother, then grabbed a beer for herself.

Tori made a face at the beer. "I'll have a glass of wine, thanks. Who's the other one for?" She turned back to the group of chattering Lunden's crew. "Anyone? Wine?"

"What kind is it?" Gus asked, ignoring Nina's exasperated reminder that he wasn't allowed to mix alcohol with his medication.

"Um," Tori said, looking at the glasses. "It's red."

"There, see?" Gus gave his wife a triumphant grin that was only a little worn around the edges. "Red wine's good for the heart, everyone knows that."

"We'll share it," Nina said, accepting the glass from Tori. "Thank you. And you," she told her husband, "get enough for the toast, and that's it. I don't want to go back to that hospital for a long, long time. Understood?"

"Yeah, yeah, yeah," Gus grumbled, but Jules noticed he didn't make much of a grab for the wine glass.

"I was just telling Juliet how much fun it was to hear the judges' comments," Tori said. "They sure seemed to like what you all cooked. I'm sure your scores will be high. Although"—she pursed her lips playfully—"I bet the scores would've been even higher if you'd dolled up a little, Juliet. I mean, I know you love the"—*air quotes*—"tomboy look, but would it kill you to slap on some makeup and brush your hair?"

Something inside Jules shriveled. One of her hands

flew up to test the messiness of her braid, unsuccessfully smoothing at the flyaway hairs.

"Jules always looks beautiful," Max said, standing up abruptly. "Can I share your beer?"

She offered it to him wordlessly, and leaned gratefully into the strength of his body.

"Beautiful, and talented, too," Gus said, taking up a position on Jules's other side, so that before she knew what was happening, she was flanked by Lunden men, their support a tangible, solid wall all around her. "We'd never have made it this far without Jules."

"Well, of course she is," Tori stammered, her cheeks redder than bronzer alone could account for. "But still. It never hurts to put your best foot forward."

Swallowing hard against the painful lump in her throat, Jules was unprepared for the way it broke apart and nearly choked her when, from across the circle of people, Nina Lunden met her gaze and said, "You must be so proud of Jules, Mrs. Cavanaugh. I know we are. We couldn't be prouder if she were our very own daughter."

"So here's to the Lunden's team," Danny said, raising his miniature bottle of Chivas. "No matter what the judges say, and how this all turns out, I'm proud to have cooked with each and every one of you, and I'd do it again in a heartbeat."

Max handed the beer back to Jules, condensation making the glass chill and slippery against her fingertips. When she took a sip, the rich, sour, yeasty taste of it rolled down her throat and spread warmly through her chest.

It felt like acceptance.

Chapter 30

Tori Cavanaugh Clarke Whatever didn't stay long after the Lunden family closed ranks around Jules. Max didn't think he'd ever been prouder to be a Lunden than in that moment.

The party got a lot less formal and a lot more fun after that, with Danny drawing Jules down on the sofa with him to laugh at the way Winslow was blowing off steam by attempting to climb Beck like a tree.

Nina went to rescue Beck, whose usual stoicism had started to fray under Win's enthusiastic overflow of frantic energy, leaving Max standing with his father.

"How are you feeling, Dad?"

"Don't start. I'm still here, aren't I?" Gus grumbled, but there was a deep contentment in his eyes.

"And believe me, we're all grateful for that. Still, I can't believe Mom let you come to the judges' panel today. Hardly what you'd call a relaxing, rejuvenating experience."

"Especially since I couldn't be in the kitchen, helping with the cooking."

Part of Max wanted to reflexively stiffen up at that,

wanted to assume a crash position and fire back something defensive, but he just couldn't. Not because he was afraid his father couldn't take it—severe angina wasn't enough to truly weaken the force of nature that was Gus Lunden—but because Max had just witnessed a few stark differences between the ways a parent can interact with a grown child. And while he and his father had never had a smooth, easy relationship, there was nothing in it of the casual thoughtlessness shown by Tori Cavanaugh. She clearly had no idea how much her criticisms hurt Jules, but obliviousness was no excuse, as far as Max was concerned.

It had taken everything Max had not to throw the woman out of the suite.

"I hope you won't be disappointed with the results," Max finally said. "I know how much it means to you, getting into this competition. Lunden's is a great restaurant, always has been. You deserve your chance to represent the East Coast."

He was a little surprised to find that he meant every word of it.

"I hope we get our shot," Gus said. "And if we do, we'll all owe you a big thank-you."

The man's voice was gruff but achingly sincere, and Max fought the urge to squirm by straightening his shoulders and standing taller.

"I'd do anything I could to help you. All of you. I hope you know that."

Gus quirked a little smile, along with one of his heavy eyebrows. "Even cook steak, huh?"

Max's heart squeezed for an instant. There was so much unsaid between them, so many questions Max wanted to ask, clarifications he wanted to make, but instead, he pulled a deep breath into his lungs and held it there, hoping against hope that he was understood.

"I did it for you," he told his father, who turned to clap a solid, strong hand on Max's shoulder.

"I know you did, son. And what you said to the judges about it, about how you honor the past by looking for new ways to build on it—I get it. I'm an old man, sue me; it took me a long time, but I did finally get it." The faded blue eyes were steady on Max's face, and there was a look in them he hadn't seen in years. "I know why you left home and what you got out of all those places you lived. And I understand why you want to get back to that life."

The chokehold around Max's heart wouldn't let up; it was getting hard to breathe.

"Dad—"

"No, let me finish. This has been a long time coming, and it's way overdue, according to your mother. I'm proud of you, Max. No matter what you choose to do with your life, whether you stay or whether you go, I'm proud of the man in front of me."

The squeezing sensation had progressed from heart to lungs to throat. Max could hardly get the words out, but they were important. "You deserve a lot of the credit for that," he said. "You and Mom. I don't think I ever really appreciated what you gave Danny and me, and Jules, too, but I do now. I love you, Dad. I'm fucking lucky to be your kid, and I know it."

Gus used the hand on his shoulder to pull him in for a brief, forceful hug. He smelled so familiar, like wood smoke, black pepper, garlic, home—Max choked in a breath and pressed his forehead to his father's shoulder, then pushed back.

Stepping away, he became aware that the rest of the group had quieted down and were sitting on and around the couch watching Gus and Max as if they were a particularly involving and dramatic soap opera.

Max's gaze went immediately to Jules, who looked as close to tears as he'd ever seen her, but was smiling hugely.

"So we're all friends again?" Danny said, breaking the emotionally charged silence. "Perfect timing! I was starting to worry you two wouldn't work your shit out before Max flew off to Italy." He gave Max a half-smile, as if to make the point that he didn't resent Max for leaving again, but Max wasn't sure he bought it.

He wasn't sure he wanted to.

"Language," Nina said, mock-frowning through her happiness.

It wasn't all that convincing, but Danny gave an outraged squawk anyway. "Hey! Max said the f-word to Dad. Why doesn't he get scolded?"

"That was in the middle of a heartfelt father-son reconciliation," Winslow explained. "The rules are different. Everybody knows that."

And they were off to the races. Everybody on the team had an opinion on when it was permissible to curse in front of "the parentals," as Winslow called them.

Before moving to join the discussion, Gus slapped Max on the back, making him sway. God, he was tired. Almost asleep on his feet.

He looked around the suite. It was a hotel room. What were the odds there was a bed through any of those doors?

Jules extracted herself from the couch, where Danny and Winslow were currently arguing over her head about whether or not "douche waffle" counted as a swear word, and came over to lace her fingers through Max's.

"You look beat," she told him. "It'll be a couple of hours before we hear anything, I'm betting. Want to go lie down?"

"Only if you come tuck me in," he said, waggling his eyebrows. The next instant, he slapped a hand to his forehead. "Crap, sorry. That's awkward. I shouldn't have . . . in front of everyone . . . I mean, obviously, you don't want to come take a nap with me. Fuck, I'm babbling. Ignore me."

He tried to smile, but it must not have been a very good attempt, because Jules's face went serious and intent. But all she said was, "Come on. Bedroom's back this way."

And with her hand firmly wrapped around his, she led him away from their family and into the quiet seclusion of the suite's bedroom.

When she closed the door, shutting out the noise and laughter and chatter from the main room, she said, "I want to be with you. And I don't care who knows about it."

There was a strength, a sureness to her that made Max hard. He licked his lips, feeling his blood start to throb heavily in his veins.

Backing toward the bed with her hand still captive, Max let gravity tip them onto it in a warm, wonderful pile.

"Thanks for keeping me company," he told her, close enough to her ear to draw a line up the outer shell with his tongue.

He loved the way she shivered when he tasted her. He loved the way she tasted.

Max loved a lot of things about Jules Cavanaugh, as it turned out, especially the way she fit against him, evenly matched from chest to belly to hips to knees, and the way she rolled them until she was on top, propping her forearms on his chest to look down into his face.

"I thought you were exhausted," she said.

Max blinked, hands stilling on her hips to hold her in place. "What, you mean too exhausted to want you? Baby. That's not how it works. At least, not with a woman as unbelievably sexy as you."

Her slow smile lit up the dimness of the room, but her gaze dropped to his chin, sort of bashful.

"So," she said, bumping his nose with hers. "You don't ever wish I was more . . . I don't know. Frilly?"

He laughed, and she froze, the sudden tension of her body glaringly obvious after the way she'd been melted into him, and with a shock, Max realized she was serious.

Oh my God. Why did I say that?

Jules wished frantically that there were some way to recall the words, swallow them down back into the dark depths of her psyche where they belonged.

"Your fucking mother," he growled, brows drawn down like thunder. "The next time I see her, she better run."

"What? No, it's not about her," Jules protested, then paused. "Okay, yes, she makes me crazy. And what exactly are you planning to do when you see her, anyway? I thought Buddhists were against violence."

"I wouldn't consider myself truly Buddhist," he hedged.

"Well, Christians are supposed to be antiviolence, too," Jules pointed out, starting to feel less like faking her own death was her only way out of this conversation.

"Okay, fine," Max said. With a whipcord twist of his body, he reversed their positions so that he lay pressing Jules into the soft mattress, surrounding her with his heat. "You got me. The next time I see your mother, I won't smack her. Probably. But I reserve the right to be pissed at her for ever making you doubt how insanely gorgeous you are."

Jules shivered under him, every inch of her skin thrilling to his nearness. "I bet you say that to all the girls," she said, breathless.

"Nope. You're the first girl whose mother I've threatened."

"It's not as if she's the only one who ever made me think maybe I should doll up sometimes. Every girl I ever knew in middle school and high school thought I was a freak for not plucking my eyebrows and wearing a pound of makeup every day. And boys—come on. Every guy I've been with has dropped hints about wearing sexier clothes, or high heels."

"Personally, I love the natural look," Max said.

"All guys say that," Jules argued, "but the girl they take to the prom is usually not the one who comes to school in a Yankees jersey and scuffed sneakers."

"I'm serious," Max protested. "I like to see your actual skin. Makeup would just be in the way."

"Sure, you say that now, but did you ever notice me when I was in high school? No. You didn't."

Wow, where was all this coming from? Appalled at herself, Jules wriggled, trying to get out from under Max, but he bore down and kept her trapped under his solid, muscular weight.

"Jules," he said. "I noticed you. But you were Danny's friend, and younger, and—"

"It's fine," she said quickly, focusing her gaze over his left ear. "I shouldn't have even brought it up. I just meant . . . yeah, my mom's not perfect. She definitely turns me into an insane person, and not just about the girly thing. But sometimes." Jules sighed. "I don't know, sometimes it's so freaking exhausting to stay angry with her."

"I know exactly what you mean," Max said, his tone throbbing with enough sincerity to turn her eyes back to his.

And thinking about the way Max and his father had finally managed to talk through some of their problems, Jules could feel herself relaxing under him, because yeah. Max did understand.

Even if he didn't know the whole story.

Suddenly, it seemed ridiculous that he didn't. What was she waiting for? What sign would ever occur to convince her it was time to open up?

The time was now, she realized. Because if not now, then when? Her time with Max was almost up. And as much as she wanted to spend whatever hours she had left storing up good memories to last her when he took off, she hated the idea of him leaving without ever really knowing her.

Taking comfort in the way his body cradled hers, Jules took in the biggest breath she could manage, and let it go.

"When I was seventeen," she started, "my mother got a new boyfriend."

By the sudden stillness of Max's form, Jules knew he'd figured out where this was going.

"That was nothing unusual, of course," she continued, watching Max's left ear again. Fascinating, that ear. There was a tiny brown birthmark dotting the lobe, right where an earring would sit if he had a piercing.

"So what was different about this guy?" Max asked, his tone careful.

"Nothing, at first." Jules let herself remember him. Oliver. "He was nicer than some. More interested in me, asking me about school and softball and stuff. And he was around a lot. He moved in, which usually was the beginning of the end for my mom's relationships, but Oliver lasted. My mom really thought he was going to ask her to marry him. She seemed happy, but kind of nervous all the time, like she was afraid to put a foot wrong."

"What was she afraid of?" Trust Max to cut to the heart of it. Jules darted a glance at his face, dreading to see pity, but his eyes were calm and gentle. He brushed the hair back from her temples, and that light touch was enough to help her go on.

"Oliver was . . . a perfectionist. Everything had to be just so, from the table setting at dinner to Mom's clothes. Me. I got pretty good grades, but anything lower than an A meant a lecture from Oliver, and my mom got extra jumpy for a few days, and it wasn't worth the hassle. So I studied hard, and I kept out of his way as much as possible so he wouldn't try to tell me how to dress, and things were mostly okay." She swallowed. "Until this one time . . . I guess I'd gotten tired of it, all the comments about my ratty jeans and baggy shirts, and I went out and spent my allowance on a dress. It was yellow. There were flowers on it, little pink ones, and it had no sleeves, just those little skinny shoulder straps. It was a summer dress, on sale."

Jules swallowed hard, remembering how embarrassed she'd been, admitting to the Macy's sales clerk that she didn't know what size she wore.

"What happened?"

"I wore it home, just sort of trying it out. My plan was to wear it to school the next Monday. There was a guy I liked—God, I don't even remember that boy's name— and the winter formal was coming up, and whatever. I wanted to try being a girl, see how it felt. See what my mom said, maybe get her to help me with some makeup. But when I got back to the apartment, she wasn't there. But Oliver was."

Tension strung wires through Max's muscles. "Did he hit you?"

His voice was deep and low enough, snarly enough, that it actually scared her for a second. "What? No. No, he liked it. The way I looked. He said . . ." Jules swallowed, not sure she could get this next part out without choking on the words.

"It's okay. Just tell me."

Jules shook her head, but opened her mouth. "*I always knew you could be pretty.* That's what he said. And he . . . touched my shoulder, where it was bare. I tried to pull away, but he got a good grip on me, I couldn't move, and he kept saying I wanted it, I must want it, or I wouldn't have dressed up for him, wouldn't have tried to be pretty for him."

"Jules," Max said, voice breaking. "Oh my God. Tell me he didn't—"

"He didn't have the chance," she assured him, working to get her breathing under control. "Mom came in and saw us, and he let me go."

Max didn't relax against her, though. Jules could feel the brittle stillness of his body along hers. "The night you left home . . . I heard you and my dad talking about it. I know about the black eye."

Shame filled Jules's head like boiling water in a tea-kettle. "Okay, so you know about that. But it wasn't Oliver. He was horrible, I hated him, God, how I hated him—but he didn't hit me."

"Then who—"

Jules forced herself to lift her chin and meet Max's fierce gaze. "It was my mom," she said.

Chapter 31

Max had never been incapacitated by pure, red-hot rage before. He didn't exactly enjoy the sensation.

Before he could unlock his tongue, Jules took up the story again.

"It was an accident. I think it was an accident; she'd never hit me like that before. But when she came in, Oliver started saying all this shit, right away, telling her how I'd come on to him, flirted with him. And there I was in a dress, which I never wore, and I was all shaken up, so I didn't defend myself right away. It's kind of a blur, actually, but somewhere in the middle of it, Oliver took off, and Mom flipped."

So many puzzle pieces were flying at Max, it was as if someone had shaken up the Jules Cavanaugh puzzle box and dumped it out on his head.

"Every time he took off, she'd get upset—I guess she was worried this time he wouldn't come back. She was always worried about that with her boyfriends, probably because of my dad. Who, you know, didn't come back."

"Jules," he said, trying to make sense of the chaotic emotions pummeling him.

"Sorry, I'm rambling," she said with a little laugh. "Anyway, so Mom's mad. And she's telling me to stop crying, yelling about the dress, and the stuff Oliver said. I tried to tell her, no, it wasn't me, it was him. That he touched me and said I was pretty, but I didn't want him to, and Mom's hand flew up out of nowhere, caught me right on the cheekbone, wham. We were both shocked, I think, her as much as me. And I said—"

Jules stopped, her throat working, and Max slid to the side, turning her so that he could enfold her fully in his arms. She tucked her head against his neck, hiding there for a long moment during which Max imagined all the horrible ways this story might end. He was pretty sure it was going to break his heart, and he would've done anything to save Jules the pain of reliving it—but she needed to get this poison out of herself and let it go.

"It's okay," he whispered. "Just say it."

"I told her. I told her that I hated her, and I'd never forgive her, and . . . And that she deserved to be alone. And she told me to get out, and not come back until I learned some manners. So I left."

Max concentrated on breathing in through his nose and out through his mouth. Winter formal, she'd said. It would've been bitterly cold, maybe snowing. She'd been seventeen. His mind shied away from images of exactly what could happen to a seventeen-year-old girl, alone on the streets of New York at night.

"Jules. God. She should've believed you. She should've protected you. I'm so sorry you had to go through that. And I'm so incredibly glad you found your way to my parents' house."

"All I could think to do was to get to Danny. I don't know what I expected him to do—but I certainly never expected your family to take me in like that. And to let me stay. It was . . . I'm still awed by the generosity of it. I mean, that's how your parents are, I know that. They would've done the same for any kid who needed help."

Max pulled back far enough to peer down into her flushed face. "Bullshit," he said, as firmly as he could.

She blinked. "What?"

"I said that's a load of crap. Yeah, my parents are good people, but they're not running a halfway house out of their apartment. Sure, they'd let people crash on their couch for a night or two, help out where they could—but none of those people ever became part of the family. My parents love you as much as they love Danny and me." With a rueful smile, Max rested his forehead against hers. "Hell, maybe more than me, at this point. And I gotta be honest, that bothered me when I first came back. As if you'd taken my place in the family, or something stupid like that."

"I know," she whispered. "I could tell you felt that way. But that's really not true—your parents are crazy about you. I could never get in the way of that, and I wouldn't want to."

"I know," he echoed her, pressing a soft kiss to her temple. "You were just making the best of a bad, shitty turn of the wheel. You deserved better than you got from your mother."

Tilting her head back, offering her throat to his searching mouth, Jules murmured, "Maybe I did. But it took two of us to get into that situation. I never talked to her, not really, not about what was going on in my head. And honestly . . . I'm just sick of being pissed about it. It happened. She is who she is, she's never going to change. I need to accept that—especially since, at the core of everything, it's what I always wished she'd do for me. Just accept me the way I am."

Max laid a line of kisses from her chin to her ear. "That's incredibly forgiving. And very Zen."

"You must be rubbing off on me."

He gave a suggestive little shove of his hips that made her gasp. "Not yet," he leered, "but give me a minute."

Jules thwapped him on the arm, but he noticed she also threw one leg over his thigh, aligning them even more closely. "I meant, you inspired me. Well, you and Gus. Watching the two of you finally get over yourselves and listen to each other, and how much lighter you both looked, after. It made me realize how heavy all this Mom stuff I've been lugging around is. And how tired I am of it."

Max stilled. She was serious. "You know," he said carefully, wanting to get this right. "Forgiveness is a funny thing. We act like it has to be earned, as if there are a certain number of hoops someone can jump through to make us forget that they hurt us. But forgiveness can't be earned. It can only be given freely, as a gift."

Her beautiful, deep amber eyes took on a faraway look. "Yeah," she said, "but who's the gift for, really? Because when it comes down to it, my mother might never understand the ways she's hurt me—and that's okay. Do I really need to make sure she has the itemized list before I forgive her? That sounds more like punishment, to me. For both of us."

"It took me years of soul-searching to figure that out," Max said, his heart swelling. "And it's a lesson I've had to learn over and over. But you're right. Forgiveness isn't about evening the score or granting pardon. It's a gift you give yourself—the gift of letting go and moving forward."

"I want that," Jules said, eyes shining. "We're going to be chosen as the East Coast team. I know it. And with the competition and the restaurant and everything, God, I haven't been this excited about the future in my whole life. I want to walk into it completely free and unencumbered by the past."

It took everything Max had not to betray the pang that

gave him with sudden stillness or tension. She wanted to be free? Did that mean free of everything, including Max?

A knock on door startled them out of their embrace.

"Yeah?" Max called.

"Win's little friend, that assistant dude came back." It was Danny. "He gave us a heads-up that the judges are calling everyone to the stage in about fifteen minutes. So put your pants back on."

"Shut up," Jules and Max yelled in unison, then looked at each other and laughed.

"So," Max said, reluctantly hauling his tired body up from the haven of the bed. "Are you going to forgive your mom?"

She raked her fingers through her hair, disordering it worse than usual. "I . . . guess I am. I mean, I have. What, is there some special ceremony or ritual I'm supposed to perform?"

"Rituals can be helpful," Max said, holding the bedroom door open for her. "But no. I think as long as you feel it in your heart, you've done the hard work already."

Max was right about one thing, Jules thought. Well, a lot of things, as it turned out, but he was really right when he said that feeling something and accepting it was the hardest part.

The whole team, including Gus and Nina, trooped down the hotel hallway together, jittering and excited as they walked toward their fate.

Jules found herself caught, balanced on the edge of her own emotions as precariously as on the edge of her favorite knife. On the one side, there was the anticipation and thrill of the Rising Star Chef competition, and everything that competing in it would mean to her adopted family.

On the other side, there was Max, and the unassailable fact that once they found out whether or not they'd be representing the East Coast, he'd leave. And there was nothing she could do to stop him.

At least—there was nothing she was willing to do, to take away his chance of studying with Vincenzo Cotto.

Beside her, Max bumped her shoulder with his, their hands sliding together as warmly and naturally as if they were magnetized to find each other.

Max glanced over at her. "You nervous?"

"Yeah. I mean, I know there's no such thing as a lock—we made some mistakes. I made some mistakes, that maple syrup. Shit." It made her mad all over again, thinking about that. She'd known, as she reached for the bottle, that it was a strong, love-it-or-hate-it flavor, and there was a danger of it overpowering the delicate balance of the salty duck confit and the sweet-tart pickled plums.

But Jules happened to love maple syrup, so she'd used it anyway. And of course, it was the one thing Claire Durand had picked on to critique.

Max squeezed her fingers tight and said, "Hey. I tasted your dish, and I thought it was perfect. Did you like it?"

"Yeah, I did."

"That's what matters. That's all you can do. Cook to your own tastes, dress how you want, live the life you choose—it's the only way to be happy."

She stopped walking so abruptly that her hand tore away from his, and he looked back over his shoulder at her, surprised.

Jules was surprised, too. She'd been through some emotional ups and downs in the past few weeks, but nothing had walloped her in the head quite like that.

"You're right," she heard herself say. "That dish was good the way it was."

"Maybe not perfect by everyone's standards." He smiled, one of those warm, wonderful ones that turned him from simply handsome to something out of a fairy tale or a myth, a piece of sacred art come to life. "But perfectly you."

Jules smiled back, her heart swelling with emotion, pounding her blood through her veins.

With a swift check of the rest of their troop's progress up the hall, Max came back to Jules and stood in front of her, reaching out to take her hands in his. Time seemed to slow down, everything around her crystallizing into a still, silent moment, as if someone had paused the movie of her life to capture this scene.

Max's smile faded, a serious, intense look she'd never seen before entering his blue eyes.

"Jules. I've been thinking. With Dad's health and the competition, and everything—the state of the restaurant . . . and you. God, you most of all."

All the breath left her body. She barely managed to croak out, "What are you saying?"

He gave a hoarse chuckle. "I'm not making any sense. Sorry. This is hard." Visibly centering himself, pulling his shoulders straight and lifting his chin, Max said, "Jules. No matter what the judges say—I'm not going to Italy. I'm going to stay here. With you."

For one heartbreaking instant, pure euphoria rushed through Jules's body, nearly lifting her off her feet. Max wanted to stay! With her!

He wanted to . . . give up his dream. The dream of Italy, the dream he'd worked toward for years. The way he'd talked about it, the longing in his voice—she couldn't forget that.

The temptation was pure torture.

But Jules had watched her mother traipse down the road of self-delusion a hundred times, and there was nothing at the end of it but resentment, loneliness, and an empty feeling of failure.

She wouldn't wish that on Max, or on herself.

Max lived life with such free-spirited joy. The people he'd met all over the world, the things they'd taught him—his boundless curiosity and adventurous nature were such integral parts of him.

If he lost that thirst for adventure, would he even be the person she loved anymore?

And if she let him stay, knowing that deep down he regretted the loss of his dreams, it would kill her.

Jules closed her eyes, unable to bear the tentative hope lighting Max's handsome face. "Thank you, Max. But it's not necessary."

He dropped her hands, leaving a cold chill behind. "What?"

"You don't need to stay here for me. I love that you offered—it means a lot to me."

Max made a sound, as if someone had elbowed him hard right in the gut. Worried, Jules forced her eyes open. He was staring at her, blank and expectant, clearly waiting for something more.

She plastered on a smile, and searched for the right words, the words that would set Max free. "Whatever happens out there, I'm glad I got the chance to know you. It sounds so lame and corny, but I've learned a lot from you. About myself, and the kind of life I want to have. And if we get the chance to continue on in the competition, I'll take what you said with me, and I know it'll help me get the team all the way to the finals. And if we get cut today, I want you to know, I'll take care of them. Your parents, and Danny, and the boys. You won't have to worry about us, because we'll be okay."

Max's face was still, his eyes dark and unreadable in the soft lighting of the hotel hallway. "So I can leave town with a clear conscience, is what you're saying. There's nothing holding me here."

The word "nothing" slid between Jules's ribs with the

lethal precision of a long, thin metal skewer, puncturing her swollen heart and making it bleed. "That's what I'm saying. You're good to go," she managed, finally allowing herself to drop her gaze.

She looked down at her chest and was vaguely surprised to see the unblemished white expanse of her chef's jacket. It seemed like it should've been soaked in red.

"Come on, you two!" Nina called down the hall. The others had made it all the way to the elevator banks, and were holding the doors open, waiting for Max and Jules, to the accompaniment of a loud, buzzing sound.

"Coming, Mom," Max said, loping off down the hall without another look at Jules.

She followed at a brisk pace, but all she really wanted to do was dig her heels into the hotel carpet. She wasn't afraid to face the judges again, no matter what they said. Max had given her that.

But she was terrified, to the center of her skewered heart, of what would happen after the judges had their say.

Chapter 32

It was about a billion degrees hotter on the stage this time, with twenty hopeful chefs crammed under the same bright-ass lights, facing down the three people whose opinions could make or break reputations in the tightly knit restaurant community.

Max tracked a bead of sweat as it trickled down his spine. He'd been cooler in Morocco.

Cooler, and less tense in general, but he was starting to wonder if a life free of stress and responsibility was all it was cracked up to be.

Footloose and fancy-free had never brought Max anything as exhilarating as Jules Cavanaugh—or as heart-breaking.

She was next to him on the stage, standing straight and tall, shoulder to shoulder with Max. There was a strange, sad set to her mouth. Probably just nerves. Max wished he could believe it had anything to do with him, with her not wanting him to leave, but that neat little speech she'd given him back in the hallway upstairs sort of put paid to that fantasy.

Jules was ready for Max to get out of town. She'd made

that pretty clear. And he couldn't even blame her—she'd gotten into this thing with him believing the whole time that it was only temporary. Part of him even understood that the temporariness of it had been a big draw.

The fact that she knew, going into it, that Max wouldn't stick around relieved her of the stress of wondering. The fact that he wasn't going to be there forever probably made it easier for Jules to let down her walls.

Or, more accurately, it had made it easier for Max to batter those walls down.

Either way. Jules had never been in it for the long haul, and even though things had changed for Max, apparently nothing had changed for her.

A hush fell over the packed ballroom as Claire Durand passed a slip of paper to Eva Jansen, who unfolded it and read the contents with a canary-swallowing smile on her pretty, feline face.

"First of all," she said into the microphone, "thank you to the judges, for your time and consideration. I know this must have been an incredibly challenging decision. And thanks to all the amazing chefs who put their skills and talents to the test here today. I saw the food you put out, and you should all be very proud of yourselves. But there can only be one team from each region in the Rising Star Chef competition."

She paused dramatically, the mic nearly pressed to her candy-apple-red mouth. "And this year, the team that will represent the East Coast in the competition for the title of Rising Star Chef will be the team from . . . Lunden's Tavern!"

Her lips kept moving, and Max barely caught the sound of their names being listed, but it was impossible to really hear over the roar of the crowd, the shouts of his brother and friends, and the din in his head.

Utter pandemonium gripped the stage. People Max had

never met were slapping him on the back, pulling him away from his teammates just by milling around like a herd of cows clogging a rural roadway. The one he could see was Winslow, who'd hopped on Beck's back again and was singing "We Are the Champions" at the top of his lungs. Through the buzzing in his ears, he could hear Jules laughing.

"You won!" His father's thick, brawny arm came around Max's shoulder and nearly lifted him off his feet with a triumphant squeeze.

Max didn't feel like he'd won anything, but he hugged his dad back and said, "Yeah. I told you we would."

"Everything's going to be different now," Gus said, his blue eyes glittering in the stage lights.

"A few things, yeah," Max acknowledged. He peered at his father's face, still a bit pale under the happy, triumphal flush.

"Don't say it," Gus warned, making Max swallow his instinctive question about how his dad was feeling. "This is the best medicine I could possibly get. I'll be fine! Good as new in a couple of weeks. I don't want you to worry about me."

"Sorry. Comes with the territory."

"You're a good son," Gus told him, which made Max feel like shit. He hadn't been, and he knew it, but his father kept talking, the sparkle in his eyes fading as his face went all solemn and man-to-man. "You came home when we needed you, and you did your part, exactly as you promised you would. No one could ask for more than that. Things are going to be different now, but we'll be okay. Just . . . come home to visit every now and then, all right? Your mother misses you."

Jesus. Was everyone he cared about determined to kick Max out the door the minute they left the stage?

He was a moron. He'd let himself forget that he'd given

up his place here a long time ago, and that it wasn't his to claim anymore. No matter how surprisingly well it still seemed to fit him, it was only on loan.

Time's up, Maxwell.

A sick twist in his guts made it impossible for Max to smile, but he managed a nod. "Great. Guess my work here is done." Glancing around at the crowd without really seeing anything, Max suddenly zeroed in on Jules at the edge of the stage, leaning down to hug his mother.

"Look, I'm going to take off," he said. "You guys don't need me anymore, and I've got a lot of things to take care of before the Italian apprenticeship starts. I'll kiss Mom good-bye on my way out. Tell the rest of the guys I said 'congrats' and 'kick ass.' And Dad . . ." Max forced himself to meet his father's gaze. "Thanks for calling me. I'm glad you did, glad I was able to help."

Gus cleared his throat and nodded, looking gruff and a little pissed, the way he always did when he was fighting down strong emotion. "Well, go on, then, if you're going. Be safe out there, kiddo."

Max's feet started to itch, his legs to tingle, in that way that had always signified that it was time for him to move on.

Keep moving, never stop, because if you stopped, you might have to sit down and think about what you were running from.

Breathing in the sharp smell of sweat from the mosh pit of chefs, judges, and audience members on the stage, Max deliberately blanked his mind and his face, and hopped down off the stage to head for his next good-bye.

This was going to be the tough one.

Part of Max wanted to chicken out, bypass his mother and Jules and send them a postcard or something from down the road. But he couldn't do that, and besides, an even bigger part of him was hoping—idiotically, foolishly, and irrationally hoping—that when he told Jules he was leaving, she'd give him a reason to stay.

But when he hugged his mother and told her he was heading home to pack, Jules said nothing. She said nothing while Nina's eyes welled up, and Max hugged his mother again so he wouldn't have to see it. She said nothing when he promised to come back and visit, to call more often, to let her know where he was staying in Le Marche once he had an address.

When Nina let go of him after one last tight squeeze, she sniffled a little and went off to find Gus, leaving Max staring up at a still-silent Jules, standing on the raised platform of the stage. The bright lights behind her made a nimbus around her head, casting her face in shadow.

"Good luck," she finally said.

Disappointment scored through Max, but he said, "You, too. Keep your head up, I'm sure you'll win this thing."

She nodded, the halo of light moving with her, turning her dark blond hair a radiant gold.

"If you make it to the finals," Max said, heart in his throat, "I'll come cheer for you."

"You'd better," she said, and he heard a hint of a smile in her voice.

"Okay, well . . ." Max lingered for a long moment.

Ask me to stay. Ask me to stay. Ask me to stay.

She didn't. Instead, she raised one hand in wave, then turned and walked away quickly, her black chef clogs thudding on the bare boards of the stage, like thunder even over the footsteps of the crowd she disappeared into.

And that was it.

There was nothing left to do but head back to the apartment, pack up his kit, and get his ass on the first flight out to Tokyo to gather the rest of his gear for the trip to Italy.

As Max walked out of the hotel and onto the busy Manhattan sidewalk, he thought about Harukai-sensei, and the noodle shop in Ginza. He thought about his little room at the back, with the pallet on the floor and the tatami mats under his feet. He remembered the serenity he'd found there, the elusive, slippery sense of peace that he'd attained after hours of meditation, and wanted that again with a sudden, ferocious need.

Max's trip back to the apartment was charmed—every light was with him, the swarms of pedestrians and window-shoppers propelling him across the streets and down into the subway, where the train pulled up the instant he hit the platform.

I get it, he wanted to yell at the universe. *I'm going, already. Quit fucking pushing me.*

When Danny found him, Max was almost completely packed. It had taken longer than he'd expected, because he'd unpacked more than he usually did for a short stay in a temporary place.

Just another sign that he'd lost sight of the big picture, Max thought, wrestling the broken zipper on his beat-up leather bag.

"So that's it," Danny said from the doorway. "You're leaving. Just like that."

"It's time," Max grunted, heaving his bag up and onto his shoulder. It was heavier than he remembered.

"Fuck you." The leashed ferocity in his brother's voice made Max's gaze fly to him. "What it's time for is for you to grow the fuck up."

The pain in Max's chest knotted into a hard ball of rage. Trying to suppress it, he ground out, "Look, I'm sorry you're not happy. And I should've said good-bye to you and the guys, but honestly, you don't need me anymore. I did what I came here to do, and I've got places to be."

"Bullshit." Danny crossed his arms over his chest, blocking the door like one of the Chinese terra-cotta warrior statues. "You're not leaving because you're done. You're not leaving because you want to learn how to make prosciutto from the master. You're running away, like you always do when things get hard."

It hit Max like a sword to the gut. He felt the truth of it all the way to his bones, but he couldn't admit it. Instead, he snarled back, "Better that than to roll over like a puppy anytime there's a fight."

Danny's mouth set in a grim line. "I'm not rolling over now, asshole."

"Well, I'm not fighting with you." Max hefted his duffel higher and straightened to his full height. He was only an inch or so taller than Danny, but by God, he *was* taller. "Get out of my way."

"Make me."

Max shook his head, and Danny's mouth twisted into a sneer. "What, you think because I don't like to fight, that I'm scared to? I'm not scared of you. At least I know who I am and what I want."

"Move, Daniel," Max growled, the short fuse of his patience burning dangerously close to the end.

"No. Not until you admit you're a coward."

Max snapped. Dropping his shoulder, he rammed his brother's chest, knocking him back into the hallway outside his room. Danny, though, didn't raise his hands in surrender. Hooking an arm around Max's neck, almost tight enough to choke off his air supply, Danny spun them both into the wall behind them. Max felt the impact all along his side, but it didn't register as pain.

Pushing off the wall, grappling with his brother, the two of them fell back into the open doorway of Max's room, hitting the floor in a tangle of fists and elbows.

Three minutes later, it was over. They lay side by side on the floor, panting and staring up at the ceiling.

Max catalogued his injuries. Split lip, sore and tangy with blood every time his tongue poked at it. The skin around his left eye felt puffy and hot, already swelling shut. His knuckles hurt; he'd gotten in a few good punches himself.

Turning his head to squint at his brother, he was both satisfied and ashamed to see the dark bruise blooming up along Danny's cheekbone.

"When did you stop being afraid of conflict?" Max asked.

"About the time you left home, and I had to deal with the assholes on the block by myself." Danny grinned, only wincing a little at the stretch. "It was right about the same time I got my growth spurt, too, so that worked out okay."

Max laughed a little, feeling the soreness in his lower abdomen from a well-placed knee. "Shit, man. See? Me leaving was the best thing that could've happened to you."

Danny sighed. "Max. When you left, I had to grow up fast. I had to take care of myself, the restaurant, Mom and Dad. You left it all on me. And I did my best. But it sucked a lot of the time."

Testing the painful spot on his ribs by rolling to a sitting position, Max pulled his knees up and rested his arms on them. Meeting his brother's solemn gaze, he said, "I'm sorry, Danny. I'm sorry I left you alone to deal with everything. But I thought I was doing the right thing—shit, you remember how much Dad and I were fighting back then. Every time we yelled, you hid in your room. I thought . . ." Max had to take a second to swallow hard. "I thought it would be better for you, for all of you, if I just took off. No more fighting."

"Sometimes fighting is good, though," Danny said, staring up at the ceiling again. "Fighting for what you want, fighting to be understood, to be heard. It's hard, but it's worthwhile." He turned his head, fixing Max with a deeply penetrating stare. "It wasn't better after you left last time, and it won't be better this time, either. For anyone. Including you. No one else wants to say that, but it's true."

"You're wrong," Max said, his heart twisting. "Jules wants me to go. She practically shoved me out the door."

With his eyes squeezed shut, Danny thumped his head once against the hardwood floor and groaned. "Judas Priest. Jules, you fucking idiot."

It was weird, but Max actually felt his knuckles tingle with the urge to connect with Danny's face again. "Shut up," he growled. "Don't talk about her like that."

When Danny opened his eyes, it was to stare up at Max with a pitying expression. "You're *both* idiots," he clarified, sitting up and scooting to rest his back against the wall under Max's classic Rolling Stones poster. It looked like the big red tongue was about to lick his head, maybe smooth down the spiky brown hair that had gotten ruffled up during the fight. "Lucky for you, I know you both better than anyone else in the world. And I'm here to tell you, Jules does not want you to leave town."

The world stopped turning, just for an instant, but it was long enough to make Max sway dizzily. "What?"

Danny rolled his eyes. "Judas *Priest*," he complained. "What the hell have the two of you been talking about, that you don't know this about her? Jules is never going to ask you to stay. She just isn't. But that doesn't mean she doesn't want it."

Max stared at his brother, who rolled his eyes again and started the laborious process of getting to his feet.

"Are you sure?" Even as the words formed in his mouth, Max was reliving the look on Jules's face when she gave him that speech back at the hotel—the way she'd wrapped around him, clinging just a little, when they were in the suite bedroom together—the revelations about her past.

"Oh my God," Max said, blinking slowly. "I'm a fucking

idiot. I guess next you're going to tell me that Dad wants me to stay, too."

Satisfaction made Danny's smile gleam like freshly polished china. The smirk made him look ten years younger, like the kid Max remembered. "Now you're starting to use your brain."

"Seriously? But Dad's spot on the team . . . he's not going to want to give that up."

Danny's jaw hardened, and Max caught a glimpse of the man who'd just knocked the sense back into his head. "Dad needs a reality check, if he thinks he's cooking on the team with us after that surgery. It might be what he wants, but you know what they say."

Danny flicked his eyes up to the Stones poster, and Max grinned. "You can't always get what you want."

"Exactly. Which doesn't mean we shouldn't try. So the question is, Maxwell—what do *you* want?"

Chapter 33

Claire left the stage after shaking hands with every single finalist. Her cheeks ached from switching between congratulatory smiles for the Lunden's crew, and heartfelt expressions of regret for the losing teams.

Finally managing to steal away to a quiet corner, she allowed her shoulders to slump as she tried to catch her breath.

The competition had barely begun, and already she was this weary? Not a good sign.

It was only that she hadn't slept well, she told herself. A restless night of remembering Kane Slater's honey-slow smile and quick, expressive hands, and sleepy, sprawled posture as he looked her in the eye and told her she could have him.

As if her incessant thoughts of him had conjured him up, Kane appeared next to her. His warm body filled the quiet space she'd found for herself with the pulsing, electric tension that always arced between the two of them.

"You okay?"

She didn't want to be affected by the concern in his tone, but Claire felt the rigid line of her shoulders soften when he leaned in, shielding her from the pandemonium of the rest of the room.

"Yes, of course," she managed. "Only a trifle fatigued. It will pass."

One corner of his mobile mouth quirked up. "I bet I could help you relax."

She stiffened. "We had an agreement, Kane. I'd use your first name in return for you ceasing the constant seduction attempts."

The other corner kicked up, spreading a full grin across his handsome, rough-jawed face. "Hey! I meant I could give you my yoga instructor's card, but your idea sounds good, too."

"Kane!" Frustration sharpened her voice more than she liked, but he never dropped his infuriating smile.

"And to be clear, I never agreed to stop trying to seduce you," he continued blithely.

"You most certainly did." Claire had spent the entire night reliving their conversation in the café.

"I most certainly didn't." He leaned in closer, until the skin of her cheek tingled in anticipation of coming into contact with the stubble lining his jaw—but he paused when he was still a breath away from her.

"I agreed to behave myself in public," he reminded her softly. "Which I'm okay with, because I'm happy to keep the world from seeing you the way I see you."

Her lungs couldn't want to draw in enough oxygen, as if he were somehow absorbing all of it.

The question rose up from the depths of her, undeniable and unstoppable as the beat of her blood. She had to know.

"And how do you see me?"

The lack of oxygen was abruptly no problem—she would've been holding her breath anyway.

"I see your brilliance and your ambition and your

strength—all the things the world sees. But here, now, I see something else, too. The woman you are inside, the woman you don't want to indulge, the woman who wants and needs and desires. That's the woman I want you to let out to play."

A few meters away, a crowd of chefs and family members shouted and laughed and chatted and celebrated or commiserated, but for Claire, they no longer existed. The cage of Kane's body, the dimness of their secluded corner, enclosed them in their own private world.

"Come on, darlin'." His drawl was soft and rough, like raw silk stroking over her skin. "I'm right here waiting for you. Come on and play with me."

A shudder ran through her, shaking her down to her bones. She lost herself staring up into his intense blue eyes for one endless moment while she struggled with the desire pounding at her heart and trying to escape from her chest.

And then she let it go in a rush that lifted her onto her toes and pressed her lips to his wide, smiling mouth.

Kane opened up to receive her, his arms and his eyes and his lips moving over her with barely leashed ferocity. The heat of him seared her nerve endings and made her want to press closer at the same time, and Claire had to force herself to break the kiss.

"Not here," she gasped against the salty skin of his neck.

His arms tightened around her shoulders, but she felt him nod. "Eva set me up with a big-ass suite upstairs. The bed's big enough for both of us, plus about five more. Want to come jump on it with me?"

Claire refused to think about her suspicion that this was all a game to him, or the fact that she'd had good reasons for refusing to give in to the attraction between them.

Only moments ago, she'd been tired, body and mind,

but now her every muscle sang with tension. Life throbbed through her veins like jet fuel, and the new surge of energy felt a thousand times better than the weighted deadness of being always correct, professional, and safe.

"Yes," Claire said, pulling back far enough to meet his gaze. "Let's go play."

Jules took another sip of her beer, the bitter taste suiting her mood perfectly. It was weird to be sitting in the middle of a raucous group of celebrating chefs, accepting congratulations and free drinks and slaps on the back, and feeling like shit.

Honestly, it ticked her off. This was supposed to be a great moment for her, a moment when she'd proved, to herself and to the huge boys' club fraternity of chefs, that she was one of them.

Chapel, the Lower East Side bar where Gus had moved the celebration after Eva Jansen kicked them off the stage at the hotel, was packed to the rafters with restaurant refugees, both front and back of house, in various stages of drunkenness. Music wailed and pounded from the tiny corner platform—it sounded like the same band that had been playing the night they made it through the qualifying round. She recognized the wild black hair on the tall, lanky bassist, the wicked slant of his grin out at the crowd.

The band kind of sucked, but you couldn't tell it by the number of guys hanging out in front of the stage, shoving each other in time to the beat. As she watched, Winslow jumped up and down several times as if he had springs installed in his sneakers, one hand out for balance. The hand clipped a slim, good-looking kid with dark red hair, who laughed and gently bumped Win back into the crowd before turning his attention to the stage once more.

Jules tilted the cold bottle to her lips again, wishing she could be as free and easy and happy and giddy as Winslow, who was bouncing back and forth between the dance floor, Beck at the bar, and that short assistant guy who'd led them to the suite . . . what was his name? Drew, over by the pinball machines in the back.

But Jules had somehow managed to isolate herself. In a room full of people she counted as friends, she'd never been more alone. It was as if the darkness of her thoughts generated a miasma around her that made it impossible for anyone to come within two feet of her. And rather than resenting it, she was fiercely glad. She wasn't sure she'd be able to manufacture a big, happy grin right now. Thank goodness Danny'd taken off about an hour ago; he'd see through her in a heartbeat.

Max was probably boarding a plane right about now, back to Tokyo.

She shook her head at herself, but it was no use trying to think of other things. Even if Max wasn't in the country anymore, he was in her head, in her heart, and she wasn't getting him out of there anytime soon.

Reaching for the strength and acceptance she'd found earlier, Jules struggled for a long, desperate moment before acknowledging the truth—it was a hell of a lot easier to be strong and serene and Zen with Max's arms wrapped around her.

Well, she'd adapt. She had to. And at least she had the satisfaction of knowing she'd sent Max on his way with a smile. Okay, maybe not a smile, but at least without tears and a big messy scene. She'd managed not to grab him by the ankles and hold on, kicking and screaming. Put it that way.

Oh, cripes, there was Danny, pushing his way through the knot of shouting, head-banging chefs by Chapel's big, wooden door. Jules straightened up, preparing to plaster on the best fake smile she could manage, and that's when she saw him.

Max Lunden.

Not on his way to the airport, not on a plane back to Tokyo; instead, he was about two feet behind his brother, using his height to scan the bar as if he were looking for something.

Or someone, because when that intense blue-gray stare settled on Jules, she felt it from the top of her head to the soles of her feet.

Confused, disoriented, Jules stood up, her heart beating louder than the drums of the band on stage. With a word to Danny, who smirked and turned away, Max was heading toward her.

One breath, two, and then he was there in front of her, as solid and real as the table between them.

"You're here," Jules said, then blushed, intensely grateful that he frowned and leaned in closer, turning his ear to her mouth.

"What?" he yelled. "Damn, it's like being trapped in the Holland Tunnel at rush hour."

"Come on," Jules said, grabbing his hand and pulling him to the exit and out onto the street. The only thought in her head was to find out what was going on.

The Lower East Side corner was quiet after the din of the bar, even with the constant rush of cars and cabs, buses and people on their way home from work. It was getting dark out already, the sun slipping behind the tall buildings and leaving the streets lit by the ambient glow of neon signs and headlights.

There was a tiny alcove surrounded by a short stone wall just up the steps that led down to Chapel. It used to be part of the abandoned church that crouched above the bar, but now it was empty. And it looked like as good a place as any to be able to talk, slightly shielded from the sidewalk and the entrance to the bar.

Jules was a woman on a mission. She had Max seated

on that stone wall beside her in a matter of seconds. She couldn't keep her eyes from going wide and hopeful, her heart hammering its way through her chest, so she did the best she could to hide it by facing forward and giving him her profile.

"What are you doing here?" she asked, tension making her voice tight.

"I came for a drink with my team," Max said. "But we seem to have left the bar."

He sounded so easy, casual—but there was something in the stiff set of his shoulders brushing hers that told Jules he was as wound up as she was.

"No flights out to Tokyo today?" she said, forcing her tone as casual as his.

He paused, then said, "Fuck it. Jules, look at me."

She shook her head, terrified to make eye contact— one good look at his stupid, beautiful, beloved face and she'd break down.

But Max was unrelenting, twisting to straddle the wall so he could face her and pull her resisting body into his arms.

"Okay, don't look at me," he said. "Just listen. I'm not going anywhere. There's a place for me right here, in Manhattan, at the restaurant, with my family, on the RSC team—and I'm claiming it." Her heart stuttered, skipping a beat, as she thought of all the things that might mean, but he wasn't finished.

"And I'm claiming my spot right next to you, Jules, because none of it means a damn without you. So suck it up, buttercup—you're not getting rid of me anytime soon."

The heart that had clenched tight enough to stall for a second soared up from her chest and into her throat. She had to look away, couldn't let him see what this was doing to her.

"What about Italy?"

"Jules, look at me."

She shook her head. This was agony. She was afraid to see the expression on Max's face when he talked about his long-held wish, but Max laid a gentle hand against the back of her neck, warm and encouraging, and Jules sighed.

Turning her head, she savored the heat soaking into her sore, abused muscles, the shiver of awareness that always took her when Max's skin touched hers. "Italy is your dream, Max. I can't ask you to give that up."

"You're not asking, I'm offering," Max pointed out. "And Italy wasn't the dream, anyway. Not really."

Jules frowned. "Don't lie to me, Max, not about this. I heard you—the longing in your voice the day in your room, when you told me about how beautiful it was, how magical. You couldn't wait to get back there."

Ducking his head to catch her evasive eyes, Max's open, candid gaze burned through her like the blaze from a handheld butane torch. "I'm not lying. I did want to get back to Italy, because I felt a glimmer of something there, something I wanted. Something I've searched the whole world for. But I wouldn't have found it at Vincenzo Cotto's studio, or in Rome, or Marrakech, or Tokyo, or anywhere else, because it was right here, all along."

Jules shook her head, just slightly, so as not to dislodge Max's loose grip at the base of her neck. "I don't understand."

Max huffed out a laugh. "Neither did I, for a long time. Years, in fact. But all along, I was looking for someplace that felt like me, where I would fit, and be enough. Where I could stop for a while and rest, and not feel the need to keep moving forward to find something new to see if it fit better, because the fit would be so perfect already."

He leaned in to press the final words to her cheek. "I was looking for a home. And I found it."

Suddenly nervous, terrified to believe what he was

telling her, Jules blurted, "But all the stuff you learned, the techniques—"

"Let me think. I can either have a life where I learn a whole bunch of cool techniques—or I can put those techniques to real use, while having a life surrounded by family and friends . . . and you. Turned out to be kind of a no-brainer."

"You could have been home this whole time! It was always here, waiting for you."

But Max shook his head, his stubbled cheek rasping against her jaw. "No. Because this place, my family—it never fit quite right before. New York isn't my home, and neither is Lunden's, or my parents' apartment."

He paused, and Jules felt his throat clench as he swallowed. She could barely breathe until he finally said, "It's you, Jules. You're my home."

Oxygen flooded her lungs, filled up her head, her whole body, until she felt light enough to float away. She wrenched herself out of his arms, but only so she could get herself turned around on the wall to face him, her legs hooking over his thighs and her arms going around his strong, warm neck.

His face, the face she'd been afraid to look at, was set in an expression that was half arrogant determination, half nervous hope. With a surge of exasperated affection, Jules realized that he was actually unsure about how she'd respond.

"You know, for a guy who's studied ancient teachings and spouts a lot of wise sayings all the time, you're pretty dumb," she told him, and watched the way joy fell over his features like a beautiful veil, obscuring every other emotion.

"Interestingly enough, you are not the first person to point this out to me today," he said, his arms tightening around her back.

Leaning away, trusting him to hold her up, Jules said, "Danny?"

Max leaned forward to nuzzle into the sensitive skin below her ear. The arch of her spine over his hard-muscled arms made her feel loose and abandoned, open and warm. "My brother's a pretty smart guy, it turns out. Which I should've known already. After all, he was the first of the Lunden men to love you."

Jules gasped as he pressed a hot, openmouthed kiss to that spot on her neck that seemed to be connected to a wire running straight through to the center of her body. Her mind already hazing over with desire, she almost missed it when Max lifted her up until she was nose to nose with him and said, "He's not the only one, though."

Her breath stilled, her lungs as afraid of breaking the moment as she was. "No?"

Max gave her a look that made her want to bite at his stubbled chin. "Nope. My parents are crazy about you, too."

"I know," she said, and she did. The knowledge filled her with a calm kind of satisfaction. Becoming one of the fraternity of chefs was cool—knowing she was a real, vital part of the Lunden family was exponentially better.

Fidgeting with his hands behind her back, fingers stroking at her spine as if he were counting the knobs of her vertebrae, Max said, "And then there's me. It's not the same—God, it better not be—but I love you as much as my family does. More, even."

Her cheeks were numb, they were spread so wide by her smile. "Oh yeah? You think you love me more? Not more than I love you, I bet."

The competitive sparkle that had fired Jules up when he first came home sparked in Max's eyes again, only this time, she could give in to the urge to kiss him. So she did.

His mouth was warm and sinful against hers, tongue

sliding deep and rubbing at hers, making her moan against his lips. Her whole body caught fire; if it started to rain, she was sure she'd sizzle.

When he finally pulled back, his eyes were dark, pupils blown wide. But he grinned and said, "I love you more than ramen noodles."

She blinked. It took her a moment to connect the dots from that mind-obliterating kiss to the conversation they'd been having before, but when she got it, she said, "I love you more than fresh plums."

Eyes alight with the joy of the game, the pleasure of being in each other's arms, the anticipation of the challenges ahead, Max said, "I love you more than Zen."

That made Jules laugh so hard she almost toppled them both off the wall. Good thing it was short enough for Max to steady them with his boots firmly on the ground.

When she caught her breath, she twined her fingers through the short spikes of his hair, looked deep into his eyes, and said, "I love you more than winning the Rising Star Chef competition."

And as passion flared in Max's gaze like the blue flame on a range, and he bent her back over his arms to kiss her again, Jules knew that it was true.

She didn't need to win any contests or prove anything to anyone. With Max in her arms, and the Lundens as her family, she'd already won.

Max lifted his head to brush the tip of his nose across her jaw and nuzzle the soft, sensitive patch of skin behind her ear. Jules shivered at the ticklish warmth of his breath, joy welling up in her throat as he whispered, "Get ready, Jules. This is the beginning of the best adventure yet."

Too Hot to Touch Recipes

MAX'S MISO-GLAZED TENDERLOIN OF BEEF

For the beef:
2½ lb beef tenderloin
1 tablespoon butter
1 tablespoon neutral oil, like grapeseed or canola

For the glaze:
2 tablespoons toasted sesame oil
1 tablespoon yuzu juice
2 teaspoons minced fresh ginger
⅓ cup black cherry jam
1 tablespoon miso paste

Preheat the oven to 350 degrees.

Pat the tenderloin dry, then salt and pepper it all over.

Combine all the glaze ingredients in a blender or food processor, and blend until smooth and thick.

Melt the butter and grapeseed oil in a roasting pan over medium high heat. When the butter has stopped frothing, put the tenderloin in the pan. Brown it on all sides, about ten minutes, regulating the heat so that it doesn't scorch or stick.

Brush the tenderloin with half of the glaze, then put the pan in the oven and roast for fifteen minutes. At that point, check the meat and apply the rest of the glaze. Roast to desired level of doneness, about fifteen to twenty more minutes for medium rare.

Allow the meat to rest for at least five minutes before slicing and serving.

BECK'S NEW YORK-STYLE GRAVLAX

2 lb whole salmon fillet, skin on (ask fishmonger to remove all pin bones)
2 cups granulated sugar
1 cup salt
4 cloves garlic, thinly sliced
1 tablespoon black pepper
4 bunches fresh tarragon
¼ cup Pernod, or other anise-flavored liqueur

Rinse the fish, checking for loose scales, and pat dry with paper towels.

Stir together the garlic, sugar, salt and pepper in a large bowl. Coat the bottom of a 9 × 13 casserole with about a third of the mixture.

Lay the fish, skin side down, across the sugar mixture in the pan. Place one bunch of tarragon around the sides of the salmon, then pour the rest of the sugar mixture over the top of the fish, making sure to cover it completely.

Spread the rest of the tarragon over the coated fish, then pour the Pernod over all and cover with plastic wrap.

You may place a weighted 8 × 11 pan on top of the covered salmon to help the curing process and absorption of the tarragon oil into the sugar, but it's not strictly necessary.

Put the pan in the refrigerator and allow to cure for two to three days. Check the salmon every twelve hours or so to make sure it's still covered, adding more sugar and salt if needed.

When ready to serve, remove the gravlax from the pan and rinse well. Pat dry with paper towels and slice thinly across the grain. Great on sandwiches, in salads, with eggs—anywhere you'd use smoked salmon!

THE FAMOUS LUNDEN'S TAVERN BRUSSELS SPROUTS

3 lbs Brussels sprouts, trimmed and halved lengthwise
3 tablespoons vegetable oil
12 ounces pancetta, diced
1 tablespoon balsamic vinegar
2 tablespoons olive oil
1 teaspoon Dijon mustard

1 teaspoon honey
1 tsp chopped fresh parsley
salt and pepper to taste

Preheat oven to 400 degrees.

Toss the trimmed, halved Brussels sprouts with the vegetable oil and salt and pepper to taste. Spread the sprouts, cut side down, in a single layer across two baking sheets. Don't crowd them too much, or they'll steam instead of roasting. Roast in the oven until tender, with crisp, browned edges, about thirty minutes. Check them at twenty—roasting times can vary depending on the size of the sprouts.

While the sprouts are in the oven, heat a large sauté pan over medium high heat. Brown the pancetta until its fat begins to render and coat the pan, about ten minutes. Remove the pancetta from the pan with a slotted spoon, and drain on paper towels.

Combine the vinegar, mustard, parsley, and honey in a small bowl. Drizzle in the olive oil, whisking vigorously until all the elements are combined into a vinaigrette. Salt and pepper to taste.

Heat the sprouts quickly in the pan coated with the rendered pancetta fat, then add them to a large serving bowl. Sprinkle with the crisp pancetta and drizzle the vinaigrette over all, then toss and serve.

The Rising Star Chef competition continues!
Read on for a preview of Louisa Edwards'

Some Like
It Hot

Coming in December 2011 from St. Martin's Paperbacks

So this is what it's like to leave home, Danny mused, narrowly avoiding a collision with a woman who seemed to have forgotten she was pulling a wheeled carry-on case behind her.

La Guardia was packed with post-holiday travelers. Every bank of waiting room benches sported at least a couple of people sleeping off their turkey and stuffing, or maybe their holiday hangovers, while the terminal seethed with chaos and confusion as flights were called, boarding was announced, and everyone rushed to find the right gate.

Danny Lunden, who'd never been out of Manhattan, soaked it all in and tried to figure out why the hell he was getting chills of excitement all down his back.

They were on their way.

A panicking voice rose above the din of

bustling passengers and PA announcements about not leaving bags unattended.

"Where's my ticket? Please tell me one of you—oh, there it is. Okay. Thanks, Danny."

Patting his jittery friend's shoulder was a little like grabbing hold of the business end of a hand mixer. "Winslow, cool it. We're all good. We're at the gate in plenty of time."

Which had to be some sort of miracle, after the adventure of wrestling luggage and carry-ons through the New York City public transit system and pushing through airport crowds walking more slowly than the tourists in Times Square. Danny did a quick head count to make sure he hadn't lost anyone in the subway tunnels or security lane.

Beck, their resident master of fish cookery, was always easy to spot in a crowd, since he topped the mere mortals around him by about four inches. The big guy caught Danny's eye and gave him a silent nod of acknowledgment. Beck was solid, as always, standing like an oak planted in the middle of a rushing river, carrying everything he'd packed for this adventure in an oversized duffel bag.

Next to him was Danny's oldest friend in the world, Jules Cavanaugh. Her dark blonde hair was caught up in a messy ponytail, and her eyes glittered with the excitement of finally embarking on this trip they'd all been anticipating ever since they won the chance to take on the Rising Star Chef competition.

She all but glowed with happiness, spilling her warm light all over the guy beside her, who was busily soaking it up like a sponge cake doused in amaretto.

Max Lunden, Danny's brother. And wasn't that a rolling pin upside the head, because Danny never thought he'd see the day when his wandering prodigal brother would settle down and commit to anything—much less to winning the RSC, his family, and a woman all in one fell swoop. But he had. Danny watched the way they leaned into each other, their wheeled bags bumping and threatening to trip them when they got too close, and tried to be glad the team had two such passionate, inventive chefs in charge, and leave it at that.

Winslow Jones, the fastest knife on the team—and the one who'd nearly been grounded by security for pleading to be allowed to carry his knife roll on the plane with him—was still vibrating under Danny's palm.

And Danny was the pastry chef. So that was everyone. He relaxed slightly, a fragment of tension going out of his shoulders.

The gang's all here.

A nasal voice over the loudspeaker broke into Danny's thoughts.

"We are now boarding flight number fourteen twenty-two to Chicago O'Hare International. First class passengers only, please."

"Well, that ain't us," Beck said, settling onto

his heels with the look of a man accustomed to waiting.

"Have you ever flown first class?" Jules asked, staring up into Max's eyes.

He laughed. "Hell no. An airplane with toilets on it is a luxury to me. I did most of my traveling through Asia on crowded buses or in the back of a truck transporting live goats or something."

"Sounds smelly." Winslow wrinkled his nose, making the dark freckles stand out on his latte-colored skin.

"You have no idea," Max told him. "But this." He gazed around the busy airport. "It's something else."

Danny looked around, too, at the walls all glass and metal, at the reasonably clean floor and the people chatting as they rode the moving walkways, and figured he knew what Max meant.

This was something outside of all their experiences. Because they weren't just embarking on some little pleasure jaunt to see the sights in the Windy City.

They were headed to meet the teams they'd be up against in the Rising Star Chef competition, the other chefs who'd be cooking their hearts out and giving it their all in the hopes of coming out on top.

The significant cash prize didn't hurt anything, either.

The newly minted East Coast team stood in

loose huddle staring at each other nervously. Someone ought to say something, Danny realized, with a visceral pang of yearning for his dad's gift of effortless inspiration, or his mom's serene calm in the face of any crisis.

"I wish Gus and Nina were here," Jules said, in one of those weird moments of reading Danny's brain like an open cookbook. She'd been doing it since they were in elementary school together, and it still freaked him out.

Shaking off the emotion as if he were flicking whipped cream off the end of a whisk, Danny did what he did best.

"Mom and Dad wish they could be here," he soothed. "But somebody's got to stay home and run Lunden's while we're off winning the Rising Star Chef and bringing glory to our restaurant. I know this is kind of a crazy situation, and we're all a little worked up, but we just have to stay focused on bringing home the prize. For Lunden's. For my parents. For all of us."

As Danny glanced around the team, making sure to lock eyes with each person in turn, he could see them all shedding their nerves and standing up a little taller. And a bit more of the tension rolled off his back, because if he could keep them all together and zeroed in on the goal, they were going to be okay.

Danny knew he'd have to work hard to take his own advice.

Stay focused. This is for the family, for the restaurant, for the future.

To Danny, they were interchangeable.

When it was their turn to board, he herded his group over to the flight attendant, produced all five tickets, and got all of them and their assorted carry-ons down the gangplank and onto the plane.

After some confusion over the seating arrangements—Max and Jules weren't technically seated together, but were still in that phase of the relationship where they couldn't bear to be parted for the hour and a half it would take them to fly from their home base of New York City to the unknown wilds of Chicago—Danny had everyone situated.

Max, Jules, and Winslow were clustered on one side of the plane, so Max could talk Win through his first takeoff and landing, while Beck and Danny were in the slightly more spacious pair of seats on the other side of the aisle, although Beck had asked to sit by the window.

Danny readily agreed, buckled himself in, stowed his satchel holding the precious tools of his trade under the seat in front of him, and was ready to go by the time the rest of the passengers finished boarding.

But they didn't go anywhere. The plane just sat there. And sat there. And sat there.

Danny craned his neck out into the aisle to get

a better view of the front of the plane. What was the problem? Were there electrical issues?

Finally one of the flight attendants, a skinny young dude with unlikely yellow hair and an earring, grabbed the handheld microphone and stood in the aisle to make an announcement.

"Sorry for the delay, ladies and gentlemen," the male attendant said smoothly, "we're just waiting on one passenger, then we can get underway."

Blithely ignoring the ripple of exasperated sighs and groans, the flight attendant hung up the mic and went back to passing out blankets and pillows.

"Well, this sucks," Danny said, impatience simmering under his skin. "Let's get the hell off the ground, already."

"If they're lying about waiting for a passenger, and there's actually some kind of systems failure, I'd personally rather they figure that shit out while we're still on the ground."

Blinking, Danny turned to study his seat partner, taking in Beck's rigid posture, the cold sweat dotting his hairline.

Crapsticks, how did I miss this?

"You're afraid of flying," Danny said, disbelief sharpening his tone.

Beck stiffened even further. Danny experienced a moment of fear that the big guy might Hulk out and break the arm right off the seat between them.

"I'm not afraid of flying," Beck grated out. "I'm not even afraid of falling—that would at least be quick and relatively painless."

Danny went into caretaker mode. "Okay, you're a tough guy, everyone knows that. I didn't mean anything by saying you were afraid."

Beck shook his head, the loose waves of his longish dark hair hiding his face for a second. "It's not that I don't—look. Everyone's afraid, sometimes. I'm no exception. Fear is a survival response; it's healthy. It can keep you alive. I just meant, it's not the flying that wigs me out so much as it's . . ." He swallowed audibly, his Adam's apple moving in the thick column of his throat. "It's kind of cramped in here. Not a lot of air movement. I don't like that."

Danny processed that quickly. There was a lot they didn't know about Beck, the taciturn chef who'd joined the Lunden's kitchen crew only a few months before Max came home. There had been rumors—mostly started by Winslow and his overactive imagination—that ranged from ex-con just out of prison to foreign prince in exile. Danny had never paid much attention to them. So long as Beck did his job, banged out the straightforward, excellent fish dishes on the Lunden's menu, and got along with the rest of the crew, Danny didn't much care where he came from.

The claustrophobia, though, was starting to lend a little credence to Win's jailbird theory.

Setting that aside for the moment, Danny said, "Would it be better if you were on the aisle? Might give you a little more room to stretch out."

Gratitude flashed in Beck's hooded eyes, but it must've been for the lack of further interrogation on his issues, because he said, "Nah, that just puts me in the middle of the big metal tube with no escape hatch. At least here, I can look out and see the open air, even if I can't touch it. I'll be fine, man. As soon as we take off and get on our way, and I can start counting down the minutes until we're in Chicago."

Danny returned the tense smile with the most reassuring expression he could manage—and when it came to reassurance, Danny was the ninja master. Usually he'd start with a pep talk, but from the way Beck was white-knuckling it, the guy needed action more than words.

Unbuckling his seat belt, Danny stood up, the familiar comfort of a sense of purpose filling him with determination.

"Where are you going?" Beck asked.

Danny straightened and stepped into the aisle. "To get some answers."

The blond flight attendant with the earring was fooling around with the coffee maker when Danny marched up the aisle to the front of the plane, but when he saw one of his passengers bearing down on him, his eyes widened.

"Sir, you need to sit down."

Danny had a couple inches on the kid, but he did his best not to loom in the cramped confines of the airplane's prep area. "Look. My friend's not a great flyer and he's starting to get anxious. Is there anything I can tell him about when we might be taking off?"

"We're nearly finished with the boarding process, and we can't push back from the gate until all passengers are seated, with their seat belts securely fastened," the attendant parroted.

"Yeah, but see, we've all been doing exactly that for the last twenty minutes, and the plane's still parked at the gate. What, exactly, are we waiting for? I mean, you've already made, like, four pots of coffee. I bet you're getting sick of the smell of burnt coffee beans."

The flight attendant's gaze flickered, and Danny pressed his advantage with a smile.

"I don't really know," the kid finally said. "I got a call from ground control to hold the plane for a late passenger; she's supposed to be on her way."

Danny stared. "You're serious. You weren't lying, trying to keep us calm while we waited to find out there's a pigeon in the engine or something?"

"We're pigeon free, as far as I know."

It obviously wasn't this kid's fault, but Danny was starting to get pissed. One of his guys was stuck feeling like shit for an extra half-hour, and as far as Danny could tell, there was no legitimate reason for it. "Is this standard practice, holding up a whole plane full of people for one single passenger?"

Earring glinting as he shook his head, the kid shrugged helplessly.

"It is when the passenger is me," purred a low voice from behind them.

Danny whirled, nearly clocking himself on the jutting refrigerator cabinet, to see a svelte woman dressed in something complicated and elegant that wrapped around her stunning body like some sort of chic lady mummy costume, only in dark blue. The color set off her pearly smooth skin, making her a study in rich jewel tones, from the sPatricket curve of her smirking mouth to the shiny brown hair angling bluntly down to her chin. She looked as if she were on her way to opening night at the Met or something, not a commuter flight to Chicago.

Recognition fired one instant after the instinctual spark of visceral desire in the pit of Danny's stomach, and he clamped down on the dizzying combination.

Clenching his teeth, Danny faced the woman whose billionaire restaurateur father had founded the Rising Star Chef competition twenty years ago.

"Thanks for waiting," she was saying to the flight attendant. "I had to avert a professional disaster, then there was a mix-up with the car service and I had to take a taxi. My assistant is so fired. Well, not really, I'd be a mess without him, but I'm cutting his chocolate budget. No more candy on his desk until he figures out how to get me to the airport on time!"

She smiled, perfect white teeth flashing. Before the dazzled flight attendant could gather his wits off the floor, Danny had stepped between them.

At a deep gut level, all he could think was *mine*.

And, close on the heels of that thought, *Uh oh*.